THE Second *Revolution*

Getting To the Promised Land

DERRICK ST. THOMAS

Ordering Information:
For orders and inquiries, please contact:
books@authorsnote360.com
www.authorsnote360.com

Printed in the United States of America

Contents

My father Ivan St Thomas was born in Boston Massachusetts, on February 8, 1920. My mother Eulalie St Thomas was born in Guyana, South America on July 19, 1922. They met while he was serving in the military during WW II. They got married in January of 1943. During the union they had four children, beginning with, Vincent, born in March of 1944. I was born in November 1945, followed by Gordon and Abby, the only girl.

In 1948, they moved to Harlem when Dad was 28 years old and Mom was 26. The marriage didn't last very long after that.

I was 12 years old when my mother moved to the Bronx. We lived in a two bedroom apartment at 766 Caldwell Ave., in the South Bronx. My father received his teaching certificate and his Master's from NYU. He was the Industrial Arts Teacher at the Catherine and Count Basie Middle School 72 in Queens when he retired. My mother worked at Lennox Hill Hospital as a nursing assistant. On Sundays my mother would have us in church all day.

In January of 1958, I enrolled in the sixth grade at Public School 38 in our neighborhood. The school only went up to the 7th grade. I made friends immediately. There was Raymond Day, Robert Hickson and especially Wolfredo Vasquez. Wolfredo was a big kid and very aggressive. A lot of the kids didn't like him. He took a liking to me and we had a good relationship. He would say things to me in Spanish and I would try to answer back in Spanish. He wanted me to learn Spanish. My only regret was I didn't take it up in high school. When I got to high school they wanted me to take French. Years later I realize I should have taken Spanish because it was more practical. I had my first fight when I was in the seventh grade. Needless to say I got my head banged on the concrete and suffered a concussion. I knew something was wrong because I went to bed when I got home. The next day I was very sick and couldn't go to school. I never told my mother what happened.

In 1959, I enrolled at Junior High School 120. I was now in the 8th grade. JHS 120 was about a 10 minute walk from home. Wolfredo was sent to 120 like most of us. However, he transferred to another school and I never saw him again. I enjoyed going to 120 because learning was fun and interesting. I developed a close relationship and hung out with Raymond Day who was very popular. He would be at my house or I would be at his. The sixties were great, we had a lot of fun growing up and partying.

A secularized form of American gospel music called Soul developed in the mid-1950s, with pioneers like Ray Charles, Jackie Wilson and Sam Cooke leading the way. In 1959, Berry Gordy founded Motown Records, the first record label to primarily feature African-American artists aimed at achieving crossover success. The label developed an innovative—and commercially successful-style of Soul music with distinctive pop elements. Its early roster of artists included The Miracles, Martha and the Vandellas, Marvin Gaye, The Temptations, The Supremes, and others.

In the summer I played basketball, stickball, and handball. Handball was fun because the girls would play with us. As I got older, I would go to the supermarket to pack groceries and make some money to buy things that I needed. We had a lot of house parties on Fridays and Saturday nights. We had to pay 50 cents to get in and you had to look good if you wanted to attract the young ladies.

I found an old discarded baby carriage and I used it to deliver groceries from the supermarket and it was very profitable. One day I was making a delivery when the lady wanted me to help her carry her groceries up to the third floor. I had no way to secure the carriage and I knew I was taking a chance leaving it. Reluctantly, I took the groceries up to her apartment and when I came back out my carriage was stolen. I never delivered groceries anymore after that.

In the summer of 1960 one of my school mates Ernest Sarkady told me that they were hiring at Orchard Beach near City Island. We applied and I got a job as a vendor selling ice cream and soda.

That went pretty good the first summer. I made a little money and I was able to buy some clothes for school and help my mother with groceries. After the summer was over I found a job delivering newspapers for the New York Post. The following summer Ernest and I went back to Orchard Beach and we got hired as busboys in the restaurant. He was the Head busboy and I was the Assistant. The work was steady and we were getting paid $1.00 an hour plus tips. That summer I saved $300. I was a big help to my mother because she didn't have to buy clothes for school. I had gained some independence. I was into basketball and I wore Converse All Stars.

I enjoyed school because it was competitive. I liked math and science. Miss Tell was our math teacher and she got us motivated. Also, she was very pretty. Earl Harper and I always competed with each other to see who would get the highest grade in algebra. I won a few times except for the simple mistakes I would make that kept me from getting perfect scores.

In 1961 I graduated from JHS 120 and went to Wm. H. Taft high school in the Bronx. The school wasn't far from Yankee Stadium. My friend Ernest Sarkady went to Dewitt Clinton High. Another notable alumni from 120 was Willie Worsley. He also went to Dewitt Clinton. After high school he went to UTEP. He played on the team that beat Kentucky for the NCAA basketball championship in 1966. I couldn't see myself in an all boy school. Raymond and Robert also attended Taft. This was at the height of integration. When I got to Taft the student population was mostly Jewish. It was like culture shock. Junior High was fun. High school was serious. My first year was a struggle. I joined the band to have fun and I learned to play the trombone.

I grew to 5'9" and I tried out for the basketball team. I got cut and I ended up on the Junior Varsity team. I took college prep courses like Geometry, French, English, History and Biology. Band and gym filled out the rest of my curriculum. For some reason Geometry gave me problems. I failed the first course and I had to take it over. I passed and went on to geometry 2. I couldn't pass 2 and I had to go to summer school. I finally passed and took the regents exam and passed. This created a problem for me in getting to play on the basketball team. I realized that keeping up my grades were important for me to graduate and play sports. Being on the varsity became less important because I was enjoying the band.

The summer of 1963 I worked at Orchard Beach and after that I worked at the 110th street Boathouse in Central Park. That was great because it was easier for me to travel to Harlem. I loved the boathouse because it had row boats that people would rent to go out on the lake. I worked mostly in the restaurant and during breaks I would take out a boat and learn to row. Arthur Bussi and I use to race around the lake. He was good send he was physically built for the task.

I was in the school hallway at the time when I saw a student coming towards me crying and she said "they shot our president". This was Friday, November 22, 1963. The Principal came over the loud speaker and told us that school was dismissed. I was stunned like everyone else because we all liked President Kennedy. The news was broadcasted all around the world. I didn't know what I was feeling at the time. Lyndon Johnson became our next President and life went on.

I was working and going to school all at the same time. In the winter of 1963 I was working at the Wolman Ice Skating Rink in Central Park. This allowed me to learn how to ice skate. By working at the restaurant I was able to get onto the rink for free. I started with hockey skates and I went to the racing skates. Skating was fun because you get to pickup girls. I met Georgette while ice skating. Coincidentally, she lived in the Bronx and not far from me. I had to walk past her building on my way to the Jackson Ave train stop. She was my first girlfriend and I gave her my class ring. On my way to school she would wait for me to pick her up and we would get on the train together. There were two other guys she was seeing. I went to her house one night and one of them was visiting her. His name was James. We were at a party and I saw her talking to a guy and I wanted to know who he was. She said it was Eddie. I told her that she would have to get serious and let these guys know what's going on between us. I decided to confront the situation and told her that she would have to choose our relationship. To my surprise she gave me my ring back.

I was caught off guard. I never expected that. I had to be a man and accept her decision. However, I moved on and forgot about it. In 1964, I was about to graduate. There were many senior activities to attend to. There was the senior prom. I didn't have a date and I went stag. I had a good time because a lot of girls went without dates. I also went to the New York World fair. It was located at Flushing Meadows in Queens. The fairs theme was "Peace through understanding," dedicated to "Man's Achievement on a shrinking globe in an expanding universe". American companies dominated the exposition as exhibitors. The theme was symbolized by a 12-story high, stainless-steel model of the earth called the Unisphere. Admission price was $2 in 1964. The fair in April of 1964 was before the turbulent years of the Vietnam War, Cultural changes, and increasing struggles for Civil Rights.

I remembered sampling a lot of different foods and also sitting in the Ford Motor Company Mustang Automobile. I didn't know what I was going to do after graduating. I took everything in stride and waited for the time to come. I had the privilege of playing in the band for our graduating class.

The girl I remembered most in high school was Jean Zinovoy, she was in my home room. She would always positively talk to me and I liked her attention. I asked her for her phone number and she gave it to me. I didn't call her because I would see her every day. She got sick one day and didn't show up for class. I called her house and she told me she had a bad cold and she was ok. I met her brother Barry at a pickup basketball game in the school yard. After school we would all meet to play ball. Barry was a big kid and a good player. That's when I found out Jean was his sister. I kept a low profile because I didn't know what to expect. Around 2004, I joined Classmates.Com and was checking out the class of 1964 when I saw her name. I sent her an email and she responded. She also told me her brother Barry had died and she was living in Florida. I didn't think I would see her again.

The 50th reunion for the class of 1964 was being organized in 2014 and I wanted to go because I never went to any of them. The person that was organizing the reunion was Barbara Katz Oster. I asked Barbara if she knew Jean and she said they were good friends. I asked her to find out if Jean was attending the reunion. Barbara told me to send Jean a message on Facebook to let her know I was looking forward to seeing her again. My wife and I went to the reunion and it was a fun filled night. They played songs from the 60s and the dance floor was packed. Jean was there and she looked real good.

I am now a high school graduate with no immediate plans, other than my normal day to day experience. College was not part of it although I know I should go. I worked at the Boat House during the summer months and was preparing to go back to the Ice Skating Rink. While watching television I saw an advertisement from the US Air Force. Without thinking it through I went to the recruitment center. They gave me a test and told me that I passed and I had a mechanical aptitude and I could be a machinist. I was sworn in and they told me I will be going to boot camp in November. I told my mother that I was leaving for the Air Force and she wasn't too happy about it. However, she told me to stay out of trouble and come home safe.

I was 19 years old when I enlisted. I was sent to Lockland Air Force Base in San Antonio, Texas for six weeks of basic training. I was somewhat in shape because they had us doing the mile run with boots on. I was surprise I didn't experience any sickness from the effects. The instructors told us if we get sick to go where the ditch is and do it there, or else you pick it up and carry it to the ditch. No vomiting on the field. An Airman was marching with us and he was having difficulty keeping in step. He was in the hospital for a hernia operation. Our training instructor was yelling and calling him names. I thought some of the things he was saying was funny and I was trying to keep from laughing. The instructor must have seen me trying to keep from laughing and he got on my case. I had to do 50 pushups and get rid of the smirk off my face. Since then I learned to keep a low profile. During the six weeks I was able to go and see where the Alamo was located.

I played pickup basketball when I got the chance and I tried bowling. The time was moving on and basic training was coming to an end. I received a promotion to E-1 or Airman third class. I also got orders to go to Chanute Air Force Base in Illinois for training as a Jet Engine mechanic. This was in December of 1964 where I spent Christmas. The training was interesting because I learned how to use different tools and take engines apart and assemble them. I met some home boys from New York and we got together and took the trip to Chicago on weekends. We stayed at the local YMCA when we got there. From there we went to the shopping areas to meet girls. I met Geraldine at the Woolworths store in downtown Chicago. She took me to meet her parents and her baby son. They were living in the projects and I adapted to the situation. I never wore my uniform when I go to visit her. We got along fine and I liked her.

After I completed my training, I was assigned to RAF Wethersfield in England. I had 30 days of leave time before reporting to my new assignment. I told Geraldine that I would keep in touch and see how things go. She wasn't very happy when I left. This was June of 1965 when I left Illinois. When I got back to the Bronx, I visited my old friends and we hung out. I wanted to see Georgette because my sister told me that she had asked for me. The day I was going to see her, I saw Kathleen sitting at the window in her building. I stopped and spoke with her for a while and I went up to her apartment. She also had a young son. We were getting serious in our relationship to the point of asking her to marry me. I wasn't thinking about Georgette anymore. I told my mother what I was planning and she went off. She told me it wasn't going to happen. There were some things about Kathleen I didn't know. My mother saw a lot of Kathleen's movements late at night while she was coming home from work. I didn't want to go against my mother and I didn't want to tell Kathleen what was going on. When the time came for me to leave for England I told Kathleen that I would write and let her know my plans. I told Kathleen about the problem with my mother and she sent my letters back. I saw her years later and she was cool.

I arrived in England in July of 1965. I was hoping to get stationed in France so I could learn to speak the language fluently since I took it in high school. In March of 1966, General Charles De Gaulle told United States forces to leave France. I had put in for a transfer to get stationed in France when I got the news. We had bases left in Germany, Italy, Spain and Libya. I went to Spain and Italy on temporary duty. RAF Wethersfield was about 60 miles south of London. The closest towns near the base were Braintree, Chelmsford, Ipswich and Sudbury. Braintree was about 6 miles from the base. I was in the Field Maintenance Squadron. They had F100 Jet fighters with the Pratt and Whitney J57 engines. I would be a mechanic in the engine shop. My crew chief was James Wool folk from Pine Bluff Arkansas. We became best friends. James was an Airman 1st class and was in the service over 4 years. He drove a Morris Cooper and I was lucky he allowed me to hang out with him. I made the most of it.

On the base were the Airman Club, the NCO Club and the Officers club. The Airman Club was for the guys under 21, and from what I heard they drank beer and there were always a fight after they got drunk. I ran with James and we went to the non-commission officers club. That was where the action took place. There were activities on Sunday, Tuesday, Friday and Saturday nights. Saturday was entertainment night. They usually have a band or DJ's playing records. Monday, Wednesday and Thursday we would go into town. I would wear jeans and my Converse All Stars with "The Saint" written on the sides. This particular night we were in Braintree outside a club when I heard someone saying "The Saint". I looked in the direction and there were a couple of girls standing by the side of the building and one of them were saying

"The Saint". I walked over to them and spoke to the one that was calling me. I said hello to her and she was excited to meet me. Her name was Theresa. She was nice and cute and wore a lot of makeup. She was aggressive and I decided to give her a play. She was excited to meet me and she fell in love with me.

I have to thank the Black Entertainers for giving us music that was entertaining and soulful. We enjoyed ourselves. As black GI's we had our clique. We had lots of women to party with and they were fun. The white GI's had problems with what they were seeing. A lot of times I heard them referring to the English girls as "Nigger lovers". They didn't know how to be cool and we never bother with them except at work or while playing sport. I stayed with basketball and I got on the base team. That allowed me to travel to other Bases to play against other service men. That made things exciting for me. I enjoyed the attention we were getting from the fans and lots of girls wanted to meet us. Theresa was becoming a distraction and I couldn't handle it. I realized it was peer group pressure. I knew I would break her heart but I had to let her go. I met Christine and we went out for a while. She was over possessive and I didn't like that situation. I was asking myself. What's up with these girls? Eventually we broke up.

There was a party in Black Notley at the nursing school where I met Gunbritt. She was from Sweden. She was about 5'10" and wore her blond hair short. She was interested in me and I went out with her. She had to go to London to finish her training. I didn't see her after that so I moved on. I met Rita while I was hoping to hear from Gunbritt. Rita was an interesting girl. She didn't like to be with just one guy. I knew about it because everybody knew everybody's business. I didn't like it and when I confronted her she gave me my walking papers. Eventually she got married to one of the Brothers. Unfortunately, he was killed in a car accident. I ran into her a few times and she didn't want to be bothered. I met Lori, and she was a trip. I introduced her to my friend Mitch and she went out with him.

In 1966 I met Sandy while I was at the NCO Club. She was from Sudbury and I liked her attitude. I asked her for a date to come back at the club the following week. One Saturday night a few months later I went to the club expecting to meet Sandy when I saw Gunbritt at the bar with her date. I waved at her and she smiled at me. Sandy was sitting at the bar and I went and sat with her. Sandy and I were getting serious and she invited me to meet her parents. I was worried because I didn't know what to expect. They were very nice to me and I felt comfortable around them. She was an only child in the family. I was in love with her and I asked her to marry me. There were a lot of interracial marriages with the Black Servicemen and the English women. I didn't think there was a problem, except it wasn't accepted in a lot of the States back home. The GI's who were in interracial marriages stayed in the military. The Air Force made sure they located them where they didn't have racial problems. I never gave much thought to the problem because I was in love and my in-laws accepted me and we got married. We spent our honeymoon at the Douglas House in London. We were lucky to get in without reservations. Sam and Dave were the entertainers that weekend. We enjoyed ourselves.

Britain was the melting pot on race, not America. There was a preference for integration over segregation. Britain was more relaxed on mixed race marriages. I had given some thoughts about staying in Britain after my discharge from the Air Force. I thought about working at the Airport in London. I couldn't stay away from home. I knew I had to go back and help with the struggle. Sam Cooke was one of my favorite artists. His song "A Change is going to come" became an anthem for the American Civil Rights Movement. In 2007, the song was selected for preservation in the Library of Congress, with the National Recording Registry deeming the song "culturally, historically, or aesthetically important."

"A Change is Going to Come" was partially inspired by an incident in which Cooke and his band tried to register at a "whites only" motel in Shreveport, Louisiana. The desk clerk explained there were no vacancies. Sam was mad and made an issue over it. He had to go to another hotel in downtown Shreveport. When he got there the cops was waiting for him and he got arrested for disturbing the peace.

In August of 1967 we had our son Steven. We lived in Braintree during our marriage. We were in a unique situation when we heard the news that marrying across racial lines were allowed in the U.S.

Loving v. Virginia

Loving v. Virginia, 388 U.S. 1 (1967), the Supreme Court in Loving v. Virginia, the U.S. Supreme Court unanimously struck Virginia's law prohibiting interracial marriages as a violation of the Fourteenth Amendment.

The Fourteenth Amendment to the U.S. Constitution ratified on July 9, 1868, defined citizenship and guaranteed the rights of citizens. The Virginia law was design to banned interracial marriage.

Decision

The U.S. Supreme Court overturned the convictions in a unanimous decision, dismissing the Commonwealth of Virginia's argument that a law forbidding both white and black persons from marry as unconstitutional.

"Marriage is one of the "basic civil rights of man," fundamental to our very existence and survival… To deny this fundamental freedom on so unsupportable a basis as the racial classifications embodied in these statutes, classifications so directly subversive of the principle of equality at the heart of the Fourteenth

Amendment, is surely to deprive all the State's citizens of liberty without due process of law. The Fourteenth Amendment requires that the freedom of choice to marry not be restricted by invidious racial discrimination. Under our Constitution, the freedom to marry, or not marry, a person of another race resides with the individual and cannot be infringed by the state.

The Supreme Court concluded that anti-miscegenation laws were racist and had been enacted to perpetuate white supremacy:

Despite this Supreme Court ruling, such laws remained on the books, although unenforceable, in several states until 2000, when Alabama became the last state to repeal its law against mixed-race marriage.

Intermarriage among people of different races is increasingly common. In 1980, just 7% of all marriages in the U.S. were between spouses of a different race or ethnicity. In 2010, that share has doubled to 15% of all new marriages in the U.S. Hispanics (26%) and Asians (28%) were most likely to "marry out," compared with 9% of whites and 17% of blacks.

Marriage was given to us by God for procreation and families. Marriage as an institution was design to grow the population. There are no laws as to who you can marry. Where there was a shortage of women, men would go looking for them for marriage and family.

In some cultures men were allowed to have more than one wife. As long as you can afford it you can have many wives as you want. In ancient Israel kings were allowed concubines to create a lineage to preserve and identify your ancestry.

During the slave era in the U.S. interracial sex amongst slave owners and black women took place for increasing the number of slaves on the plantation. The result of mix race off springs is common. Slaves were freed and laws were passed forbidding race mixing. Segregation was the rule and people stayed among them.

Even though these laws were on the books in several states, it did not prevent interracial marriages from happening in other states. Escaped slaves were marrying into the Indian tribes. The Seminole natives of Florida and the Cherokee people. Many couples left the U.S. for Europe and other countries to get married interracially. This is the way it is and you can't stop it.

Same-Sex marriage

Same-Sex marriage (also known as gay marriage) is marriage between two people of the same biological sex and/or gender identity. The legalization of samesex marriage is characterized as "redefining marriage" by many opponents. The first laws enabling same-sex marriage in modern times were enacted during the first decade of the 21st century. On June 26, 2015—the Supreme Court ruled on Friday that the U.S. Constitution provides same-sex couples the right to marry, handing a historic triumph to American gay rights movement.

The Court ruled 5-4 that the Constitution's guarantees of due process and equal protection under the law mean that States cannot ban same-sex marriages. With the landmark ruling, gay marriages become legal in all 50 States.

Same sex relationship has been around for centuries. Egyptians, Romans, Greeks all had some form of same sex relationship. I believe that Genetics has a lot to do with sexual orientation. Adam and Eve made a lot of children and they went on to marry each other.

Sodom and Gomorra entertained homosexual activities when God destroyed it. Lot and his two daughters left after the destruction. The daughters got their father drunk and were having sex with him until they conceived. They were afraid for the future. Some societies do not allow relationships of this kind. People had to suppress their feelings to survive. They would get killed or whipped to get rid of the emotional effects of homosexuality of lesbianism.

The laws had to be written and passed to protect gay people from being attacked. People rights are gay rights. In terms of procreation and population growth adoption is the acceptable norm for raising children in same sex relationship. People have a right to marry whoever they want. Same for gay marriage. We have to show love and understanding in dealing with people and their differences.

Mass killings in the Pulse Club in Florida were against gay people. Somebody brother or sister was killed that night in Florida. It was a terrorist act against innocent people. Furthermore, that is the way you were born. An individual told me that he knew he was gay when he was growing. His parents used to beat him to stop acting like a girl. Eventually they gave up and accepted him for who he is. All 50 states have laws on the books to protect the gay person.

1968 was a tough year in America. Martin Luther King Jr., and Bobby Kennedy were assassinated. The TET offensive convinced many that the Vietnam War had gone badly off the rails. Rioting erupted in the cities across America. All the hope that had motivated young people through the early Civil Rights Movements and the John F. Kennedy era seemed to be crashing down in a destructive orgy of frustration, disillusionment, and violence. The 1960's, which had started with such promise, seemed headed for a bad end. Into the breach stepped James Brown, (May 3, 1933-December 25, 2006) the Hardest Working Man in show business, normally apolitical in his song writing materials, released "Say it Loud (I'm Black and I'm Proud)." Perhaps the definitive statement of a new pride and consciousness in the younger generation. If the Black Power era had a soundtrack this song would surely have been its lead single. Many whites heard it only as militant and angry. What's wrong with (I'm white and I'm Proud).

In the song, Brown addresses the prejudice towards blacks in America, and the need for black empowerment. He proclaims that "we demand a channel to do things for ourselves, we're tired of beating our head against the wall/and working for someone else. Martin Luther King Jr., (January 15, 1929–April 4, 1968), gave his Black and Proud speech to address the problem.

I was promoted to the rank of E-4 and I was contemplating my future. I didn't want to reenlist, but I was willing to take an extension to go to Thailand where some of my friends went. James was discharged and as far as I knew he went home. I gave him my home address in the Bronx to look me up when I got out. My request for an extension came back with orders to go to Pleiku Air Base in Vietnam. My wife and her parents were dead set against me going. I decided to finish out my time and go home. Besides my brother Vincent did two tours in Vietnam with the Army. I made the right choice because in 1968 Vietnam had gotten explosive and I didn't want to get killed.

In October of 1968 I was discharged from the Air Force. I went back to the Bronx and was looking around for a job. I applied to the Post Office and was hired for the holidays. I was planning to take the exam to get a permanent position. I got a letter from James and he said he was in East Hartford CT, working for Pratt & Whitney Aircraft Company in the inspection department and the company is hiring. I answered his letter and he came to the Bronx and got me. I applied to Pratt & Whitney and they hired me on the spot. This was January 1969. I worked as a technician in the experimental department for jet engines.

The work at Pratt & Whitney was exciting and rewarding. I found what I was looking for and I thank the military for giving me the experience. I rented a 2 bedroom apartment in East Hartford so that Sandy and Steven could join me. My first car was a 1967 Pontiac Catalina convertible. After that I bought a 1970 Dodge Charger R/T with the 440 engine. I paid $4000 for it. I was at the Mall in Farmington when it got stolen. When I got it back, the engine was blown but still running. I drove it to the Bronx and parked it in my mother's garage. I felt it would become a collector item down the road. Years later my mother sold her house and they got rid of the Charger. In 1971 I took a transfer to work at the South Windsor Engineering Facilities. I was working with fuel cell technology to generate electricity for space travel. In 1972 I moved to a new duplex apartment in Manchester. It was beautiful because it had a walk in basement into a back yard. I bought a pool table for the basement where I could entertain my friends.

Everything was great up until December 1974. The company had a big lay-off. I was collecting unemployment, when I started to think about going to college. A lot was going on that I didn't understand and getting an education seems to be the logical decision to take. The G I Bill gave me ten years to complete my college education. I enrolled at Manchester Community College in the summer of 1975. I took a history of civilization course for starters. I received a 'B' for the course and I felt encouraged to continue. In the fall of 1975, I enrolled full time. I also got a part time job with the Veterans out-reach program to counsel veterans how to use their education benefits. I wanted to study Business Administration for a start. I spoke to a very helpful guidance counselor. She even told me I had good scores on my SAT's which I didn't even remember from high school. I knew I took it and I didn't pay much attention to it.

I graduated from Manchester Community College with an Associate Degree in 1977. I applied and got accepted to the University of Connecticut. At the time I entered college I was sporting an Afro hair style. The Afro became a powerful political symbol which reflected black pride and it was a hairstyle that was easier to maintain without requiring frequent trips to the barber shop. I wore it with my military jacket and it was cool. That was the style and it was a way of projecting the militant look. I didn't make a lot of friends. At times I was the only black student in the classroom or meetings. Colleges were begging minorities to enroll back in that time. UCONN had about 3 to 4 percent Black enrollment out of 25,000 student population. I felt privilege and proud to be going there even though they had some problems trying to get minorities to enroll. The basketball teams had good representations. They won four NCAA championships. The women won ten championships. I was motivated to get an education and that was all that mattered.

My VA benefits was going to end in October of 1978. To keep my benefits flowing I had to take classes in the fall, spring and summer. It came down to finishing 4 years of college in 3 years. When I got to UCONN, I changed my major to Management and Labor Relations. Working in Human Resources had some appeal. I was undecided about what I wanted to do. I saw some possibilities of being an Arbitrator for the Unions. I was a Union Steward at Pratt & Whitney before I got laid-off. I saw the opportunity in the labor relation part of my courses. At the same time I was under immense pressure to finish school and find a job. I also realized that I would have to go to Law School to become an arbitrator. It was too much for me to deal with and I put Law School on the backburner.

Before I got educated, I considered myself politically independent. I did not consider myself Republican or Democrat. I just wanted to be a proud citizen of the United States and live by the principles on which the country was founded. We live in a democracy that gives us equality before the law. I was going along with the status quo when I realized I had no say in my future. Empowerment to take action is by voting. You are making your voice heard. It is our right, it is our duty, and it is our responsibility.

The right to petition elected officials for redress of grievances; due process; civil liberties; human rights; and elements of civil society outside the government. As voters we have the right to demand from our elected officials to answer for their behavior. The participation of the people in naming their political representatives. Politicians today expect to gain financially and are mainly interested in the influence they can gain to increase their wealth in office and for when they leave office. Some politicians become so entrenched in their governmental powers; they often feel themselves above the law. A lot of politicians become lobbyists, to influence those working in government to benefit the interest of those they represent. Politicians always know what's best for us because they make decisions for us without asking. I believe that voting gives you the power to make change, in our history and voicing your opinion. Voting is essential to have your say in what matters in this country.

It is also expensive to run for political office in this country. A lot of Democratic countries have compulsory voting in national elections as a right of citizenship. Political parties can derive financial benefits from compulsory voting, since they do not have to spend resources convincing the electorate that it should in general turn out to vote. The big concern here is voter suppression.

I finished college in the fall of 1978 with enough credit to graduate in 1979. Pratt & Whitney did call me to go back to work while I was pursuing my degree. If I had stayed there for 10 years I would have been vested and be eligible for a pension. Some of my friends got early retirement at age 55. I was told that if I had maintained my union dues I would have been able to go back to my job or get a better situation. "Oh well." During my job search, I spoke to recruiters on campus that was looking for black college graduates. I was offered a position of a Systems Analyst with one company. The problem was I didn't want to relocate. I decided to take a position with Metropolitan Life Insurance Company in Manchester. They sent me to Rhode Island for training and I got my Life and Casualty License.

I stayed with Met Life for 3 years. I went to work for an investment company in East Hartford.

I had to get the Series 7 license to be a Stock Broker. I intended to get enough experience in the business and go and start my own company. The opportunity came when I met Roy Whitt. He was my client and a business owner. He was building a Supermarket on Albany Avenue in Hartford. He needed help with the financing of the project and with his accountant Lennox Miller a business plan was developed. We went to the SBA with it to get the financing. The financing was in place and we went to work building the structure. Roy suggested that we include an office to provide Insurance and Investment Services. I felt that was a great idea because it would provide a great benefit to the Black community. After the building was ready I put up my sign to advertise my services. I sold car insurance, life insurance and investment saving plans. I was advising people to save money in mutual funds, some as low as $25 a month. I was getting community support and referrals. I felt proud because I was the only one in the community providing the services.

We were on our way towards building an empire. I bought a 1983 Mercedes Benz 240D. The car cost me $18,000. It was worthwhile investment because it measured my success and the image I wanted. I was very busy keeping the business going. I had two secretaries working with me and I was enjoying the challenges of the business. It was early in the morning when I got the call. The supermarket was on fire. I saw it on the morning news, the market was destroyed. They said it was arson. We were out of business. I had to go back to the investment company and work from there. I made my last payment on the Mercedes when I got into an accident and totaled it. The insurance company gave me $10,000 for it. I bought a used 300D to replace it.

I was trying to piece things together and I saw myself going in different directions. I was hanging out with a different crowd and it ruined my marriage. I decided to go back to New York and take some time off. I wanted to keep things simple. I knew I was walking away and a lot of people would be disappointed. I needed to find peace within. Someone suggested I should start with God.

I was watching television and I saw this message about another testament of Jesus Christ. I called the number associated with it and two missionaries came over to my apartment with the Book of Mormon. They gave me a lesson plan and I read the book and found it interesting. They invited me to church and I liked what was happening to me. I joined the church in 1990 and got baptized. I felt the spirit and wanted to get involve and be proactive among the members. First I had to overcome the negatives of being a Mormon. When I told people that I was a Mormon, I got a lot of negative feedback.

My problem was I didn't know enough about the church to defend the bad things that I would hear. I took it upon myself to investigate. I started with Joseph Smith who was the founder of the church. As a young man of fourteen years, Joseph already had a desire to find the truth. Like the rest of his family he was deeply religious, and when the time came for him to be baptized, Joseph had to decide which of the many Christian denomination to join. After careful study, he still felt confused. He later wrote, "So great were the confusion and strife among the different denominations, that it was impossible for a person young as I was…to come to any certain conclusion who was right and who was wrong. During this war of words and tumult of opinions, I often said to myself: What is to be done? Who of all these parties are right; or, are they all wrong together? If any one of them be right, which is it, and how shall I know it? Joseph turned to the Bible for guidance. He read, "If any of you lack wisdom, let him ask of God, that gives to all men liberally, and upbraided not; and it shall be given him". (James 1:5). In response to a humble prayer, God called Joseph to re-establish the Church of Jesus Christ.

I was in the Richmond Hill, Queens, branch and I was given a calling to be the Young Men's President. The organizations promote the growth and development of each young man through instruction, activities, and give support to the parents and the home. This was a great calling because I got to meet with parents and they were very supportive. During this time I got married and was starting a new family.

A new branch of the Church opened in Brooklyn, East New York. I lived in Brooklyn at the time and I was asked to be the First Counselor to the Bishop for that branch. The congregation was mostly African-Americans and new converts to the church.

The atmosphere was fantastic and the members were glad to see me in the position of leadership.

Two years later I bought a house in queens and I had to be released from the calling. I went back to my old branch where I served as a home teacher. That required going to the homes of members once a week to check on their needs and give them spiritual blessings.

I wanted to go back to Connecticut because it was a good place to raise my children and I had a lot of friends living there. I contacted some of them and they were delighted with my decision. My friend Jesse found a house for me in Bloomfield and he sent a truck to get our furniture. That was the help we needed. We packed up, sold the house and moved to Connecticut. We lived in the town of Bloomfield for a year and then we moved to Windsor. We joined the church and enjoyed peace of mind. After the kids finished high school, we moved back to New York to start over again.

The Church of Jesus Christ of Latter-day Saints has the largest Genealogy Records available. I was able to locate my ancestors as far back as the 1800s. My paternal grandparents migrated from Barbados to live in Boston. However, my main concern was the racial attitudes of members in the white branches I visited.

Pres. Hinckley calls racism 'ugly and unacceptable'

On April 2, 2006 I went to the LDS General Conference and President Gordon B Hinckley opened the session by telling the members that racism was unacceptable. He wanted everyone to acknowledge the difference in each of us and to be Christ like in dealing with other races. He admonishes members to show more kindness in their lives.

Membership in the LDS Church has surpassed 15 million according to statistical report and the number of operational temples worldwide at 144.

The Legacy of Slavery

The Missouri Compromise was a federal law in the United States that regulated slavery in the countries Western territories. The compromise, devised by Henry Clay, was agreed to by the pro-slavery and anti-slavery factions in the United States Congress and passed as a law in 1820. It prohibited slavery in the former Louisiana Territory, except within the boundaries of the proposed state of Missouri. The Missouri Compromise criticized by many southerners because it established the principle that could make laws regarding slavery, northerners on the other hand, condemned it for acquiescing in the expansion of slavery. It was repealed by the Kansas Nebraska Act of 1854. The Supreme Court indicated that the Missouri Compromise was unconstitutional in the 1857 Dred Scott v. Sanford ruling.

After the civil war Lincoln issued the Emancipation Proclamation 1862, declaring that all the slaves in the rebel states was free. The 13 Amendment ended slavery. The 14 Amendment ratified 9 July 1868, made blacks citizens and all native born Americans citizens which why the children of illegal immigrants become citizens when born here.

Andrew Johnson was the 17th president of the United States serving from 1865 to 1869. Became president as he was the vice president at the time of the assassination of Abraham Lincoln. Once in office, Johnson focused on quickly restoring the southern States to the Union. In 1866 Johnson vetoed the Freedman's Bureau bill and the Civil Rights bill, legislation aimed at protecting blacks. That same year, when Congress passed the 14th Amendment granting citizens to blacks, the president urged Southern States not to ratify it (the amendment nevertheless was ratified in July 1868).

The Bureau of Refugees, Freedmen, and Abandoned Lands, usually referred to as simply the Freedman's Bureau, was a U.S. federal government agency established in 1865 to aid Freedmen (freed Slaves) in the South during the reconstruction era of the United States, which attempted to change society in the former Confederate.

Racial attitude against blacks from the plantations forced labor led to racial bias in the deep South, exploitation of blacks on the farms, Jim Crow Laws and lynching in the cotton belt areas. Picking cotton was labor intensive and unprofitable venture.

However, after Eli Whitney unveiled the Cotton Gin, processing cotton became much easier resulting in greater availability and cheaper cloth. The invention had the by-product of increasing the number of slaves needed to pick the cotton thereby strengthening the arguments for continuing slavery. The cotton states of the Deep South chose to recede.

The first branch of the Ku Klux Klan was established in Pulaski, Tennessee, in May, 1866. A year later a general organization of local Clans was established in Nashville in April, 1867. Most of the leaders were former members of the Confederate Army. The first grand wizard was Nathan Forrest. Klansmen tortured and killed black Americans and sympathetic whites. Between 1868 and 1870 the Ku Klux Klan played an important role in restoring white rule in North Carolina, Tennessee and Georgia.

Share Cropping—By the early 1870s, the system known as sharecropping had come to dominate agriculture across the cotton-planting south. Under this system, black families would rent small plots of land, or shares, to work themselves; in return, they would give a portion of their crop to the landowner at the end of the year.

Black Codes: Blacks were left without land and forced to work as laborers on large white owned farms and plantation to earn a living. Many clashed with former slave masters bent on reestablishing a gang labor system similar to the one that prevailed under slavery. To regulate the labor force and reassert white supremacy in the post-war South, former confederate state legislatures soon passed restrictive legislation denying blacks legal equality and political rights and requiring them to sign yearly contracts.

The battle to change attitudes against being black is an everyday task.

Dred Scott

Dred Scott was 46 or 47-year old slave who sued for his freedom after the death of his owner because he had lived in a territory where slavery was forbidden (the northern part of the Louisiana Purchase, from which slavery was excluded under the terms of the Missouri Compromise). Scott filed suit for freedom in 1846 and went through two State trials, the first denying and the second granting freedom. Eleven years later the Supreme Court denied Scott his freedom in a sweeping decision that set the United States on course for Civil War. The court ruled that Dred Scott was not a citizen who had a right to sue in the federal courts, and that Congress had no constitutional power to pass the Missouri Compromise.

In 1857 Dred Scott decision, decided 7-2, held that a slave did not become free when taken into a free state; Congress could not bar slavery from a territory; and people of African descent imported into the United States and held as slaves, or their descendants could not be citizens. Furthermore, a state could not bar slave owners from bringing slaves into that State. This decision, seen as unjust by many Republicans including Abraham Lincoln, was also seen as proof that the slave Power had seize control of the Supreme Court. The decision, written by Chief Justice Roger B. Taney, barred slaves and their descendants from citizenship. Taney wrote the notorious 1857 Dred Scott ruling denying citizenship to blacks, noting that the Constitution's framers considered them "beings of an inferior order." The decision enraged abolitionist and encouraged slave owners helping to push the country towards civil war.

Dred Scott was considered property and property could not be taken without Due Process of Law. Black people were not considered citizens when the Constitution was drafted in 1787. However, there were free black citizens in the U.S. during that time. Dred Scott spent time in Illinois a Free State and Wisconsin a free territory. He was doomed from the beginning, he was not considered a person and when he asked for his freedom it was denied. He was not going to get his freedom unless his owner granted it. Living in a non-slave territory does not make you free. Your owner could take you anywhere because you are his property.

During the Lewis and Clarke expedition, a slave by the name of York was owned by Meriwether Lewis. He was also an explorer with the expedition. York tasted freedom and he took it because he never went back to Virginia with his owner. Either he was set free or he took his freedom. Last we heard he was living with the Indians.

Rebellions that led to the Civil War
Nathanial "Nat" Turner

Nat Turner (1800-1831) was a black American slave who led the only effective, sustained slave rebellion (August 1831) in U.S. history. Spreading terror throughout the white South, his action set off a new wave of oppressive legislation prohibiting the education, movement, and assembly of slaves and stiffened proslavery, anti-abolitionist convictions that persisted in that region until the civil war (1861-65).

Nat Turner was hanged, beheaded, skinned, and chopped up. Body parts scattered and no burial. His crime? Plotting a revolt to free his people.

Turner went into hiding for several months and white militias retaliated against many slaves because of widespread fear. The injustices against the slaves forced Turner to do something about it. Whites felt they were treating their slaves very well and they didn't think they would want to be free. Slaves were always trying to escape from their masters. When they were caught they were punished mercilessly.

Turner was a man of God and couldn't accept slavery as God's will for his people. He had to do something. He became a religious leader among his fellow slaves. He learned from the bible that he had to lead his people to freedom. He saw the bible as a book to save your soul. Yet the same people who believe in the bible would do terrible things to the slaves in the name of punishment.

Turner claimed that God spoke to him in visions to free the slaves. He was an inspiration to the slaves because they weren't educated and they were looking for a leader to get them out of their condition towards freedom. Although the rebellion failed the damage was done and it led others to be inspired.

John Brown

John Brown (1800-1859) was a white American abolitionist who believed armed insurrection was the only way to overthrow the institution of slavery in the United States. During the 1856 conflict in Kansas, Brown commanded forces at the Battle of Black Jack and the Battle of Osawatomie. Brown's followers also killed five slavery supporters at Pottawatomie. In 1859, Brown led an unsuccessful raid on the federal armory at Harpers Ferry that ended with his capture. Brown's trial resulted in his conviction and sentence of death by hanging. Historians agree John Brown played a major role in the start of the Civil war.

John Brown was a Civil Rights activist willing to use military force if necessary. He came from a religious background and felt slavery had to be abolished. He took part in the Underground Railroad to help slaves escape to Free States and Canada. The Underground Railroad was a network of secret routes and safe houses. He gave land to free African Americans and help protect them from slave hunters.

Brown was inspired by Frederick Douglas who he met in Springfield Mass. Brown also settled in the Black community of North Elba, New York. Years later he moved to Kansas where he became involved in the slave issue. The Kansas-Nebraska Act of 1854, cause conflict of a slave or Free State.

In 1858, Brown liberated a group of enslaved people from a Missouri homestead and helped guide them to freedom in Canada. He believed that his actions were just and sanctioned by God. He planned to arm the slaves and strike terror in the hearts of slave owners. When Brown and his men raided the Federal Arsenal the slaves living in the area did not joined the raid.

The only black man that was killed in the raid was Hayward Shepherd. He was not a slave. A year later the secession from the Union started.

The Confederate flag has always been a symbol of white supremacy and racism.

Throughout history, the Confederate flag has been repeatedly used as a symbol to oppress black people. It was flown by Southern armies during the Civil War as they fought to keep slavery. And it was later brought back in the 1960s, to intimidate civil rights advocates and defend segregation.

South Carolina, the first state to secede, said in its official statement that it saw any attempts to abolish slavery and grant rights to black Americans as "hostile to the South" and "destructive of its beliefs and safety.

Mississippi, meanwhile, was even more explicit in its statement, saying that its "position is thoroughly identified with the institution of slavery":

These statements leave no doubt that the South fought in the Civil War to protect the institution of slavery.

Convinced that their way of life, based on slavery, was irretrievably threatened by the election of President Abraham Lincoln (November 1860). The Confederate States of America consisted of the governments of 11 Southern States which were South Carolina, Mississippi, Florida, Alabama, Georgia, Louisiana, Texas, Virginia, Arkansas, Tennessee and North Carolina.

The 13th Amendment, adopted late 1865, officially abolish slavery, but freed blacks' status in the post-war South remained precarious, and significant challenges awaited during the Reconstruction period (1865-77). Former slaves received the rights of Citizenship and the "equal protection" of the constitution in the 14th Amendment (1868) and the right to vote in the 15th (1870), but the provisions of the Constitution were often ignored or violated, and it was difficult for former slaves to gain a foothold in the post-war economy thanks to restrictive black Codes and regressive contractual arrangements such as sharecropping.

Supporters of the Confederate flag claim it's flown to honor the dead who fought in the Civil War and pay tribute to the South's heritage. The problem is this heritage is mired in racism—as demonstrated by States' justifications for seceding at the start of the Civil War.

Despite seeing an unprecedented degree of black participation in American political life, Reconstruction was ultimately frustrating for African Americans, and the rebirth of white supremacy including the rise of racist organization such as the Ku Klux Klan-had triumphed in the South by 1877. Almost a century later, resistance to the lingering racism and discrimination in America that began during the slavery era would lead to the civil rights movements of the 1960s which would achieve the greatest political and social gains for blacks since Reconstruction.

Slavery was morally wrong and people became victims. People in the south are still celebrating the old days for enslaving black people by putting up statutes of a Confederate General in a park or Confederate flags flying at the state house honoring a crime against black people. Black people look at this and say "people are saluting their heritage from slavery and genocide". Making heroes of white supremacist and accepting their views of bigotry.

These people need to start acting civilized and work to create social harmony for the good of the community and society and stop offending people.

The Jim Crow Laws

The Jim Crow Laws were racial segregation laws enacted between 1876 and 1965 in the United States at the state and local level. They mandated de jure racial segregation in all public facilities in Southern States of the former Confederacy, with, starting in 1890, a "separate but equal" status for African Americans. The separation in practice led to conditions for African Americans that were inferior to those provided for White Americans, systematizing a number of economic, educational and social disadvantages. De jure segregation mainly applied to the Southern United States, while Northern segregation was generally de facto—patterns of segregation in housing enforced by covenants, bank lending practices and job discrimination, including discriminatory union practices for decades. Some examples of Jim Crow Laws were the segregation of public schools, public places and public transportation, and the segregation of restrooms, restaurants and drinking fountains for whites and blacks. The US military was also segregated, as were federal work places, initiated in 1913 under President Woodrow Wilson, the first Southern President since 1856. His administration practiced overt racial discrimination in hiring, requiring candidates to submit photos. Legal practices of Jim Crow Laws ended with the passage of the Voting Rights Act of 1965.

Birth of a Nation

On March 21, 1915 President Woodrow Wilson attended a special screening at the White House of The Birth of a Nation. The novel was written by Wilson's good friend Thomas Dixon.

The film presented a distorted portrait of the South after the Civil War, glorifying the Ku Klux Klan and denigrating blacks. It falsified the period of Reconstruction by presenting blacks as dominating Southern whites and sexually forcing themselves upon white women. The Klan was portrayed as the South's savior from the alleged tyranny. This portrayal was untrue. During reconstruction, whites dominated blacks and assaulted black women.

President Wilson remarked that "It is like writing history with lightning, and my only regret is that it is all terribly true."

African American audiences openly wept at the film's malicious portrayal of blacks, while Northern white audiences cheered.

The film incited riots in major cities like Boston and Philadelphia. It was denied release in Chicago, Ohio, Denver, Pittsburg, Saint Louis and Minneapolis.

The NAACP fought against the film and tried unsuccessfully to get it banned. The characters in the movie were white men in black faces. The Klan successfully used it to recruit new members. The Klan is still a white terrorist organization that carried out hundreds of murders. The number of lynchings in America had risen sharply in 1915.

WEB Du Bois felt that censorship was justified. Writing to the head of the NAACP in 1921 he called The Birth of a Nation "a special case. A new art was used, deliberately, to slander and vilify a race." To Du Bois, it was "a public menace…not art, but vicious propaganda."

Dixon said "that one purpose of his play was to create a feeling of abhorrence in white people, especially white women against colored men—to prevent the mixing of white and Negro blood by intermarriage," and added "that he wished to have all Negroes removed from the United States."

In its effort to ban the movie, it had unintended consequences for black representation in motion pictures. Oscar Micheaux's Within Our Gates, which excoriated lynch mobs and the Klan, was banned in several places for the same reasons as Birth.

Membership in the NAACP doubled to 10,000 by the end of 1915 and had reached 80,000 by the close of the decade.

Key events

Immediately following the Civil War, the federal government began a program known as Reconstruction aimed at rebuilding the states of the former Confederacy. The federal programs also provided aid to the former slaves and attempted to integrate them into society. During and after this period, blacks made substantial gains in their political power and many were able to move from poverty into the middle class. At the same time resentment by many whites toward these gains led to unprecedented violence and the rise of the Ku Klux Klan.

The year 1896 held the landmark Supreme Court decision Plessey v. Ferguson, (1896), which upheld "separate but equal" racial segregation, which proved a major setback to civil rights efforts. Throughout the post-war period anti-progressives waged efforts to curtail these efforts. This case and other events in the 1890s marked a turning point beyond which the civil rights progress in the 19th century was dramatically reversed. The most important civil rights leaders of this period were Frederick Douglas and Booker T. Washington.

Benjamin "Pap" Singleton was an American activist and businessman best known for his role in establishing African American settlements in Kansas. A former slave from Tennessee who escaped to freedom in 1846, he became a noted abolitionist, community leader, and spokesman for African American civil rights. He returned to Tennessee during the Union occupation in 1862, but soon concluded that blacks would never achieve economic equality in the white-dominated South.

Following the end of Reconstruction, many blacks feared the Ku Klux Klan, the White League and the Jim Crow laws which continued to make them second-class citizens. Motivated by Benjamin "Pap" Singleton, as many as forty thousand left the South to settle in Kansas, Oklahoma and Colorado. This was the first general migration of blacks following the Civil War. In the 1880s, blacks bought more than 20,000 acres of land in Kansas, and several of the settlements made during this time (e.g. Nicodemus, Kansas, which was founded in 1877) still exist today. This sudden wave of migration came as a great surprise to many white Americans, who did not realize that black southerners were free in name only. Many blacks left the South with the belief that they were receiving free passage to Kansas, only to be stranded in St. Louis, Missouri. Black churches in St. Louis, together with Eastern philanthropists, formed the Colored Relief Board and the Kansas Freedmen's Aid Society to help those stranded in St. Louis to reach Kansas.

Disfranchisement

Mississippi passed a new constitution in 1890 that included provisions for poll taxes, literacy tests (which depended on the arbitrary decisions of white registrars), and complicated record keeping to establish residency, which severely reduced the number of blacks who could register. It was litigated before the Supreme Court. In 1898, in Williams v. Mississippi, the Court upheld the state. Other Southern states quickly adopted the "Mississippi plan", and from

1890—1908, ten states adopted new constitutions with provisions to disfranchise most blacks and many poor whites. States continued to disfranchise these groups for decades, until mid-1960s federal legislation provided for oversight and enforcement of constitutional voting rights.

Blacks were most adversely affected, and in many southern states black voter turnout dropped to zero. Poor whites were also disfranchised. In Alabama, for instance, by 1941, 600,000 poor whites had been disfranchised, as well as 520,000 blacks.

It was not until the 20th century that litigation by African Americans on such provisions began to meet some success before the Supreme Court. In 1915 in Guinn v. United States, the Court declared Oklahoma's 'grandfather clause' to be unconstitutional. Although the decision affected all states that used the grandfather clause, state legislatures quickly employed new devices to continue disfranchisement. Each provision or statute had to be litigated separately. The NAACP, founded in 1909, litigated against many such provisions.

Criminal law and lynching

In 1880, the United States Supreme Court ruled in Strauder v. West Virginia, 100 U.S. 303 that African Americans could not be excluded from juries. But, beginning in 1890 with new state constitutions and electoral laws, the South effectively disfranchised blacks in the South, which routinely disqualified them for jury duty which was limited to voters. This left them at the mercy of a white justice system arrayed against them. In some states, particularly Alabama, the state used the <u>criminal justice system</u> to reestablish a form of peonage, through the convict-lease system. The state sentenced black males to years of imprisonment, which they spent working without pay. The state leased prisoners to private employers, such as Tennessee Coal, Iron and Railroad Company, a subsidiary of United States Steel Corporation, which paid the state for their labor. Because the state made money, the system created incentives for the jailing of more men, who were disproportionately black. It also created a system in which treatment of prisoners received little oversight.

Extrajudicial punishment was more brutal. During the last decade of the 19th century and the first decades of the 20th century, white vigilante mobs lynched thousands of black males, sometimes with the overt assistance of state officials, mostly within the South. No whites were charged with crimes in any of those murders. Whites were so confident of their immunity from prosecution for lynching that they not only photographed the victims, but made postcards out of the pictures.

Initially the KKK presented itself as another fraternal organization devoted to betterment of its members. The KKK's revival was inspired in part by the movie Birth of a Nation, which glorified the earlier Klan and dramatized the racist stereotypes concerning blacks of that era. The Klan focused on political mobilization, which allowed it to gain power in states such as Indiana, on a platform that combined racism with anti-immigrant, anti-Semitic, antiCatholic and anti-union rhetoric, but also supported lynching. It reached its peak of membership and influence about 1925, declining rapidly afterward as opponents mobilized.

Senate apologizes for inaction on lynching's in 2005

At least 4,749 Americans are known to have been lynched during a time when the Senate failed to act on some 200 anti-lynching bills.

A resolution was sponsored by Senators Mary Landrieu of Louisiana and George Allen of Virginia, leading 78 other senators to apologize for the U.S. Senate's inability to get the 200 anti-lynching bills over the years.

Although the resolution was a noble step in the right direction, it puts focus on the fact that Black Life had been viewed as worthless and expendable in this country for centuries. The inexcusable crimes against African Americans and the spectacle that typically surrounded their deaths are lasting images that cannot simply be pushed aside because of a gathering of law makers and their apology.

An Alabama-based civil rights organization will construct a monument in Montgomery to commemorate victims of lynching's across the South. The

Equal Justice Initiative will also construct a museum nearby focused on African-American history.

The memorial will be the first in the country to pay tribute to the more than 4,000 black victims of lynching who were killed between 1877 and 1950. The 6-acre monument will feature a series of columns, each representing a county where, "racial terror lynchings" took place, according to the Equal Justice Initiative. The names of the victims will be engraved on the columns.

Bryan Stevenson, the organizations director, said in an interview with the Associated Press, that by acknowledging the darker aspects of the country's history, hopefully the U.S. can work toward a more unified future. We want to "liberate America" from limiting who we are and what we can be.

Segregated economic life and education

This period saw the maturing of independent black churches, whose leaders were usually also strong community leaders. Blacks had left white churches and the Southern Baptist Convention to set up their own churches free of white supervision immediately during and after the American Civil War. With the help of northern associations, they quickly began to set up state conventions and, by 1895, joined several associations into the black National Baptist Convention, the first of that denomination among blacks. In addition, independent black denominations, such as the African Methodist Episcopal Church and AME Zion Church, had made hundreds of thousands of converts in the South, founding AME churches across the region. The churches were centers of community activity, especially organizing for education.

Continuing to see education as the primary route of advancement and critical for the race, many talented blacks went into teaching, which had high respect as a profession. Segregated schools for blacks were underfunded in the South and ran on shortened schedules in rural areas. Despite segregation, in Washington, DC by contrast, as Federal employees, black and white teachers were paid on the same scale. Outstanding black teachers in the North received advanced degrees and taught in highly regarded schools, which trained the next generation of leaders in cities such as Chicago, Washington, and New York, whose black populations had increased in the 20th century due to the Great Migration

Northern alliance's had helped fund normal schools and colleges to teach African-American teachers, as well as create other professional classes. The American Missionary Association, supported largely by the Congregational and Presbyterian churches, had helped fund and staff numerous private schools and colleges in the South, who collaborated with black communities to train generations of teachers and other leaders. Major 20th-century industrialists, such as George Eastman of Rochester, New York, acted as philanthropists and made substantial donations to black educational institutions such as Tuskegee Institute.

In 1787, Richard Allen and others of African descent withdrew from St. George's Methodist Church in Philadelphia because of unkind treatment and restrictions placed upon the worshipers of African descent. After Allen left St. George's Methodist Church, he and his followers purchased a blacksmith shop for thirty-five dollars. From the blacksmith shop they worshipped and helped the sick and the poor. The blacksmith shop was converted into a church. They called the new church Bethel.

In 1816, Black members of Charleston's Methodists Episcopal Church withdrew over disputed burial ground, and under the leadership of Morris Brown. The Rev. Morris Brown organized a church of persons of color and sought to have it affiliated with Allen's church.

In 1822 the church was investigated for its involvement with a planned slave revolt. Denmark Vesey, one of the churches founders, organized a major slave uprising in Charleston. During the Vesey controversy, the AME Church was burned. Worship services continued after the church was rebuilt until 1834 when all black churches were outlawed. The congregation continued the tradition of the African church by worshipping underground until 1865 when it was formally reorganized, and the name Emanuel was adopted, meaning "God with us."

The Black Church

The Black church in the United States was the result of rejection by White Christians. What these white Christians did not seem to know is that Africans were members of the church from the beginning. Black people did not first discover Christianity through slaveholders or white missionaries. African people and places are mentioned over 850 times in the Bible. Africans played a significant role in the life of Jesus. The beginning and end of Jesus' life was marked by the involvement of Africans. Shortly after his birth Jesus' family fled to Africa to escape the murderous threats of King Herod. At his death an African, Simon of Cyrene, carried the cross of Jesus.

When the authors of the Bible described the formation of Christian congregations, Africans were there from the beginning as members of churches in the Middle East, Asia, and Europe. Tradition says that the Ethiopian treasury official noted in the Book of Acts in the New Testament who was traveling down the Gaza road back to home in what today is the Sudan launched the first churches in Africa.

As the center of community life, Black churches were integral leaders and organizers in the civil rights movement. Their history as a focal point for the Black community and as a link between the Black and White worlds made them natural for this purpose. Rev. Martin Luther King, Jr. was but one of many notable Black ministers involved in the movement. Ralph David Abernathy, Bernard Lee, Fred Shuttles worth, and C.T. Vivian are among the many notable minister-activists. They were especially important during the later years of the movement in the 1950s and 1960s.

The NAACP

W.E.B. Du Bois (February 23, 1868-August 27. 1963) was an American Sociologist, historian civil rights activist, Pan-Africans, author, writer and editor. Born in Great Barrington, Massachusetts. After completing graduate work at the University of Berlin and Harvard, where he was the first African American to earn a doctorate, he became a professor of history, sociology and economics at Atlanta University. Du Bois was one of the co-founders of the National Association for the Advancement of Colored People (NAACP) in 1909.

W.E.B. Du Bois said, on the launch of his ground breaking 1903 treatise The Souls of Black Folk, "For the problem of the Twentieth Century is the problem of the color-line." He has been proven right.

Viewed in historic and cross-national perspective, the legal and political transformation of American race relations since WW II represents a remarkable achievement, powerfully confirming the virtue of our political institutions official segregation, which some southerners as late as 1960 were saying would live forever, is dead. The caste system of social domination enforced with open violence has been eradicated. Whereas two generations ago most Americans were indifferent or hostile to blacks' demands for equal citizenship rights, now the ideal of equal opportunity is upheld by our laws and universally embraced in our politics.

A large and stable black middle class has emerged, and black participation in the economic, political and cultural life of this country, at every level and in every venue, has expanded impressively. This is good news. In the final years of this traumatic, exhilarating century, it deserved to be celebrated.

W. E. B. Du Bois joined with other black leaders and white activists, such as Mary White Covington, Oswald Garrison Villard, William English Walling, Henry Moskowitz, Julius Rosenthal, Lillian Wald, Rabbi Emil G. Hirsh, and Stephen Wise to create the National Association for the Advancement of Colored People (NAACP) 1909. Du Bois also became editor of its magazine The Crisis. In its early years, the NAACP concentrated on using the courts to attack Jim Crow Laws and disfranchising constitutional provisions. It successfully challenged the Louisville, Kentucky ordinance that required residential segregation in Buchanan v. Warley, 245 U.S. 60. It also gained a Supreme Court ruling striking down Oklahoma's grandfather clause that exempted most illiterate white voters from a law that disfranchised African-American citizens in Guinn v. United States (1915).

The NAACP lobbied against President Woodrow Wilson's introduction of racial segregation into Federal government employment and offices in 1913. They lobbied for commissioning of African Americans as officers in World War I. In 1915 the NAACP organized public education and protests in cities across the nation against D.W. Griffith's silent film Birth of a Nation, a film that glamorized the Ku Klux Klan. Some cities refused to allow the film to open.

The NAACP devoted much of its energy between the first and second world wars to fighting the lynching of blacks and investigating the serious race riots in numerous cities throughout the United States in what was called the "Red Summer" of 1919, resulting from postwar economic and social tensions. The organization sent Walter F. White, who later became its general secretary, to Phillips County, Arkansas in October 1919 to investigate the Elaine Race Riot. In that year, it was unusual for being a rural riot: more than 200 black tenant farmers were killed by roving white vigilantes and federal troops after a deputy sheriff's attack on a union meeting of sharecroppers left one white man dead. The NAACP organized the appeals for twelve men sentenced to death a month later, based on their testimony having been obtained by beating and electric shocks. They obtained a groundbreaking Supreme Court decision in Moore v. Dempsey, 261 U.S. 86. This case significantly expanded the Federal courts' oversight of states' criminal justice systems in the years to come.

The NAACP also spent more than a decade seeking federal legislation barring lynching. It regularly displayed a black flag stating "A Man Was Lynched Yesterday" from the window of its offices in New York to mark each outrage. Efforts to pass an anti-lynching law foundered on Southern Democratic power in Congress. For instance, while Republicans achieved passage in the House of an anti-lynching law in 1922, Southern Democratic senators filibustered the bill in the Senate and defeated it in the 1922, 1923 and 1924 legislative sessions. The Southern Democratic block controlled important chairmanships in both houses of Congress and defeated all lynching legislative proposals.

The NAACP led the successful fight, in alliance with the American Federation of Labor, to prevent the nomination of John Johnston Parker to the Supreme Court. They opposed him because of his opposition to black suffrage and his anti-labor rulings. This alliance and lobbying campaign were important for the NAACP, both in demonstration the NAACP's ability to mobilize widespread opposition to racism and as a first step toward building political alliances with the labor movement.

The NAACP's legal department, headed by Charles Hamilton Houston and Thurgood Marshall, undertook a campaign spanning several decades to bring about the reversal of the "separate but equal" doctrine announced by the Supreme Court's decision in Plessy v. Ferguson. Instead of appealing to the legislative or executive branches of government, they focused on the judiciary, reasoning that Congress was dominated by Southern segregationists, while the Presidency could not afford to lose the Southern vote. The NAACP's first cases did not challenge the principle directly, but sought instead to show that the state's segregated facilities were not equal.

Even those more modest goals helped lay the foundation for the ultimate reversal of the doctrine in Plessy v. Ferguson by showing the irrational nature of the distinctions that the states drew to preserve segregation and the humiliating impact it had on the black subjects of "separate but equal" treatment. The Supreme Court's unanimous decision in Brown v. Board of Education (1954), holding that state-sponsored segregation of elementary schools was unconstitutional, was a first step in dismantling segregation in the South. It was a historic milestone in reframing the national debate over segregation by putting state-sponsored discrimination beyond constitutional defense.

Spring 1951 was the year in which great turmoil was felt amongst Black students in reference to Virginia State's educational system. At the time in Prince Edward County, Monton High School was segregated and students had decided to take matters in their own hands to fight against two things: the overpopulated school premises and the unsuitable conditions in their school. This particular behavior coming from Black people in the South was most likely unexpected and inappropriate as White people had expectations for Blacks to act in a subordinate manner. Moreover, some local leaders of the NAACP had tried to persuade the students to back down from their protest against the Jim Crow laws of school segregation. When the students did not accept the NAACP's demands, the NAACP automatically joined them in their battle against school segregation. This became one of the five cases that made up what is known today as Brown v. Board of Education.

On May 17, 1954, the United States Supreme Court handed down its decision regarding the case called Brown v. Board of Education of Topeka, Kansas, in which the plaintiffs charged that the education of black children in separate public schools from their white counterparts was unconstitutional. The opinion of the Court stated that the "segregation of white and colored children in public schools has detrimental effect upon the colored children. The impact is greater when it has the sanction of the law; for the policy of separating the races is usually interpreted as denoting the inferiority of the Negro group"

The lawyers from the NAACP had to gather some plausible evidence in order to win the case of Brown vs. Education. Their way of addressing the issue of school segregation was to enumerate several arguments. One of them pertained to having an exposure to interracial contact in a school environment. It was said that it would, in turn, help to prevent children to live with the pressures that society exerts in regards to race. Therefore, having a better chance of living in democracy. In addition, another was in reference to the emphasis of how 'education' comprehends the entire process of developing and training the mental, physical and moral powers and capabilities of human beings". In Goluboff's book, it has been stated that the goals of the NAACP was to bring to the Court's awareness the fact that African American children were the victims of the legalization of school segregation and were not guaranteed a bright future. Without having the opportunity to be exposed to other cultures, it impedes on how Black children will function later on as adults trying to live a normal life.

The Court ruled that both Plessy v. Ferguson (1896), which had established the segregationist, "separate but equal" standard in general, and Cumming v. Richmond County Board of Education (1899), which had applied that standard to schools, were unconstitutional. The following year, in the case known as Brown v. Board of Education, the Court ordered segregation to be phased out over time, "with all deliberate speed".

After the Court's decision, a myriad of things have come about to promote the education of all Black people. What was most interesting was the fact that, at the time, the Black press had taken the initiative to become involved in the encouragement of all Black individuals holding different professional jobs by exposing them in their articles. Not only that, but some of the poor Black people were used as examples as well and gained as much respect as those with a diploma. Regular praises were given out to people with very modest lives. For instance, a Black journalist named Ethel Payne interviewed in 1954 a lady called Mrs. Sarah Belling. Belling worked as a bookkeeper and had a son named Spotswood who "had been the plaintiff in one of the school desegregation cases consolidated as Brown vs Topeka Board of Education" Mrs. Belling was somewhat put on a pedestal for wanting her son to get a good education and for being involved in her church. Following her encounter with the journalist, Mrs. Belling's story was published in the press.

Rosa Parks and the Montgomery Bus Boycott, 1955-1956

On December 1, 1955, Rosa Parks (the "mother of the Civil Rights Movement") refused to give up her seat on a public bus to make room for a white passenger. She was secretary of the Montgomery NAACP chapter and had recently returned from a meeting at the Highlander Center in Tennessee where nonviolent civil disobedience as a strategy had been discussed. Parks was arrested, tried, and convicted for disorderly conduct and violating a local ordinance. Parks later said that she was thinking of Emmett Till when she refused to give up her seat four days later. After word of this incident reached the black community, 50 African-American leaders gathered and organized the Montgomery Bus Boycott to demand a more humane bus transportation system. However, after any reforms were rejected the NAACP, led by E.D. Nixon, pushed for full desegregation of public buses. With the support of most of Montgomery's 50,000 African Americans, the boycott lasted for 381 days until the local ordinance segregating African-Americans and whites on public buses was lifted. Ninety percent of African Americans in Montgomery took part in the boycotts, which reduced bus revenue by 80%. A federal court ordered Montgomery's buses desegregated in November 1956, and the boycott ended.

A young Baptist minister named Martin Luther King, Jr., was president of the Montgomery Improvement Association, the organization that directed the boycott. The protest made King a national figure. His eloquent appeals to Christian brotherhood and American idealism created a positive impression on people both inside and outside the South.

Rosa Parks Biography
Born Rosa Louise McCauley (1913-2005)

Although she had become a symbol of the Civil Rights Movement, Rosa Park suffered hardship as a result. She lost her job at the department store and her husband lost his after his boss forbade him to discuss his wife or their legal case. They were unable to find work and eventually left Montgomery. Rosa Parks moved her family—husband and mother—to

Detroit, Michigan. There she made a new life for herself, working as a secretary and receptionist in U.S. Representative John Conyer's congressional office in Detroit. She also served on the board of the Planned Parenthood Federation of America. In 1987, along with Elaine Eason Steele, a long-time friend, she founded the Rosa and Raymond Parks Institute for Self-Development. The institute runs the "Pathways to Freedom" bus tours, introducing young people to important civil rights and Underground Railroad sites throughout the country. In 1992, she published Rosa Parks: My Story, an autobiography recounting her life in the segregated South. In 1995, she published her memoirs entitled Quiet Strength which focuses on the role religious faith played in her life.

Legacy

Rosa Parks received many accolades during her lifetime including the Spingarn Medal, the NAACP's highest award. She also received the Martin Luther King Jr. Award. On September 9, 1996, President Bill Clinton awarded Rosa Parks the Presidential Medal of Freedom, the highest honor given by the U.S. executive branch. The next year she was awarded the Congressional Gold Medal, the highest award given by the U.S. legislative branch. In 1999, Time magazine named Rosa Parks one of the 20 most influential people of the 20th century.

On October 24, 2005, at the age of 92, Rosa Parks quietly died in her apartment. She had been diagnosed the previous year with progressive dementia. Her death was marked by several memorial services, among them lying in state at the Capitol Rotunda in Washington D.C. where an estimated 50,000 people viewed her casket. Rosa was interred between her husband and mother at Detroit's Woodlawn Cemetery in the chapel's mausoleum. Shortly after her death the chapel was renamed the Rosa L. Parks Freedom Chapel.

In 1994, Parks was robbed and assaulted in her home at the age of 81. Damon Keith, a Detroit native and federal judge worked to find Parks a new, safer apartment at the Riverfront apartments in Detroit. Mike Ilitch the founder of Little Caesars pizza and owner of the Detroit Tigers and Red Wings paid for Parks' housing indefinitely. He continued paying for the apartment until Parks died in 2005.

Slaves in the Civil War

Enslaved African Americans did not wait for Lincoln's action before escaping and seeking freedom behind Union Lines. From early years of the war, hundreds of thousands of African Americans escaped to Union Lines, especially in Union-controlled areas like Norfolk and the Hampton Roads region in 1862 Virginia, Tennessee from 1862 on, the line of Sherman's march, etc. So many African Americans fled to Union lines that commanders created camps and schools for them, where both adults and children learned to read and write. The American Missionary Association entered the war effort by sending teachers south to such contraband camps, for instance, establishing schools in Norfolk and on nearby plantations. In addition, nearly 200,000 African-American men served with distinction as soldiers and sailors with Union troops. Most of those were escaped slaves.

Blacks were permitted to join the Union Army in 1863. They were paid $10 a month. White soldiers were paid at least $13. Officers were paid more. Blacks were charged$3 monthly fees for clothing. They refused the lower wages by protesting not to accept it until they got equal pay. The Union army was multicultural. One in ten blacks made up the Union Army. Many blacks joined the Army in exchanged for freedom.

Runaway slaves were treated as property rather than human beings. Their desire for freedom however, brought on the movement toward emancipation. Blacks used opportunities to gain freedom during the civil war.

In the South, slaves were hired to work in Iron factories, on railroad lines, Salt works and Iron forges to sustain the Confederate war effort. Slaves were put to work in the army hospitals as nurses, cooks, and laundresses. White men enlisted in the Confederate army. Whites would terrorize the slaves to keep them under control.

Slaves, freedmen spied on South during Civil War William A Jackson

Jackson served as a coachman to Confederate President Jefferson Davis. As a servant in Davis' home, Jackson overheard discussions the president had with his military leadership. His first report of Confederate plans and intentions was in May 1862 when he crossed into union lines. The information was sent to the War Department in Washington.

William Jackson was a runaway slave who became a Union agent. He funnels information to the Union from conversations he overheard. Davis and his military leaders assumed that Jackson did not understand and didn't care about the matters being discussed. Jackson was able to extract some of the most guarded military secrets of the confederacy.

Mary Touvestre

Mary Touvestre was a freed slave who worked as a housekeeper for a Confederate engineer who was repairing and transforming the USS Merrimac into the Virginia, the Confederate's first iron-clad (Warship). She overheard the engineer talking about the importance of the ship and realized that it could be a significant weapon against the Northern blockade.

At great personal risk, Touvestre stole the plans for the ship and fled to Washington, where she met with the Department of the Navy. The Union Navy was working on a similar ship, the USS Monitor. Touvestre, Wells said in an 1873 letter, "told me the condition of the vessel, and took from her clothing a paper, written by a mechanic who was working on the 'Merrimac', describing the character of the work, its progress and probable completion."

The Union navy intensified its construction of the Monitor and sailed it down to Virginia leading to the world's first ironclad naval battle, a stalemate that kept the rebel from breaking the federal blockade of Norfolk. Because of Touvestre information, the Union was able to prevent damage to the blockade to allow much needed supplies to slip through from Europe to the Confederacy.

Mary was born in the Shenandoah Valley of Western Virginia. As a slave she was sold to one of the farms in the area. She was trained as a seamstress. She had to be able to fit and study garments on customers to determine alterations. She had to have the ability to sew garments by hand, take up and let down hems, alters, repair and create clothing to meet customer needs. As a seamstress she had to know about design and the techniques to produce precise technical plans for garments.

From her training, she was able to understand the importance of the blue print of the ship that the engineer was discussing. Her technical background helped her to recognize the importance of the plans she stole. Her talent was unrecognized and as usual slaves were taken for granted as inferior.

John Scobell

John Scobell, the first African American secret service agent was a freed slave and was recruited by U.S. Secret Service Chief Allan Pinkerton.

In the Confederate circles he navigated, John Scobell was considered just another Mississippi slave: singing, shuffling, illiterate and completely ignorant of the Civil War going on around him.

Confederate officers thought nothing of leaving important documents where Scobell could see them, or discussing troop movements in front of him. Whom would he tell? Scobell was only the butler, or the deckhand on a rebel sympathizers steamboat, or the field hand belting out Negro spirituals in a powerful baritone.

In reality, Scobell was not a slave at all.

He was a spy sent by the Union army, one of a few black operatives who quietly gathered information in a high-stakes game of cat-and-mouse with Confederate spy-catchers and slave masters who could kill them on the spot. These unsung Civil War heroes were often successful, to the chagrin of Confederate leaders who never thought their disregard for blacks living among them would become a major tactical weakness.

"The chief source of information to the enemy," Gen. Robert E. Lee, commander of the Confederate Army, said in May 1863, "is through our negroes."

Little is known about the black men and women who served as Union intelligence officers, other than the fact that some were former slaves or servants who escaped from their masters and others were Northerners who volunteered to pose as slaves to spy on the Confederacy. There are scant references to their contributions in historical records, mainly because Union spymasters destroyed documents to shield them from Confederate soldiers and sympathizers during the war and vengeful whites afterward.

"These kinds of spies and operatives come up over and over again, many of them unnamed and rarely do they receive glory," said Hari Jones, curator of the African American Civil War Museum in Washington, who lectures on the Civil War's African American spies.

Jones and other experts are hoping the 150th anniversary of the Civil War will include some measure of remembrance for these officers.

Allan Pinkerton, head of the Union Intelligence Service at the onset of the Civil War, detailed his recruitment of black spies in his autobiography, including a couple of successful missions by Scobell and the extraction of valuable papers from a Union defector. Scobell in particular, Pinkerton said, was a "cool-headed, vigilant detective" who easily duped the Confederates around him by assuming "the character of the light-hearted, happy darkey."

"From the commencement of the war, I have found the Negroes of invaluable assistance and I never hesitated to employ them when after investigation I found them to be intelligent and trustworthy," Pinkerton said.

John Scobell was a slave in Mississippi and was given his freedom by his former Master James MacFarland Scobell. According to Allan Pinkerton, the former slaves were the most willing to cooperate and often had the best knowledge of Confederate fortifications, camps and supply points. John Scobell became a Pinkerton agent in 1861. He was well educated by his owner. He was quick-witted and an accomplish role player, which permitted him to function in several different identities on various missions including food vendor, cook, or laborer.

Scobell was a member of the "Legal League," a Negro organization in the South supporting freedom for slaves. Members supported Scobell by acting as couriers to carry his information to Union Lines.

Harriet Tubman

She was not only a conductor of the Underground Railroad, but also a spy for the Union. Her capability as a spy allowed her to guide a raiding party for Gen. David Hunter against confederate forces and freed 750 slaves. She also helped abolitionists John Brown recruit men for his raid on Harpers Ferry, and in the post-war era was an active participant in the struggle for women's suffrage.

Harriet Tubman was much more famous for her underground activities with the Underground Railroad. Her intelligence activities are well documented. In 1863, Union officials had found a more dramatic and active role for Tubman to play. The Union forces in South Carolina badly needed information about Confederate forces opposing them. Intelligence on the strength of enemy units, location of encampments, and designs of fortifications was almost nil. All these requirements could be met by short-term spying trips behind enemy lines, and it fell to Tubman to organize and lead these expeditions.

Tubman selected a few former slaves knowledgeable about the areas to be visited and established her spy organization. Often disguised as a field hand or poor farm wife, she led several spy missions herself, while directing others from Union lines. Information she provided was used effectively in military operations.

Tubman also served as a nurse for the Union army during the Civil War.

When Tubman died in 1913, she was honored with a full military funeral in recognition for work during the war.

In a 2015 poll, Harriet Tubman was chosen to replace Andrew Jackson on the $20 bill. It is left to President Obama to authorize the redesign of the currency.

However, Harriet Tubman's fate on the $20 bill is in question. Obama's Treasury secretary proposed putting the American hero on the $20 bill; Trump's Treasury secretary isn't convinced. Trump was asked about the issue on his campaign, and deemed Tubman "fantastic," but suggested bringing back the

$2 bill, a largely useless denomination of currency, in order to put her on it without displacing anyone else.

Elevating Tubman to U.S. Currency, on the other hand, would be "pure political correctness," he said.

Another spy, **Mary Elizabeth Bowser**, was born a slave to the Van Lew family, who freed her and sent her to school. Bowser then returned to Richmond, where Elizabeth Van Lew was running one of the war's most sophisticated spy rings.

Somehow, Van Lew got Bowser a job inside the Confederate White House as a housekeeper, Bowser then proceeded to sneak classified information out from under Confederate President Jefferson Davis' nose.

According to the memoirs of Thomas McGiven, the Union spymaster in Richmond whose cover was that of a baker who delivered to the Confederate White House, Bowser "had a photographic mind. Everything she saw on the Rebel President's desk she could repeat word for word. Unlike most colored, she could read and write. She made the point of always coming out to my wagon when I made deliveries at the Davis' home to drop information."

Stories about Bowser, who is also known as Ellen Bond, Mary Jones or Mary Jane Richards, show up as early as May 1900 in Richmond newspapers, and her name was revealed in 1910 in an interview with Van Lew's niece, according to Elizabeth Varon, author of a book about Van Lew.

There is no proof that Bowser existed beyond these recollections. Van Lew, like Pinkerton before her, requested that Union forces turn over all her intelligence records at the end of the Civil War and destroyed them, leaving no proof of her vast network.

Jefferson Davis' wife, Varina, publicly denied that a black female spy could have infiltrated their White House.

But Varon's book suggests that Bowser's true name was Mary Richards, she survived the Civil War and married a man named Garvin. Richards even writes in an 1867 letter that during the Civil War she was "in the service…as a detective."

Others are not as well-known.

Union forces weren't the only ones operating a black spy network in the South.

Black abolitionists also ran a vast private network called the "loyal League," "Lincoln's Legal Loyal League" or the "4Ls," which spied for the North and spread word about the war among the black slaves. Scobell was a member of the 4Ls, Pinkerton said, and used the network to get information to Washington, D.C.

"I traveled to about the plantations within a certain range, and got together small meetings in the cabins to tell the slaves the great news. Some of these slaves in turn would find their way to still other plantations—and so the story spread. We had to work in dead secrecy," with "knocks and signs and passwords, "said George Washington Albright of Holly Springs, Miss., in 1937.

Utmost secrecy was needed for these spies because of the consequences for those who were caught.

James Bowser, a free black from Nansemond County, Va., decided to help the Union army by spying on the South, according to Virginia Hayes Smith of Norfolk, Va., an elderly black lady who related Bowser's story to Virginia Writers Project field interviewers in 1937. Her recollections were subsequently published in the book "Virginia Folk Legends."

Bowser's white neighbors, some of whom coveted Bowser's farmland, heard rumors of his activities, Smith said. A mob of planters attacked Bowser's house at night and dragged out Bowser and his son.

"After severely beating both father and son, the horde made Bowser lies on the ground and stretches his neck over a log like a chicken on a chopping block," said Smith, "Then someone cut his head off. The plan was to kill the boy in the same manner, but the more thoughtful ones disagreed. They suggested that he be left to carry the news of this ghastly example back to the other Negroes. The mob gave in."

Another Virginian, a free black bricklayer named Martin Robinson, was killed on the spot.

Robinson was considered "faithful and reliable" by the Union hierarchy, and already had helped Union officers escape from the infamous Libby Prison in Richmond, wrote Louis M. Boudrye. Chaplain of the 5th New York Calvary.

Union forces wanted to attack Richmond in 1864 to free Union soldiers and spies held by

Confederates at Belle Isle, a small island in the middle of the James River. Colonel Ulric Dahlgren was to cross the James River eight miles to the south and press north into the city while other Union forces attacked from other directions. Robinson, who lived in the area, was sent by the Bureau of Military Intelligence to take Dahlgren's troops and horses to the best place to cross the river.

When they arrived, the river was impassable. Robinson panicked. Dahlgren decided Robinson had deliberately deceived him. However, the river normally would have been passable had it not been for flooding from heavy rains, Confederate veteran Richard G. Crouch said in 1906.

"The colonel ordered him to be hung—a halter strap was used for the purpose, and we left the miserable wretch hanging by the roadside," Boudrye said.

Integrating the Armed Forces

Today, many Americans consider the U.S. Army the country's most successful effort at racial integration. General Colin Powell, became the country's first African American Secretary of State, has become a symbol of the Army's relative openness. He rose through the Army's ranks to become the first black head of the Joint Chiefs of Staff.

Yet the integration of the armed forces is a relatively recent development. As recently as the end of 1950, when the Korean War was entering its seventh month, African American troops were trained at a segregated facility at Fort Dix, New Jersey, near New York City. Even later, in the fall of 1954, an all-African American unit, the 94th Engineer Battalion, was stationed in Europe.

African Americans have participated actively in the country's wars. An African American minuteman, Prince Easterbrooks, a slave, was wounded at the battle of Lexington, and, altogether, some 5,000 African Americans fought for American independence during the Revolution despite British promises of freedom to any slaves who defected to the Loyalist side.

It was not until the Civil War that African Americans were required to fight in racially separate units. In 1869, Congress made racial separation in the military official government policy. This policy remained intact through the Spanish American War, World War I (when two African American divisions participated in combat), and World War II.

Originally known as the 15th New York National Guard, the New York National Guard 369th infantry regiment is one of the most under-appreciated contributors to World War I within this country. Only in France did they receive proper recognition. 500 of its members received the French "Croix de Guerre", or "War Cross."

This regiment gained the nickname "The Harlem Hell fighters" by the Germans, who were surprised to see an entirely Black regiment fight so well.

The Harlem Hell Fighters, despite fighting the longest of any American Regiment, were not allowed to march in the Paris parades. U.S. pressure also disallowed it a place in the French national war memorial. Prior to World War I there should have been no hesitation for the government to use and trust a Black. The Harlem Hell Fighters met with uninviting MPs upon their return to New York, who were instructed not to salute any 369th soldiers.

President Woodrow Wilson's administration had encouraged the military to turn its back on the Black soldiers, despite their successes in battle. Pershing issued a directive to the French Military Mission, warning them of the dangers of relying on Black troops. Pershing wrote a document listing out reasons for the French to keep a close watch on the Black soldiers. He stated that the Black man is an "inferior," lacks "civic and professional conscience" and is a "constant menace to the American. And this is how the U.S. Military regarded Black units.

Pershing continued "we must not eat with them, must not shake hands or seek to talk or meet with them outside the requirements of military service." Pershing also added that "we" must not commend them too highly the Black American troops, especially not in front of white American troops. The French reaction to Pershing's directive was one of indifference. Pershing added that an effort must be made to prevent the local population from "spoiling the Negroes."

It was during World War II that the policy of racial segregation within the military began to break down under pressure from African American leaders, who pointed out the contradiction of a country fighting Nazi racism having a segregated military. In March 1943, the War department ordered the desegregation of recreational facilities at military facilities. In mid-1944, the War Department ordered all bases to be operated in a non-discriminatory fashion. Military necessity helped to shatter racial barriers. In December, 1944, 250,000 German troops launched a massive counteroffensive, later known as the Battle of the Bulge, in Belgium. With only 80,000 Allied troops available in the area to resist the German forces, black troops volunteered. Although black and white troops served in separate platoons, this experience helped the Army break with its usual practice of placing African American troops in separate units and assigning them to non-combat duties.

In February 1948, President Harry S. Truman directed the U.S. armed forces to desegregate as quickly as possible. In July, he issued Executive Order 9981 calling on the military to end racial discrimination. It would take several years—and another war—before the military actually ended segregation. Three factors would ultimately lead to integration: the growing recognition that segregation undercut the United States' moral stature during the Cold War; the need to reduce racial tensions within the military; and the manpower needs produced by the Korean War.

Following President Truman's Executive Order, two boards were established to make recommendations about integration. A presidential commission chaired by Charles Fahy recommended an end to discrimination in jobs, schooling assignment, and recruitment. An Army board headed by lieutenant General S.J. Chamberlin called on the Army to remain segregated and retain racial quotas. In the end, the Army agreed to open all jobs and military training schools on a non-segregated basis. There were isolated examples at unit-level integration, including at Camp Jackson, South Carolina in early 1951.

It was the Korean War that finally led to the desegregation of previously all-white combat units. After six months of fighting, insufficient white replacement troops were available and black enlistments were high. In February 1951, the Chamberlain board was asked to reexamine its conclusions. Although it acknowledged that integrated units had fewer racial tensions than a combination of segregated units, it continued to call for a 10 percent Army quota of African Americans. At this time, 98 percent of the Army's black soldiers served in segregated units. In May, General Matthew Ridgway requested permission to desegregate his command.

In March, 1951, the Army asked Johns Hopkins University's Operations Research Office to analyze the impact of integrating its forces. Extensive surveys of troops and analysis of combat performance in Korea revealed that:

- Integration raised the morale of African American soldiers and did not reduce that of white soldiers;
- Integration was favored by black soldiers and was not opposed by most white soldiers;
- Experience in integrated units increased white support for integration;
- Integration improved fighting effectiveness.

An essential finding is that integration reduced racial tensions within the military. In December 1951 the Chief of Staff ordered all Army commands to desegregate.

Ignoring Black American Veterans

The current controversy surrounding the plight of veterans in the United States is an important issue for all families in America who have benefited from the service of millions of men and women who have served in the military. Every Memorial Day, the nation pauses to remember and honor all of those who have served the nation and who today continue to serve in the armed services. But the growing contradictions surrounding the U.S. Veterans Administration (VA) about systematic failures to provide timely and adequate health care for veterans is alarming.

Too often, however, the status and interests of Black American veterans get loss in the national public debate when issues of the VA are raised. Since the Vietnam War in the 1960s and 1970s, the percentage of Black Americans serving in the U.S. armed services peaked at 30 percent. Today, the percentage is at approximately 20 percent. Now that so many Black American veterans and other veterans are now returning home from the long and awful wars in Iraq and Afghanistan, the VA is now overwhelmed with the increased demands for health care and war-related disabilities.

The Department of Veterans Affairs health care group is the largest health care provider in the U.S., overseeing 1,700 hospitals, nursing homes, multipurpose health clinics, and other medical facilities. The VA is a massive bureaucracy that has had major dysfunctional problems for decades. Accordingly, the crisis at the VA is not a new one. Yet, with a Black American president of United States, old problems are viewed with a different level of urgency and priority. The truth is that past U.S. presidents were aware of the VA's long term systemic dysfunctions, but they did not correct or remedy the VA's problems. It is president Obama's responsibility as commander-in-chief to take all necessary leadership and actions to quickly resolve this crisis. Some reports have found evidence that allegedly indicates that deaths of veterans have occurred as a result of the administrative failures of the VA. One White House official reported that President Obama was "madder than hell" about the VA scandal. An Obama White House aide told "Face the Nation" on CBS that "Obama is demanding that Veterans Affairs Secretary Eric Shinseki and others in the administration continue to fix these things until they're functioning the way that our veterans believe they should."

I believe that all veterans should be treated with equal respect. All veterans should receive all the benefits that they are entitled, including good health care without bureaucratic red tape and prolonged waiting list. We are all aware that before and after the enactment of the Affordable Care Act (ACA), the problem of racism and racial discrimination in the delivery of quality health care remains a serious problem. While 10 million or more people have health care as a result of ACA, there are still millions of Black Americans and Latino Americans who do not have health care insurance coverage.

Black American veterans are facing a double whammy. They are confronted with the inadequacies of the VA as well as the racism in society that makes it more difficult to get quality health care in traditional public and private health care systems. And for Black female vets, there's a triple whammy. This is why it is urgent to call urgent attention to the struggles and challenges that confront Black veterans.

Military service purportedly offers the benefits of job training, funding for higher education, and access to a steady middle-class career with excellent benefits. America's poor support of our veterans population has resulted with Black female vets suffering from the lack of effective resources to aid their transition to civilian status has contributed to their high presence in the homeless population. Black women in combat zones have higher rates of PTSD, because they were victims of assaults that are never reported.

Black veterans have long history of being neglected by the Veterans Administration and other military support group. In some cases they may return home to marital infidelity, financial difficulties, applying for benefits they are not receiving.

Documents indicate that more African Americans in Vietnam were placed in combat positions because officials argued that Blacks were more suitable for frontline combat "because of their surroundings and the environment they grew up in." The government reasoned, that blacks were more accustomed to fighting and shooting and stabbing in the ghettos and more suitable to send into the jungle. Blacks were leading the way in combat missions and suffered from PTSD.

When white and black soldiers return home they have difficulty adjusting to the society they knew so well before. They find that there are few that can understand what they went through, few with whom they can discuss it. The former soldier may take refuge in drugs. Too many went to prison because of inadequate health care and unemployment and war-related problems.

Obama making strides in Veterans health care

President Obama has cut Veteran Homelessness nearly in half, by 47 percent. With the help of Michelle Obama and Jill Biden for using their initiative on military families to challenge mayors and county officials nationwide to end veterans' homelessness.

His initiative of enrolling one million veterans to make precision medicine or tailored treatment a reality is making a difference. Increased spending on veterans, expanded and better health care for female veterans, tax credit for hiring veterans and strides toward reducing the homeless issues and streamline claims and appeals are all working.

Caring for Veterans through Research and Collaboration, "highlights the importance of collaboration between Veterans medical centers around the country with researchers, academic partners, and other federal agencies to translate research finding into advancements for veterans' health care.

Tax Credit for hiring veterans: Many employers have come to learn that Veterans make excellent employees. They usually are easily trainable and possess desirable characteristics, such as honesty, loyalty, and responsibility. The tax law encourages employers to hire certain targeted groups of workers by offering a tax credit tied to the wages to these new employees, and certain Veterans are treated as a target group.

Veteran homelessness: VA has many benefits and services to assists homeless veterans such as disability benefits, education, health care, rehabilitation services and residential care. VA provided health care services to more than 100,000 homeless veterans and provided services to 70,000 veterans in its specialized homeless program. More than 40,000 homeless veterans receive compensation or pension benefits annually. 55% of veterans have used VA homeless services.

Report says too many whites, men leading military

An independent report for Congress said, the U.S. military is too white and too male at the top and needs to change recruiting and promotion policies and lift its ban on women in combat.

Seventy-seven percent of senior officers in the active-duty military are white, while only 8 percent are black, 5 percent are Hispanic and 16 percent are women, the report by an independent panel said, and quoting data from September 2008.

One barrier that keeps women from the highest ranks is their inability to serve in combat units. Promotion and job opportunities have favored those with battlefield leadership credentials.

The report ordered by Congress in 2009 calls for greater diversity in the military's leadership so it will better reflect the racial, ethnic and gender mix in the armed forces and in American society.

"This problem will only become more acute as the racial, ethnic and cultural makeup of the United

States continues to change," said the report from the Military Leadership Diversity Commission, whose more than two dozen members included current and former military personnel as well as businessmen and other civilians.

Having military brass those better mirrors the nation can inspire future recruits and help create trust among the general population, the commission said.

Among recommendations is that the military eliminate policies that exclude women from combat units, phasing in additional career fields and units that they can be assigned to as long as they are qualified. A 1994 combat exclusion policy bans women from being assigned to ground combat units below the brigade level even though women have for years served in combat situations.

Michelle Howard vice chief of Naval operations will be a 4 star no. 2-ranking officer. She will be the first black woman to hold a four-star rank in America's military. She joins five other African–American four-star commanders. The highest possible rank—already serving in the Army, Airforce and Navy.

Today, about one in five soldiers are black, compared with nearly 27% in 1985 and 1995, according to Army figures. The smallest representations of blacks are in the Marine Corps. The Army now devotes a third of its recruiting marketing campaign to attracting minorities and winning over parents, educators, clergy and coaches. Years ago the military was looked at as the place for minorities to go to have an opportunity to succeed and improve them, to get a better education.

Factors hindering diversity efforts are one that still exists in many areas of society. The military reflects society and all its biases. To achieve diversity in the military, minority cultivation is required at the military academies. Minorities have to be brought into the ranks of command positions and with time will be commanders of the future.

Stretching the definition of diversity, the report also said the military must harness people with a greater range of skills and backgrounds in, for instance, cyber systems, languages and cultural knowledge to be able to operate in an era of new threats and to collaborate with international partners and others.

Blacks in the Republican Party

Dr. Martin Luther King, Jr. was a republican; in that era, almost all black Americans were Republican. Why? From its founding in 1854 as the anti-slavery party until today, the Republican Party has championed freedom and civil rights for blacks.

Abraham Lincoln the country's first Republican President. From the 1860s through the early 20th century Blacks exclusively identified and tied their cultural ambitions to the Republican Party. It was this party who was responsible for their coveted freedom and liberties not the Democrats. Industrialization and the great migration to the Northern Cities to escape the brutality of the South and seek better opportunities cause blacks to settle in the cities and created urban communities.

In early 1933 the nation needed immediate relief, recovery from economic collapse, and reform to avoid future depressions, so relief, recovery and reform became Franklin D. Roosevelt's goals when he took the helm as president. At his side stood a Democratic Congress, prepared to enact the measures carved out by a group of his closest advisors. One recurring theme in the recovery plan was Roosevelt's pledge to help the "forgotten man at the bottom of the economic pyramid." The "New Deal" was coined during his Nomination Acceptance Speech in 1932, when he said, I pledge myself, to a new deal for the American people. "Roosevelt summarized the New Deal as an organized form of self-help for all classes and groups and sections of our country." FDR and the "New Deal" received 71% of the Black vote.

Harry S. Truman was the 33rd President of the United States. He was Republican appointed. He received 40% of Black votes. He was the last running mate of President Franklin D. Roosevelt in 1944. Truman succeeded to the Presidency on April 12, 1945, when Roosevelt died after months of declining health. During the 1948 Presidential election he received 77% of the black vote; Due to the fact that he desegregate the armed forces. In 1948, Blacks saw themselves as Republicans.

President Eisenhower was the 34th President of the United States from 1953 until 1961. He was Republican appointed. He received 40% of black votes. He appointed Earl Warren who served as the 14th Chief Justice of the United States (19531969). He is known for the sweeping decisions of the Warren Court, which ended school segregation and transformed many areas of American law, especially regarding the rights of the accused, ending public-school-sponsored prayer, and requiring "one-man-one vote" rules of appointment. He made the Court a power center on a more even base with Congress and the presidency especially through four landmark decision (Brown v. Board of Education 1954), Gideon V. Wainwright (1963), Reynold v. Sims (1964), and Miranda v. Arizona (1966).

In the 2008 and 2012 elections, blacks came out in droves to vote for President Obama who is black. Mr. Obama isn't running and black voters is an untapped well for Republicans. Obama was given a pass because of obstruction in the Republican ranks. Blacks were ignored on matters concerning their communities by the Democrats.

The Republican agenda to get blacks in the party calls for low taxes, low regulation "economic freedom zones in black neighborhoods, restoring voting rights for convicted felons and reforming a federal prison sentencing system that has been criticized as being unfair to blacks. Blacks voted Republican because they came up with responses to black issues.

Blacks and the Democratic Party

Blacks mostly voted Republican from after the Civil War and through the early part of the 20th Century. That's not surprising when one considers that Abraham Lincoln was the first Republican president, and the white segregationist politicians who governed Southern States in those days were Democrats. The Democratic Party didn't welcome blacks then, and it wasn't until 1924 that blacks were even permitted to attend Democratic conventions in any official capacity. Most blacks lived in the South, where they were mostly prevented from voting at all. And as one Pundit so succinctly stated, the Democratic Party is as it always has been, the party of the four S's: Slavery, Secession, Segregation and now Socialism.

The election of Roosevelt in 1932 marked the beginning of a change. He got 71 percent of the black vote for president in 1936 and did nearly that well in the next two elections, according to historical figures kept by the Joint Center for Political and Economic Studies. But even then, the number of blacks identifying themselves as Republicans was about the same as the number who thought of themselves as Democrats.

It wasn't until Harry Truman garnered 77 percent of the black vote in 1948 that a majority of blacks reported that they thought of themselves as Democrats. Earlier that year Truman had issued an order desegregating the armed services and an executive order setting up regulations against racial bias in federal employment.

Even after that, Republican nominees continued to get a large slice of the black vote for several elections. Dwight D. Eisenhower got 39 percent in 1956, and Richard Nixon got 32 percent in is narrow loss to John F. Kennedy in 1960.

But then President Lyndon B. Johnson pushed through the landmark Civil Rights Act of 1964 (outlawing segregation in public places) and his eventual Republican opponent, Sen. Barry Goldwater, opposed it. Johnson got 94 percent of the black vote that year, still a record for any presidential election.

The following year Johnson signed the 1965 Voting Rights Act. No Republican presidential candidate has gotten more than 15 percent of the black vote since.

Martin Luther King Jr. was born Jan 15, 1929, in Atlanta on Auburn Ave. The Rev. Martin Luther King Sr. was pastor of the Ebenezer Baptist Church at Jackson Street and Auburn Avenue. Young Martin went to Atlanta's Morehouse College, a Black institution whose students acquired what was sometimes called the "Morehouse swank." The President of Morehouse, Dr. B.E. Mays, took a special interest in Martin, who had decided, in his junior year, to be a clergyman.

He was ordained a minister in his father's church in 1947. It was in this church he was to say, some years later: "America, you're strayed away. You've trampled over 19 million of your brethren. All men are created equal. Not some men. Not white men. All men. America, rise up and come home."

Before Dr. King had his own church he pursued his studies in the integrated Crozier Theological Seminary, in Chester, Pa. He was one of six Blacks in a student body of about a hundred. He was named the outstanding student and won a fellowship to study for a doctorate at the school of his choice. The young man enrolled at Boston College in 1951. For his doctoral thesis he sought to resolve the differences between the Harvard theologian Paul Tillich and the neo-naturalist philosopher Henry Nelson Wieman. During this period he took courses at Harvard, as well.

While he was working on his doctorate he met Coretta Scott, a graduate of Antioch College, who was doing graduate work in music. He married the singer in 1953. They had four children, Yolanda, Martin Luther King 3rd, Dexter Scott and Bernice.

To many millions of African Americans, the Rev. Dr. Martin Luther King Jr. was the prophet of their crusade for racial equality. He was their voice of anguish their eloquence in humiliation, their battle cry for human dignity. He forged for them the weapons of nonviolence that with stood and blunted the ferocity of segregation. His strong beliefs in Civil Rights and nonviolence made him one of the leading opponents of American participation in the war in Vietnam. To him the war was unjust, diverting vast sums away from programs to alleviate the condition of the Negro poor in this country. He called the conflict "one of history's most cruel and senseless wars."

Inevitably, as a symbol of integration, he became the object of unrelenting attacks and vilification. His home was bombed. He was spat upon and mocked. He was struck and kicked. He was stabbed, almost fatally, by a deranged black woman. He was frequently thrown into jail. Threats became so common place that his wife could ignore burning crosses on the lawn and ominous phone calls. Through it all he adhered to the creed of passive disobedience that infuriated segregationists.

Dr. King's belief in nonviolence was subjected to intense pressure in 1966, when some black groups, adopted the slogan "black power" in the aftermath of civil rights marches into Mississippi and race riots in the Northern Cities.

Scores of millions of Americans-white as well as blacks sat before television sets in the summer of 1963 to watch the awesome march of some 200,000 Blacks on Washington were deeply stirred when Dr. King, in the shadow of the Lincoln Memorial, gave his famous "I have a dream speech."

And all over the world, men were moved as they read his words of Dec 10, 1964, when he became the third member of his race to receive the Nobel Peace Prize.

Dr. King was jailed for 5 days in Birmingham. While he was in prison he issued a 9,000-word letter that created considerable controversy among white people, alienating some sympathizers who thought Dr. King was being too aggressive.

Desegregati4ng Little Rock, 1957

Because of Brown vs. Board of Education 1954 declaring segregation in public schools unconstitu-tional, the court had mandated that all public schools in the country be integrated "with all deliberate speed" because segregation was so wide spread the Court issued a second decision in 1955, known as Brown 11, ordering school districts to integrate "with all deliberate speed:

Daisy Bates and others from the Arkansas NAACP recruited nine students to attend Central High School in Little Rock. The group came to be known as the Little Rock Nine.

Little Rock, Arkansas, was in a relatively progressive Southern State. A crisis erupted, however, when Governor of Arkansas Orval Faubus called out the National Guard on September 4 to prevent entry to the nine African-American students who had sued for the right to attend an integrated school, Little Rock Central High School. The nine students had been chosen to attend Central High because of their excellent grades. On the first day of school, only one of the nine students showed up because she did not receive the phone call about the danger of going to school. She was harassed by white protesters outside the school, and the police had to take her away in a patrol car to protect her. Afterward, the nine students had to carpool to school and be escorted by military personnel in jeeps.

Faubus was not a proclaimed segregationist. The Arkansas Democratic Party, which then controlled politics in the state, put significant pressure on Faubus after he had indicated he would investigate bringing Arkansas into compliance with the Brown decision. Faubus then took his stand against integration and against the Federal court order that required it.

Faubus' order received the attention of President Dwight D. Eisenhower, who was determined to enforce the orders of the Federal courts. Critics had charged he was lukewarm, at best, on the goal of desegregation of public schools. Eisenhower federalized the National Guard and ordered them to return to their barracks. Eisenhower then deployed elements of the 101st Airborne Division to Little Rock to protect the students.

The students were able to attend high school. They had to pass through a gauntlet of spitting, jeering whites to arrive at school on their first day, and to put up with harassment from fellow students for the rest of the year. Although federal troops escorted the students between classes, the students were still teased and even attacked by white students when the soldiers weren't around. One of the Little Rock Nine, Minnijean Brown, was suspended for accidentally spilling a bowl of chili on the head of a white student who was harassing her in the school lunch line. Later, she was expelled for verbally abusing a white female student.

Only one of the Little Rock Nine, Ernest Green, got the chance to graduate; after the 1957-58 school years was over, the Little Rock school system decided to shut public schools completely rather than continue to integrate. Other school systems across the South followed suit.

Martin Luther King Jr. attended graduation ceremonies at Central High School in May 1958 to see Ernest Green, the only senior among the Little Rock Nine, receive his diploma. Other than Green the rest of the Little Rock Nine completed their high school careers at other high schools across the country. Ernest Green served as assistant secretary of the Federal Department of Labor under President Jimmy Carter. In 1999, President Clinton awarded each member of the group the Congressional Gold Medal.

The nine also all received perso0nal invitations to attend President Barack Obama's inauguration in 2009.

Sit-ins, 1960

The sit-ins in the 1960s were started by Black students on college campuses throughout the South and in the North. Two Black colleges in Greensboro NC. Bennett College for women and North Carolina Agricultural and Technical (NCA&T) discusses strategies and tactics for opposing segregation. They got information from the Oklahoma City NAACP which had previously used nonviolent direct-action to desegregate local restaurants. The young women decided to target the Woolworth's lunch counter in downtown Greensboro because it is part of a national chain that blacks all over the country patronize. On February 1, 1960, four black men from NCA&T sat down at Woolworth's "whites only" lunch counter and ask to be served coffee and doughnuts. They are refused.

When word spread that Black students were using the sit-ins to get rid of segregation the NAACP endorses their actions. The Ku Klux Klan got involve by heckling and harasses the students. The students are not deterred. Their number grew to include white students. The sit-ins swept across the South.

As students across the south began to "sit-in" at the lunch counters of a few of their local stores, local authority figures sometimes used brute force to physically escort the demonstrators from the lunch facilities.

The "sit-in" technique was not new—as far back as 1939, African-American attorney Samuel Wilbert Tucker organized a sit-in at the then-segregated Alexandria, Virginia library. In 1960 the technique succeeded in bringing national attention to the movement. The success of the Greensboro sit-in led to a rash of student campaigns throughout the South. Probably the best organized, most highly disciplined, the most immediately effective of these was in Nashville, Tennessee.

On March 9, 1960 an Atlanta University Center group of students released An Appeal for Human Rights as a full page advertisement in newspapers, including the Atlanta Constitution, Atlanta Journal, and Atlanta Daily World. This student group, known as the Committee on the Appeal for Human Rights (COAHR), initiated the Atlanta Student Movement and began to lead in Atlanta with Sit-ins starting on March 15, 1960.

By the end of 1960, the sit-ins had spread to every southern and border state and even to Nevada, Illinois, and Ohio.

Demonstrators focused not only on lunch counters but also on parks, beaches, libraries, theaters, museums, and other public places. Upon being arrested, student demonstrators made "jail-no-bail" pledges, to call attention to their cause and to reverse the cost of protest, thereby saddling their jailers with the financial burden of prison space and food.

In April, 1960 activists who had led these sit-ins held a conference at Shaw University in Raleigh, North Carolina that led to the formation of the Student Nonviolent Coordinating Committee (SNCC). SNCC took these tactics of nonviolent confrontation further, to the freedom rides.

The sit-ins challenge Black leadership and their reliance on legislation and litigation. The people set the direction of the freedom movement. The movement continues until the Civil Rights Act of 1964 makes segregated public facilities illegal.

Freedom Rides, 1961

In 1946 (Morgan v. Virginia) the Supreme Court prohibited racial segregation in interstate transportation. That same year the Congress of Racial Equality (CORE) wanted to test segregation in interstate travel. The first freedom ride was called the Journey of Reconciliation.

White segregationists resisted CORE's efforts starting in North Carolina when the police effectively stop the journey when most of the demonstrators were arrested. In 1960 the Supreme Court reiterated the ruling prohibiting racial segregation in interstate transportation in (Boynton v. Virginia).

Freedom Rides were journeys by Civil Rights activists on interstate buses into the segregated southern United States to test the United States Supreme Court decision Boynton v. Virginia, (1960) 364 U.S. that ended segregation for passengers engaged in inter-state travel. Organized by CORE, the first Freedom Ride of the 1960s left Washington D.C. on May 4, 1961, and was scheduled to arrive in New Orleans on May 17.

During the first and subsequent Freedom Rides, activists traveled through the Deep South to integrate seating patterns and desegregate bus terminals, including restrooms and water fountains. That proved to be a dangerous mission. In Anniston, Alabama, one bus was firebombed, forcing its passengers to flee for their lives. In Birmingham, Alabama, an FBI informant reported that Public Safety Commissioner Eugene "Bull" Connor gave Ku Klux Klan members fifteen minutes to attack an incoming group of freedom riders before having police "protect" them. The riders were severely beaten "until it looked like a bulldog had got a hold of them." James Peck, a white activist, was beaten so hard he required fifty stitches to his head.

Mob violence in Anniston and Birmingham temporarily halted the rides, but SNCC activists from Nashville brought in new riders to continue the journey from Birmingham. In Montgomery, Alabama, at the Greyhound Bus Station, a mob charged another bus load of riders knocking John Lewis unconscious with a crate and smashing Life photographer Don Urbrock in the face with his camera. A dozen men surrounded Jim Zwerg, a white student from Fisk University, and beat him in the face with a suitcase, knocking out his teeth.

The freedom riders continued their rides into Jackson, Mississippi, where they were arrested for "breaching the peace" by using "white only" facilities. New freedom riders were organized by many different organizations. As riders arrived in Jackson, they were arrested. By the end of summer, more than 300 had been jailed in Mississippi.

In the face of mob violence freedom riders stayed committed to nonviolence. Their courage and commitment provided momentum to the desegregation movement. Public sympathy and support for the freedom riders led the Kennedy administration to order the Interstate Commerce Commission (ICC) to issue a new desegregation order to ban discrimination on buses and at bus terminals. When the new ICC rule took effect on November 1, passengers were permitted to sit wherever they chose on the bus; "white" and "colored" signs came down in the terminals; separate drinking fountains, toilets, and waiting rooms were consolidated; and lunch counters began serving people regardless of skin color.

The student movement involved such celebrated figures as John Lewis, a single-minded activist; James Lawson, the revered "guru" of nonviolent theory and tactics; Diane Nash, an articulate and intrepid public champion of justice; Bob Moses, pioneer of voting registration in Mississippi; and James Bevel, a fiery preacher and charismatic organizer and facilitator. Other prominent student activists included Charles McDew, Bernard Lafayette, Charles Jones, Lonnie King, Julian Bond, Hosea Williams, and Stokely Carmichael.

Voter registration organizing

The 14th Amendment to the U.S. Constitution was ratified in the Reconstruction era to prevent the South from doing away with many of the liberties granted to the African-Americans after the war. The 15th Amendment give citizens the right to vote. As the South became powerful it didn't allow blacks to get the freedom they deserved or share in the power.

After the Freedom Rides, local black leaders in Mississippi such as Amzie Moore, Aaron Henry, Medgar Evers, and others asked SNCC to help register black voters and to build community organizations that could win a share of political power in the state. Since Mississippi ratified its constitution in 1890, with provisions such as poll taxes, residency requirements, and literacy tests, it made registration more complicated and stripped blacks from the polls. After so many years, the intent to stop blacks from voting had become part of the culture of white supremacy. In the fall of 1961, SNCC organizer Robert Moses began the first such project in McComb and the surrounding counties in the Southwest corner of the state. Their efforts were met with violent repression from state and local lawmen, White Citizens' Council, and Ku Klux Klan resulting in beatings, hundreds of arrests and the murder of voting activist Herbert Lee.

White opposition to black voter registration was so intense in Mississippi that Freedom Movement activists concluded that all of the state's civil rights organizations had to unite in a coordinated effort to have any chance of success. In February 1962, representatives of SNCC, CPRE, and the NAACP formed the Council of Federated Organizations (COFO). At a subsequent meeting in August, SCLC became part of COFO.

In the spring of 1962, with funds from the Voter Education Project, SNCC/COFO began voter registration organizing in Mississippi Delta area around Greenwood, and the areas surrounding Hattiesburg, Laurel, and Holly Springs. As in McComb, their efforts were met with fierce opposition—arrests, beatings, shootings, arson, and murder. Registrars used the literacy test to keep blacks off the voting roles by creating standards that even highly educated people could not meet. Besides, employers fired blacks who tried to register and landlords evicted them from their homes. Over the following years, the black voter registration campaign spread across the state.

In the Presidential race of 1964 President Johnson was elected and pushed for legislation to get stronger voting-rights laws. On March 7, 1965, many Americans were outraged when peaceful participants in a voting rights march from Selma, Alabama to the state capital in Montgomery were met by Alabama state troopers who attacked them with nightsticks, tear gas and whips after they refused to turn back. Some protesters were severely beaten, and others ran for their lives. The incident was captured on national television.

The voting rights bill was passed and President Johnson signed the bill into law with Martin Luther King Jr. and other civil rights leaders present at the ceremony.

Integration of Mississippi Universities, 1956—1965

Clyde Kennard was a black Korean War veteran who wanted to get a college education. He attempted to enroll at Mississippi Southern College (now the University of Southern Mississippi) at Hattiesburg. To prevent him from enrolling, trumped up criminal charges was brought against him. Kennard was wrongfully convicted as an accessory to a burglary of $25 worth of chicken feed from farmers Co-op. Johnny Lee Roberts, who admitted to stealing the goods and portrayed Kennard as his accomplice. Kennard was eventually sentenced to seven years in the state prison.

While in prison he developed Colon Cancer which was misdiagnosed as sickle cell anemia. After three years in prison he was paroled by Governor Ross Barnett and given clemency on medical grounds. Johnny Lee Roberts recanted his testimony attesting that Kennard was innocent. The University of Southern Mississippi, years later, named its student center after Clyde Kennard. In 2006, Judge Robert Helfrich ruled that Kennard was factually innocent of all charges.

The Korean War Veterans Memorial was confirmed by the U.S. Congress and President George H.W. Bush conducted the groundbreaking memorialon June 14th, 1992.

James Meredith was an Air Force veteran of 9 years. In 1961, he applied to the University of Mississippi. He was initially accepted, but his admission was later withdrawn when the registrar discovered his race. Meredith filed suit alleging discrimination and took it to the Supreme Court, which ruled in his favor. In 1962 he enrolled at the University of Mississippi but not without rioting from white students. President Kennedy had to send in the National Guard to keep the peace. In 1963, Meredith graduated with a degree in Political Science.

Another Army veteran in the fight against segregation was Medgar Evers. He applied to the University of Mississippi Law School in 1954 and was rejected. Thurgood Marshall served as his attorney for the legal challenge to racial discrimination. The case led to the 1954 Brown v. Board of Education case which legally ended segregation in schools.

Evers became the first field secretary for the NAACP in Mississippi. He recruited new members for the NAACP and organized voter registration efforts. On June 12, 1963 Evers was shot and killed in the driveway of his home. He was buried with full military honors in Arlington National Cemetery, and the NAACP posthumously awarded him their 1963 Spingarn Medal. In 2009, the U.S. Navy also bestowed his name on one of their vessels.

Albany Movement, 1961-1962

The Albany Movement was a desegregation campaign formed on November 17, 1961, in Albany, Georgia. Local activists from the Student Nonviolent Coordinating Committee (SNCC), the National Association for the Advancement of Colored People (NAACP), the Ministerial Alliance, the Federation of Women's Clubs, and the Negro Voters League joined together to create the movement.

The Albany Movement challenged all forms of racial segregation and discrimination in the City. Martin Luther King Jr. and the Southern Leadership

Conference (SCLC) joined the movement in December 1962. King was arrested and the condition of his release was to leave town. Upon his leaving, the City would comply with the ICC ruling and release jail protestors on bail. After Kings Departure, the city failed to uphold its agreement and protest continue into 1962.

The campaign was a failure because of the canny tactics of Laurie Pritchett, the local police chief, and divisions within the black community. The goals may not have been specific enough. Pritchett contained the marchers without violent attacks on demonstrators that inflamed national opinion. He also arranged for arrested demonstrators to be taken to jails in surrounding communities, allowing plenty of room to remain in his jail. Pritchett also foresaw King's presence as a danger and forced his release to avoid King's rallying the black community. King left in 1962 without having achieved any dramatic victories. The local movement, however, continued the struggle, and it obtained significant gains in the next few years.

Birmingham Campaign, 1963-1964

The Albany movement was shown to be an important education for the SCLC, however, when it undertook the Birmingham campaign in 1963. Executive Director Wyatt Tee Walker carefully planned strategy and tactics for the campaign. It focused on one goal—the desegregation of Birmingham's downtown merchants, rather than total desegregation, as in Albany. The movement's efforts were helped by the brutal response of local authorities, in particular Eugene "Bull" Connor, the Commissioner of Public Safety. He had long held much political power, but had lost a recent election for mayor to a less rabidly segregationist candidate. Refusing to accept the new mayor's authority, Connor intended to stay in office.

The campaign used a variety of nonviolent methods of confrontation, including sit-ins, kneel-ins at local churches, and a march to the county building to mark the beginning of a drive to register voters. The city, however, obtained an injunction barring all such protests. Convinced that the order was unconstitutional, the campaign defied it and prepared for mass arrests of its supporters. King elected to be among those arrested on April 12, 1963.

Images of children being blasted by high-pressure fire hoses, clubbed by police officers, and attacked by police dogs appeared on television and in Newspapers, triggering international outrage. White business structure was weakening under adverse publicity and the unexpected decline in business due to the boycott.

The Birmingham campaign 1963-1964 led to the removal of "Whites Only" and "Blacks Only" signs in restrooms and on drinking fountains, a plan to desegregate lunch counters, an ongoing "program of upgrading Negro employment", the formation of a biracial committee to monitor the progress of the agreement, and the release of jailed protesters on Bond.

Birmingham segregationists responded to the agreement with a series of violent attacks. Ku Klux Klan members bombed Birmingham's Sixteenth Street Baptists Church, killing four young girls. Martin Luther King Jr. delivered the eulogy for three of them.

Widespread public outrage led the Kennedy Administration to intervene more forcefully in negotiations between the white business community and the SCLC. On May 10, the parties announced an agreement to desegregate the lunch counters and other public accommodations downtown, to create a committee to eliminate discriminatory hiring practices, to arrange for the release of jailed protesters, and to establish regular means of communication between black and white leaders.

Other events of the summer of 1963:

On June 11, 1963, George Wallace, Governor of Alabama, tried to block the integration of the University of Alabama. President John F. Kennedy sent a force to make Governor Wallace step aside, allowing the enrollment of two black students. That evening, President Kennedy addressed the nation on TV and radio with his historic civil rights speech. The next day, Medgar Evers was murdered in Mississippi. The next week, as promised, on June 19, 1963,

President Kennedy submitted his Civil Rights bill to Congress.

March on Washington, 1963

A. Philip Randolph had planned a march on Washington, D.C. in 1941 to support demands for elimination of employment discrimination in defense industries; he called off the march when the Roosevelt Administration met the demand by issuing Executive Order 8802 barring racial discrimination and creating an agency to oversee compliance with the order.

Randolph and Bayard Rustin were the chief planners of the second march, which they proposed in 1962. The Kennedy Administration applied great pressure on Randolph and King to call it off but without success. The march was held on August 28, 1963.

Unlike the planned 1941 march, for which Randolph included only black-led organizations in the planning, the 1963 march was a collaborative effort of all of the major civil rights organizations, the more progressive wing of the labor movement, and other liberal organizations. The march had six official goals:

- "meaningful civil rights laws,
- A massive federal works program,
- Full and fair employment,

- Decent housing,
- The right to vote, and
- adequate integrated education."

Of these, the march's major focus was on passage of the civil rights law that the Kennedy Administration had proposed after the upheavals in Birmingham.

More than 200,000 had gathered by the Washington Monument where the march was to begin. Black and White, rich and poor, young and old, Hollywood stars and everyday people were represented. Money was raised by the sale of buttons for the march at 25 cents and thousands of small cash donations. Bayard Rustin later said. "Credit for mobilizing the March on Washington could go to "Bull Connor, his police dogs, and his fire hoses."

James Farmer speech was written while imprisoned in Louisiana. He said the fight for legal and economic equality would not stop "until the dogs stop biting as in the South and the rats stop biting as in the North.

The march on Washington was a success. It had been powerful, yet peaceful and orderly beyond any ones expectations. It was the high tide of the Civil Rights movement.

After the march, King and other civil rights leaders met with President Kennedy at the White House. While the Kennedy Administration appeared sincerely committed to passing the bill, it was not clear that it had the votes in Congress to do it.

But when President Kennedy was assassinated on November 22, 1963, the new President Lyndon Johnson decided to use his influence in Congress to bring about much of Kennedy's legislative agenda.

St. Augustine, Florida, 1963-1964

Dr. Robert Hayling is generally considered the "father" of the St. Augustine movement. Hayling served as an Air Force officer and then became the first black dentist in Florida to be elected to the American Dental Association. He set up business in St. Augustine in 1960 and joined the NAACP. In March of 1963, the NAACP led a protest of the segregated celebration of the city's 400th anniversary. The protest did not affect making changes to the Jim Crow Laws.

In September 1963, the Klan seized Robert Hayling and three other NAACP activist (Clyde Jenkins, James Jackson, and James Hauser) and beat them with fists, chains, and clubs. Charges against the Klansmen were dismissed but Hayling was convicted of "criminal assault" against the KKK mob.

In 1964, Dr. Hayling and other activists urged the Southern Christian Leadership Conference to come to St. Augustine. The first action came during spring break, when Hayling appealed to northern college students to come to the Ancient City, not to go to the beach, but to take part in demonstrations. Four prominent Massachusetts women—Mrs. Mary

Parkman Peabody, Mrs. Esther Burgess, Mrs. Hester Campbell (all of whose husbands were Episcopal bishops), and Mrs. Florence Rowe (whose husband was vice president of John Hancock Insurance Company) came to lend their support, and the arrest of Mrs. Peabody, the 72 year old mother of the governor of Massachusetts, for attempting to eat at the segregated Ponce de Leon Motor Lodge in an integrated group, made front page news across the country, and brought the civil rights movement in St. Augustine to the attention of the world.

Widely publicized activities continued in the ensuing months, as Congress saw the longest filibuster against a civil rights bill in its history. Dr. Martin Luther King was arrested at the Monson Motel in St. Augustine on June 11, 1964, the only place in Florida he was arrested. He sent a "Letter from the St. Augustine Jail" to a northern supporter, Rabbi Israel Dresner of New Jersey, urging him to recruit others to participate in the movement. This resulted, a week later, in the largest mass arrest of rabbis in American history—while conducting a pray-in at the Monson.

A famous photograph taken in St. Augustine shows the manager of the Monson Motel pouring acid in the swimming pool while blacks and whites are swimming in it. The horrifying photograph was run on the front page of the Washington newspaper the day the senate went to vote on passing the Civil Rights Act of 1964.

Mississippi Freedom Summer, 1964

The 1964 Freedom Summer project was designed to draw the Nation's attention to the violent oppression experienced by Mississippi blacks who attempted to exercise their constitution rights, and to develop a grassroots freedom movement that could be sustained long after student activists left Mississippi.

In the summer of 1964, COFO (Council of Federated Organization) brought nearly 1,000 activists to Mississippi—most of them white college students—to join with local black activists to register voters, teach in "Freedom Schools," and organize the Mississippi Freedom Democratic Party (MFDP).

Robert Moses who became director of the Council of Federated Organizations capitalized on the successful use of white student volunteers in Mississippi during the 1963 mock election called the "Freedom Vote". Moses proposed that northern white student volunteers take part in a large number of simultaneous local campaigns in Mississippi during the summer of 1964.

He sent letters to prospective volunteers alerting them to conditions in Mississippi, explaining the likelihood of arrest, the need for Bond money and subsistence funds, and the requirement that drivers in Mississippi get license for themselves and their cars. They were asked to read Kings Memoir of the Montgomery bus boycott, Stride toward Freedom and Lillian Smith's novel Killers of the Dream.

Many of Mississippi's white residents deeply resented the outsiders and attempts to change their society. State and local governments, police, the White Citizens' Council and the Ku Klux Klan used arrests, beatings, arson, murder, spying, firing, evictions, and other forms of intimidation and harassment to oppose the project and prevent blacks from registering to vote or achieving social equality.

On June 21, 1964, three civil rights workers disappeared. James Chaney, a young black Mississippian and plasterer's apprentice; and two Jewish activists, Andrew Goodman, a Queens College anthropology student; and Michael Schwerner, a CORE organizer from Manhattan's Lower East Side, were found weeks later, murdered by conspirators who turned out to be local members of the Klan, some of them members of the Neshoba County sheriff's department. This outraged the public leading the U.S. Justice Department along with the FBI (the latter which had previously avoided dealing with the issue of segregation and persecution of blacks) to take action. The outrage over these murders helped lead to the passage of the Civil Rights Act.

Throughout the Summer Project, some 17,000 Mississippi blacks attempted to become registered voters in defiance of the red tape and forces of white supremacy arrayed against them—only 1,600 (less than 10%) succeeded. But more than 80,000 joined the Mississippi Freedom Democratic Party (MFDP), founded as an alternative political organization, showing their desire to vote and participate in politics.

Though Freedom Summer failed to register many voters, it had a significant effect on the course of the Civil Rights Movement. It helped break down the decades of people's isolation and repression that were the foundation of the Jim Crow system. Before Freedom Summer, the national news media had paid little attention to the persecution of black voters in the Deep South and the dangers endured by black civil rights workers. The progression of events throughout the South increased media attention to Mississippi. The deaths of affluent northern white students and threats to other northerners attracted the full attention of the media spotlight to the state. Many black activists became embittered, believing the media valued lives of whites and blacks differently. Perhaps the most significant effect of Freedom Summer was on the volunteers, almost all of whom—black and white—still consider it to have been one of the defining periods of their lives.

Civil Rights Act of 1964

Although President Kennedy had proposed civil rights legislation and it had support from Northern Congressmen, Southern Senators blocked consideration of the bill by threatening filibusters. After considerable parliamentary maneuvering and 54 days of filibuster on the floor of the United States

Senate. Richard Russell (D-GA) launched a filibuster to prevent its passage. Said Russell: "We will resist to the bitter end any measure or any movement which would tend to bring about social equality and intermingling and amalgamation of the races in our (Southern) states.

President Johnson got a bill through the Congress. On July 2, 1964, President Johnson signed the Civil Rights Act of 1964, that banned discrimination based on "race, color, religion, or national origin" in employment practices and public accommodations. The bill authorized the Attorney General to file lawsuits to enforce the new law. The law also nullified state and local laws which required such discrimination.

There were white business owners who claimed that Congress did not have the constitutional authority to ban segregation in public accommodations. However, the Supreme Court held that Congress drew its authority from the Constitution Commerce Clause.

The Civil Rights Act of 1964, which ended segregation in public places and banned employment discrimination based on race, color, religion, sex or national origin, is considered one of the crowning legislative achievements of the civil rights movement.

Mississippi Freedom Democratic Party, 1964

Blacks in Mississippi had been disfranchised by statutory and constitutional changes since the late 1800s. Because Mississippi blacks were barred from participating in the meetings of the State's Democratic Party, they decided to form their party.

In 1964, organizers launched the Mississippi Freedom Democratic Party (MFDP) to challenge the all-white official party. When Mississippi voting registrars refused to recognize their candidates, they held their primary. They selected Fannie Lou Hamer, Annie Devine, and Victoria Gray to run for Congress, and a slate of delegates to represent Mississippi at the 1964 Democratic National Convention.

The presence of the Mississippi Freedom Democratic Party in Atlantic City, New Jersey, was inconvenient, however, for the convention organizers. They had planned a triumphant celebration of the Johnson Administration's achievements in civil rights, rather than a fight over racism within the Democratic Party. All-white delegations from other Southern states threatened to walk out if the official slate from Mississippi was not seated. Johnson was worried about the inroads that Republican Barry Goldwater's campaign was making in what previously had been the white Democratic stronghold of the "Solid South", as well as support which George Wallace had received in the North during the Democratic primaries.

Johnson could not, however, prevent the MFDP from taking its case to the Credentials Committee. There Fannie Lou Hamer testified eloquently about the beatings that she and others endured and the threats they faced for trying to register to vote. Turning to the television cameras, Hamer asked, "Is this America?"

Johnson offered the MFDP a "compromise" under which it would receive two non-voting, at-large seats, while the white delegation sent by the official Democratic Party would retain its seats. The MFDP angrily rejected the "compromise."

The MFDP kept up its agitation within the convention, after it was denied official recognition. When all but three of the "regular" Mississippi delegates left because they refused to pledge allegiance to the party, the MFDP delegates borrowed passes from sympathetic delegates and took the seats vacated by the official Mississippi delegates. National party organizers removed them. When they returned the next day, they found convention organizers had removed the empty seats that had been there the day before. They stayed and sang "freedom songs".

The 1964 Democratic Party convention disillusioned many within the MFDP and the Civil Rights Movement, but it did not destroy the MFDP. The MFDP became more radical after Atlantic City. It invited Malcolm X, of the Nation of Islam, to speak at one of its conventions and opposed the war in Vietnam.

Dr. King Awarded Nobel Peace Prize

The Nobel Peace Prize for 1964 was awarded to the Rev. Dr. Martin Luther King Jr. The 35-year-old civil rights leader is the youngest winner of the prize that Dr. Alfred Nobel Instituted since the first awarded in 1901. The prize honors acts "for the furtherance of brotherhood among men and to the abolishment or reduction of standing armies and for the extension of these purposes." Dr. King said that "every penny" of the prize money, which amounts to about $54,000, would be given to the civil rights movement.

The United States Ambassador in Oslo, Miss Margaret Joy Tibbetts, said: "As an American and representative of the American people, I want to express joy and gratitude that one of my fellow countrymen has been awarded this prize. She praised the role of Dr. King "among his fellow countrymen." He is also the 12th American to receive the peace Prize. The first, in 1950, was Dr. Ralph J. Bunche, Under Secretary of the United Nations.

In 1960 the former leader of the African National Congress in South Africa, Chief Albert Luthuli, received the award. Dr. King is the 12th American to be awarded the peace prize. Dr. Nobel, the Swedish scientist who established it, was the inventor of dynamite.

Boycott of New Orleans by American Football League Players, January 1965

After the 1964 professional American Football League season, the AFL All-Star Game had been scheduled for early 1965 in New Orleans' Tulane Stadium. After numerous black players were refused service by several New Orleans hotels and businesses, and white cabdrivers refused to carry black passengers, black and white players alike lobbied for a boycott of New Orleans. Under the leadership of Buffalo Bills players, including Cookie Gilchrist, the players put up a unified front. The game was moved to Houston and its Jeppesen Stadium.

The discriminatory practices which prompted the boycott were illegal under the Civil Rights Act of 1964 which had been signed in July 1964. This new law likely encouraged the AFL players in their cause. It was the first boycott by a professional sports event of an entire city.

Selma and the Voting Rights Act, 1965

SNCC had undertaken an ambitious voter registration program in Selma, Alabama, in 1963, but by 1965 had made little headway in the face of opposition from Selma's sheriff, Jim Clark. After residents asked the SCLC for assistance, King came to Selma to lead several marches, at which he was arrested along with 250 other demonstrators. The marchers continued to meet violent resistance from police. Jimmie Lee Jackson, a resident of nearby Marion, was killed by police at a later march in February 1965. Jackson's death prompted James Bevel, director of the Selma Movement, to initiate a plan to march from Selma to Montgomery, the state capital.

March 7, 1965 attempting to march peacefully from the small town of Selma, Alabama to Montgomery, the state capital, to protest a brutal murder and the denial of their constitutional right to vote. Six hundred people were attacked by state troopers and mounted deputies dressed in full riot gear.

The national broadcast of the news footage of lawmen attacking unresisting marchers' seeking the right to vote provoked a national response, as had scenes from Birmingham two years earlier. The marchers were able to obtain a court order permitting them to make the march without incident two weeks later.

On March 21, more than one thousand people from all over the United States again left Brown Chapel African Methodist Episcopal Church in Selma and set out for Montgomery. This time they were watched over by regular Army and Alabama National Guard Units ordered by President Johnson to protect the marchers against further violence.

At the successful completion of the march on March 25, Martin Luther King Jr., addressed a crowd estimated at 25,000 in front of the Alabama State Capitol.

Viola Liuzzo (April 11, 1925—March 25, 1965) was a civil rights activist from Michigan. In March 1965 Liuzzo, then a housewife and mother of 5 with a history of local activism, heeded the call of Martin Luther King Jr. and traveled from Detroit, Michigan to Selma, Alabama in the wake of the Bloody Sunday attempt at marching across the Edmund Pettus Bridge. Liuzzo participated in the successful Selma to Montgomery marches and helped with coordination and logistics. Driving back from a trip shuttling fellow activists to the Montgomery airport, she was shot by members of the Ku Klux Klan. Her murder helped accelerate passage of the historic Voting Rights Act.

Eight days after the first march, President Johnson delivered a televised address to support the voting rights bill he had sent to Congress. In it he stated:

But even if we pass this bill, the battle will not be over. What happened in Selma is part of a far larger movement which reaches into every section and state of America. It is the effort of American Negroes to secure for themselves the full blessings of American life.

Their cause must be our cause too. Because it is not just Negroes, but it is all of us, who must overcome the crippling legacy of bigotry and injustice. And we shall overcome. Johnson signed the Voting Rights Act of 1965 on August 6. The 1965 act suspended poll taxes, literacy tests, and other subjective voter tests. It authorized Federal supervision of voter registration in states and individual voting districts where such tests were being used. African Americans who had been barred from registering to vote finally had an alternative to taking suits to local or state courts. If voting discrimination occurred, the 1965 act authorized the Attorney General of the United States to send Federal examiners to replace local registrars. Johnson reportedly told associates of his concern that signing the bill had lost the white South as voters for the Democratic Party for the foreseeable future.

The act had an immediate and positive impact for African Americans. Within months of its passage, 250,000 new black voters had been registered, one third of them by federal examiners. Within four years, voter registration in the South had more than doubled. In 1965, Mississippi had the highest black voter turnout at 74% and led the nation in the number of black public officials elected. In 1969, Tennessee had a 92.1% turnout; Arkansas, 77.9%; and Texas, 73.1%.

Several whites who had opposed the Voting Rights Act paid a quick price. In 1966 Sheriff Jim Clark of Alabama, infamous for using cattle prods against civil rights marchers, was up for reelection. Although he took off the notorious "Never" pin on his uniform, he was defeated. At the election, Clark lost as blacks voted to get him out of office. Clark later served a prison term for drug dealing.

Blacks' regaining the power to vote changed the political landscape of the South. When Congress passed the Voting Rights Act, only about 100 African Americans held elective office, all in northern states of the U.S. By 1989, there were more than 7,200 African Americans in office, including more than 4,800 in the South. Nearly every Black Belt county (where populations were majority black) in Alabama had a black sheriff. Southern blacks held top positions within city, county, and state governments.

Atlanta elected a black mayor, Andrew Young, as did Jackson, Mississippi, with Harvey Johnson, and New Orleans, with Ernest Morial. Black politicians of the national level included Barbara Jordan, who represented Texas in Congress, and Andrew Young was appointed United States Ambassador to the United Nations during the Carter administration. Julian Bond was elected to the Georgia Legislature in 1965, although political reaction to his public opposition to U.S. involvement in Vietnam prevented him from taking his seat until 1967. John Lewis represents Georgia's 5th congressional district in the United States House of Representatives, where he has served since 1987.

Memphis, King Assassination and the Poor People's March, 1968

Rev. James Lawson invited King to Memphis, Tennessee, in March 1968 to support a strike by sanitation workers. They had launched a campaign for union representation after two workers were accidentally killed on the job.

A day after delivering his famous "Mountaintop" sermon at Lawson's church, King was assassinated on April 4, 1968. Riots broke out in more than 110 cities across the United States in the days that followed, notably in Chicago, Baltimore, and in Washington, D.C. The damage done in many cities destroyed black businesses.

Martin Luther King Jr. had led the civil rights movement since the mid-1950s, using a combination of powerful words and non-violent tactics such as sit-ins, boycotts and protest marches (including the massive march on Washington in 1963) to fight segregation and achieve significant civil and voting rights advances for African Americans. He worked on issues as poverty and unemployment and the Vietnam War.

President Lyndon B. Johnson urged Americans to "reject the blind violence" that had killed King, whom he called the "apostle of nonviolence." He called on congress to pass the Civil Rights Act of 1968, also known as the Fair Housing Act.

A campaign to establish a national holiday in his honor was started. President Ronald Reagan signed the holiday bill into law in 1983. A permanent memorial to King is located on the Mall in Washington D.C.

The day before King's funeral, April 8, Coretta Scott King and three of the King children led 20,000 marchers through the streets of Memphis, holding signs that read, "Honor King: End Racism" and "Union Justice Now". National Guardsmen lined the streets, perched on M-48 tanks, bayonets mounted, with helicopters circling overhead. On April 9 Mrs. King led another 150,000 in a funeral procession through the streets of Atlanta. Her dignity revived courage and hope in many of the Movement's members, cementing her place as the new leader in the struggle for racial equality.

Rev. Ralph Abernathy succeeded King as the head of the SCLC and attempted to carry forth King's plan for a Poor People's March. It was to unite blacks and whites to campaign for fundamental changes in American society and economic structure. The march went forward under Abernathy's plainspoken leadership but did not achieve its goals.

Kennedy Administration, 1961-1963

During the years preceding his election to the presidency, John F. Kennedy's record of voting on issues of racial discrimination had been scant. Kennedy openly confessed to his closest advisors that during the first months of his presidency his knowledge of the civil rights movement was "lacking".

When John F. Kennedy became president in 1961, African Americans throughout much of the South were denied the right to vote, barred from public facilities, subjected to insults and violence, and could not expect justice from the courts. In the North, black Americans also faced discrimination in housing, employment, education, and many other areas.

A few weeks during the 1960 election, Martin Luther King Jr., was arrested while leading a protest in Atlanta Georgia. Kennedy phoned Coretta Scott King to express his concern while a call from Robert Kennedy to the judge helped secure her husband's safe release.

More than 70 percent of African Americans voted for Kennedy and helped him to the White House. He appointed unprecedented numbers of African Americans to high level positions in the administration and strengthen the Civil Rights Commission. Vice President Lyndon Johnson was in charge of the President's Committee on Equal Employment Opportunity. Attorney General Robert Kennedy turned his attention to voting rights.

During the Freedom Rides in the 1960s, Attorney General Robert Kennedy sent federal Marshalls to protect freedom riders and order ICC to order desegregation of Interstate travel. President Kennedy mobilize the National Guard to allow James Meredith to enter the University of Mississippi. He provided troops to quell the protest in Alabama and the integration of the University of Alabama.

President Kennedy was assassinated before the passing of the comprehensive Civil Rights Bill. President Johnson worked on getting the Civil Rights Bill to pass. Provisions of the legislation included: (1) protecting African Americans against discrimination in voter qualification tests; (2) outlawing discrimination in hotels, motels, restaurants, theaters, and all other public accommodations engaged in interstate commerce; (3) authorizing the U.S. Attorney General's Office to file legal suits to enforce desegregation in public schools; (4) authorizing the withdrawal of federal funds from programs practicing discrimination; (5) outlawing discrimination in employment in any business exceeding 25 people and creating an Equal Employment Opportunity Commission to review complaints.

The Civil Rights Act was passed on July 2, 1964 giving Blacks full legal equality.

For the first two years of the Kennedy Administration, attitudes to the President and Attorney-General, Robert F. Kennedy, were mixed. Many viewed the Administration with suspicion. A well of historical cynicism toward white liberal politics had left a sense of uneasy disdain by African–Americans toward any white politician who claimed to share their concerns for freedom. Still, many had a strong sense that in the Kennedys there was a new age of political dialogue beginning.

Although observers frequently assert the phrase "The Kennedy Administration" or even, "President Kennedy" when discussing the legislative and executive support of the Civil Rights movement, between 1960 and 1963, many of the initiatives were the result of Robert Kennedy's passion. Through his rapid education in the realities of racism, Robert Kennedy underwent a thorough conversion of purpose as Attorney-General. Asked in an interview in May 1962, "What do you see as the big problem ahead for you, is it Crime or Internal Security?" Robert Kennedy replied, "Civil Rights." The President came to share his brother's sense of urgency on the matters to such an extent that it was at the AttorneyGeneral's insistence that he made his famous address to the nation.

When a white mob attacked and burned the First Baptist Church in Montgomery, Alabama, where King held out with protesters, the Attorney-General telephoned King to ask him not to leave the building until the U.S. Marshals and National Guard could secure the area. King proceeded to berate Kennedy for "allowing the situation to continue". King later publicly thanked Robert Kennedy's commanding the force to break up an attack which might otherwise have ended King's life.

The relationship between the two men changed from mutual suspicion to one of shared aspirations. For Dr. King, Robert Kennedy initially represented the 'softly softly' approach that in former years had disabled the movement of blacks against oppression in the U.S. For Robert Kennedy, King initially represented what he then considered an unrealistic militancy. Some white liberals regarded the militancy itself as the cause of so little governmental progress.

King initially regarded much of the efforts of the Kennedys as an attempt to control the movement and siphon off its energies. Yet he came to find the efforts of the brothers to be crucial. It was at Robert Kennedy's constant insistence, through conversations with King and others that King came to recognize the fundamental nature of electoral reform and suffrage—the need for black Americans to actively engage not only protest but political dialogue at the highest levels. In time the President gained King's respect and trust, via the frank dialogue and efforts of the Attorney-General. Robert Kennedy became very much his brother's key advisor on matters of racial equality. The President regarded the issue of civil rights to be a function of the Attorney-General's office.

With a very small majority in Congress, the President's ability to press ahead with legislation relied considerably on a balancing game with the Senators and Congressmen of the South. Indeed, without the support of Vice-President Lyndon Johnson, who had years of experience in Congress and longstanding relations there, many of the Attorney-General's programs would not have progressed.

By late 1962, frustration at the slow pace of political change was balanced by the movement's strong support for legislative initiatives: housing rights, administrative representation across all US Government departments, safe conditions at the ballot box, pressure on the courts to prosecute racist criminals. King remarked by the end of the year, "This administration has reached out more creatively than its predecessors to blaze new trails [in voting rights and government appointments]. Its vigorous young men have launched imaginative and bold forays and displayed a certain elan in the attention they give to civil rights issues.

> "We preach freedom around the
> world, and we mean it, and we
> cherish our freedom here at home,
> but are we to say to the world, and
> much more importantly, to each

other that this is the land of the free except for the Negroes; that we have no second-class citizens except Negroes; that we have no class or caste system, no ghettoes, no master race except concerning Negroes? Now the time has come for this Nation to fulfill its promise. The events in Birmingham and elsewhere have so increased the cries for equality that no city or State or legislative body can prudently choose to ignore them."—President Kennedy,

Assassination cut short the life and careers of both the Kennedy brothers and Dr. Martin Luther King, Jr. The essential groundwork of the Civil Rights Act 1964 had been initiated before John F. Kennedy was assassinated. The dire need for political and administrative reform had been driven home on Capitol Hill by the combined efforts of the Kennedy brothers, Dr. King (and other leaders) and President Lyndon Johnson.

In 1966, Robert Kennedy undertook a tour of South Africa in which he championed the cause of the anti-Apartheid movement. His tour gained international praise at a time when few politicians dared to entangle themselves in the politics of South Africa. Kennedy spoke out against the oppression of the native population. He was welcomed by the black population as though a visiting head of state. In an interview with LOOK Magazine he said:

> At the University of Natal in Durban, I was told the church to which most of the white population belongs teaches apartheid as a moral necessity. A questioner declared that few churches allow black Africans to pray with the white because the Bible says that is the way it should be. After all, God created Negroes to serve. "But suppose God is black", I replied. "What if we go to Heaven and we, all our lives, have treated the Negro as an inferior, and God is there, and we look up and He is not white? What then is our response?" There was no answer. Only silence.—Robert Kennedy

American Jewish community and the Civil Rights movement

The NAACP was formed on February 12, 1909 after a race riot in Springfield, Illinois. The NAACP was also formed in response to the practice of lynching, which was prevalent in the South at that time. The founders of the NAACP were a diverse group.

W.E.B. DuBois held a position on the governing board and was largely directed, funded and control in its early decades by Jews like Henry Moskowitz and Joel Spingarn.

"The Jewish struggle for equality and fair treatment," was linked to the struggles of Blacks for greater opportunity. They recognized in the black struggle for civil rights elements that could benefit them. They saw the struggle as a way for them to stop anti-Semitism which is a virulent and murderous form of hatred.

Spingarn announced a yearly award named after himself, the "Spingarn Medal," for the highest and noblest achievement of an American Negro.

Many in the Jewish-American community supported the Civil Rights Movement. Statistically Jews were one of the most actively involved non-black groups in the Movement. Many Jewish students worked in concert with African Americans for CORE, SCLC, and SNCC as full-time organizers and summer volunteers during the Civil Rights era. Jews made up roughly half of the white northern volunteers involved in the 1964 Mississippi Freedom Summer project and approximately half of the civil rights attorneys active in the South during the 1960s.

Jewish leaders were arrested while heeding a call from Rev. Dr. Martin Luther King, Jr. in St. Augustine, Florida, in June 1964, where the largest mass arrest of rabbis in American history took place at the Monson Motor Lodge—a nationally important civil rights landmark that was demolished in 2003 so that a Hilton Hotel could be built on the site. Abraham Joshua Heschel, a writer, rabbi and professor of theology at the Jewish Theological Seminary of America in New York was outspoken on the subject of civil rights. He marched arm-in-arm with Dr. King in the 1965 March on Selma.

Brandeis University, the only nonsectarian Jewish-sponsored college university in the world, created the Transitional Year Program (TYP) in 1968, in part response to Rev. Dr. Martin Luther King's assassination. The faculty created it to renew the University's commitment to social justice. Recognizing Brandeis as a university with a commitment to academic excellence, these faculty members created a chance to disadvantaged students to participate in an empowering educational experience. Over 1000 students have participated in the program since its 1968 founding.

The American Jewish Committee, American Jewish Congress, and Anti-Defamation League actively promoted civil rights.

Allies: The UFT and the civil rights movement

The United Federation of Teachers released a report detailing how some New York City charter schools constitute what is essentially a separate and unequal public school system. This is an issue that should greatly trouble everyone who cares about the education of our children—all our children—and it is an injustice that the UFT is fighting hard to correct.

We have been down similar roads before. Fifty years ago, New York City schools faced the ugly specter of racial division. Some neighborhoods—and subsequently their schools—became increasingly segregated as whites fled the inner cities. A 1955 report documented the stark disparities between schools in different neighborhoods. From class size to building conditions to per-pupil expenditures, minority students were being severely shortchanged.

My father Ivan St Thomas was a member of the UFT when he became a teacher. He was very encouraged with their policy on civil rights. He was the shop teacher at Catherine and Count Basie Middle School 72 in Jamaica Queens.

In the Brown vs Board of Education the teachers Guild honor the NAACP lawyer who litigated Brown, Thurgood Marshall, with the Unions prestigious Davey Award. In 1956, it was largely the Guild's doing that put an end to segregated Jim Crow locals, using the threat of expulsion. The UFT also raised money for civil rights groups like the NAACP, the student Nonviolent Coordination Committee (SNCC) and the Congress of Racial Equality (CORE).

"Leading the UFT in this troubled time and undergoing his baptism of fire was its new president, Albert Shanker. At least for the early years of his presidency, no issue more dominated the union's agenda than civil rights. Throughout his career, Shanker would not be deterred from his lifelong commitment to racial integration."

On the national front, Shanker and the UFT continued to work and March with civil rights leaders to help strengthen the movement. UFT members raised money to buy station wagons to transport black voters to the polls in Selma, Ala. Shanker, along with Charles Cogen, the first UFT president, and other union officers personally delivered the keys to Martin Luther King Jr. and joined his March on Montgomery to protest the beating of civil rights volunteers.

The UFT was a prominent voice in other causes as well, including: Cesar Chavez's boycotts against California growers in support of migrant workers, the founding of the A. Philip Randolph Institute to join the labor and civil rights movements and the introduction of a multicultural curriculum in the city schools. City teachers stood against intolerance, supported freedom riders, boycotts and protest and prejudice where they found it.

The Labor movement and civil rights

A. Philip Randolph April 15, 1889-May 16, 1979 was a giant in the American Labor Movement and a leader in the Civil Rights Movements. He organized and led the Brotherhood of Sleeping Car Porters, the first predominantly African-American labor union. In 1937, he won membership in the

AFL, making the BSCP the first African-American union in the United States.

Randolph protested against discrimination in the war industry workforce. President Roosevelt issued an executive order that banned racial discrimination at government defense factories and established the first Fair Employment Practices Committee.

Randolph fought against racial segregation in the U.S. Armed Forces. His actions eventually led President Harry S. Truman to issue a 1948 executive order to desegregate the Armed Forces. In 1955, Randolph became a vice president of the newly merged entity AFL-CIO (Congress of Industrial Organizations). After finding systematic racial prejudices in the AFL-CIO he formed the Negro American Labor Council in 1959.

The CIO was particularly vocal in calling for elimination of racial discrimination by defense industries during World War II. They were also forced to combat racism within their membership, putting down strikes by white workers who refused to work with black co-workers. While many of these "hate strikes" were short-lived: a wildcat strike launched in Philadelphia in 1944 when the federal government ordered the private transit company to desegregate its workforce lasted two weeks and was ended only when the Roosevelt administration sent troops to guard the system and arrested the strike's ringleaders.

The labor movement, with some exceptions, had historically excluded African Americans. While the radical labor organizers who led organizing drives among packinghouse workers in Chicago and Kansas City during World War I and the steel industry in 1919 made determined efforts to appeal to black workers, they were not able to overcome the widespread distrust of the labor movement among black workers in the North. With the ultimate defeat of both of those organizing drives, the black community and the labor movement largely returned to their traditional mutual mistrust.

The BSCP became the only black-led union within the American Federation of Labor in 1935. Randolph chose to remain within the AFL, when the Congress of Industrial Organizations split from it. The CIO was much more committed to organizing African-American workers and made strenuous efforts to persuade the BSCP to join it, but Randolph believed more could be done to advance black workers' rights, particularly in the railway industry, by remaining in the AFL, to which the other railway brotherhoods belonged. Randolph remained the voice for black workers within the labor movement, raising demands for elimination of Jim Crow unions within the AFL at every opportunity. BSCP members such as Edgar Nixon played a significant role in the civil rights struggles of the following decades.

Many of the CIO unions, in particular the Packinghouse Workers, the United Auto Workers and the Mine, Mill and Smelter Workers made advocacy of civil rights part of their organizing strategy and bargaining priorities: they gained improvements for workers in meatpacking in Chicago and Omaha, and in the steel and related industries throughout the Midwest. The Transport Workers Union of America, which had strong ties with the Communist Party at the time, entered into coalitions with Adam Clayton Powell, Jr., the NAACP and the National Negro Congress to attack employment discrimination in public transit in New York City in the early 1940s.

Another example of civil rights unionism is the Local 22 strike of 1943. In this instance, workers of the Reynolds Tobacco plant in Winston-Salem, NC united and achieved great stride to end workplace racism. Job security for senior workers, vacations, wage increases and grievance procedures were secured. Participation in unions exposed many African American workers to voting for the first time and led to successes in local elections.

Randolph and the BSCP took the battle against employment discrimination even further, threatening a March on Washington in 1942 if the government did not take steps to outlaw racial discrimination by defense contractors. Randolph limited the March on Washington Movement to black organizations to maintain black leadership; he endured harsh criticism from others on the left for his insistence on black workers' rights in the middle of a war. Randolph only dropped the plan to march after winning substantial concessions from the Roosevelt administration.

In 1963, Randolph was a principal organizer of the March on Washington for jobs and freedom. He was presented with the Presidential Medal of Freedom by President Lyndon B. Johnson

Fraying of Alliances

The Civil Rights Movement was a coalition of thousands of local efforts nationwide. Some Blacks felt that leaders should take their activism at a slower pace and work on reforming issues within the black community. Some Blacks defended segregation in terms of the Status Quo they enjoyed. They had social and economic mobility. Community leaders, Church ministers, business men and educators wanted to retain the privileges they gained from whites, such as monetary gains.

Some blacks felt the backlash from whites would create negative situations. For Martin Luther King Jr. and other leading activist and groups in the movements these viewpoints acted as an obstacle against their ideas.

King reached the height of popular acclaim during his life in 1964, when he was awarded the Nobel Peace Prize. His career after that point was filled with frustrating challenges. The liberal coalition that had gained passage of the Civil Rights Act of 1964 and the Voting Rights Act of 1965 began to fray.

King was becoming more estranged from the Johnson Administration. In 1965 he broke with it by calling for peace negotiations and a halt to the bombing of Vietnam. King felt that the Vietnam War was sapping resources from domestic social programs. His action sets him against President Johnson who has been an ally. He moved further left in the following years, speaking of the need for economic justice and thoroughgoing changes in American society. He also attacked housing discrimination and issues of employment which were unsuccessful.

Race riots, 1963 and beyond

By the end of World War II, more than half of the country's black population lived in Northern and Western industrial cities rather than Southern rural areas. Migrating to those cities for better job opportunities, education and to escape legal segregation, African Americans often found segregation that existed rather than in law.

In the 1950s blacks entered the industrial job market which collapsed. Whites moved out of the cities into the expanding suburbs. Blacks mainly stayed in the cities occupying older housing in the inner city neighborhoods. Unemployment was higher and crimes were frequent. Blacks rented the stores and businesses where they lived. The housing tenements were dilapidated, poorly maintained schools were the worst academically. The racial makeup of the police department in the cities was mostly whites and a factor to racial tensions.

Harlem riot of 1964 happened when police shot an unarmed black teenager in Harlem in July 1964. Residents were frustrated with racial inequalities and started rioting in Bedford-Stuyvesant neighborhood in Brooklyn. Rioting also broke out in Philadelphia for similar reasons.

In the aftermath of the riots of July, 1964, the federal government funded a pilot program called Project Uplift, in which thousands of young people in Harlem were given jobs during the summer of 1965. The project was inspired by a report generated by HARYOU called Youth in the Ghetto. Harlem Youth Opportunities Unlimited (HARYOU) was given a major role in organizing the project, together with the National Urban league and nearly 100 smaller community organizations. Permanent jobs at living wages, however, were still out of reach of many young black men.

In 1965, President Lyndon B. Johnson signed the Voting Rights Act, but the new law had no immediate effect on living conditions for blacks. A few days after the act became law, a riot broke out in the South Central Los Angeles neighborhood of Watts. Like Harlem, Watts was an impoverished neighborhood with very high unemployment. Its residents had to endure patrols by a largely white police department. While arresting a young man for drunk driving, police officers argued with the suspect's mother before onlookers. The conflict triggered a massive destruction of property through six days of rioting. Thirty-four people were killed and property valued at about $30 million was destroyed, making the Watts riot one of the worst in American history.

Riots among blacks occurred in 1966 and 1967 in cities such as Atlanta, San Francisco, Oakland,

Baltimore, Seattle, Tacoma, Cleveland, Cincinnati, Columbus, Newark, New York City and Detroit.

The Detroit riot of 1967 saw blacks looted and destroyed property for five days. Forty three people had been killed, hundreds injured and thousands left homeless. In April 1968 after the assassination of Dr. Martin Luther King, Jr. in Memphis, Tennessee rioting broke out in cities across the country from frustration and despair.

With black militancy on the rise, increased acts of anger were now directed at the police. Black residents growing tired of police brutality continued to riot. Some young people joined groups such as the **Black Panthers**, whose popularity was based in part on their reputation for confronting police officers.

Bobby Seale and Huey Newton co-found the Black Panthers in Oakland, California. Unlike the civil rights activist who preaches non-violence, the Black Panthers authorized the use of violence as self-defense.

The Panthers were an urban self-defense militia organized to stop police brutality in the black community and they were eager defenders of the second Amendment. They were an unofficial social service agency that fed school children in poor neighborhoods and provided free, medical case. They were a social-justice movement and a political party, and in both of those modes they began to reach beyond their base in inner-city African-American neighborhoods.

They symbolized black anger, black militancy and black power that galvanized the entire African

American community. Before they would become powerful J. Edgar Hoover and the FBI crushed the Panthers because they consider the Panthers as the greatest internal threat to American society.

In Detroit, a comfortable black middle class had begun to develop among families of blacks who worked at well-paying jobs in the automotive industry. Blacks who had not moved upward were living in much worse conditions, subject to the same problems as blacks in Watts and Harlem. When white police officers shut down an illegal bar on a liquor raid and arrested a large group of patrons, furious residents rioted.

One significant effect of the Detroit riot was the acceleration of "white flight", the trend of white residents moving from inner-city neighborhoods to predominantly white suburbs. Detroit experienced "middle class black flight" as well. Cities such as Detroit, Newark, and Baltimore now have less than 40% white population as a result of these riots and other social changes. Changes in industry caused continued job losses, depopulation of middle classes, and concentrated poverty in such cities.

As a result of the riots, President Johnson created the National Advisory Commission on Civil Disorders in 1967. The commission's final report called for major reforms in employment and public assistance for black communities. It warned that the United States was moving toward separate white and black societies.

Affirmative Action altered the hiring process of more black police officers in every major city. Blacks make up a proportional majority of the police departments in cities such as Baltimore, Washington, New Orleans, Atlanta, Newark, and Detroit. Civil rights laws have reduced employment discrimination. The conditions that led to frequent rioting in the late 1960s have receded, but not all the problems have been solved.

With industrial and economic restructuring, tens of thousands of industrial jobs disappeared since the later 1950s from the old industrial cities. Some moved south, as has much population and others out of the US altogether. Civil unrest broke out in Miami in 1980, in Los Angeles in 1992, and in Cincinnati in 2001.

Black power, 1966

At the same time King was finding himself at odds with factions of the Democratic Party, he was facing challenges from within the Civil Rights Movement to the two key tenets upon which the movement had been based: integration and non-violence. Stokley Carmichael, who became the leader of SNCC in 1966, was one of the earliest and most articulate spokespersons for what became known as the "Black Power" movement after he used that slogan, coined by activist and organizer Willie Ricks, in Greenwood, Mississippi on June 17, 1966.

SNCC, now headed by Stokley Carmichael, rejects its historical strategy of non-violence to embrace a doctrine of "Black Power," which emphasizes Black Nationalism and self-reliance. Violence is accepted as a legitimate form of self-defense.

In 1966 SNCC leader Stokley Carmichael began urging African American communities to confront the Ku Klux Klan armed and ready for battle. He felt it was the only way to ever rid the communities of the terror caused by the Klan.

Several people engaging in the Black Power movement started to gain more of a sense in black pride and identity as well. In gaining more of a sense of a cultural identity, several blacks demanded that whites no longer refer to them as "Negroes" but as "Afro-Americans." Up until the mid-1960s, blacks had dressed similarly to whites and straightened their hair. As a part of gaining a unique identity, blacks started to wear loosely fit dashikis and had started to grow their hair out as a natural afro. The afro, sometimes nicknamed the "fro," remained a popular black hairstyle until the late 1970s.

Black Power was made most public however by the Black Panther Party which founded by Huey Newton and Bobby Seale in Oakland, California, in 1966. This group followed the ideology of Malcolm X, a former member of the Nation of Islam, using a "by-any-means necessary" approach to stopping inequality. They sought to rid African American neighborhoods of Police Brutality and created a ten-point plan amongst other things. Their dress code consisted of black leather jackets, berets, slacks, and light shirts. They wore an afro hairstyle. They are best remembered for setting up free breakfast programs, referring to police officers as "pigs", displaying shotguns and a black power fist, and often using the statement of "Power to the people".

Black Power was taken to another level inside prison walls. In 1966, George Jackson formed the Black Guerilla Family in the California prison of San Quentin. The goal of this group was to overthrow the white-run government in America and the prison system. In 1970, this group displayed their dedication after a white prison guard was found not guilty of shooting and killing three black prisoners from the prison tower. They retaliated by killing a white prison guard.

In 1968, Tommie Smith and John Carlos, while being awarded the gold and bronze medals, respectively, at the 1968 Summer Olympics, donned human rights badges and each raised a black-gloved Black Power salute during their podium ceremony. Incidentally, it was the suggestion of white silver medalist, Peter Norman of Australia, for Smith and Carlos to each wear one black glove. Smith and Carlos were immediately ejected from the games by the USOC, and later the IOC issued a permanent lifetime ban for the two. However, the Black Power movement had been given a stage on live, international television.

King was not comfortable with the "Black Power" slogan, which sounded too much like Black

Nationalism to him. The SCLC and NAACP did not endorse Black Power. SNCC activists, in the meantime, began embracing the "right to self-defense" in response to attacks from white authorities, and booed King for continuing to advocate non-violence.

When King was murdered in 1968, Stokley Carmichael stated that whites murdered the one person who would prevent rampant rioting and that blacks would burn every major city to the ground. In every major city from Boston to San Francisco, racial riots broke out in the black community following King's death and as a result, "White Flight" occurred from several cities leaving Blacks in a dilapidated and nearly unrepairable city.

Parchman Farm and the Freedom Riders (1961)

In the spring of 1961, Freedom Riders went to the Southern States to work for desegregation of public facilities which were declared unconstitutional by the Supreme Court. The southern states ignored the rulings because the Federal Government didn't enforce the order. Forty-five male freedom riders 29 Blacks and 16 Whites were arrested in Mississippi and sent to Parchman Farm Penitentiary.

The freedom riders were stripped of their clothing and given tee shirts and boxer shorts to wear. One shower per a week and no mail were allowed. To break their spirit, their mattresses and bug screens were removed and the lights stayed on 24 hours. By the end of June, 163 freedom riders had been convicted and sent to Parchman Farm. Most of them were bailed out after a month. Parchman Farm became well known for the part it played in the United States Civil Rights Movement.

In 1970 Civil Rights lawyer Roy Haber began taking statements from inmates, which eventually totaled fifty pages of details of murders, rapes, beatings and other abuses suffered by the inmates from 1969 to 1971 at Mississippi State Penitentiary. In a landmark case known as Gates v. Collier (1972) four inmates represented by Haber sued the superintendent of Parchman Farm for violating their rights under the United States Constitution. Federal Judge William C. Keady found in favor of the inmates, writing that Parchman Farm violated the civil rights of the inmates by inflicting cruel and unusual punishment. He ordered an immediate end to all unconstitutional conditions and practices. Racial segregation of inmates was abolished. And the trustee system, which allows certain inmates to have power and control over others, was also abolished.

The prison was renovated in 1972 after the scathing ruling by Judge Keady in which he wrote that the prison was an affront to "modern standards of decency." Among other reforms, the accommodations were made fit for human habitation and the system of "trusties" (in which lifers were armed with rifles and set to guard other inmates) was abolished.

In integrated correctional facilities in northern and western states, blacks represented a disproportionate amount of the prisoners and were often treated as second class citizens at the hands of white correctional officers. Blacks also represented a disproportionate number of death row inmates. Eldridge Cleaver's book Soul on Ice was written from his experiences in the California correctional system and further fueled black militancy.

Cold War

There was an international context for the actions of the U.S. Federal government during these years. It had stature to maintain in Europe and a need to appeal to the people in the Third World. In Cold War Civil Rights: Race and the Image of American Democracy, Historian Mary L. Dudziak showed how, in the ideological battle of the Cold War, Communist critics could easily point out the hypocrisy of the United States portrayal of itself as the "leader of the free world" when so many of its citizens were the object of racial discrimination. She argued that this was a major factor in pushing the government to support civil rights legislation.

American racism was a major concern of U.S. allies, a chief Soviet propaganda theme, and an obstacle to American Cold War goals throughout Africa, Asia, and Latin America. Each lynching harmed foreign relations, and "the Negro problem" became a central issue in every administration from Truman to Johnson.

Stories like, an African-American veteran of world War ll lynched in Georgia, African diplomats denied restaurant service; black artists living in Europe and supporting the civil rights movement from overseas. Conservative politicians viewing desegregation as a communist plot. Civil rights activists gained tremendous advantage as the government sought to polish its international image.

In 1958, a black American farmhand James 'Jimmy' E. Wilson was an American farmhand who was sentenced to death by an Alabama court after he was convicted of violent robbery for a small amount of two dollars. He was convicted by an all-white jury.

The case became a source of embarrassment for the United States at the height of the Cold War, as it suggested that American promotion of democratic principles was hypocritical when it did not seem to uphold the same standards in its states.

Because of the international attention the case was receiving, Wilson sentence was commuted to a life sentence. Wilson was paroled on October, 1973 at age 70 after 16 years in prison.

Black Colleges and Universities

Before the Civil War, higher education for African American students was virtually nonexistent. The few who did receive schooling, such as Frederick Douglas, often studied in informal and sometimes hostile settings. Some were forced to teach themselves entirely. Some schools for elementary and secondary training existed, such as the Institute for Colored Youth, a school started in early 1830s by a group of Philadelphia Quakers. A college education was also available to a limited number of students at schools like Oberlin College in Ohio and Berea College in Kentucky.

The Institute for Colored Youth was founded in 1837 in Philadelphia, Pennsylvania. The institute was founded by Richard Humphreys to design and establish a school to educate people of African descent. The goal was to teach them in the Arts, trades and agriculture in order to prepare them to train as teachers. The name was change to Cheyney University.

The first College founded solely for African–American students was Ashmun Institute in Southern Chester County, Pennsylvania on January 1, 1857. It was chartered to give theological, classical, and scientific training to African Americans. In 1866, the institution was renamed Lincoln University.

Oberlin College was founded as an institution to promote Christian values. In 1835 it became the first predominantly white collegiate institution to admit African American male students and two years later it opened its doors to all women, becoming the first coeducational college in the country. Mary Jane Patterson earned a B.A. degree in education from Oberlin, becoming the first African American woman to earn a degree from an American College. By 1900, one third of all black professionals in the U.S. had undergraduate degrees from Oberlin. Oberlin's commitment to the abolition of slavery made it a welcoming and safe environment for 19th century black students.

Berea College in Kentucky was founded in 1855 by abolitionist John G. Fee. Berea was one of the first fully integrated colleges in the South, enrolling an essentially equal number of blacks and whites from 1865 to 1892.

A need to improve education

Southern slaveholders generally opposed slave literacy. In 1740 South Carolina enacted laws prohibiting teaching a slave to read or write. In other parts of the South expansion of earlier laws forbidding the education of slaves. In the absence of formal education, slaves in both the rural and urban south often found alternative paths to learning. Slaves learned from parents, spouses, family members, and fellow slaves and some were even personally instructed by their masters or hired tutors.

In the North, where black education was not forbidden, African-Americans had greater access to formal schooling and were more likely to have basic reading and writing skills than Southern blacks. Quakers played an important part elevating literacy rates among Northern blacks by rigorously promoting education programs in the years before and after the Revolutionary War.

In the antebellum North, black schools struggled to stay afloat under constant financial hardships and back of white support. In both the North and South, labor demands made it difficult for slave children to engage in extensive learning or to attend school consistently. Knowing the benefits of education, emancipated blacks worked vigorously to establish schools and colleges during the reconstruction period and, despite segregation, intimidation, and violent opposition, continued to pursue equal education in the years to follow.

In the years following the Civil War, with the 13th Amendment's abolition of slavery and reconstruction in the South, things began to change. In 1862, Senator Justin Morrill spearheaded a movement to improve the state of public higher education throughout the United States, emphasizing the need for institutions to train Americans in the applied sciences, agriculture, and engineering. The Merrill Land-Grant Act gave federal lands to the states to open colleges and universities to educate farmers, scientists, and teachers. The program was to benefit students of all races. Although many such institutions were created, few were open or inviting to blacks, particularly in the South.

Alcorn University was founded in 1871 and was the first black land grant college established in the United States. Congress required that states with segregated educational institutions designate black land grant colleges to receive land grants money for white colleges. Only Alcorn State University in Mississippi was created explicitly as a black land-grant college. It would be 28 years before Senator Morrill rectified this problem. The solution came with the second Morrill Land-Grant Act of 1890, which specified that States using federal land-grant funds must either make their schools open to both blacks and whites or allocate money for segregated black colleges to serve as an alternative to white schools. Sixteen exclusively black institutions received 1890 land-grant funds.

Most of these public schools were founded by state legislatures between 1870 and 1910. Before this, it was the initiative of many blacks themselves, along with the support of the American Missionary Association (AMA) and the Freedmen's Bureau that was responsible for setting up private colleges and universities for the education of blacks. African American churches ran their own elementary and secondary education for southern blacks, preparing them for vocations or advanced studies. This created a demand for higher education, particularly for the institutes to train teachers for work in black schools. Between 1861 and 1870, the AMA founded seven black colleges and 13 normal (teaching) schools. Many of these institutions along with the private historical black colleges and universities founded later by the AMA, the Freedmen's Bureau, and black churches-became the backbone of black higher education, producing African American leaders for generation to come.

The Course of American Education

The time spent on education—the belief being that in a democracy it was only right and fair that all people regardless of skin color should have the right to a decent education.

Within the south, the general philosophy that had developed since the civil war, was that if African Americans were kept ill-educated they would remain 'in their place' in society. An educated "boy" could become a danger. There was also a belief in some areas that African-Americans were not intelligent enough to deserve an education. The shadow of "Jim Crow" cast itself over education in the south.

The result of this was very much linked to the poverty most African Americans found themselves in—without a good education no-one could advance themselves in Southern society. Therefore a poor education guaranteed a poor lifestyle for the African-Americans.

Two graduates from the first generation of students to attend these new black institutions of higher learning came to take forefront in the early twentieth century, each backing a different course for the black college to take.

Booker T. Washington, a freed slave from Virginia, attended the Hampton Normal and Agricultural Institute. There, he was exposed to one of the best examples of elementary and secondary black vocational education in the nation. Hampton, founded by the AMA and the Freedmen's Bureau, focused its efforts on preparing young blacks throughout the South to fill jobs in the skilled trades. Washington became an apprentice of Hampton's president and decided to lead his school after graduating. In 1881, he took the helm at the fledgling Tuskegee Institute. Tuskegee quickly became famous for its practical curriculum and focus on preparing blacks for many agricultural and mechanical trades. Washington gained notoriety and was soon a celebrity among blacks and whites as the proponent of black advancement through vocational training and racial conciliation. He believed firmly that the best way for freed slaves and other blacks to attain equality in the United States was through the accumulation of power, wealth, and respect utilizing hard work in practical trades. The inscription on the Tuskegee University monument to Booker T. Washington reads, "He lifted the veil of ignorance from his people and pointed the way to progress through education and industry".

W.E.B.DuBois took a very different view of how blacks ought to function in society. Raised in Massachusetts and first exposed to segregation during his undergraduate work at Fisk University in Nashville, Tennessee, DuBois believed that it was essential that blacks receive training not only in vocational fields, but also in the liberal arts. A fierce advocate for civil rights, DuBois feuded very openly with Washington over the proper strategy for educating black university students. DuBois felt quite strongly that Washington's universal vocational training only perpetuated the servitude of slavery. He believed equality and a sense of purpose would only come if talented blacks were allowed to study the arts and sciences. Then they could become leaders and teachers for the next generation. It is impossible to say which of these views triumphed. Each, in its way, lives on today in modern HBCUs. Many colleges and universities seem to be embracing both schools of thinking—students receive practical, technical training grounded in the liberal arts.

Frederick Douglas Patterson, October 10, 1901-April 26, 1988. Became president of what is now Tuskegee University (1935-1953) and founder of the United Negro College Fund (1944 to present).

By the age of 31, Patterson had attained three educational degrees. A Doctorate of Veterinary Medicine, A Master of Science from Iowa State, and a Doctorate of Philosophy from Cornell University.

In 1944 founded two institutions which would largely shape his overall legacy: the school of Veterinary Medicine at Tuskegee University which has graduated approximately 75 percent of the United States black veterinarians. The United Negro College Fund (UNCF) which administers 37 private historically black colleges and universities throughout the United States and administers 10,000 scholarships every year. Since its inception in 1944 UNCF has raised over $3.6 billion.

Served on President Harry S. Truman's President's Commission on Higher Education from 1946-47. This Commission called for an important shift in American college education away from European Concepts, and towards equality of opportunity.

Dr. Patterson would receive the Presidential Medal of Freedom from President Ronald Reagan on June 23, 1987. In 1988, he was awarded the Spingarn Medal from the NAACP.

Historical Black Colleges and Universities Gain Credibility

Throughout the debate, attendance at HBCUs increased substantially, as did financial support from the government and individual philanthropists such as John D. Rockefeller and Andrew Carnegie. HBCUs also gained credibility and respect when the Southern Association of Colleges and Schools began formally surveying and accrediting them in 1928.

The Higher Education Act of 1965 defines an HBCU as any historically black college or university that was established before 1964, whose principal mission was, and is, the education of black Americans, and that is accredited by a nationally recognized accrediting agency or association determined by the secretary (of education) to be a reliable authority as to the quality of training offered. There are 80 HBCU's eligible to be included on the list. Sixty-nine is ranked.

Bluefield State opened in the late 19th Century as the Bluefield Colored Institute, created to educate the children of black coal miners in segregated West Virginia. Today Bluefield State College is 90 percent white. Many black folks who migrated to West Virginia to work the coal sent their children to the Bluefield Colored Institute. Brown v. Board of Education made segregation illegal.

When the coal mining industry became obsolete from new technology, black people headed north for factory jobs. Korean war veterans came back to West Virginia went to the inexpensive Black School. Bluefield State had gone from an all-black college to a mostly white commuter school.

To qualify as an HBCU and receive federal funding, an institution must have served a predominantly black student population before 1964. There is no mechanism in federal law for removing that "historically black" designation. Once an HBCU, always an HBCU.

New Challenges

Historical black colleges and universities would soon face many new challenges, though. The Great Depression and World War ll, left many black colleges in a financial crisis. Despite improvements in funding in previous years, most land-grant HBCUs were still dismally underfunded when compared to their white counterparts. Private HBCUs were in an even tougher bind. The depression had wiped out many of their sources of philanthropy. Fundraising was becoming very difficult and distracting administrators from issues of improving education. In 1943, Dr. Fredrick D. Patterson, president of the Tuskegee Institute, published an open letter to the presidents of private HBCUs urging them to band together, pooling their resources and fundraising abilities. The next year, the United Negro College Fund began its activities soliciting donations to private HBCUs, with far greater efficacy than any one of its member colleges alone.

In 1944 William Trent, a long-time activist for education for blacks, joined w2ith Tuskegee Institute President Frederick D. Patterson and Mary McLeod Bethune to found the UNCF, a nonprofit that united college presidents to raise money collectively through an "appeal to the national conscience". As the first executive director from the organization's start in 1944 until 1964. Trent raised $78 million for historically black colleges so they could become "strong citadels of learning, carriers of the American dream seedbeds of social evolution and revolution. In 1972, the UNCF adopted as its motto the maxim "A mind is a terrible thing to waste."

Though set up to address funding inequities in education resources for African Americans, the UNCF administered scholarships are open to all ethnicities. It provides scholarships to students attending its member colleges as well as those going elsewhere. Graduates of UNCF scholarships have included many blacks in the field of business, politics, health care and the arts.

Brown v. The Board of Education

On May 17, 1954 the United States Supreme Court handed down its ruling in the landmark Case of Brown v. Board of Education to Topeka, Kansas. The court's unanimous decision overturned provisions of the 1896 Plessey v. Ferguson decision, which had allowed for "separate but equal" public facilities, including public schools in the United States.

Declaring that "separate educational facilities are inherently unequal," the Brown v. Board decision helped break the back of state-sponsored segregation, and provided a spark to the American civil rights movement. Chief Justice Earl Warren rejected the Plessey doctrine, declaring that "separate educational facilities" were "inherently unequal" because the intangible inequalities of segregation deprived black students of equal protection under the law.

Ten years later, public HBCUs and black students across the nation became the beneficiaries of the Supreme Court's decision in the case of Brown v. The Board of Education. The court's ruling that "separate but equal" schooling was anything but equal meant that states would be forced to better fund the HBCUs and open their other universities to black college-bound student. The case, won by lawyers trained at Howard University, didn't bring immediate relief in many cases, as states protested the ruling. The Civil Rights Act of 1964 gave the federal government greater power to enforce desegregation.

White people have resisted equal and integrated schools since the Supreme Court famously overturned school segregation in 1954. At first, the resistance was overt, as when former governor Orval Faubus of Arkansas called in the National Guard to prevent black students from attending Central High School in Little Rock.

Once it became clear there was no way to forcibly re-segregate public schools, white people across the South simply started enrolling their kids in all-white private schools, known as "segregation academies." White flight and geographic segregation has created a public school system that is nearly as segregated as it was in the 1960s and, of course, schools in predominantly black neighborhoods are generally underfunded. High school graduation rates have risen in the last four years for all students and especially for black students.

Higher education Act and Presidential Support

President Dwight D. Eisenhower laid the foundation for the Higher Education Act with the 1958 National Defense Education Act (NDEA). Title ll of the NDEA established a federal student aid program, which, Eisenhower surmised, would "reduce the waste of talent" and aid National security.

Six years later, President Lyndon B. Johnson established a task force to study the role of the federal government in providing student aid. The 1964 task force believed that whether a student could afford to attend college should not be the determining factor in whether he did so. One of the factors that drove the task force was a study showing that one in six high school students who took the National Merit Scholarship test did not attend college, many do to financial constraints. It was a finding that "in Johnson's eyes…reflected a loss of human capital."

The Higher Education Act was first signed into Law in 1965 by President Lyndon Johnson as one of many programs comprising his Great Society initiative, and has been reauthorized nine times since then, most recently in 2008.

The purpose of the HEA is allocating federal student loan and grants to ease the cost of college— Part of President Johnson's goal to keep "the doors to higher education open for all academically qualified students regardless of their financial circumstances."

In 1965, the federal government provided aid to HBCUs through the Higher Education Act. It was followed by another important judicial decision, Adams v. Richardson. This case found ten states in violation of the Civil Rights Act for supporting segregated schools. The states were ordered to work actively to integrate institutions, so long as that integration was not carried out at the expense of HBCUs, which were deemed to play an important and unique role in the education of African Americans.

The Carter, Reagan, and Bush administrations thought that HBCUs were significant too. President Carter established a program aimed at strengthening and expanding the capacity of the historical black college or university. Regan issued an executive order at further reversing the effects of previous discriminatory treatment towards black colleges. Congress supported the Regan order with increased federal funding to HBCUs. Reagan's successor, George Bush, also issued an executive order, this time building on the Reagan order and establishing a commission in the Department of Education responsible for advising the president on matters regarding historically black colleges and universities.

February 27, 2017 President Donald Trump signed an executive order aimed at signaling his commitment to historically black colleges and universities, saying that those schools will be "an absolute priority for this White House."

HBCU presidents are hoping Congress will bolster Trump's actions to strengthen the schools with dramatically increased funding in the upcoming federal budget. They are calling for $25 billion for infrastructure, college readiness, financial aid and other priorities. Under President Barack Obama's administration, HBCU's received $4 billion over seven years. Many of the college presidents also went to Capitol Hill to lobby Congress for more funding.

Thurgood Marshall College Fund President Johnny Taylor said the $25 billion is needed to make up for years of underfunding and would cover the country's more than 100 HBCUs.

Sen. Tim Scott, R-S.C., said he and Rep. Mark Walker, R-N.C., planned to personally push for more money for black colleges, and "hopefully they will be more successful than they have been in the last few years.

United States v. Fordice

Mississippi launched its public University system in 1848 by establishing the University of Mississippi [Ole Miss], an institution dedicated to the higher education exclusively of white persons. In succeeding decades, the State erected additional post-secondary, single-race educational facilities.

Alcorn State University opened its doors in 1871 as "an agricultural College for the education of Mississippi's black youth." Creation of four more exclusively white institutions followed: Mississippi State University (1880), Mississippi University for Women (1885), University of Southern Mississippi (1912), and Delta State University (1925). The State added to more solely black institutions in 1940 and 1950, Jackson State University and Mississippi Valley State University.

The first black student (James Meredith) was not admitted to the University of Mississippi until 1962, and then only by Court Order. For the next 12 years, the segregated public university system in the State University, Mississippi University for Women, University of Southern Mississippi, and Delta State University each admitted at least one Black student during these years, but student composition of these institutions was still almost completely white.

During this period, Jackson State and Mississippi Valley State were exclusively black; Alcorn State had admitted five white students by 1968.

Another pivotal court ruling came in 1992 with the United States Supreme Court's ruling in United States v. Fordice. The court's decision required that Mississippi do away with the remnants of a dual, segregated system of education. This was similar to the Adams decision except that no special circumstances were outlined for the treatment of HBCUs. Supporters of black colleges worried that the decision might hurt African American students in the long run if the support and attention they received at HBCUs was taken away. Desegregation is important, in their view, but should never be viewed as a reason for putting black students in a disadvantageous situation.

The historical black college or university provides a unique education for African Americans. Students who attend HBCUs graduate with greater frequency than African American students at predominantly white universities, and these students get more academic and social support. HBCUs must be protected because they are not only an important part of our history, but also an important part of our future.

HBCUs have traditionally awarded a large percentage of the education degrees earned by Blacks throughout the United States and continue to do so, awarding 37 percent in 1990. As of 1994, the leading producers of Bachelor of Science degrees to African-Americans have been Southern University at Baton Rouge, North Carolina A&T State University, Howard University, Prairie View A&M University, Tuskegee University, and Grambling State University.

The existence of HBCUs does not threaten racial equality. HBCUs provide a choice for students seeking environments "that are consistent with their values and experiences.

DERRICK ST. THOMAS

The High-Ranking Liberal Arts Colleges Where Black Students Stand the Best Chance of Admission

Long-term statistics show that at the vast majority of the nation's 25 highest-ranking liberal arts colleges, no fewer one third of all black applicants are accepted for admission. These acceptance rates have held in each of the past 10 years. Also, more than one half of all black applicants have been admitted at 11 of these high-ranking colleges. Over the past decade at Middlebury College in Vermont, an average of 68 percent of all black applicants has been admitted.

Middlebury College is a private liberal arts college located in Middlebury, Vermont. The college was founded in 1800 by Congregationalists making it the first operating college or university in Vermont. The college is the first American institution of higher education to have granted a bachelor's degree to an African-American, graduating Alexander Twilight in the class of 1823.

Middlebury works to promote a college wide approach to issues of diversity, access, and equity. Through strategic planning and programmatic development, (AIM) Alliance for Inclusive Middlebury will help the community foster an inclusive campus so that no one should experience it as an outsider.

In the fall of 2004 all 25 high-ranking liberal arts colleges in JBHE survey provided detailed information on their acceptance rates for black students. For the current academic year the black acceptance rate was greater than 50 percent at seven of the 25 highest-ranked liberal arts colleges. At this highly selective college in Vermont, 58, or 71.6 percent, of the 81 black applicants were accepted for admission. The other six highly ranked liberal arts colleges that accepted more than one half of their black applicants in 2004 were Macalester College, Trinity College, Oberlin College, Pomona College, Mount Holyoke College, and Haverford College.

Journal of Blacks in Higher Education

When JBHE published its first issue in 1993, one of its stated missions was to provide college-bound African-American students with information that would better equip them to make informed decisions on their best chances for success in higher education. To this end JBHE have amassed a huge database of information on the standing and prospects of blacks in higher education.

Brand names in higher education continue to rule the day. American society places great importance on the credential obtained by graduating from one of the nation's highest-ranked colleges or universities. For blacks, a diploma from Harvard, Stanford, or Williams College provides a solid boost in efforts to gain admission to graduate or professional school or to secure a good job at one of the nation's most successful corporations. Blacks with a diploma from one of the nation's most selective and prestigious colleges or universities tend to be well on their way to success in life.

In 2004 JBHE reported that the number of blacks earning bachelor's degrees in the United States reached an all-time high. More than 131,000 African Americans earned a four-year college degree. For blacks, as well as whites, business management was the most popular major by a large margin. Blacks earned 33,044 bachelor's degrees in the field of business management and administration in 2003-2004 academic years. This was 25.5 percent of all bachelors' degree earned by blacks.

The next most popular field of study for blacks who earned degrees was the social science. This includes sociology, economics, and political science. Education was the second most popular major among whites. The fields of psychology, communications, and health sciences were popular majors among both racial groups. It is noteworthy to point out that computer science was the first most popular major among blacks but was not among the 10 most popular majors for whites.

Acceptance Rates for Black Students

For the past decade, JBHE has been collecting data on the acceptance rates of black applicants at the nation's highest-ranked universities and liberal arts colleges. A small number of the nation's top-ranked universities have been unwilling to divulge information on their black student acceptance rates. But our data on black student acceptance rates at the nation's leading liberal arts colleges is considerably stronger than is the case for the large research universities.

Wesleyan University in Middletown, CT. has enrolled the highest percentage of black first-year students. Followed by Amherst College. At Amherst 15.8 percent of the freshman class in fall 2014 was black according to the report by JBHE. Amherst College showed the highest percentage of black students in its entering freshman class.

Columbia University leads the universities in the statistical ranking for enrolling the highest percentage of black students in first-year classes. Columbia has shown leadership in advancing affirmative action in college admissions. The University of North Carolina in Chapel Hill showed improvement in the freshman class followed by Stanford, Duke and Yale.

At the lower end of the acceptance rate rankings, only 10, or 23.3 percent, of the 43 black applicants to Harvey Mudd College in California were accepted for admission. Bates College, Grinnell College, Wesleyan University, Davidson College, and Colgate University all accepted less than one third of the black students who applied in 2004.

Over the Past Decade

While the 2004 data on black acceptance rates gives college-bound blacks students a good clue on their chances of admission to the nation's high-ranking liberal arts colleges, long-term information in the JBHE database on acceptance rates over the past decade yields a more comprehensive view. This is so because single-year data often contains a statistical blip that is not indicative of overall opportunity. A particular college could have a very strong black applicant pool one year resulting in a very high acceptance rate. Similarly, a college might have an off year in attracting outstanding young black applicants, which would result in a low acceptance rate for blacks that year.

The 10-year average of the black acceptance rate at the nation's highest-ranked liberal arts colleges. Middlebury sits at the top with 71.6%. Probably one reason for the high black student acceptance rate at Middlebury is the fact that the college has consistently had to cope with a low black student yield. Therefore, it appears to accept a large number of black applicants to maintain some level of racial diversity on its remote Vermont campus.

JBHE research also shows that nearly two thirds of all black applicants to Macalester College in Minnesota are accepted. At Carleton College, also in chilly Minnesota, an average of 58 percent of black applicants has been approved for admission over the past decade. But note that there have been wide fluctuations in the black acceptance rate. In 1997, 80 percent of all blacks were admitted. For the past two years the black acceptance rate has averaged 42.9 percent, considerably lower than the 10-year average.

At Williams College and Amherst College, two of the most selective liberal arts colleges in the nation, more than 50 percent of all black applicants have been accepted over the past decade. The acceptance rate at these top-ranking colleges for applicants of all races stands at about 20 percent.

A note of caution: It is important to remember that the black acceptance rate at all of the high-ranking liberal arts colleges averages at least 36 percent over the past decade. Even the colleges with relatively low acceptance rates are still accepting many dozens of black students each year. Collegebound black students with top-notch academic qualifications should not be discouraged from applying to any of these schools. Moreover, the vast majority, if not all, of the high-ranking liberal arts colleges actively recruit black students. They all seek greater racial diversity in their student bodies. While it appears that a black applicant is twice as likely to be admitted to Middlebury College as to Davidson College, a black applicant to Davidson with a strong academic resume is also likely to meet with success.

Top 50 Colleges for Black Students, 2003

Based on responses from nearly 1,855 African-American professionals in higher education, Black Enterprise magazine has ranked the top 50 colleges and universities where African-American students are most likely to succeed. The ranking considers factors such as black population (at least 3%), academic strengths, social environment, and graduation rates.

1. Morehouse College, Atlanta, Ga.
2. Hampton University, Hampton, Va.
3. Spellman College, Atlanta, Ga.
4. Howard University, Washington, D.C.
5. Xavier University, New Orleans, La.
6. Florida A&M University, Tallahassee, Fla.
7. Stanford University, Palo Alto, Calif.
8. Columbia University, New York, N.Y.
9. Georgetown University, Washington, D.C.
10. Clark Atlanta University, Atlanta, Ga.
11. Harvard University, Cambridge, Mass.
12. Duke University, Durham, N.C.
13. Berea College, Berea, Ky.
14. Williams College, Williamstown, Mass.
15. University of North Carolina, Chapel Hill, N.C.
16. Oberlin College, Oberlin, Ohio.
17. Emory University, Atlanta, Ga.
18. Wesleyan University, Middletown, Conn.
19. North Carolina A&T University, Greensboro, N.C.
20. University of Maryland, College Park, Md.
21. Tuskegee University, Tuskegee, Ala.
22. Fisk University, Nashville, Tenn.
23. University of Pennsylvania. Philadelphia, Pa.
24. George Washington University, Washington, D.C.

25. Cornell University, Ithaca, N. Y.
26. Wellesley College, Wellesley, Mass.
27. University of Michigan, Ann Arbor, Mich.
28. Univ. of Southern California, Los Angeles, Calif.
29. Mount Holyoke College, South Hadley, Mass.
30. Amherst College, Amherst, Mass.
31. Wake Forest University, Winston-Salem, N.C.
32. New York University, New York, N.Y.
33. Swarthmore College, Swarthmore, Pa.
34. Florida State University, Tallahassee, Fla.
35. Morgan State University, Baltimore, Md.
36. Johnson C. Smith University, Charlotte, N.C.
37. Southern University and A&M College, Baton Rouge, La.
38. Johns Hopkins University, Baltimore, Md.
39. Vassar College, Poughkeepsie, N.Y.
40. Yale University, New Haven, Conn.
41. Temple University, Philadelphia, Pa.
42. Brown University, Providence, R.I.
43. Dillard University, New Orleans, La.
44. Tennessee State University, Nashville, Tenn.
45. Ohio State University, Columbus, Ohio.
46. Florida International University, Miami, Fla.
47. California State University, Los Angeles, Calif.
48. Bethune-Cook man College, Daytona Beach, Fla.
49. Mass. Institute of Technology, Cambridge, Mass.
50. University of California Los Angeles, Los Angeles, Calif.

- is a private liberal arts college that was the first institution of higher education in the United States to admit African American students. Oberlin was also the first college to grant bachelor's degrees to women in a coeducational program.

Affirmative Action: Factious Past, Uncertain Future

Executive Order 10925, signed by President John F. Kennedy on March 6, 1961, required government contractors to "take affirmative action to ensure that applicants are employed and that employees are treated during employment without regard to their race, creed, color, or national origin. It established the President Committee on Equal Employment Opportunity (PCEEO), which was chaired by then Vice President Lyndon Johnson.

The first implementation of Affirmative Action was meant to give equal opportunities in the workforce to all U.S. citizens, not to give special treatment to those discriminated against.

Affirmative action, however, was not limited to the employment context. Most notably, it extended to the admissions offices of colleges, universities, and professional and graduate schools.

Those whom affirmative action was intended to benefit came to include not only blacks, the original focus of Executive Order 10,925, but also in most cases, Hispanics, Asian-Pacific Americans, and

Native Americans. By the early 1970s, affirmative action had come to mean for most people most of the time, treating, as opposed to not treating, those belonging to the designated or protected groups concerning their race, creed, color or national origin.

Indeed, it meant treating members of protected groups in such a way as to hire, promote, or admit the designated minorities in enough instances that the total numbers of those so advanced were not trivial.

However, its supporters propose to Justify affirmative action, treating people about their minority status is what affirmative action means in practice today. It has become a way of life throughout the public sector and in many parts of the private sector. It is a way of life that many institutions, especially those of higher education are proud of.

Even affirmative action's most severe critics must concede that it has done some good. It has helped employers and other gatekeepers of opportunity understand that the United States is indeed a nation of many peoples and races. Unlike preferential affirmative action, other means such as Head Start are more compatible with the best in the American political tradition, and they enjoy the majority support of the American people.

There is no getting around the fact that affirmative action is unfair action when it unambiguously deprives non-discriminatory actors of their opportunities. Plaintiffs Allan Bakke, Brian Weber and Marco Defunis, Jr., are cases that show affirmative action is a barrier to those who otherwise, because of their superior qualifications, would have advanced had they been members of the necessary racial groups.

In early 1992, the United States Court of Appeals in the Fourth Circuit struck down a blacks-only scholarship fund at the University of Maryland at College Park.

More attention must focus on, among other things improving the quality of education in all schools. Especially deserving of improvements are those schools in which minorities are predominant, particularly the elementary grades, Kindergarten, pre-Kindergarten, and apprentice programs in which those without adequate job skills can learn them.

"For years now, large majorities of Americans have expressed opposition to preferential treatment based on race." At the same time, Americans remain strongly opposed to racial discrimination and are willing to help minorities at the wholesale level through race-neutral programs such as Head Start.

The Supreme Court ruled in 2003 that universities can consider race as a factor, if the goal is to achieve diversity. But in that case, former Justice Sandra Day O'Conner famously wrote that within 25 years, race-based affirmative action would become obsolete.

The Supreme Court upheld a University of Texas admissions plan that allows race and ethnicity to be considered as one of many factors in admission. The Court noted that the Texas Plan—which automatically grants admission to roughly the top 10 percent of students across the State, then uses race as one of many factors in considering the rest—was unique and very much a product of Texas politics, law and demographics.

In affirming the value of diversity, including race and ethnicity, in higher education, the court recognized that there was not one, immutable way of defining and achieving it. The U.S. Supreme Court, however, is pushing universities to pursue alternative means to achieve diversity—such as giving a preference to economically disadvantaged students of all races, for admitting the top proportion of students from all high schools in a state.

As the U.S. student population experiences dramatic demographic changes—and as our society's income inequality continues to rise—promoting racial, ethnic, and economic inclusion at selective colleges has become more important than ever. To be economically competitive and socially just, America needs to draw upon the talents of students from all backgrounds.

The Supreme Court has long recognized that diversity in all of its forms—including racial, ethnic, and socioeconomic—is valuable for two reasons: (1) to improve the education of students and (2) to demonstrate that pathways to leadership are open to all in a democratic society.

The Court also recognized a second interest: To cultivate a set of leaders with legitimacy in the eyes of the citizenry, the path to leadership must be visibly open to talented and qualified individuals of every race and ethnicity. We must have confidence in the openness and integrity of the educational institutions that provide this training.

On June 4, 1965, President Lyndon Johnson gave the commencement address at Howard University in Washington, D.C. In that speech, he set down the intellectual argument in favor of a system that is now known as affirmative action. "You do not take a person who, for years, has been hobbled by chains and liberate him, bring him up to the starting line of a race and then say, 'you are free to compete with all the others,' and still justly believe that you have been completely fair, "he said."

Julian Bond, the famed Civil Rights leader, was just 26 at the time. That speech makes a profound impact on him and many other civil rights leaders. Bond argues that it began a process that was—and still is—necessary. He says people of color and women are in jobs and schools to which they didn't have access before.

"The forthcoming of affirmative action in its many forms and ways made it possible for these formally excluded groups to be included," he said. "So it's been a great success."

Julian Bond a former chairman of the NAACP, co-founder of the Southern Poverty Law Center and a prominent fighter for social justice since the 1960s civil rights movement died at age 75 on Saturday August 15, 2015.

"Justice and equality was the mission that spanned his life—from his leadership of the Student nonviolent Coordinating Committee, to his pioneering service in the Georgia legislature and his steady hand at the helm of the NAACP serving for 10 years.

In 1965, Bond was elected as a Democrat to the Georgia House of Representatives. But members of the legislature refused to seat him, citing his vocal opposition to the Vietnam War. Before Bond was allowed to join the Georgia House a year later, he had to twice win re-election to his vacant seat, and the U.S. Supreme Court unanimously ruled that his rights had been violated. He ended up serving 20 years in the Georgia House and Senate.

Policy Changes

More than a decade after California law banned race-conscious admissions, outreach and financial aid at public universities, the State's most selective public university system has seen a significant impact on its ability to increase enrollments of African American, Latino and American Indian students.

A ruling by the Supreme Court ending race-based preferences in college admissions would have a limited effect in California because state law already prohibit it. But as other states consider the effects of a Supreme Court ruling on their college populations, they might observe what happened in the Golden State.

The University of California board of Regents in 1995 passed a resolution that eliminated race, religion, sex, color, ethnicity or national origin as criteria for admission to the university. The following year, California voters approved Proposition 209, which went further by also prohibiting race-conscious outreach and financial aid.

The percentage of underrepresented minority students admitted to the UC system dropped significantly as soon as prop. 209 passed. Today, despite some policies and strategies employed by the university to diversify its student population, these groups remain a substantially smaller proportion of those admitted to and enrolled at the university's most selective campuses—UC Berkeley and UCLA—than they were before the elimination of race conscious policies.

Anne De Luca, associate vice chancellor and acting director of undergraduate admissions at UC Berkeley said Prop. 209 put the university at a disadvantage compared with some of its competitors, such as Stanford, MIT or Cal Tech, because those institutions can more freely reach out to underrepresented minority students and woo them with bigger financial aid packages.

The assumption, says Laird, Author of The Case for Affirmative Action University Admissions, was that race was the sole factor Berkeley had considered before the ban. Proponents of the legislation thought admissions offices would turn to other factors, such as socioeconomic status, and new ways of recruiting students. "The fact was that Berkeley had included

Low socioeconomic status among its diversity variables for at least 30 years, "Laird says.

The university system had also been forming outreach and academic development programs since the mid-1960s, he says. "The notion that somehow we could find something we hadn't thought of was naive, and in some cases, simply disingenuous," he says. 'Reverse Discrimination'? An often-used critique of affirmative action is that implementing a quota system is unfair, but Laird criticizes that notion.

"We've gotten ourselves into this kind of absurd position where we say as a society, by and large, we value the goal racial and ethnic diversity," he says. "However, we are not going to consider race and ethnicity to achieve this racial and ethnic diversity." The argument unfairness also tends to accompany the idea of "reverse discrimination," a term Laird calls a "very persuasive sound bite."

"The notion that somehow dialing back slightly the needle on white privilege in higher education constitutes the same form of legal discrimination that took place for 300 years against African-Americans and, to a large extent, against Native Americans, and... More recently, against Latino Students, is a false equivalency, and I think very careless thinking, "he says.

Why Affirmative Action has failed

The pending Supreme Court case that has put affirmative action back in the News—a reverse discrimination lawsuit by a disappointed white applicant against the University of Texas—focuses mainly on the same debate about fairness to various racial groups that has gone on for more than 40 years.

But, meanwhile, the broader public debate is being transformed by previously unheralded evidence that the large racial preferences into which affirmative action has devolved are not working well—and are at war with the egalitarian principles that were once their goal.

This new evidence makes three points: First, racial preferences are exposing many or most of their supposed beneficiaries to a serious risk of academic struggle. Second, university leaders are systematically misleading these black and Hispanic recruits (and everyone else) about their academic prospects. Third, most of these preferred students are more affluent than many of the better-qualified Asians and whites who disfavored on account of race.

Academic struggle results when black and Hispanic students (as well as athletes and children of big donors) who got B's in high school are put into competition with Asian and white students who got A's. The research shows that most of the B students will have trouble keeping up, suffering heavy blows to their self-confidence, and will end up learning less than if they had gone to schools for which they were well-qualified.

We call this the mismatch effect.

Several studies have tracked black and Hispanic students who initially aspired to become scientists or engineers. Soon after arriving at elite Colleges where they were academically mismatched, these students felt lost and got bad grades.

Their professors were racing through tough courses at a pace designed to challenge their far better-prepared classmates. These victims were only half as likely to get science degrees as comparably qualified students at less selective schools.

Another study shows that black students who aspire to be professors are far less likely to achieve their goals if they go to selective schools where they are mismatched rather than schools for which they are well-qualified.

Little-noticed University of California statistics show that a 1996 ballot initiative outlawing racial preferences was on balance good for black and Hispanic students. Those who would probably have done badly if admitted through racial preferences to Berkeley and UCLA did better at somewhat less selective campuses, such as Riverside and Santa Cruz.

UC-wide, black and Hispanic grades, science degrees and graduation rates improved markedly. The total number of black and Hispanic students receiving bachelor's degrees from UC has soared since racial preferences were outlawed.

Some scholars scoff at such evidence by claiming that black and Hispanic students can fully assess which college is in their own best interests. But by hiding the enormous size of their racial preferences, by assuring marginally qualified students that they will do fine academically and gain ground on their better-prepared classmates and by ostracizing scholars who shine a light on mismatch problems, the universities do their best to deny their "diversity recruits" the opportunity to make informed choices. Lastly, data showing that most racial-preference recipients are catapulted over working-class and poor Asians and whites who are less affluent and better qualified compels the conclusion that the current regime is perverting a once-egalitarian cause by increasing economic inequality.

Justice Samuel Alito highlighted this problem during the Oct. 10 oral argument in the Texas Case, expressing incredulity at the university's contention that it needs racial preferences to bring in affluent black and Hispanic students because those brought in by a law admitting the top 10% of every high school class were mostly underprivileged: "I thought the whole purpose of affirmative action was to help students who come from underprivileged backgrounds." Not any more, it's not.

But we hope to see the original ideals of affirmative action revived as word of findings about mismatch, the dishonest practices of universities and the comforting-the-comfortable thrust of the current racial—preference regime filter through the academy.

The Supreme Court could speed that process by requiring that schools using racial preference discloses to applicants and the public their size, operation and effects on academic performance. Transparency is the best route to reform.

Affirmative action-induced low grades are a serious problem—as demonstrated by research over the last decade. For example, in one study of top law schools, more than 50 percent of African-American law students (many of whom had been admitted according to affirmative action policies) were in the bottom 10 percent of their class. And the dropout rate among African-American students was more than twice that of their white peers (19.3 percent vs. 8.2 percent)

More Academic Mismatch

When a student's entering credentials put him or her at the bottom of the class, it should come as no surprise when he or she switches to an easier major, drops out, or fails out. It's become increasingly clear that affirmative action is doing more harm than good to the very people it is intended to help. Because of affirmative action policies, fewer minorities enter careers in science, technology, engineering and math (STEM) fields.

Study after study shows that minorities tend to be more interested in STEM fields than their white counterparts. But admitting students with lower high school grades and SAT Math scores into schools with elite science and math programs is a recipe for disaster.

Thus students should be encouraged to apply to universities where their credentials are matched with those of their fellow students. Merit-based admission are a "win-win" situation. Students end up at institutions where they are more likely to graduate and in the field of study they want to pursue. A case in point is the race-blind admissions in the University of California system.

California's Race-Blind Admissions lead to Higher Grades and Fewer Dropouts.

In 1996, the people of California passed an initiative amending the state Constitution to bar state schools from "discriminating against, or granting preferential treatment to, any individual o9r group based on race, sex, color, ethnicity, or national origin." Before this amendment went into effect, California struggled with affirmative action-induced high failure rates and low grades.

Professor Heriot notes that UC-San Diego, a selective institution topped only by flagship institutions like Berkeley, had only one African-American student with a 3.5 GPA or higher after freshman year in 1997.

Failure rates at state schools were also disappointing, with 15 percent of African-American and 17 percent of American-Indian students in academic jeopardy, as compared with 4 percent of white students. The problem was not that there were no minority students capable of making the UC-San Diego Honor Roll—it's just that those students were going to places like Berkeley and Stanford, where they too were not on the Honor Roll.

After race-blind admissions went into effect, the media broke into pandemonium. Accusations that Berkeley was now "lily-white" were levied. Yet this was not the case. While minority students did drop from 58.6 percent of the student body to 48.7 percent, white students made up a bare majority, and Asian-Americans came in second at 38 percent. What happened to the other minorities? They went to institutions like UC-San Diego, UC-Riverside, and UC-Santa Cruz. These schools are all part of the prestigious University of California System, attended by only the top 12.5 percent of California high school graduates.

At UC-Riverside, the results were impressive: African-American and Hispanic student admissions skyrocketed by 42 percent and 31 percent, respectively. Failure rates collapsed, and grades improved.

At UC-San Diego, 20 percent of African–American students now made the Honor Roll, and failure rates for African-Americans and American

Indians dropped to 6 percent. Under merit-based admissions, grades were higher and dropouts were lower, and between 1997 and 2003, 50 percent more African-Americans and Hispanics graduated with a degree in STEM field.

Sadly, in these successes, the California schools sought new ways to get around the state constitution's requirement of race-blind admissions.

The Harms Are Clear

The Harms of affirmative action are clear. Academic mismatch perpetuates low grades and high dropout rates for minority students who need a racial preference to gain admission. Basing admissions on race rather than merit also contributes to the dearth of minorities in STEM fields. No person should be disadvantaged by the color of his or her skin, no matter how sincere the intentions of affirmative action proponents.

Mismatched

- Black College freshmen are more likely to aspire to science or engineering careers than are white freshmen, but mismatch causes blacks to abandon these fields at twice the rate of whites.

- Blacks who start college interested in pursuing a doctorate and an academic career are twice as likely to be derailed from this path if they attend a school where they are mismatched.
- About half of black college students rank in the bottom 20 percent of their classes (and the bottom 10 percent in law school)
- Black law school graduates are four times as likely to fail bar exams as are whites; mismatch explains half of this gap.
- Interracial friendships are more likely to form among students with relatively similar levels of academic preparations; thus, blacks and Hispanics are more socially integrated on campuses where they are less academically mismatched.

Affirmative Action Has Helped White Women that anyone

Originally, women weren't even included in legislation attempting to level the playing field in education and employment. In 1967, President Johnson amended the 1961 Kennedy executive order and a subsequent measure included sex, recognizing that women also faced many discriminatory barriers and hurdles to equal opportunity. In a nation where white women and black people were onced considered property—not allowed to own property themselves and not allowed to vote—it was clear to all those who were seeking fairness and opportunity that both groups faced monumental obstacles.

According to one study in 1995, 6 million women, the majority of whom were white, had jobs they wouldn't have otherwise held but for affirmative action.

Another study shows that women made greater gains in employment at companies that do business with the federal government, which are therefore subject to federal affirmative—action requirements, than in other companies—with female employment rising 15.2 % at federal contractors but only 2.2% elsewhere. And the women working for federal-contractor companies also held higher positions and were paid better. Even in the private sector, the advancement of white women eclipse those of people of Color. After IBM established its own affirmative—action program, the numbers of women in management positions more than tripled in less than 10 years. Data from subsequent years show that the number of executives of color at IBM also grew, but not nearly at the same rate.

The successes of white women make a case not for abandoning affirmative action but for continuing it. As the numbers in the Senate and the Fortune 500 show, women still face barriers to equal participation in leadership roles.

Women are now more likely to graduate with bachelor's degrees and attending graduate school than men are and outnumber men on many college campuses. In 1970, just 7.6 percent of physicians in America were women; in 2002, that number had risen to 25.2 percent. But—and this is a big but—those benefits are more likely to accrue to white women than they are to women of color, and that imbalance has very real effects on employment and earnings later in life.

In other words: affirmative action works, and it works way better for white women than it does for all other women in America. White women benefit enormously from affirmative action. By opposing it, they're advocating for making life harder not only for racial and ethnic minorities—but also for themselves.

A Different Measurement

In the aftermath of anti-affirmative action legislation, with the recognition of the value that diversity brings to higher education and the workforce, and with the looming shortage of workers to meet labor demands, institutions of higher learning, private and public corporations and organizations and professional associations have a renewed interest in the best recruitment and retention practices and programs to prepare ethnically and racially diverse students to enter professional careers.

Gov. Andrew M. Cuomo pledge to cover tuition costs at state colleges for hundreds of thousands of middle- and low-income New Yorkers. Under the governor's plan, college students who have been accepted to a state or city university in New York—including two-year community colleges—would be eligible, provided they or their family earn $125,000 or less a year.

Tennessee and Oregon have programs to cover the costs of community college. The governor's plan would include four year schools, including dozens of campuses that are part of the state university system, as well as the city's university system.

If New York is successful other States will follow.

Demographics

In 2000, minorities comprised approximately 30% of the population of the United States (US Census Bureau). By 2050, it is projected that the minority population will represent approximately 50% of the total U.S. population, meaning ethnically and racially diverse people may no longer be a numerical minority. (US Census Bureau). There has been an oscillating pattern of minority enrollment in colleges. The rates have begun to slow considerably, calling attention to the need for college and university officials and professionals associations to renew their efforts to recruit and retain minority students in higher education.

Predicted labor shortages in corporate America and many professions make it essential that corporate world increase the number of minorities and women with the skills necessary to fulfill their labor demand.

As the proportion of white male's available decreases in the 21st century, the lack of a skilled labor force can curtail America's economic growth significantly.

Corporate America must seek to increase diversity in the workplace or face a decline in international competitiveness. America's economic future mandates that issues of access and inequities in the education of minority students become a national concern.

Poverty is one of the more debilitating barriers minority students face. Education can help lift minority communities out of poverty. Lack of role models within their own families is another major obstacle minority student face in graduation from high school and advancing to higher education. Educators should focus their attention on students who maybe the first in their families to graduate high school, much less attend college.

Government, business, and foundations should steer more funds to the institutions these students typically attend. It is critical that all our children be afforded access to free, high quality Pre-k, and that states and municipalities have the resources they need to prepare, develop and support early childhood education. "Providing universal preschool education to children free of charge will improve the future of thousands of children, giving them an educational and social foundation upon which they can grow and thrive.

Congress needs to improve the quality of Pre-k throughout the nation by seeking to allow federal money and support for universal Pre-k. "Education is the key that unlocks a child's potential. Unlocking that potential at an earlier age is not a luxury, it is a necessity to closing the opportunity gap and ensuring the kind of holistic development that social scientists have proven is a difference—maker in our young people's futures." Said Eric Adams Brooklyn Borough President.

<u>Recruitment Issues and Strategies</u>

One of the realities confronting the U.S. is that a major proportion of racial and ethnic minority students in this country have unequal access to higher education. Many experience a variety of personal, environmental, and institutional barriers that result in limited or no access to college and university education. Some of these barriers include financially difficulty and lack of financial aid, the need to work full-time, lack of family support, lack of information about the college preparation and application process, low scores on traditional college admission test, and often, an absence of role models who have gone to college. Social and institutional discrimination may cause children and youth to restrict their career interest and avoid particular career paths.

Financial Difficulty

Lack of financial aid in the form of grants and scholarships is a major deterrent to minority student choice to attend college. A large proportion of federal grants to minority students have been replaced by loans. Minority student are reluctant to incur large debts. Colleges and universities with a commitment to increasing minority enrollment must find ways to provide financial aid to students when they are making admission decisions.

Americans are split when it comes to public opinion and affirmative action. Some argue that class—not race—should be the main factor in affirmative action. Rich Kahlemberg, a senior fellow at the Century Foundation, is one of the leading proponents of this idea. He argues that if you look at the most selective colleges and universities in America, you'll find that there are 25 times as many rich kids as there are poor ones.

He says you achieve ethnic diversity by only using class as an admissions factor by defining socioeconomic status in a sophisticated way. "In addition to looking at concentrated poverty, it's important to look at wealth," Kahlenberg says. He says that since an individual's net worth is accumulated over generations, the wealth gap by race is much larger than the income gap.

The Century Foundation looked at 10 leading universities in this country where race has been dropped from admissions, usually because there was a voter initiative to ban the use of race at public institutions, "he says." And in seven of the 10 cases, universities were able to get as much or more racial and ethnic diversity—that is, African American and Latino representation—as they had using race and ethnicity in the past." Universities nationwide may have to remodel their admissions, depending on the outcome of Fisher v. University of Texas. But the Supreme Court could also offer up a narrow opinion that only applies to the State of Texas, making Justice O'Conner's 25-year prediction more plausible.

The Minority Report: How Minority Students are faring at Community Colleges.

Despite all of our society's socioeconomic progress, there still exists a major performance gap between students of different ethnic and income backgrounds. A recently published report paints a disturbing picture of how minority and low-income students are performing in community colleges.

The report, titled "Charting a Necessary Path" and prepared by the Washington, D.C. based non-profit group the Education Trust, indicates that students from historically under-represented back-grounds-defined as students of African American, Latino, and Native American descent-as well as students from low-income families, complete associate's degree programs and transfer to four-year degree pro-grams at significantly lower rates than their peers.

Few Minority Students who Enter Community College Attain Bachelor's Degrees

The press release accompanying the study reports that although 80 percent of freshmen entering community college intend to eventually earn a bachelor's degree, only 7 percent of low-income and minority community college students attain a bachelor's degree within ten years. As the press release explains, low-income and minority students are "overrepresented in terms of enrollment" in community colleges but "underrepresented among completers" of community college.

Low Rate of Transfer to Four-Year Institutions

The rate at which historically underrepresented minorities transfer from community colleges to four-year institutions is also worrisome, according to the report. Only 12 percent of students from underrepresented minority groups transfer to bachelor's degree programs within four years of enrolling in a community college.

Low Community College Completion Rates

College completion rates vary widely along racial lines with black and Hispanic students earning credentials at a much lower rate than white and

Asian students do, according to a report release by the National Student Clearing House Research Center. The Center evaluated data from students nationwide who entered a college or university in fall 2010. The data represents students at two- and four-year colleges, students who studied part- and full-time, as well as those who graduated after transferring institutions.

Altogether, 54.8 percent of those students completed a degree or certificate within six years of entering a postsecondary institution, but broken down by race and ethnicity, those rates fluctuate by up to 25 percent. White and Asian students completed their programs at similar rates—62 percent and 63.2 percent respectively. While Hispanic and black students graduated at rates of 45.8 percent and 38 percent, respectively.

These numbers likely won't surprise most people who track higher education closely as they fall in line with what other studies have found over the years, but "it will certainly reinforce the point that there's more work to be done.

The study recognizes, however, that attaining a bachelor's degree is not the goal of all students. It also tracks community college "completion" rates, which it defines as either earning a certificate or associate's degree or transferring to a four-year college. The study indicate that across racial and socio-economic groups, about one-third of students who enter two-year institutions achieve completion within four years. Troublingly, the two-year college completion rate for African-American, Latino, and Native American students is only 24 percent.

What can be done to close the Performance Gap

The troubling statistics certainly call for an evaluation of what community colleges can do to close the performance gap. Effective education policy includes returning authority to the states and empowering parents with the opportunity to choose a safe and effective education for their children.

Pell Grants

"A Pell Grant is a subsidy the U.S. federal government provides to students who need it to pay for college. Federal Pell Grants are limited to students with financial need, who have not earned their first bachelor's degree, or who are enrolled in certain post-baccalaureate programs, through participating institutions."

Reporting on the study's findings, the Washington Post notes that the "one bright spot" in the research concerns the Pell Grant, a federal program that helps low-income students through college. The education Trust's report indicates that community college students who are Pell Grant recipient achieve completion at a rate of 32 percent, which is the same as the general population.

Coordinated Programs with Strong Leadership

According to Campus Progress, a branch of the think tank Center for American Progress, one of the study's authors, Jennifer Engle, believes that "a coordinated effort of increased financial aid, specialized counseling, and leadership from the university system's administrators" helps to close the graduation rate achievement gap between minority and non-minority students.

Civil Rights Issue

The press release accompanying the report notes that the trends revealed by the study are "alarming, but reversible." The study was performed as part of the Access to Success Initiative, a program that includes 24 Public higher-education systems, which have committed themselves to halving the achievement gap between minority students and their peers by the year 2015. Closing the achievement gap is "the civil rights issue of our day "says William E. Kirwin, chancellor of the University System of Maryland. Having a college degree is more important today than ever before: Kirwin notes that in this era, "a college degree is the path to a meaningful career and a high quality of life."

Besides, community colleges, as the press release acknowledges, serve as "important access points to higher education" for many low-income and minority students. Thus, the fact that minority and low-income students at community colleges lag so significantly behind their non-minority and higher-income peers points to a racial and socioeconomic divide that does not sit well with those who advocate for racial and economic equality.

Closing the achievement gap is not only a civil rights issue, but also essential for the United States to remain economically competitive in the 21st century. The journal inside higher Ed, notes that if our nation is to again become one of the world's leaders in terms of the number of citizens with a post-secondary education-which is a goal set by President Obama-we must attend to the success rates of minority and low-income students, "whose share of the country's population is growing by the day."

The commissioner of higher education in Louisiana, for instance, told Inside Higher Ed that while the white population of her state is expected to grow by 4 to 6 percent over the next several years, the number of low-income and minority residents of the state is expected to grow by 70 percent. If the state could eradicate its achievement gap so that all minority and low-income residents were showing educational achievements similar to that of the state's general population," the personal income of Louisiana's population would be $10 billion higher," the higher education commissioner said. Similar patterns of population growth can be seen across the United States.

For both moral and economic reasons, the educational achievement gap that affects minority and low-income community college students affects us all.

President Barack Obama's proposal to send many students to Community College for free has widespread public support, a new HuffPost/YouGov poll finds. Sixty percent of Americans say they're in favor of Obama's proposal to give two years of free community college tuition to students with a C+ or better average who are making progress toward a degree, with 32 percent and another 8 percent unsure. More broadly, half of Americans say it's a good idea for the government to pay for students to attend college for free, while 30 percent say it's a bad idea, and 20 percent aren't sure.

A substantial 45 percent of Americans say they know someone who wants to go to college and can do so, but can't afford to do so. Forty-three percent have taken at least one class at a community college themselves, although few received a degree from one.

But personal experience with community college didn't have much bearing on opinions, with support for the proposal hovering at about 60 percent among both those who'd attended and those who never had. Instead, opinions divided down the usual party lines, with 86 percent of Democrats and just 39 percent of Republicans in support.

GOP lawmakers have hammered the proposal as being costly and vague on the details of funding, with a spokesman for House Speaker John Boehner

(R-Ohio) calling it "more like a talking point than a plan."

Obama, who will need to secure congressional approval called for bipartisan support, highlighting a similar state-level initiative backed by Tennessee Gov. Bill Haslam (R).

The national plan is part of the Obama administration's effort to make attending college "the norm in the same way high school is the norm now," White House domestic policy director Cecilia Munoz told reporters.

By a nearly three-to-one margin, 61 to 23 percent, Americans say it's a good idea to encourage every high school graduate to attend college. More than 70 percent of Democrats, black Americans, and Hispanic Americans said everyone should be encouraged to enroll in higher education.

Racist Incidents

Racist incidents continue to pop up at Colleges and Universities. The current college generation—young people who came of age under the nation's first black president—is said to have more accepting racial attitudes, but putting an end to racism among them has proved elusive.

Bucknell University expelled three students for making racist comments during a March 20, 2015 campus radio broadcast. At Duke University, a noose was found hanging from a tree. A former University of Mississippi student indicted on federal civil rights charges last week, accused of tying a noose on the statue of the university's first black student and draping it with an old Georgia state flag that includes a confederate battle emblem.

The wide usage of sharable video has also been a factor. In February, students at Oklahoma were caught on video singing a chant that included references to lynching and used a racial slur to describe how the Sigma Alpha Epsilon fraternity would never accept black members.

At the University of Maryland, a student resigned from Kappa Sigma fraternity this year after being suspended after a 2014 email containing racially and sexually suggestive language about black, Indian and Asian women was made public. This followed an Instagram photo of a University of Maryland sorority member late last year with a birthday cake containing racially explicit text.

The Pew Research Center work has found that millennial are more likely than older generations to say society should make every possible effort to improve the position of blacks and other minorities. They are also more likely to support interracial marriage and have friends of other races. Such data also shows divides. Little more than half of white and blacks millennial in one Pew survey said all, most or some of their friends are black or white, respectively.

Benjamin Reese, president of the National Association of Diversity Officers in Higher Education, said efforts to put appropriate focus on the issue of diversity has unintentionally "diluted the focus on the unfinished business regarding race.

LeBron's foundation to spend $41 million to send kids to college

Sandusky, Ohio—LeBron James is giving kids from Akron—ones with challenging backgrounds like his—the chance to go to college for free. The NBA star has partnered with the University of Akron to provide a guaranteed four-year scholarship to the school for students in James' "I Promise" program who qualify. The scholarship will cover tuition and the university's general service fee—currently $9,500 per year. James told ESPN he plans to provide this for 1,100 kids, which would cost his foundation a total of $41.8 million at the school's current rates.

It's the latest example of James, who often refers to himself "as just a kid from Akron," giving back to a community that helped raise him. "It's the reason I do what I do," said James, who announced the program Thursday while hosting an event for students at Cedar Point Amusement Park. "These students have big dreams, and I'm happy to do everything I can to help them get there. They're going to have to earn it, but I'm excited to see what these kids can accomplish knowing that college is in their futures."

The school and the LeBron James family Foundation are still finalizing the criteria for the scholarships. The students will have to graduate high school within Akron's public school system and achieve standard testing requirements as well as fulfill a community service obligation.

James has had a long-standing relationship with the university. As his celebrity soared in high school, James played many game on the school's campus and the four-time MVP deepened his connection with Akron soon after he turned professional.

"It means so much because, as a kid growing up in the inner City and a lot of African-American kids, you don't think past high school," said James, who bypassed college to jump to the NBA. "You don't know your future. You hear high school all the time, and you graduate high school and then you never think past that because either it's not possible or your family's not financially stable to even be able to support a kid going to college."

In recent months, James and members of his foundation net with Akron president Dr. Scott Scarborough hoping to establish a program that would have long-term impact on the community. The result was an initiative they believe will inspire the area's youth to achieve and reach their potential.

Michele Campbell, the executive director of the LeBron James family Foundation, said James, who grew up in a single-parent home, became visibly emotional when discussing the impact the program will have on the kids and their families. "He has a chance to change their futures, "Campbell said, "Not everybody can be an NBA superstar, so to be able to provide the frame work to make your dreams come true is overpowering."

The University is renaming its education department the LeBron James Family Foundation College of Education. The first class eligible for the scholarships will graduate in 2021. The scholarship program was welcomed, positive news for Akron, which announced $40 million in widespread cuts—including the loss of the baseball team—this summer due to financial troubles. "Every institution has to go through an adjustment from time to time and you look at what you've funded in the past and you look at the things that are new opportunities and new initiatives for the future and this fits in our sweet spot," he said. "This is a program that focuses on the local area. This is a program that rewards earning your way into college. I think LeBron's philosophy is that things are earned not given and that aligns well with our emphasis on experience and learning and career service and education.

"We're excited about this and it does represent what the University wants to be about in the future. In the end, this is a University that makes students of all ages dreams come true, so this seems to fit nicely with what LeBron wants for his kids and what we want for the University."

JP Morgan Chase is providing a program to track the progress of students in the program.

Sean "Diddy" Combs has opened a school in Harlem, the neighborhood where he grew up is where he's now trying to improve education. The Capital

Preparatory Harlem Charter School is modeled after a similar school in Connecticut that was founded by educator Steve Perry.

Combs believe that his school is the best way to help children in the neighborhood. Capital Prep Harlem sits at East 104th Street and will host grades six through 12. "If I have anything to do with it, they're going to have a fair playing field," he said. "And they're going to be the future leaders of our country."

African Americans
in Government

African Americans in Congress

After the Civil War and the abolition of slavery, the 14th Amendment (1868) granted African Americans citizenship, and the 15th Amendment (1870) gave black men (but not women) the right to vote. In February 1870, Hiram Revels (Republican–Mississippi) became the first black senator, taking the seat once occupied by Jefferson Davis, President of the Confederacy. In December 1870, Joseph Rainey (Republican-South Carolina) became the first black representative.

Several Southern states sent African Americans to Congress during Reconstruction. But later efforts by white Southerners to restrict black voting, often through violence and intimidation, resulted in the defeat of most black incumbents. After 1901 no blacks served in Congress until the election of Oscar De-Priest (Republican-Illinois) in 1928. By then, Washington had become a segregated city, and DePriest had to struggle even for his staff members to eat in the Capitol restaurants. In 1934, Arthur Mitchell (Democrat-Illinois), also an African American, defeated DePriest, signifying a dramatic shift in African-American voters from the party of Lincoln to the party of Franklin D. Roosevelt. William Dawson (Democrat-Illinois) succeeded Mitchell and later became the first black member of Congress to chair a major committee. During the 1940s. Dawson and Adam Clayton Powell, Jr. (Democrat-New York) were the only black members of Congress. But beginning in the 1950s, the number of blacks winning election to the House slowly grew, first from Northern cities and then from Southern rural districts. In 1968, Shirley Chisholm (Democrat-New York) became the first black woman elected to Congress. By Contrast to the growing number of black representatives, Edward Brooke (Republican-Massachusetts) and Carol Mosely–Braun (Democratic-Illinois) have been the only black senators to serve during the 20th century.

As their ranks increased, African-American representatives formed the Congressional Black Caucus. Begun in 1971, the Black Caucus has sought a leadership role among African Americans, speaking for their concerns and promoting their legislative interests. The Black Caucus has worked for civil rights and equal opportunity in education, employment, and housing but also has taken stands on Presidential nominations and matters of foreign policy.

African Americans in the Executive Branch

Despite the abolition of slavery in 1865 and the extension of the vote in 1870, African Americans remained largely outsiders in American democracy. Post-Civil War Reconstructionist politics was full of fierce dispute over the role blacks should have in the political system: many Republicans worked to empower African Americans politically while reactionary Democrats sought to rebuild the antebellum South. Presidents began appointing African Americans to positions within the executive branch during the late 19th century. Former U.S. senator Blanche K. Bruce served as registrar of the Treasury, and the abolitionist Frederick Douglass was appointed U.S. minister to Haiti. Republican Presidents also appointed southern blacks as postmasters and to other federal patronage positions.

John Mercer Langston was elected clerk of a town in rural Ohio in 1855, making him the first black elected to public office. In organizing black political clubs around the country and helping to shape the post-Civil War Republican party's progressive relationship toward blacks, Langston had an important role in mobilizing African Americans. He was twice suggested as a candidate for Republican Vice President.

African Americans shifted political allegiance to the Democratic Party during the Great Depression and New Deal in the 1930s. Under President Franklin D. Roosevelt, high-level African-American appointees in several agencies met regularly in what was popularly known as the Black Cabinet to discuss racial policy. Mary McLeod Bethune was the founder of the National Council of Negro Women in 1935, and Roosevelt appointed her director of the Division of Negro Affairs of the National Youth Administration in 1936, a position she held until 1944. Along with the rest of the Black Cabinet, Bethune forced politicians to see African Americans as a significant population of voters who deserved representation.

Another member of the Black Cabinet, Robert Weaver, became the first African American appointed to the Presidential cabinet, when Lyndon Johnson named him as secretary of housing and urban affairs in 1966.

The first African American to run for President was Jesse Jackson. Although he lost the Democratic Party nomination in 1984, and 1988, his campaigns proved that a black candidate could command a large audience and reflect a broad range of political interests. In 1984 Jackson garnered 21 percent of the popular vote in the primaries, and in 1988 his campaign registered more than 2 million new voters.

Jackson also opened the door for future black Presidential hopefuls. In 1996 Colin Powell, the first African American to serve as chairman of the Joint Chiefs of Staff (1989-93), made a Presidential bid but ultimately decided not to run. Alan Keyes, a former member of Ronald Reagan's administration and a U.S. ambassador to the United Nations Social and Economic Council, also made two bids for the Republican nomination, in 1996 and 2000.

African Americans in the Federal Judiciary

In 2000, 10.3 percent of the country's federal judges were African American, while more than 12 percent of the total U.S. population was African American. The Supreme Court included one black justice, Clarence Thomas. Only one other African American had ever sat on the Court: Thurgood Marshall, who served from 1967 to 1991.

Half of the 13 U.S. appellate courts included not one of African-American ancestry in 2000. The Fourth Circuit, which serves Maryland, Virginia, West Virginia, North Carolina, and South Carolina, has never had a black judge, even though 23 percent of the region's population is black. Civil rights organizations, such as the National Association for the Advancement of Colored People (NAACP) have persistently called for the appointment of more African Americans and other minorities to the federal judiciary.

Marshall, Thurgood

Marshall, Thurgood, 1908-93, U.S. lawyer and Associate Justice of the U.S. Supreme Court (1967-91). He received his law degree from Howard Univ. in 1933. In 1936 he joined the legal staff of the National Association for the Advancement of Colored People. As its chief counsel (1938-61), he argued more than 30 cases before the U.S. Supreme Court, successfully challenging racial segregation, most notably in higher education. His presentation of the argument against the "separate but equal" doctrine achieved its greatest impact with the landmark decision handed down in <u>Brown v. Board of Education of Topeka</u> (1954). His appointment to the U.S. Court of Appeals in 1961 was opposed by some Southern senators and was not confirmed until 1962. President Lyndon B. Johnson appointed him to the Supreme Court two years later; he was the first black to sit on the high court, where he consistently supported the position taken by those challenging discrimination based on race or sex, opposed the death penalty, and supported the rights of criminal defendants. His support for affirmative action led to his strong dissent in <u>Regents of the University of California v. Bakke</u> (1978). As appointments by Presidents Nixon and Reagan changed the outlook of the Court, Marshall found himself increasingly in the minority; in retirement he was outspoken in his criticism of the court.

Famous Firsts by African Americans

In December 1943, the singer and activist Paul Robeson became the first black man to address baseball team owners of the subject of integration. At the owners' annual winter meeting, Robeson argued that baseball, as a national game, had an obligation to ensure that segregation did not become a national pattern. The owners gave Robeson a round of applause. Still, Robeson is credited with helping to pave the way for Jackie Robinson's entry into major league baseball four years later.

Jack Roosevelt "Jackie" Robinson

Robinson 01/31/1919-10/24/72 became the first African American to play in Major League Baseball in the modern era. Robinson broke the baseball color line when the Brooklyn Dodgers started him at first base on April 15, 1947. The Dodgers ended racial segregation that had relegated black players to The Negro Leagues for six decades.

Robinson was inducted into Baseball Hall of Fame in 1962. In 1997, MLB "universally" retired his uniform number, 42, across all major league teams; he was the first pro athlete in any sport to be so honored. On April 15, 2004, MLB has adopted a new annual tradition, "Jackie Robinson Day", on which every player on every team wears #42.

In recognition of his achievements on and off the field, Robinson was posthumously awarded the Presidential Medal of Freedom and the Congressional Gold Medal.

According to historian Doris Kearns Goodwin, Robinson's "efforts were a monumental step in the civil-rights revolution in America. His accomplishments allowed black and white Americans to be more respectful and open to one another and more appreciative of everyone's abilities.

Harlem Globetrotters

Harlem Globetrotters defeated the NBA's Minneapolis Lakers for the first time in 1948. This unexpected victory of an all-black basketball team over an all-white, World Championship team would create in the years that followed. While mainstream, professional sports were still predominantly a foreign land to African Americans in the 1940s; holes were beginning to appear in the dike. The Globetrotters' win over the Lakers combined with Jackie Robinson's headfirst slide over the color barrier in baseball, gave blacks a solid one-two punch against the cultural restraints that had previously bound them in the sports world. The Globetrotters showed the world that blacks could compete with whites on the basketball court, and do so in a way that entertained as well as inspired. The NBA was paying attention. Soon thereafter, Globetrotter Nat "Sweetwater" Clifton became the first African American to sign an NBA contract, joining the New York Knicks in 1950, with many others soon to follow.

African-American firsts: Government

- **Local elected official:** John Mercer Langston, 1855, town clerk of Brown helm Township, Ohio.
- **State elected official:** Alexander Lucius Twilight, 1836, the Vermont legislature.
- **Mayor of major city:** Carl Stokes, Cleveland, Ohio, 1967-1971. The first black woman to serve as a mayor of a major U.S. city was Sharon Pratt Dixon Kelly, Washington, DC, 1991-1995.
- **David Norman Dinkins:** born July 10, 1927, is an American politician who served as the 106th Mayor of New York City, from 1990 to 1993. He was the first and to date, only African American to hold that office. Before entering politics, Dinkins served in the U.S. Marine Corps, graduated Cum laude from Howard University, and received a law degree from Brooklyn Law School. He served as Manhattan Borough president before becoming mayor.
- **Governor (appointed):** P.B.S. Pinchback served as governor of Louisiana from Dec. 9, 1872-Jan. 13, 1873, during impeach-

ment proceedings against the elected governor.

- **Governor (elected):** <u>L. Douglas Wilder,</u> Virginia, 1990-1994. The only other elected black governor has been Deval Patrick, Massachusetts, 2007-
- **U.S. Representative:** <u>Joseph Rainey</u> became a Congressman from South Carolina in 1870 and was reelected four more times. The first black female U.S. Representative was **<u>Shirley Chisholm,</u>** Congresswoman from New York, 1969-1983. Ran for president of the United States in 1972. She said "she ran because someone had to do it first, in this country everybody is supposed to be able to run for president, but that's never been true. I ran because most people think the country is not ready for a black candidate, nor ready for a woman candidate. Someday… The next time a woman runs, or a black, a Jew, or anyone from a group that the country is 'not ready' to elect to its highest office, I believe he or she will be taken seriously from the start. The door is not open yet, but it is ajar."
- **U.S. Senator:** <u>Hiram Revels</u> became Senator from Mississippi from Feb. 25, 1870, to March 4, 1871, during Reconstruction. <u>Edward Brooke</u> became the first African–American Senator since Reconstruction, 1966-1979. <u>Carol Mosley Braun</u> became

the first black woman Senator serving from 1992-1998 for the state of Illinois. (There have only been a total of five black senators in U.S. history: the remaining two are <u>Blanche K. Bruce</u> (1875-1881) and <u>Barack Obama</u> (2005-2008).

- **U.S. cabinet member:** <u>Robert C. Weaver,</u> 1966-1968, Secretary of the Department of Housing and Urban Development under Lyndon Johnson; the first black female cabinet minister was <u>Patricia Harris,</u> 1977, Secretary of the Department of Housing and Urban Development under Jimmy Carter.
- **U.S. Secretary of State:** Gen. <u>Colin Powell,</u> 2001-2004. The first black female Secretary of State was <u>Condoleezza Rice,</u> 2005-2009.
- **Major Party Nominee for President:** Sen. <u>Barack Obama,</u> 2008. The Democratic Party selected him as its presidential nominee.
- **U.S. president:** Sen. <u>Barack Obama.</u> Obama defeated Sen. John McCain in the general election on November 4, 2008, and was inaugurated as the 44th president of the United States on January 20, 2009.

African-American First: law

- **Editor, Harvard Law Review:** Charles Hamilton Houston, 1919. Barack Obama became the first President of the Harvard Law Review.
- **Federal Judge:** William Henry Hastie, 1946; Constance Baker Motley became the first black woman federal judge, 1966.
- **U.S. Supreme Court Justice:** Thurgood Marshall, 1967-1991. Clarence Thomas became the second African American to serve on the Court in 1991.

African-American First: Diplomacy

- **U.S. diplomat:** Ebenezer D. Bassett, 1869, became minister-resident to Haiti; Patricia Harris became the first black female ambassador (1965; Luxembourg).
- **U.S. Representative to the UN:** Andrew Young (1977-1979).
- **Nobel Peace Prize winner:** Ralph J. Bunche received the prize in 1950 for mediating the Arab-Israeli truce. He was involved in the formation and administration of the United Nations. In 1963, he was awarded the Medal of Freedom by President John F. Kennedy. Martin Luther King, Jr., became

the second African-American Peace Prize winner in 1964.

African-American Firsts: Military

- **Combat pilot:** Georgia-born <u>Eugene Jacques Bullard.</u> 1917, denied entry into the U.S. Army Air Corps because of his race, served throughout World War 1 in the French Flying Corps. He received the Legion of Honor, France's highest honor, among many other decorations.
- **First Congressional Medal of Honor winner:** <u>Sgt. William H. Carney</u> for bravery during the Civil War. He received his <u>Congressional Medal of Honor</u> in 1900.
- **General:** <u>Benjamin O. Davis,</u> Sr., 1940-1948.
- **Lt. Col. Merryl Tengesdal:** The only black female pilot to ever fly the U-2, an aircraft built to go to extremely high altitudes to collect intelligence which it brings back to decision makers worldwide for analysis.
- **Vernice Armour:** The first African–American female naval aviator in the Marine Corps and the first African–American female combat pilot in the U.S. Armed Forces. She flew the AH-1W Super Cobra attack helicopter in the 2003 inva-

sion of Iraq and eventually served two tours in support of Iraqi Freedom.

- **Chairman of the Joint Chiefs of Staff:** <u>Colin Powell,</u> 1989-1993.

African-American firsts: Science and Medicine

- **First patent holder:** <u>Thomas L. Jennings,</u> 1821, for a dry-cleaning process. Sarah E. Goode, 1885, became the first African–American woman to receive a patent, for a bed that folded up into a cabinet.
- **M.D. degree:** James McCune Smith, 1837, University of Glasgow; Rebecca Lee Crumpler became the first black woman to receive an M.D. degree. She graduated from the New England Female Medical College in 1864.
- **Inventor of the blood bank:** Dr.Charles <u>Drew,</u> 1940.
- **Heart surgery pioneer:** <u>Daniel Hale Williams,</u> 1893.
- **First astronaut:** Robert H. Lawrence, Jr., 1967, was the first black astronaut, but he died in a plane crash during a training flight and never made it into space. Guion Bluford, 1983, became the first black astronaut to travel in space; <u>Mae Jemison, 1992,</u> became the first black female astronaut.

Frederick D. Gregory, 1998, was the first African-American shuttle commander.

African-American Firsts: Scholarship

- **College graduate (B.A.):** Alexander Lucius Twilight, 1823, Middlebury College; first black woman to receive a B.A. degree: Mary Jane Patterson, 1862, Oberlin College.
- **Ph.D.:** Edward A Bouchet, 1876, received a Ph.D. from Yale University. In 1921, three individuals became the first U.S. black women to earn PhDs: Georgiana Simpson, University of Chicago; Sadie Tanner Mossell Alexander, University of Pennsylvania; and Eva Beatrice Dykes, Radcliffe College.
- **Rhodes Scholar:** Alain L. Locke. 1907.
- **College president:** Daniel A. Payne, 1856, Wilberforce University, Ohio.
- **Ivy League president:** Ruth Simmons, 2001, Brown University.

African-American Firsts: Literature

- **Novelist:** Harriet Wilson, Our Nig (1859).
- **Poet:** Lucy Terry, 1746, "Bar's Fight." It is her only surviving poem.

- **Poet (published):** <u>Phillis Wheatley,</u> 1773, Poems on Various Subjects, Religious and Moral. Considered the founder of African–American literature.
- **Pulitzer Prize winner:** <u>Gwendolyn Brooks,</u> 1950, won the Pulitzer Prize in poetry.
- **Pulitzer Prize winner in Drama:** Charles Gordone, 1970, for his play No Place to Be Somebody.
- **Nobel Prize for Literature winner:** <u>Toni Morrison,</u> 1993.
- **Poet Laureate:** <u>Robert Hayden,</u> 19761978; first black woman Poet Laureate: <u>Rita Dove,</u> 1993-1995.

African-American First: Music and Dance

- **Member of the New York City Opera:** <u>Todd Duncan,</u> 1945.
- **Member of the Metropolitan Opera Company:** <u>Marian Anderson,</u> 1955.
- **Male Grammy Award winner:** <u>Count Basie,</u> 1958.
- **Female Grammy Award Winner:** <u>Ella Fitzgerald,</u> 1958.
- **Principal dancer in a major dance company:** <u>Arthur Mitchell,</u> 1959, New York City Ballet.

African-American Firsts: Film

After World War 1 ended, most film-making moved to California. This was the beginning of the Jazz Age which did little to change the roles that African American actors received. They were offered conventional roles like Hattie McDaniel's servant role and other low wage roles such as convicts or boxer's trainers. Oscar Micheaux, January 2, 1884–March 25, 1951 was an African American author, film director and independent producer of more than 44 films. He opened doors for future black filmmakers and collaborated with important figures like Paul Robeson and the novelist Charles Chesnutt, a whole scholarly industry has grown up around Micheaux.

African American filmmakers such as George and Noble Johnson, The Colored Players of Philadelphia and Oscar Micheaux continued to make movies that were an African American version of already successful movies. Oscar Micheaux became an entrepreneur selling his novels door to door focusing on themes that other African American filmmakers and writers would not touch such as African American success stories and tales of lynching.

Sound Films

Sound reached film during the Great Depression and African Americans were unable to find the capital to invest and upgrade ghetto theaters to enjoy the new enhancement. It would take a period before African American audiences would benefit from Sound Films.

Oscar Micheaux, after experiencing going bankruptcy, remade "The Exile", "The Girl from Chicago" and "Swing" and was able to rebound. During this time, some African American filmmakers joined with their white counterparts and made movies and musicals that voiced African American Concerns.

After the Second World War, African American filmmakers began to have a stronger voice. Movies that addressed racial tensions, documentaries and even an African American Physician role in Ralph Cooper's "Am I Guilty" in 1940.

Actors such as Sidney Poitier and Harry Belafonte became familiar faces in film beginning in the 1950s with "Odds Against Tomorrow", "Guess Who's Coming to Dinner"' Lilies of the Field" and "No Way Out." These movies were a reflection of Civil Rights struggles that were occurring in the 50s and 60s.

The 1960s' films focused on Blaxploitation films such as "Shaft", "Blacula" and "Cool Breeze" that all followed the same pattern. The Civil Rights movement played out in "The battle of Algiers", "To Kill a Mockingbird", "The Pawnbroker", and Sounder" to begin the age of angry films. These films depicted the feelings that African Americans felts after the assassination of Martin Luther King Jr.

Present Day Films

The pathway to current day filmmakers like Spike Lee, Robert Townsend and others were paved by filmmakers from the late 1900s. From the late 1970s, African American actors and filmmakers made movies on their terms. African American actors continue to evolve as well with current blockbuster actors like Will Smith and Halle Berry commanding large salaries and ticket sales.

- **First Oscar:** Hattie McDaniel, first Black Oscar winner who received the award in 1940 for her portrayal of the loyal maid in "Gone with the Wind." (1895-1952)
- **Oscar, Best Actor/Actress:** Sidney Poitier broke all kinds of New Ground when he became the first black man ever to win a Best Actor Oscar in 1964, for Lillies of the field. He managed to have box office hits with movies about race relations: To Sir, With Love, in the Heat of the Night, and Guess Who's Coming to Dinner.
- **Oscar, Best Actress Nominee:** Dorothy Dandridge, 1954, Carmen Jones.
- **Film director:** Oscar Micheaux, 1919, wrote, directed, and produced The Homesteader, a feature film.
- **Hollywood Director:** Gordon Parks directed and wrote The Learning Tree for Warner Brothers in 1969.

Russell Simmons Blasts Hollywood's Racial 'Segregation'

Due to racial discrimination in the 19th and early 20th centuries, Hollywood tended to avoid using African-American actors/actress/. In the 19th century Blackface became a popular form of entertainment. Blackface let Hollywood use different characters without actually having to employ anyone with a darker skin tone. In 1930, the craze of Blackface died out because of its connotations with bigotry and racism.

African-American actresses and actors are more common on the big screen, but they are still scarce in bigger blockbuster movies, "with the stakes high, many studio executives worry that films that focus on African-American themes risk being too narrow in their appeal to justify the investment. The then and now 2014 Academy Awards were a turning point for African-American films, with the iconic film 12-Years a Slave taking home the Oscar for Best Picture.

Spike Lee and Tyler Perry have become household names in the black communities with African American films. The popularity of both directors are signifying less racial tensions in Hollywood.

Hip-hop mogul Russell Simmons had harsh words about the business environment he has encountered in Hollywood now that he's turned his focus to producing movies, TV shows and digital content.

"The reality is the lack of integration is deafening," he said Wednesday 01/21/2015 during a

Q&A at the NATPE Confab. "The segregation in Hollywood is incredible."

In a candid 45-minute conversation with *Variety* co-editor in chief Andrew Wallenstein, the Def Jam founder was critical of Hollywood "progressives" who have no understanding of African-American culture, even if they are well-meaning and liberal in their political views. He said he's seen ample evidence of bias in the development process that tends to keep black creative from working in an organically integrated way with white talent.

"I speak English," he said. "Not only can I make Eddie Murphy cool again, I can make Jim Carrey cool again." Simmons also called on African-Americans to be more proactive in demanding more opportunities. "I kind of blame black people for not forcing their way in doors," he said. "You have to take the initiative and push your way in the door too… Everybody has to take responsibility for the new incarnation of Hollywood."

Simmons was critical of the lack of diversity in most Hollywood talent agencies, noting that he recently moved from CAA to WME. "I didn't realize they're all the same," he said, adding that both agencies seem to have "the one black agent. "He later added that despite his criticism, he was happy to be at WME.

Simmons said he had 11 more projects in various stages of development and he is emphasizing stories that present an integrated world. He described a comedy project that he billed as akin to "Legally

Blonde," with a white man in love with a black woman who gets an introduction to African-American life when he follows her to school at Howard University, the historically black college. Another project stars J.B. Smooves as a man who goes to Sweden, solves a crime and becomes the Monarch.

"There's a lack of integration from a cultural standpoint," he said. "There's a white space" where creative talent of different races and ethnic backgrounds should be working more together. "America wants to see Hollywood more integrated than 'Jerry Springer.'"

Simmons lamented the fact that a group of comedians who broke out in part through his Def Comedy Jam series—including Smoove, Mike Epps, Bernie Mac, Martin Lawrence, Chris Tucker, Kevin Hart and Dave Chappelle—saw their careers stall about 15 years ago through lack of opportunities in film and TV.

He cited the problem of executive "gatekeepers" who chose to pick "more accessible" African–American talent rather than those comedians whose material is more rooted in the specific black experience. He cited the duo of Key and Peele, stars of the Comedy Central sketch series, as an example.

Moreover, Simmons noted that TV has shied away from difficult questions of race and class for years. "No one has even discussed race and politics as good as Norman Lear in 30 years," he said.

Simmons said he just delivered a pilot to HBO as part of a first-look deal he has there that he produced with director Steve McQueen and writer Matthew Carnahan. The untitled project revolves around a black man with a mysterious past who enters New York High society. He said he was "pretty sure" it will get picked up.

While Simmons is forging ahead with projects through his Def Pictures film and Television, he's also energized by the lower-budget work underway at his All Def Digital banner. He's working with some YouTube, Vine and Instagram stars on a range of short-and long-form content, which is attractive because he can own that content and the talent is raw and ripe for breakout stardom.

"Maybe I'll make all my movies and TV for myself," he said. With racial issues in the headlines again, following a string of police-related deaths of unarmed black men, Simmons said the entertainment biz should help move the country forward.

"Hollywood should lead the way in healing," he said, generating a round of applause. "Hollywood should not be afraid of the subject matter Norman Lear dealt with 35 years ago."

African-American First: Television

- **Network television show host:** <u>Nat King Cole,</u> "The Nat King Cole Show"; <u>Oprah Winfrey</u> became the first black woman television host in 1986, The Oprah Winfrey Show."

- **Star of a network television show:** <u>Bill Cosby,</u> 1965, "I Spy".

African-American Firsts: Sports

- **Major League baseball player:** <u>Jackie Robinson,</u> 1947, Brooklyn Dodgers.
- **Elected to the Baseball Hall of Fame:** <u>Jackie Robinson,</u> 1962.
- **NFL quarterback:** <u>Willie Thrower,</u> 1953.
- **NFL football coach:** <u>Fritz Pollard,</u> 1922-1937.
- **Golf champion:** <u>Tiger Woods,</u> 1997, won the Masters golf tournament.
- **NHL hockey player:** <u>Willie O'Ree,</u> 1958, Boston Bruins. (Canadian)
- **World cycling champion:** <u>Marshall W. "Major" Taylor,</u> 1899.
- **Basket Ball:** <u>Wilt Chamberlain</u> is the only NBA player ever to score 100 points or more in a game, a feat he achieved in 1962.
- **Tennis champion:** <u>Althea Gibson</u> became the first black person to play in and win Wimbledon and the United States national tennis championship. She won both tournaments twice, in 1957 and 1958. In all, Gibson won 56 tournaments, including five Grand Slam singles events. The first black male champion was <u>Arthur Ashe</u> who won the 1968 U.S. Open, the 1970

Australian Open, and the 1975 Wimbledon championship.

- **Heavyweight boxing champion:** <u>Jack Johnson,</u> 1908.**<u>Mohammed Ali,</u>** Gold medalist 1960 Olympics and heavy weight boxing champion at age 22.
- **Olympic gold medalist (summer games):** George Poage, 1904, won two bronze medals in the 200 m hurdles and 400 m hurdles.
- **Olympic gold medalist (summer games):** John Baxter "Doc" Taylor, 1908, won a gold medal as part of the 4 x 400 m relay team.
- **Olympic gold medalist (summer games; individual):** <u>DeHart Hubbard,</u> 1924, for the long jump; the first woman was <u>Alice Coachman,</u> who won the high jump in 1948.
- **Olympic medalist (winter games):** Debi Thomas, 1988, won the bronze in figure skating.
- **Olympic gold medalist (winter games):** Vonetta Flowers, 2002, bobsled.
- **Olympic gold medalist (winter games; individual):** Shani Davis, 2006, 1,000 m speedskating.

Other African-American Firsts

- **Licensed Pilot:** Bessie Coleman, 1921.

- **Millionaire:** <u>Madame C. J. Walker.</u>
- **Billionaire:** Robert Johnson, 2001, owner of Black Entertainment Television: <u>Oprah Winfrey,</u> 2003.
- **Portrayal on a postage stamp:** <u>Booker T. Washington,</u> 1940 (and also 1956).
- **Miss America:** <u>Vanessa Williams,</u> 1984, representing New York. When controversial photos surfaced and Williams resigned, Suzette Charles, the runner-up and also an African American, assumed the title. She represented New Jersey. Three additional African Americans have been <u>Miss Americas:</u> Debbye Turner (1990), Marjorie Vincent (1991), and Kimberly Aiken (1994).
- **Explorer, North Pole:** Matthew A. Henson, 1909, accompanied Robert E. Peary on the first successful U.S. expedition to the North Pole.
- **Explorer, South Pole:** George Gibbs, 1939-1941 accompanied Richard Byrd.
- **Flight around the world:** Barrington Irving, 2007, from Miami Gardens, Florida, flew a Columbia 400 plane named Inspiration around the world in 96 days, 150 hours (March 23-June 27).

The History of Black History

The story of Black History Month begins in Chicago during the summer of 1915. An Alumnus of the University of Chicago with many friends in the City, Carter G Woodson traveled from Washington, D.C. to participate in a national celebration of the fiftieth anniversary of emancipation sponsored by the State of Illinois. Thousands of African Americans travelled from across the Country to see exhibits highlighting the progress their people had made since the destruction of slavery.

Awarded a doctorate in Harvard three years earlier, Woodson joined the other exhibitors with a black history display. On September 9th, Woodson met with others to form the Association for the Study of Negro Life and History (ASNLH). In 1916, he publishes the Journal of Negro History. As early as 1920, Woodson urged black civic organizations to promote the achievements that researchers were uncovering.

1924 was the creation of Negro History and literature week. He believed the black community should focus on the countless black men and women who had contributed to the advance of human civilization. Americans have recognized black history annually since 1926, first as "Negro History Week" and later as "Black History Month." What you might not know is that black history had barely begun to be studied-or even documented-when the tradition originated. Although blacks have been in America at least as far back as colonial times, it was not until the 20th century that they gained a respectable presence in the history books.

Blacks Absent from History Books

We owe the celebration of Black History Month, and more importantly, the study of black history, to <u>Dr. Carter G. Woodson.</u> Born to parents who were former slaves, he spent his childhood working in the Kentucky coal mines and enrolled in high school at age twenty. He graduated within two years and later went on to earn a Ph.D. from Harvard. The scholar was disturbed to find in his studies that history books largely ignored the black American population-and when blacks did figure into the picture, it was generally in ways that reflected the inferior social position they were assigned at the time.

Woodson chose the second week of February for Negro History Week because it marks the birthdays of two men who greatly influenced the black American population Frederick Douglass and Abraham Lincoln. And Lincoln, however great had not freed the slaves—the Union Army, including hundreds of thousands of black soldiers and sailors, had done that.

Established Journal of Negro History

Woodson, always one to act on his ambitions, decided to take on the challenge of writing black Americans into the nation's history. He established the Association for the Study of Negro Life and History (now called the Association for the Study of Afro-American Life and History) in 1915, and a year later founded the widely respected journal of Negro History. In 1926, he launched Negro History Week as an initiative to bring national attention to the contributions of black people throughout American history.

Woodson chose the second week of February for Negro History Week because it marks the birthdays of two men who greatly influenced the black American population. <u>Frederick Douglass</u> and <u>Abraham Lincoln.</u> However, February has much more than Douglass and Lincoln to show for its significance in black American history. For example:

- **February 23, 1868:** <u>W. E. B. Dubois,</u> important civil rights leader and co-founder of the NAACP, was born.
- **February 3, 1870:** The <u>15 th Amendment</u> was passed, granting blacks the right to vote.
- **February 25, 1870:** The first black U.S. senator, <u>Hiram R. Revels</u> (1822-1901), took his oath of office.

- **February 12,1909:** The <u>National Association for the Advancement of Colored People (NAACP)</u> was founded by a group of concerned black and white citizens in New York City.
- **February 1, 1960:** In what would become a <u>civil-rights movement</u> milestone, a group of black Greensboro, N.C., college students began a sit-in at a segregated Woolworth's lunch counter.
- **February 21, 1965:** <u>Malcolm X,</u> the militant leader who promoted Black Nationalism, was shot to death by three Black Muslims.

Malcolm X

Malcolm X, (1925-1965) was a black leader who, as a key spokesman for the Nation of Islam, epitomized the "Black Power" philosophy. By the early 1960s, he had grown frustrated with the non-violent, integrated struggle for civil rights and worried that blacks would ultimately lose control of their own movement. The Nation promoted black supremacy, advocated the separation of black and white Americans, and rejected the civil rights movements for its emphasis on integration.

His teachings included the beliefs

- That white people are devils

- That black people are the original people of the world
- That blacks are superior to whites, and
- That the demise of the white race is imminent

Many whites and some blacks were alarmed by Malcolm X and the statements he made during this period. He and the Nation of Islam were described as hate mongers, black supremacists, racists, violence-seekers, segregationists, and a threat to improved race relations. He was accused of being anti-Semitic. One of the goals of the civil rights movement was to end disenfranchisement of African Americans, but the nation of Islam forbade its members from participating in voting and other aspects of the political process.

Civil rights organizations denounced him and the Nation as irresponsible extremist whose views did not represent African Americans. While the civil rights movement fought against racial segregation. Malcolm X advocated the complete separation of African Americans from whites. He proposed that African Americans should return to Africa and that, in the interim, a separate country for black people in America should be created. He rejected the civil rights movement strategy on nonviolence, expressing the opinion that black people should defend and advance themselves "by any means necessary".

His speeches had a powerful effect on his audiences, who were generally African Americans in northern and western cities. Many of them—tired of being told to wait for freedom, justice, equality and respect—felt that he articulated their complaints better than the civil rights movement.

Near the end of his life, Malcolm X publicly recognized that "Dr. King wants the same things I want—freedom." He went to Washington and witnessed debates on the Civil Rights Bill of 1964. He threw himself into the civil rights struggle. He was with voter registration efforts. He spoke at the invitation of Student Non-Violent Coordination Committee in Selma Alabama. Joined with King for civil rights.

Quotes by Malcolm X

"Be peaceful, be courteous, obey the law, respect everyone, but if someone puts his hand on you, send him to the cemetery. "Nobody can give you freedom. Nobody can give you equality or justice or anything. If you're a man, you take it. "I believe in a religion that believes in freedom. Any time I have to accept a religion that won't let me fight a battle for my people. I say to hell with that religion. "If you are not ready to die for it, put the word 'freedom' out of your vocabulary. "The future belongs to those who prepare for it today. "A man who stands for nothing will fall for anything. "Education is the passport to the future, for tomorrow belongs to those who prepare for it today. "You're not supposed to be so blind with patriotism that you can't face reality. "Wrong is wrong no matter who says it. "I am for violence if non-violence means we continue postponing a solution to the American Black man's problem just to avoid violence. "If you don't stand for something you will fall for anything. "There is no better than adversity. "Every defeat, every heartbreak, every loss, contains its seed, its lesson on how to improve your performance the next time. "I'm for truth, no matter who tells it. "I'm for justice, no matter who it's for or against. "If you have no critics you'll likely have no success. "I don't even call it violence when it's in self-defense; I call it intelligence. "I believe in human beings, and that all human beings should be respected as such, regardless of their color. "Stumbling is not falling. "My Alma mater was books, a good library… I could spend the rest of my life reading, just satisfying my curiosity. "Power in defense of freedom in greater than power in behalf of tyranny and oppression. "In all our deeds, the proper value and respect for time determines success or failure. "Power never takes a back step only in the face of more power. "You can't separate peace from freedom because no one can be at peace unless he has his freedom. "You show me a capitalist, and I'll show you a bloodsucker. "The Negro revolution is controlled by foxy white liberals, by the Government itself. "But the Black Revolution is controlled only by God. "Without education, you are not going anywhere in this world. "You don't have to be a man to fight for freedom. All you have to do is to be an intelligent human being.

Carver Federal Savings Bank

Founded on November 5, 1948, and named for agricultural researcher and scientist George Washington Carver, Carver Federal Savings bank formally began operations on 125th Street in Harlem, providing residents a place to save and obtain mortgages to buy homes in their communities on January 5, 1949. In February 1961, Carver opened its first branch in the Bedford-Stuyvesant section of Brooklyn and continued expanding its operations in Manhattan, Brooklyn and Queens into the 1990s.

On September 28, 2006 Carver successfully acquired Brooklyn-based community Capital Bank to complement its savings and real estate lending with small business and non-profit lending across a 10-branch network. On October 24, 1994, Carver Bancorp, Inc. became a publicly traded company and on July 10, 2007 was listed on the NASDAQ stock exchange (CARV). Carver Bancorp, Inc. is the holding company of Carver Federal Savings Bank.

Today, Carver is the largest African-and Caribbean-American operated bank in the United States and channels its capital resources into under-served neighborhoods by reinvesting over 80% of its deposits into the communities we call home. The bank remains rooted in expanding wealth enhancing opportunities in the communities it serves, by expanding access to capital and financial advice, to consumers, businesses and non-profit organizations, including faith-based institutions. Carver remains headquartered in Harlem, and predominantly all of its 8 branches and stand-alone 24/7 ATM Centers are located in low-to-moderate income neighborhoods.

Many of these historically underserved communities are now experiencing unprecedented growth and diversification of incomes, ethnicity and economic opportunity, after decades of public and private investment. A measure of its progress in achieving this goal includes the Bank's "Outstanding" Community Reinvestment Act rating, awarded by the Office of Thrift Supervision following its most recent Community Reinvestment Act examination in February 2009. The examination report noted that Carver's loan originations were within low-to moderate-income geographies, which far exceeded peer institutions.

Carver has been designated by the U.S. Treasury Department as a Community Development Financial Institutions (CDFI) because of our community focused banking services and our dedication to the economic viability and revitalization of underserved neighborhoods. Carver continues to invest in developing and executing a community bank that meets the needs of today's customer.

Our customers aren't just benefactors of our legacy, they're building it.

William R. Hudgins, a former door-to-door salesman in Harlem who helped start the Carver Federal Savings Bank, now the largest black-owned bank in the nation, and was its president for 18 years, died on Friday at his home in Manhattan.

Mr. Hudgins, who along with <u>Jackie Robinson</u> later helped start the Freedom National Bank, was 100.

With seven other Harlem leaders, Mr. Hudgins founded what was originally known as the Carver Federal Savings and Loan Association in 1948, when blacks were facing what an article in The New York Times called "a wall of bias" in obtaining loans from major financial institutions.

"There was always black homeownership and business ownership in Harlem in the '40s, '50s '60s, but the question was who provided the loan money," Earl G. Graves Sr., the publisher of Black Enterprise Magazine, said yesterday. "It was usually family, friends, persons you knew in the church that you attended or, in the West Indian community, sousous, informal credit unions."

"Bill Hudgins recognized the need, "Mr. Graves said. The Carver bank, named for the botanist George Washington Carver, was started on a financial shoe-string of $250,000 with $14,000 in cash and the rest in pledges from community residents. By 1962, it had lent more than $30 million to about 3,000 home buyers and maintained more than 32,000 savings accounts.

Last year, with branches in Manhattan, Queens, the Bronx and Brooklyn, Carver held assets of $648 million and deposits of $488 million, according to Black Enterprise Magazine.

In 1966, Mr. Hudgins joined with another group of black leaders, including Mr. Robinson, who by then had retired as a baseball player, to form the

Freedom National Bank. He was its president until 1971. Freedom National went out of business in 1990

William Randolph Hudgins was born in Petersburg, Va., on April 30, 1907. At the age of 2 he was adopted by William and Agnes Hudgins. His adoptive father was a carpenter and owned a delivery truck; his adoptive mother was a music teacher.

A tall, thin young man, Mr. Hudgins came to Harlem in his early 20s. He first worked door to door as a Fuller Brush salesman, then took a job at a local dry-cleaning store that specialized in refurbishing costumes from Broadway shows. In 1943, he parlayed the value from several real estate investments to start Best Yet Hair Products, a mail-order business that sold high-quality wigs made from human hair.

Because of his business success in the late 1940s, Mr. Hudgins became the first African-American chosen to join the merchants' division of the Uptown Chamber of Commerce in Manhattan, now called the Greater Harlem Chamber of Commerce.

Although Freedom National Bank was less successful than the Carver bank, a Time magazine article in 1966 offered a glimpse of the mission that Mr. Hudgins envisioned for his banking enterprises. "Almost like a small-town banker, Hudgins gets personally involved in many loan applications," the article said. "Doubtfuls usually wind up in his second-floor office to plead their cases, and frequently get their loans after careful investigation."

Black Owned Banks

All-American Bank...Birmingham, Alabama. Broadway Federal Bank...Los Angeles, California. Commonwealth National Bank...Mobile Alabama. Industrial Bank...Washington D.C. Axiom Bank... Midland Florida. Carver State Bank...Savannah, Georgia. Citizens Trust Bank...Atlanta Georgia. Illinois Service Federal...Chicago, Illinois. Seaway Bank...Chicago Illinois. Metro Bank...Louisville, Kentucky. Liberty Bank...New Orleans, Louisiana. Harbor Bank of Maryland...Baltimore, Maryland. One United Bank...Boston, Massachusetts. First Independence Bank...Detroit, Michigan. City National Bank of New Jersey...Newark, New Jersey. Mechanics and Farmers Bank...Durham, North Carolina. United Bank of Philadelphia... Philadelphia, Pennsylvania. South Carolina Community Bank...Columbia, South Carolina. Citizen's Savings Bank...Nashville Tennessee. Tri State Bank of Memphis...Memphis Tennessee. Unity National Bank of Houston...Houston, Texas. First State Bank...Danville, Virginia. Columbia Savings and Loan...Milwaukee, Wisconsin. North Milwaukee State Bank...Milwaukee, Wisconsin.

Foreordination

When we come into mortality, we bring the talents, capacities, and abilities acquired by obedience to law in our prior existence. Some people are born with special abilities or strengths that become apparent at an early age. We call them prodigies. These are quite common in languages, mathematics and music it seems. Mozart composed and published sonatas when but eight years of age because he was born with musical talent.

In the premortal spirit world, God appointed certain spirits to fulfill specific missions during their mortal lives. This is called foreordination. Jesus Christ was foreordained to carry out the Atonement, becoming "the lamb slain from the foundation of the world," (Revelation 13:8, 1 Peter 1:19-21). The scriptures tell of others who were foreordained. The prophet Abraham learned about his foreordination when he received a vision in which he saw "many of the noble and great ones" among the spirits in the pre-mortal spirit world. He said, "God saw these souls that they were good, and he stood in the midst of them, and he said: These I will make my rulers; for he stood among those that were spirits, and he saw that they were good; and he said unto me; Abraham, thou art one of them; thou was chosen before thou wast born (Abraham 3:22-23). The lord told Jeremiah, "Before I formed thee in the belly I knew thee; and before thou camest forth out of the womb I sanctified thee, and I ordained thee a prophet unto the nations" (Jeremiah 1:5).

John the Baptist was foreordained to prepare the people for the Savior's mortal ministry (Isaiah 40:3, Luke 1:13-17). As people prove themselves worthy, they will be given opportunities to fulfill the assignments they then received.

Others foreordained to their early missions were Enoch, Moses Jeremiah, Joseph Smith, and other latter-day prophets, and many others (Doctrine and Covenants 138:53-56). During their mortal lives, their spirits have been inclined toward desires they expressed in the pre-mortal life, and they have carried out their foreordained missions based on their faith and following the promptings of the Holy Ghost through exercising their agency in righteous ways.

God is in charge of the affairs of nations, even those that are evil. The affairs of nations and the lives of those in it are governed by his sovereign hand. He is the author of history and writes every page to accomplish his eternal purposes, to glorify himself, to redeem a people from among these worlds' sinners, and to bestow his good on us.

God chose that Barack Obama would be the president of the United States. Some have resisted this, when he first came into office, the head of the Senate Republicans said, "My number one priority is making sure president Obama's a one term president."

U.S. President: Senator Barack Obama. Obama defeated Sen. John McCain in the general election on November 4, 2008, and was inaugurated as the 44th president of the United States on January 20, 2009.

Barack Hussein Obama, Jr. winner of the 2008 U.S. presidential election. After a historic and bruising 22-month long campaign, Sen. Barack Obama was elected the 44th president of the United States on November 4, 2008. He prevailed over Sen. John McCain in what was probably the most pivotal U.S. election since World War ll. He took the oath of office on January 20, 2009 and became the first black U.S. president.

Two days into his presidency, Obama reversed some of the most controversial policies of the Bush administration. He signed executive orders that ended the Central Intelligence Agency's secret interrogation program, began the process to close the Guantanamo Bay detention camp; and established a cabinet-level panel that will formulate a plan to detain and question terrorism suspects in the future. Obama's orders said that the C.I.A. can only use the 19 interrogation methods mentioned in the Army Field Manual. The move ended Bush's policy of allowing the C.I.A. to use methods that were not permitted by the military. "We believe we can abide by a rule that says we don't torture, but we can effectively obtain the intelligence we need," Obama said.

On February 13, 2016 Justice Scalia died while serving on the Supreme Court. Scalia died while serving on the Supreme Court. Scalia's death was also the seventh occasion since 1900 in which a seat on the Supreme Court of the United States was vacant during a year in which a presidential election was set to occur. Article ll of the U.S. Constitution gives the president the power to nominate justices to the Supreme Court, subject to the advice and consent "of the Senate. At the time of Scalia's death, the sitting president was President Obama, a member of the Democratic Party, while the Republicans held a 54-46 seat majority in the Senate. Because of the composition of the Supreme Court at the time of Scalia's death, and the belief that President could replace Scalia with a much more liberal successor, some believed that an Obama appointee could potentially swing the Court in a liberal direction for many years to come, with potentially far-reaching political consequences.

The situation led to conflict between the White House and Republican leadership. Republican leaders have claimed that the vacancy should not be filled until after the next president is elected, and threatened that the Republican—controlled Senate might delay the appointment of a new justice until after the inauguration of a new president.

On February 23, 2016, the 11 Republican members of the Senate Judiciary Committee signed a letter to Senate majority leader Mitch McConnell stating their intention to withhold consent on any nominee made by President Obama, and that no hearings would occur until after January 20, 2017, when the next President takes office.

In an August 2016 Speech in Kentucky, Senator McConnell said, "One of my proudest moments was when I looked Barack Obama in the eye and I said, Mr. President, you will not fill the Supreme Court vacancy.

Once Trump won, Republicans assumed he could undo everything Obama did. After Trump's election, Republicans giddily predicted a quick erasure of Obama's legacy. The most important parts of Obama's legacy revolved around actions that could not be overturned: The Economic Stimulus, Massive green energy investments, Education reform, Wall Street Regulation, and Affordable Care. All these reforms required legislations.

Campaign Battle

By taking advantage of the internet and the power of text messaging on mobile phones, Obama ran an innovative campaign that appealed to young voters. Shunning public financing for his election, Obama raised an unprecedented amount of money, much of it from small donors. Until the financial crisis struck in mid-September, the wars in Iraq and Afghanistan dominated the campaign. Obama presented himself as the candidate for change and stressed that McCain presidency would mirror the policies of the Bush administration.

As a political newcomer, Obama faced an uphill battle in convincing voters that he would be ready to lead the nation. Indeed, throughout the long and often bitter campaign for the Democratic nomination, he and Sen. Hillary Clinton ran neck-and-neck in the primaries and caucuses. Obama and Clinton competed fiercely for the support of working-class voters, and each candidate tried to paint the other as elitist. Obama met sharp criticism for his association with his former pastor, the combative and controversial Rev. Jeremiah Wright. Obama denounced Wright after several of his divisive sermons popped up in the media. Wright's charged statements prompted Obama to address the race issue, and he earned wide praise for his speech on race relations, "A More Perfect Union."

Running as the candidate of change, Obama made hope the center of his campaign. His platform focused on advocating for working families and poor communities, education, caring for the environment and ethics reform.

Barack Obama has made history by beating Hillary Clinton for the Democratic nomination and becoming the first African-American with a viable chance of winning the white House. Obama's victory effectively brought to an end Clinton's bid to become the first US female president.

It also confirms Obama's reputation as a political giant slayer, who after less than four years in the US Senate brought down the couple credited with creating the Democrats' most powerful political machine.

Formative years

Mr. Obama's father was a black Kenyan; his mother a white American from Kansas. Mr. Obama was born in Hawaii and spent part of his childhood in Jakarta, Indonesia before returning to Honolulu and enrolling at Punahou, an elite prep school. Mr. Obama lived with his grandparents in an apartment near the school.

After his parents divorced, Obama's Harvard-educated father then returned to Kenya, where he worked in the economics ministry. Obama's mother pursued studies in anthropology. In class he excelled in debate and composition. He also played basketball for Punahou high school.

Obama left Hawaii for college, enrolling first at Occidental College in Los Angeles for his freshman and sophomore years, and then at Columbia University in New York City. He read deeply and widely about political and international affairs, graduating from Columbia with a political science major in 1983. After spending an additional year in New York as a researcher with Business International Group, a global business consulting firm, Obama accepted an offer to work as a community organizer in Chicago's largely poor and black South side.

Obama's main assignment as an organizer was to launch the church-funded Developing Communities Project and, in particular, to organize residents of Altgeld Gardens to pressure Chicago' city hall to improve conditions in the poorly maintained public housing project and reduce the unemployment rate in high-crime neighborhoods.

His efforts met with some success, but he concluded that, faced with a complex city bureaucracy, "I just can't get things done here without a law degree." In 1988 Obama enrolled at Harvard Law School, where he excelled as a student, graduating magna cum laude and winning election as president of the prestigious Harvard Law Review for academic year 1990-1991, as the first African American president in the long history of the Law Review. After receiving his degree from Harvard Law School, he returned to Chicago and practiced as a Civil Rights lawyer. He also taught at the University of Chicago.

Personal Life

Mr. Obama's mother Anne Dunham, deeply admired the civil rights movement of the 1950s and 1960s and taught her son, "To be black was to be the beneficiary of a great inheritance, a special destiny, glorious burdens that only we were strong enough to bear."

During a summer Internship at Chicago's Sidley and Austin law firm after his first year at Harvard, Obama met Michelle Robinson a Chicago native who also graduated from Harvard Law School. Michelle worked in corporate law for three years before pursuing a career in public service. She has worked for the city of Chicago, and she co-founded Public Allies, which helps young adults acquire skills to work in the public sector. In 2005 she was appointed vice president of community and external affairs at the University of Chicago Medical Center.

The Obama's married on October 3, 1992 after dating for 2 years. Barack and Michelle Obama have two daughters: Malia Ann, born July 4, 1998 and Natasha (known as Sasha) had born on June 10, 2001.

Political Career

After directing Illinois Project Vote, a voter registration drive aimed at increasing black turnout in the 1992 election, Obama accepted positions as an Attorney with the Civil Rights law firm of Miner, Barnhill and Galland and as a lecturer at the University of Chicago Law School.

He launched his first campaign for political office in 1996 after his district's State senator, Alice Palmer, decided to run for congress. With Palmer's support, Obama announced his candidacy to replace her in the Illinois legislature. His advocacy work on the local level in Chicago led to a run for the Illinois Senate. Obama served for four years as a state senator and used his position to create programs such as the state Earned Income Tax Credit that provided more than $100 million in tax cuts to families over three years. He also generated and expansion in early childhood education and worked to pass legislation that requires all interrogations and confessions in capital cases to be videotaped.

Obama's eloquent keynote speech at the 2004 Democratic National Convention earned him praise and cemented his reputation as one of the party's freshest and most inspirational new faces. In 2004, he was elected to the U.S. Senate, winning with 70% of the vote against the conservative black Republican, Alan Keyes. Obama became the only African–American serving in the U.S. Senate (and the fifth in U.S. history). Obama's idealism, commitment to civil rights and telegenic good looks generated enormous media attention for his Senate campaign. He worked with Republicans on issues such as weapons control and ethics reform, yet voted with other Democrats against President Bush's surge of 20,000 troops to Iraq and favor of a resolution that required combat troops to be fully withdrawn by March 2008.

He served on the Senate Health, Education, Labor, and Pensions Committee; the foreign Relations Committee; the Veteran's Affairs Committee; and the Environment and Public Works Committee.

2008 Presidential Democratic Candidate Acceptance Speech

Obama accepted the Democratic presidential nomination before some 83,000 people at Invesco Field rather than the convention hall in Denver. His acceptance coincided with the 45th anniversary of the March on Washington, during which Rev. Martin Luther King Jr. gave his pivotal "I Have a Dream" speech. In his speech, Obama attacked John McCain on several fronts, including national security and his support for many of the policies of the Bush administration, and outlined his plans for the economy, the environment, and health Care. Calling McCain out of touch with the economic woes of working-class America, Obama said, "It's not because John McCain doesn't care. It's because John McCain doesn't get it."

Obama spoke of the core issues facing the United States at the time, among them the economy, the Iraq War and the Onset of Global warming, a message to America's enemies and friends, and the coming energy crisis.

To our future as Americans:

This is our time, to put our people back to work and open doors of opportunity for our kids; to restore prosperity and promote the cause of peace; to reclaim the American dream and reaffirm that fundamental truth, that out of many, we are one, that while we breathe we hope. And where we are met with cynicism and doubts and those who tell us that we can't, we will respond with the timeless creed that sums up the spirit of people: Yes, we can.

After his election, Obama sought to mend fences by making Hilary Clinton his Secretary of State.

Obama took office in a severe recession for the U.S. economy. His first major piece of legislative was the American Recovery and Reinvestment Act, a $787 billion spending bill, or "stimulus package," designed to create jobs and reignite the economy. He also acted quickly to bring about the change from the policies of the Bush administration that he had promised during the campaign. Two days after his inauguration he signed an executive order to close the controversial detention facility in Guantanamo Bay Cuba within the year. Soon to follow were executive orders that reversed Bush's policies on stem cell research and interrogation techniques for enemy detainees.

Wins the Nobel Prize

The 2009 Nobel Peace Prize was awarded to the United States President Barack Obama for his "extraordinary efforts to strengthen international diplomacy and cooperation between peoples." The Norwegian Nobel Committee cited Obama's promotion of nuclear nonproliferation and a "new climate in international relations fostered by Obama, especially in reaching out to the Muslim world." The award came as somewhat as a shock to the White House and beyond, as few of Obama's proposed international policy changes have yet to be realized. Indeed, North Korea continues to taunt the world with missile tests and nuclear bravado, Iran only recently agreed to engage in talks about its nuclear program, and his Afghanistan policy is a work in progress. However, Thorbjorn Jagland, the chairman of the Norwegian Nobel Committee, said, "We would hope this [the Peace Prize] will enhance what he is trying to do."

Obama is the fourth President of the United States to have been awarded a Nobel Prize. The list includes Theodore Roosevelt, Woodrow Wilson and Jimmy Carter.

Obama donated the monetary award of $1.4 million to charitable organizations.

A Best Selling Author

Barack Obama is a 6 time bestselling Author with 2 bestselling books. 4 time bestseller. The Audacity of Hope and a 2 time bestseller. Dreams from my Father.

Obama published an autobiography, Dreams from My Father, in 1995; it became a best-seller during his 2004 Senate campaign. His next autobiography, The Audacity of Hope, became a best-seller after its Oct. 2006 publication and won both the Black

Caucus of the American Library Association Literary Awards and the NAACP Image Awards in 2007.

Eric Holder Jr.

Eric Himpton Holder Jr. was born in the Bronx New York, to parents with roots in Barbados. Eric Himpton Holder Sr. (1905-1970) was born in Saint Joseph, Barbados and arrived in the United States at the age of 11. He later became a real estate broker. His mother, Miriam, was born in New Jersey, while his maternal grandparents were immigrants from Saint Philip, Barbados.

Holder grew up in East Elmhurst, Queens, and attended public school until the age of 10. When entering the 4th grade he was selected to participate in a program for intellectually gifted students.

In 1969, he graduated from Stuyvesant High School in Manhattan and attended Columbia University, where he played freshman basketball. He earned a B.A. degree in American History in 1973. Holder received his J.D. from Columbia Law School, graduating in 1976. He worked for the NAACP Legal Defense and Educational Fund during his first summer and the United States Attorney during his second summer.

In 1969, while a freshman at Columbia, Holder was one of several dozen students who staged an occupation of the Reserve Officers' Training Corps office, renaming it as the Malcolm X Student Center.

Career

After graduating from Columbia Law School, Holder joined the U.S. Justice Department's new Public Integrity Section, where he worked from 1976 to 1988. During his time there, the assisted in the prosecution of Democratic Congressman John Jenrette for bribery discovered in the Abscam sting operation. In 1988, Ronald Reagan appointed Holder to serve as a Judge of the Superior Court of the District of Columbia

On December 1, 2008 President elect Obama announced that Holder would be his nominee for Attorney General of the United States. He was formally nominated on January 20, 2009 and was overwhelmingly approved by the Senate Judiciary Committee on January 28 with a bipartisan vote of 17 to 2. He was officially confirmed by the entire senate on February 2, 2009, by a vote of 75 to 21 becoming the nation's first African-American A ttorney General.

President Obama's First Two Years in Office

"LET'S BE THE GENERATION THAT
MAKES FUTURE GENERATIONS
PROUD OF WHAT WE DID HERE."
—PRESIDENT BARACK OBAMA

The challenges that President Obama and this administration inherited were immense-two wars, an economy in freefall, record deficits, and a health care system in crisis. Although there is still more work to do, we have made an incredible amount of progress over the past two years. Together, we have begun to lay a new foundation for growth, building an economy that works for all Americans.

"We meet at a moment of great uncertainty for America. The economic crisis we face is the worst since the Great Depression… I know folks are worried. But I also know this—we can steer ourselves out of this crisis."

I'm here today to tell you that there are better days ahead. I know these are tough times. I know that many of you are anxious about the future. But this isn't a time for fear or panic. This is a time for resolve and leadership. I know that we can steer ourselves out of this crisis. Because that's who we are. Because this is the United States of America. This is a nation that has faced down war and depression; great challenges and great threats. And at every moment, we have risen to meet these challenges—not as Democrats, nor as Republicans, but as Americans.

With resolve, with confidence, with that fundamental belief that here in America, our destiny is not written for us, but by us. That's who we are, and that's the country we need to be right now.

—Barack Obama—October 2008

REBUILDING OUR ECONOMY

RECOVERY ACT

Many argue today that Obama's $800 billion plan, the one that eventually became law, was not enough. With a bigger boost, the economy would have recovered much more quickly and years of needless suffering could have been allayed. In truth, of course, the political headwinds against stimulus were extraordinary. Republicans dismissed it as an irresponsible shopping spree that would leave the country in even greater debt. Representative John A. Boehner of Ohio, the minority leader in the House, physically threw the bill on the ground, arguing that it was "nothing more than a spending, spending and more spending." But Democrats, led by the "deficit Hawk" wing of the party, also fought against anything too ambitious, and Obama, still in the first month of his presidency, was left in the position of negotiating with his party, such that he was just barely able to get the $800 billion on a straight party line vote.

The Recovery Act represented the largest infrastructure investment since President Eisenhower, the largest education investment since President Johnson and the largest clean-energy bill ever. It has saved or created as many as 3.7 million jobs across America while creating a foundation for future growth.

WALL STREET REFORM

Wall Street reform empowered consumers and investors, put a stop to predatory lending practices, brought shadowy Wall Street trades into the light, and ended taxpayer-funded bailouts.

Dodd-Frank

The Dodd-Frank Wall Street Reform and Consumer Protection Act is a massive piece of financial reform legislation passed by the Obama administration in 2010 as a response to the financial crisis of 2008. Named after sponsors U.S. Senator Christopher J. Dodd and U.S. Representative Barney Frank, the act's numerous provisions, spelled out over roughly 2,300 pages, are being implemented over a period several years and are intended to decrease various risks in the U.S. financial system.

The act established many new government agencies tasked with overseeing various components of the act and by extension various aspects of the banking system.

President Donald Trump has pledged to repeal Dodd-Frank, and on June 8, 2017, the house of Representatives voted to replace it with Financial CHOICE ACT, which will roll back significant pieces of Dodd-Frank. The CHOICE Act, however, is not expected to pass the Senate in its entirety.

MIDDLE-CLASS TAX CUTS

As part of the stimulus, formally known as the American Recovery and Reinvestment Act, single workers collected a $400 tax credit, and working couples got $800. The credit didn't come in the form of a check; it worked out so that most workers had about $400 less in federal income taxes withheld from the paychecks spread out over the entire year.

Most workers received a tax cut under that plan, except for some high earners. The tax cuts phased out for couples who make more than $250,000 or a single person making over $200,000, according to an analysis from the nonpartisan Tax Policy Center.

The Recovery Act reduced taxes for 95 percent of working families, putting more money in the pockets of Americans who need it most. President Obama also worked to prevent a middle-class tax increase, while extending vital unemployment benefits for Americans who lost their jobs through no fault of their own.

CREDIT CARD REFORM

The Credit Cardholders' Bill of Rights includes several provisions aimed at limiting how credit card companies can charge consumers but does not include price controls, rate caps, or fee settings. Key provisions include: (1) Giving consumers enough time to pay their bills. Credit Card Companies have to give consumers at least 21 days to pay from the time the bill is mailed. Credit Card Companies cannot "trap" consumers by setting payment deadlines on the weekend or in the middle of the day, or changing their payment deadlines each month. (2) No retroactive rate increases. Credit Card Companies must give consumers at least 45 days, notice if their rates are about to go up, and cannot change any terms of the contract within a year. Low introductory rates must last at least six months. (3) Easier to pay down debt. Credit Card Companies must apply payments to a consumer's highest interest rate balances first. Statements must show consumers how long it would take to pay off their existing balance if the consumer made only the minimum payment, and must show the payment amount and total interest cost to pay off the entire balance in 36 months. (4) Eliminates "fee harvester cards." The act restricts fees on low balance cards sold to card holders with bad credit.

For many of these cards, the up-front fees charged exceeded the remaining credit. The act also restricts the fees that can be charged for gift cards and other prepaid cards. (5) Eliminates excessive marketing to young people. Consumers under the age of 21 must prove that they have an independent income or get a co-signer before applying for a credit card. The Act also prevents credit card companies from mailing offers to consumers under 21 unless they "opt in," and prohibits companies from wooing students with T-shirts, free pizza and other gifts at university-sponsored events.

These reforms put a stop to unfair credit card practices. Reform banned retroactive rate hikes, implemented new protections for students and young people, and required credit card companies to explain their terms in plain language.

BUILDING A CLEAN-ENERGY ECONOMY

New emissions and fuel efficiency standards for American cars and historic investments in clean-energy technologies are helping pave the way to a more sustainable future, creating new jobs and entire industries here in America.

When President Obama signed the American Recovery and Reinvestment Act (Recovery Act). Not only did the Recovery Act stimulate the economy and raise GDP by an estimated 2-3 percent following the depts. Of the Great Recession, but it also made the largest single investment in clean energy in history, providing more than $90 billion in strategic clean-energy investments and tax incentives to accelerate job creation and the deployment of low carbon technologies. This historic investment toward a 21st century clean-energy economy included the seed funding for ARPA-E, a new agency within DOE with the mission to advance potentially transformational energy technologies that are too early in their development to attract private-sector investment.

We need to double down on these core investments to maintain American leadership and accelerate the transition to a clean-energy economy.

The President's ambitious actions to cut carbon pollution will ensure that America takes a comprehensive approach to the climate technology challenge, including a balanced mix of basic science, applied research and development, lab to market support, and incentives for widespread deployment—including smart pollution standards that reward innovation in cutting emissions. Now more than ever, the stage is set for rapid progress toward a low-carbon economy, with momentum building all along the innovation pipeline.

REBUILDING THE AMERICAN AUTO INDUSTRY

In 2008, the entire auto industry was in very bad shape. Layoffs at auto plants and among auto parts suppliers were on track to reach 250,000 workers. Gasoline prices were up and buying power was down. General Motors was virtually out of cash to pay its bills and Chrysler was not far behind.

In November 2008, the New York Times ran the headline "GM Teetering on bankruptcy pleads for federal bailout." The Center for Automotive Research, an independent research group that gets some funding from automakers, predicted harsh outcomes if GM and Chrysler went belly up. Beyond the immediate jobs lost, there would be a partial collapse of the supplier industry that would lead to a 50 percent drop in production at Ford and the Americanbased foreign car plants. Imports would replace 70 percent of the lost GM and Chrysler production, the group predicted.

When President Obama took office, he created a task force with a sweeping mandate to determine the fate of GM and Chrysler. The companies' first proposals to the task force included downsizing, but the task force wanted deeper changes. In March 2009, Obama rejected those plans and said if the firms wanted federal money, they had to go through bankruptcy.

That happened quickly. The car companies filed for bankruptcy in June and emerged in July. Both Chrysler and General Motors are significantly profitable, earning more now than they have in years.

The Obama administration acted decisively to invest in America's auto industry, preventing hundreds of thousands of job losses across the country and revitalizing the backbone of America's manufacturing sector.

An economy that had been shrinking for nearly a year is now growing. After nearly two years of job loss, our economy added more than one million private sector jobs in 2010. "The stimulus alone represents a strikingly progressive presidential legacy—rivaling the biggest reforms of the Clinton presidency. And it passed on Obama's 24th day in office."—Tim Dickinson October 2010

"The bailout of the auto industry protected against absolute devastation in the economies of the Midwest… And it is now turning out to be a huge financial boon for taxpayers." Norm Ornstein October 2010

"Let's be the generation that finally tackles our health care crisis. Let's be the generation that says right here, right now, that we will have universal health care in America by the end of the next president's first term."—Barack Obama September 2008

HISTORIC HEALTH REFORM

AFFORDABLE CARE ACT

The issue of health insurance reform in the United States has been the subject of political debate since the early part of the 20th Century.

In the 2008 Presidential election Barack Obama called for universal health care. His plan called for the creation of a National Health Insurance Exchange that would include both private insurance plans and a Medicare—like government run option. Coverage would be guaranteed regardless of health status and premiums would not vary based on health status either. It would have required parents to cover their children, but did not require adults to buy insurance.

On November 7, the House of Representatives passed the Affordable Health Care for America Act on a 220-215 vote and forwarded it to the Senate for passage. On December 24, the bill then passed by a vote of 60-39 with all democrats and two independents voting for, and all republicans voting against. The bill was endorsed by the AMA and AARP. The House passed the Senate bill with a vote of 219 to 212 on March 21, 2010 with 34 Democrats and all 178 voting against it.

The following day, Republicans introduced legislation to repeal the bill. Obama signed the ACA into law on March 23, 2010.

The Affordable Care Act provides stability and security to Americans who have insurance and provides affordable options for those who don't. It lowers costs for families, businesses, and America as a whole, provides the largest middle-class tax cut for health care in our history, and puts an end to the worst insurance industry abuses.

Supreme Court upholds Nationwide Health Care Law subsidies

Washington—The Supreme Court on Thursday June 25, 2015 upheld the Nationwide tax subsidies underpinning President Barack Obama" health care overhaul, rejecting a major challenge to the landmark law in a ruling that preserves health insurance for millions of Americans.

The Justices said in a 6-3 ruling that the subsidies that 8.7 million people currently receive to make insurance affordable do not depend on where they live, as opponents contended. The outcome was the second major victory for Obama in politically charged Supreme Court tests of his most significant domestic achievement and it came the same day the Court gave him an unexpected victory by preserving a key tool the administration uses to fight housing bias.

Obama greeted news of the decision by declaring the health care law "is here to stay." He said the law is no longer about politics, but the benefits millions of people are receiving.

CHILDREN'S HEALTH INSURANCE

The expansion of the State Children's Health Insurance Program (SCHIP) extended coverage to another 4 million low-income children. Increasing the total number of children covered by the program to more than 11 million. "All progressives since Theodore Roosevelt wanted [health care reform], all Democrats since Harry Truman fought for it, and only Barack Obama got it… This is his huge accomplishment."—Douglas Brinkley October 2010

"I will end this war in Iraq responsibly, and finish the fight against al Qaeda and the Taliban in Afghanistan. I will build new partnerships to defeat the threats of the 21st century: terrorism and nuclear proliferation; poverty and genocide; climate change and disease. And I will restore our moral standing, so that America is once again that last, best hope for all who are called to the cause of freedom, who long for lives of peace, and who yearn for a better future." Barack Obama August 28th, 2008

NATIONAL SECURITY

ENDING COMBAT OPERATIONS IN IRAQ

President Obama declared an end on August 31, 2010 to the seven year American Combat mission in Iraq, saying that the United States has met its responsibility to that country and that it is now time to turn to pressing problems at home.

Mr. Obama balanced praise for the troops who fought and died in Iraq

We have ended our combat mission in Iraq and removed nearly 100,000 troops so that we can focus on fighting alQaeda and rebuilding our nation at home.

<u>TOWARD A WORLD WITHOUT NUCLEAR WEAPONS</u>

The President reached the most important arms control agreement with Russia in two decades. New START will reduce our nuclear arsenals, put inspectors on the ground in Russia, and renew America's leadership in pursuit of a world without nuclear weapons. President Obama also rallied the world behind a plan to secure all nuclear material from terrorists within four years, fulfilling a key campaign promise.

<u>A NEW STRATEGY FOR AFGHANISTAN AND PAKISTAN</u>

The United States and our allies have gone on the offense in Afghanistan, in Pakistan, and around the world to ensure that al Qaeda and other terrorists do not have any safe place from which to plan future attacks on America.

> "In foreign policy, [President Obama] has set the stage for engagement and multilateralism. He has reset relations with Russia, made overtures to the Muslim world in his Cairo speech, and provided a philosophic discussion of war, peace, and human rights in his Nobel speech."—

Doris Kearns Goodwin January 2010

"Now is the time to finally meet our moral obligation to provide every child a world-class education, because it will take nothing less to compete in the global economy... I will not settle for an America where some kids don't have that chance." Barack Obama August 2008

EDUCATION

REFORMING STUDENT LENDING

President Obama signed legislation to expand College access for millions of young Americans by revamping the student loan program in what he called "one of the most significant investments in higher education since the G.I. Bill."

The new law will eliminate fees paid to private banks to act as intermediaries in providing loans to college students and use much of the nearly $68 billion in savings over 11 years to expand Pell grants and make it easier for students to repay outstanding loans after graduating.

The law also invests $2 billion in community colleges over the next four years to provide education and career training programs to workers eligible for trade adjustment aid after dislocation in their industries.

The law will increase Pell grants along with inflation in the next few years, which should raise the maximum grant to $5,975 from $5,550 by 2017, according to the White House, and it will also provide 820,000 more grants by 2020.

Students who borrow money starting in July 2014 will be allowed to cap repayments at 10 percent of income above a basic living allowance, instead of 15 percent. Moreover, if they keep up payments, their balances will be forgiven after 20 years instead of 25 years-or after 10 years if they are in public service, like teaching, nursing or serving in the military.

SPURRING INNOVATION

Programs like "Race to the Top" and "Educate to Innovate" are giving American schools and states the tools and resources they need to be successful.

President Obama spoke to the audience in Elkhart County, Indiana. "For as the world grows more competitive, we can't afford to run the race at half-strength or half-speed. If we hope to lead this century like we did the last Century, we have to create the conditions and the opportunities for places like Elkhart to succeed. We have to harness the potential—the innovative and creative spirit—that's waiting to be awakened all across America.

Continuing his efforts to establish a 21st century clean energy economy, the President announced an unprecedented $2.4 billion Investment in 48 new advanced battery and electric drive projects, funded through the Recovery Act. The projects were selected through a highly competitive process by the Department of Energy will accelerate the development of U.S. manufacturing capacity for batteries and electric drive components as well as the deployment of electric drive vehicles, helping to establish American leadership in creating the next generation of advanced vehicles.

"If we want to reduce our dependence on oil, put America back to work and reassert our manufacturing sector as one of the greatest in the world, we must produce the advanced, efficient vehicle of the future." Said President Obama.

A NEW GI BILL

To mark the end of combat in Iraq and the return of U.S. troops in time for the holidays, President Barack Obama and First Lady Michelle Obama spoke at Fort Bragg, N.C., on December 14, 2011.

Michelle Obama thanked service members and their families for their sacrifices and touted her husband's work in supporting returning veterans. She mentioned improved mental health care for veterans and tax cuts for business that hire veterans. She also said this of her husband: "He's helped more than half a million veterans and military family members go to college through the Post-9/11 G.I. Bill."

The bill, officially called the Post-9/11 Veterans Educational Assistance Act of 2008, was introduced by Sen. Jim Webb, a Democrat from Virginia and Vietnam War Veteran. It paid for veterans who served at least three years after September 11, 2001, to attend a public college or university for free for four years, provided a monthly housing stipend and covered up to $1,000 a year for books.

Service members who agreed to serve four more years in the military had the option of transferring the benefit to their spouses or children. With the backing of numerous veterans groups, the bill was hailed as the most comprehensive educational benefits program since the original G.I. Bill was enacted in the World War ll era.

Obama, then a senator campaigning for president, supported the bill, along with most other members of Congress.

CIVIL RIGHTS

REPEALING "DON'T ASK, DON'T TELL"

President Obama signed legislation that will bring an end to "Don't Ask, Don't Tell," strengthening our national security and ending this discriminatory law.

Obama's first assistant Attorney General for Civil Rights, Thomas Perez, and his successors have helped direct the U.S. Justice Department to address abuses.

The Civil Rights Division actively pursued cases involving equal opportunities for employment and education and civil rights. The agency established a dedicated a Fair Lending Unit to stop discriminatory lending practices against minorities, and pursued cases to ensure citizens with disabilities and overseas military personnel have the opportunity to vote.

PROTECTING AGAINST HATE CRIMES

Obama fulfilled a pledge to support the Matthew Shepard and James Byrd Jr. Hate Crimes Prevention Act, which he signed in August 2009. The law broadened federal jurisdiction in prosecuting hate crimes and expanded the definition of a hate crime to include bias-motivated crimes based on a victim's actual or perceived "gender, sexual orientation, gender identity, or disability."

Before the law was passed, there were 45 states with their hate crimes prevention laws, but they did not all cover the same categories of crimes. The Justice Department went through a top-down cultural shift that emphasized these sorts of crimes, he said, and many U.S. attorneys committed themselves to carrying out the law. The Federal Bureau of Investigation also prepared a new hate crimes training manual with guide lines for treating cases that is now used as an example for local law enforcement.

FAIR PAY FOR WOMEN

The Lilly Ledbetter Fair Pay Act of 2009 is a federal statute in the United States that was the first bill signed into law by President Barack Obama on January 29, 2009. The Act amends the Civil Rights Act of 1964. The new act states that the 180-day statute of limitations for filing an equal-pay lawsuit regarding pay discrimination resets with each new paycheck affected by that discriminatory action.

For 10 years, Lilly Ledbetter fought to close the gap between women's and men's wages, sparring with the Supreme Court, lobbying Capitol Hill in a historic discrimination case against Goodyear Tire and Rubber Company. Ledbetter won a jury verdict of more than $3 million after having filed a gender pay discrimination suit in federal court, but the U.S. Supreme Court later overturned the lower court's ruling.

The Supreme Court's decision was nullified when President Obama, signed into law the first new law of his administration: The Lilly Ledbetter Fair Pay Act of 2009.

> "Less than halfway through his first term, Obama has compiled a remarkable track record... On

the social front, he has improved pay parity for women and hate-crime protections for gays and lesbians."—Tim Dickinson October 2010

AS WE APPROACH THE HALFWAY POINT OF PRESIDENT OBAMA'S FIRST TERM, the list of accomplishments already dwarfs that of many of his predecessors. The actions taken by this administration and by Democrats in Congress have eased the burden on middle-class families, making it easier for working parents to meet their families' daily needs while opening doors of opportunity for their children. Together, these accomplishments form a foundation for a new generation of prosperity, a new era of possibility, and a new century of American greatness.

> "This president has delivered more sweeping, progressive change in 20 months than the previous two Democratic administrations did in 12 years."—Tim Dickinson October 2010

Obama signs law for Indian tribes black farmers

American Indians and black farmers will be paid $4.6 billion to address claims of government mistreatment over many decades under landmark legislation President Barack Obama signed Wednesday December 15, 2010.

The legislation "closes a long and unfortunate chapter in our history," Obama said, "It's finally time to make things right."

At a signing ceremony at the White House the president declared that approval of the long-delayed legislation "isn't simply a matter of making amends, it's about reaffirming our values on which this nation was founded: the principles of fairness and equality and opportunity."

Obama promised during his campaign to work toward resolving disputes over the government's past discrimination against minorities. The measure he signed settles a pair of long-standing class-action lawsuits. The measure also settles four long-standing disputes over Native American water rights in Arizona, New Mexico and Montana.

Elouise Cobell, a member of the Blackfeet Tribe from Browning, Mont., and the lead plaintiff in the Indian royalties case, called the signing ceremony "breathtaking," adding that she did not expect it to happen in her lifetime. Cobell filed the suit nearly 15 years ago and led efforts to reach the $3.4 billion settlement a year ago and then push it through the House and Senate.

At least 300,000 Native Americans say they were swindled out of royalties overseen by the Interior Department since 1887 for oil, gas, grazing and timber rights. The plaintiffs will share the settlement.

Cobell said she was driving her car in Montana when she learned the Senate had approved the measure last month. "I pulled over and I cried," she said.

Even with Obama's signature, the settlement must still go through a gauntlet of court hearings, a media campaign to notify beneficiaries, waiting periods for comments and appeals. The first check is not expected to reach tribal plaintiffs until August.

Even so, Cobell said the day was historic.

"This day means a lot to the elders, because it means they receive justice," she said. "The money is secondary. They got justice. The United States government gave them justice."

Sen. Blanche Lincoln, D-Ark., used similar language to describe the black farmer's case, which marks the second round of funding from a class-action lawsuit originally settled in 1999. The case, which involves allegations of widespread discrimination by local Agriculture Department offices in awarding loans and other aid, is named after Timothy Pigford, a black farmer from North Carolina who was an original plaintiff.

The new settlement, totaling nearly $1.2 billion, is intended for people who were denied payments in the earlier settlement because they missed deadlines for filing. Individual amounts depend on how many claims are successfully filed.

"The time is long overdue to fund the discrimination settlement for farmers who have experienced decades of injustice," Lincoln said.

The settlement will not erase the anxiety and frustrations many black farmers experienced, Lincoln added, but "it will help compensate their financial losses and begin laying the foundation in restoring their faith in the United States government."

With pressure on small family farms through the 20th century, both whites and African American farmers were struggling to survive in the South. The USDA made its loans dependent on applicants' credit, but African Americans were discriminated against and had difficulty gaining credit. They had been disenfranchised by southern laws and policies since the turn of the century and excluded from the political system, a condition that was maintained for much of the 20th Century.

Southern states had established one-party political rule by whites under the Democratic Party. In Mississippi, where black farmers made up to 2/3 of the total of farmers in the Delta in the late 19th century, most lost their land by 1910 and had to go to sharecropping or tenant farming. Divested of political power, African Americans were even less able to gain credit.

While the law and regulations implementing them were color blind, the people carrying them out were not. The denial of credit and benefits to black farmers and the preferential treatment of white farmers essentially forced black farmers out of agriculture through the 20th century. African-American farmers were subject to humiliation and degradation by USDAA county officials.

Some Republicans have warned that black farmers might make up stories of discrimination that are hard to prove. Rep. Steve King, R-Iowa, likened the program to "modern-day reparations" for African–Americans and argued that the claims process is rife with fraud.

Agriculture Secretary Tom Vilsack and Attorney General Eric Holder said the bill includes new safeguards to prevent fraud, including an extended court approval process and government audits.

Holder called fraud concerns "legitimate," but he said the settlement rights a historical wrong.

Bachmann criticizes black farmer settlement

Republican presidential candidate Michele Bachmann pointed to one program in particular Monday when talking about wasteful government spending: a multibillion dollar settlement paid to black farmers, who claim the federal government discriminated against them for decades in awarding loans and other aid.

The issue came up after Bachmann and Republican Rep. Steve King of Iowa toured flooded areas along the Missouri River. During a news conference, they fielded a question about whether farmers affected by the flooding also should be worried by proposed U.S. Department of Agriculture cuts.

The two responded by criticizing a 1999 settlement in what is known as the Pigford case, after the original plaintiff, North Carolina farmer Timothy Pigford. Late last year, President Barack Obama signed legislation authorizing a new, nearly $1.2 billion settlement for people who were denied payments in the earlier one because they missed deadlines for filing.

King has likened the Pigford settlement to "modern-day reparations" for African-Americans. He said Monday a large percentage of the settlement "was just paid out in fraudulent claims" and criticized the Obama administration's plan to resolve separate lawsuits filed by Hispanic and female farmers.

"That's another at least $1.3 billion," King said "I'd like to apply that money to the people that are under water right now."

Bachmann seconded King's criticism, saying, "When money is diverted to inefficient projects, like the Pig ford project, where there seems to be proof-positive of fraud, we can't afford $2 billion in potentially fraudulent claims when that money can be used to benefit the people along the Mississippi River and the Missouri River."

John Boyd, president of the National Black Farmers Association, which represented black farmers in the Pig ford settlement, called the criticism unfair.

"Why continue to take from those people who haven't taken part in federal programs equally and give to another group of farmers who have taken part in federal programs?" Boyd asked. "I think taking resources from a group of people who have been historically denied any relief at the Department of Agriculture is a bad idea. For the flood victims that deserve redress. They should provide those people with relief, too."

Boyd said he and others worked to put antifraud provisions in the legislation signed last year. They require each claim of discrimination to be judged individually to determine its merit—a process that Boyd said has not yet even begun.

"We worked with Republicans…to get those issues addressed," he said. "Even after we got them addressed, Ms. Bachmann and Mr. King have continued to look at black farmers in a very negative way.

"I think it's bad for the American people. I think if Ms. Bachmann wants to be president of the United States, she should treat all people fairly."

Bachmann's criticism wasn't limited to the U.S. Department of Agriculture. The Minnesota congresswoman also took a swipe at the president, who has not visited areas of Iowa, Nebraska or other states flooded by the river.

"The devastation is beyond what people can imagine," Bachmann said. "Surely this is worthy of a presidential visit to come see this level of devastation in western Iowa."

Heavy rain and a large snowmelt from the Rocky Mountains have poured water into the Missouri, flooding more than 500,000 acres in seven states. The high water is expected to linger through August, putting pressure on levees that protect homes, cities and farms.

"This flood that we have seems to have disappeared from the minds of people from across the country," King said. "If you're not here to see it…you don't hear very much about it."

Democratic Rep. Marcia Fudge of Ohio, chairwoman of the Congressional Black Caucus, told the Jackson Mississippi Clarion-Ledger "I am pleased this chapter of discrimination in the history of the Department of Agriculture is closed and bureaucracy will no longer keep these farmers from receiving their due justice."

Many farmers who had filed claims have since died. Of the 18,000 claims approved, about 4,000 to 5,000 were estate claims. The National Black Farmers Association is working with some families whose deceased parents had filed claims.

About $1 billion in payments has been issued to approximately 18,000 claimants leaving about $9.5 million left over will be available for distribution to law schools or nonprofit organizations.

The relevant provision in the settlement says the left-over money must go to either of two places: first is "a law school that has a low-income taxpayer clinic or program that provides tax advice or assistance to Class Members who have received an award under the Settlement Agreement and that has been approved by the Court." Second is "a tax-exempt non-profit organization, other than a law firm, legal services entity, or educational institution, that is providing agricultural, business assistance, or advocacy services, including assistance under Pigford and Consolidated Case, to African American farmers.

African Americans by the Numbers From the U.S. Census Bureau Population Distribution

Note: Unless otherwise noted, the estimates in this section refer to the population that is either single-race black or black in combination with one or more other races.

Black and African Americans constitute the third largest racial and ethnic group in the United States (after White Americans and Hispanic and Latino Americans) Most African Americans are of West and Central African descent and are descendants of enslaved peoples within the boundaries of the present United States. The vast majority of African Americans also have some European and Native American ancestry. According to US Census Bureau data, African immigrants generally do not self-identify as African American.

The overwhelming majority of African immigrants identify instead with their respective ethnicities. Immigrants from some Caribbean, Central American and South American nations and their descendants may or may not also self-identify with the term.

41.1 million

As of July 1, 2008, the estimated population of black residents in the United States, including those of more than one race. They made up 13.5 percent of the total U.S. population. This figure represents an increase of more than half a million residents from one year earlier.

65.7 million

The projected black population of the United States (including those of more than one race) for July 1, 2050. On that date, according to the projection, blacks would constitute 15 percent of the nation's total population.

18

Number of states with an estimated black population on July 1, 2008, of at least 1 million. New York, with 3.5 million, led the way. The 17 other states on the list were Alabama, California, Florida, Georgia, Illinois, Louisiana, Maryland, Michigan, Mississippi,

New Jersey, North Carolina, Ohio, Pennsylvania, south Carolina, Tennessee, Texas and Virginia.

38%

Percentage of Mississippi's population that is black, highest of any state. Blacks also make up more than a quarter of the population in Louisiana (32 percent), Georgia (31 percent), Maryland (30 percent), South Carolina (29 percent) and Alabama (27 percent). They comprise 56 percent of the population in the District of Columbia.

67,000

The increase in Georgia's black population between July 1, 2007, and July 1, 2008, which led all states. Texas (64,000), Florida (41,000) and North Carolina (45,000) also recorded large increases.

24

Number of states or equivalents in which blacks were the largest minority group in 2008. These included Alabama, Arkansas, Delaware, District of Columbia, Georgia, Illinois, Indiana, Kentucky, Louisiana, Maine, Maryland, Michigan, Minnesota, Mississippi, Missouri, New York, North Carolina,

Ohio, Pennsylvania, South Carolina, Tennessee, Virginia, West Virginia and Wisconsin.

1.4 million

The number of blacks in Cook County, Ill., as of July 1, 2008, which led the nation's counties in the number of people of this racial category. Orleans Parish, La., had the largest numerical increase in the black population between July 1, 2007, and July 1, 2008 (16,400). Neighboring St. Bernard Parish had the largest percent increase over the period (97 percent).

Among counties with total populations of at least 10,000, Claiborne County, Miss., had the largest percent of population that was black (84.4 percent). Claiborne led 82 majority-black counties or equivalents, all but one of which (St. Louis city, Mo.) was in the South.

30%

The proportion of the black population younger than 18 as of July 1, 2008. At the other end of the spectrum, 8 percent of the black population was 65 and older.

Serving Our Nation
2.3 million

Number of single-race black military veterans in the United States in 2008. More military veterans are black than any other minority group.

Education

Note:
83%

Among single-race blacks 25 and older, the proportion who had at least a high school diploma in 2008.

20%

Percentage of single-race blacks 25 and older who had a bachelor's degree or higher in 2008.

1.4 million

Among single-race blacks 25 and older, the number who had an advanced degree in 2007 (e.g., master's, doctorate, medical or law). In 1998, 857,000 blacks had this level of education.

2.5 million

Number of single-race black college students in fall 2008. This was roughly double the corresponding number from 15 years earlier.

Voting

About 2.1 Million

The increase in the number of black voters between the 2004 and 2008 presidential elections, to 16.1 million. The total number of voters rose by 5.4 million, to 131.1 million.

55%

Turnout rate in the 2008 presidential election for the 18- to 24-year-old citizen black population, an 8 percent increase from 2004. Blacks had the highest turnout rate in this age group.

65%

Turnout rate among black citizens in the 2008 presidential election, up about 5 percentage points from 2004. Looking at voter turnout by race and

Hispanic origin, non-Hispanic whites and blacks had the highest turnout levels.

Businesses

$88.6 billion

Revenues for black-owned businesses in 2002. The number of black-owned businesses totaled nearly 1.2 million in 2002. Black-owned firms accounted for 5% of all nonfarm businesses in the United States.

129,329

The number of black-owned firms in New York in 2002, which led all states. New York City alone had 98,080 such firms, which led all cities.

10,716

The number of black-owned firms operation in 2002 with receipts of $1 million or more. These firms accounted for 1% of the total number of black-owned firms in 2002, and 55% of their total receipts, or $49 billion.

969

The number of black-owned firms with 100 or more employees in 2002. Firms of this size accounted for 24% of the total revenue for black-owned employer firms in 2002, or $16 billion.

Income, Poverty, and Health Insurance

$34,218

The annual median income of single-race black households in 2008, a decline of 2.8 percent (in 2008 constant dollars) from 2007.

24.7%

Poverty rate in 2008 for single-race blacks, statistically unchanged from 2007.

19.1%

The percentage of single-race blacks lacking health insurance in 2008, statistically unchanged from 2007.

Families and Children

63%

Percentage of families among households with s single-race black householder. There were 8.5 million black family households.

44%

Among families with single-race black householders, the percentage that is married couples.

1.2 million

Number of single-race black grandparents living with their grandchildren younger than 18. Of this number 50 percent were also responsible for their care.

Homeownership—the American Dream

Since the earliest reporting of homeownership rates in the United States, black or African American households and households of other racial/ethnic subpopulations consistently have been less likely than white households to own homes. This is true regardless of income level, although the gap between the homeownership rates of high-income whites and high income African Americans is the smallest of the gaps by income group. In addition to being less likely than whites to own homes, African Americans own homes with lower median value than whites: These trends persist despite initiatives undertaken since the mid-1990s to increase homeownership among households with low income or worse members belong to racial /ethnic subpopulations.

In 1940, the black homeownership rate was half the white rate; since then the black rate has remained substantially lower than the white rate, despite increases in both rates. Between 1940 and 2000, the homeownership rate for Black households more than doubled, increasing from 22.8 percent to 46.3 percent.

Nationally, the percentage of households with a householder who is single-race black who lived in owner-occupied homes. The rate was higher in certain states, such as Mississippi, where it reached 59 percent.

There were 24,685 black-owned firms in Missouri in 2007, up from 16,758 in 2002, according to data from the U.S. Census Bureau's 2007 Survey of Business Owners. This was 47.4 percent increase in the number of black-owned firms in the state. These firms accounted for nearly $2.41 billion in sales and receipts in 2007.

In the U.S., there were 1.9 million black-owned firms in 2007, up 63 percent from 2002. Sales and receipts from black-owned firms totaled $135.7 billion in 2007. Black-owned firms made up 7.1 percent of all firms and 0.4 percent of all sales and receipts in the U.S.

States with largest of black-owned businesses were New York (204,004), Georgia (183,864), Florida (181,496) Texas (154,283) and California (137,891). California had the largest gross sales from black-owned firms. Missouri ranked 19th among the states in total number of black-owned firms.

Seven States had more than 100,000 black-owned businesses. Eighteen States had fewer than 5,000 black-owned businesses, as a percent of all firms, were located mostly in the Southern and Eastern portions of the United States. The area with the largest percentage of black-owned businesses was the District of Columbia at 28.2 percent. Other states with a large percentage of black-owned businesses were Georgia (20.4%), Maryland (19.3%), Mississippi (18.0%) and Louisiana (15.9%). In Missouri, blacks owned 4.9 percent of all firms in 2007, up from 3.8 percent of all firms in 2002.

Black segregation in US drops to lowest in century

America's neighborhoods became more integrated last year (2009) than during any time in at least a century as a rising black middle class moved into fast-growing white areas in the South and West.

Still, ethnic segregation in many parts of the U.S. persisted, particularly for Hispanics.

Segregation among blacks and whites fell in roughly three-quarters of the nation's 100 largest metropolitan areas as the two racial groups spread more evenly between inner cities and suburbs, according to recent census data.

The findings are expected to be reinforced with fresh census data being released Tuesday on race, migration and economics. The new information is among the Census Bureau's most detailed releases yet for neighborhoods.

"It's taken a Civil Rights movement and several generations to yield noticeable segregation declines for blacks," said William H. Frey, a demographer at the Bookings Institution who reviewed the census data. "But the still-high levels of black segregation in some areas, coupled with uneven clustering patterns for Hispanics, suggest that the idea of a post-racial America has a way to go."

The race trends also hint at the upcoming political and legal wrangling over the 2010 census figures, to be published in the spring. The data will be used to reallocate congressional districts, drawing new political boundaries. New Hispanic dominated districts could emerge, particularly for elected positions at the state and local level. States are required under the Voting Rights Act to respect the interests of minority voting blocs, which tend to support Democratic candidates.

Milwaukee, Detroit and Syracuse, N.Y., were among the most segregated, all part of areas in the Northeast and Midwest known by some demographers as the "ghetto belt." On the other end of the scale, cities that were least likely to be segregated included Fort Myers, Fla., Honolulu, Atlanta and Miami.

Hispanic integration was mixed. There was less Hispanic-white segregation in cities and suburbs in many large metros such as Buffalo, Washington, D.C., and Chicago, according to preliminary census figures. But in many smaller neighborhoods, large numbers of more recently arrived Hispanic immigrants are believed to be clustering together for social support, experts said.

The findings on segregation are partly based on a demographic index that tracks the degree to which racial groups are evenly spread between city and suburb. The index ranges from 0 to 100, with 60 or above generally considered highly segregated. That index found that for large U.S. metros in 2009, the black-white segregation reading was 27, down from 33 in 2000 and the lowest in generations.

Other findings:

Overall, Asians showed less residential segregation from whites compared with blacks and Hispanics, but results varied widely by geography. Asians were most segregated in large metros such as Greensboro, N.C., and Stockton, Calif. They were most integrated in Phoenix, Washington, D.C., and Las Vegas, due partly to the movement of more affluent Asians to suburbs.

New Orleans was among metros with the largest decline in city-suburb segregation among blacks and whites since 2000, due largely to the exodus of low-income blacks from the city after Hurricane Katrina.

Other large metros showing less segregation included those with technology-based economies, such as Boston, Seattle, Houston, Austin, Tex., and San Francisco, which attracted middle-and upper-income blacks to their suburbs.

Still, the recent gains in racial integration are somewhat limited, said John Logan, a sociologist at Brown University who has studied residential segregation. He noted that black-white segregation remained generally high in areas of the Northeast and Midwest. In those areas, there is slow population growth and white flight from increasingly minority neighborhoods is still common.

As for Hispanics and Asians, while residential movement out of ethnic neighborhoods has been increasing, those numbers have generally been surpassed by the arrival of new immigrants into traditional enclaves.

"The political implications of these trends are great in the long run-majority black districts will become harder to sustain, while more majority Hispanic districts will emerge, especially for state and local positions" Logan said.

The figures come from previous censuses and the 2009 American Community Survey, which samples 3 million households.

Due to incomplete 2009 data, the analysis of racial segregation omits seven metro areas: Sarasota, Fla., Greenville, S.C., Harrisburg, Pa., Jackson, Miss., McAllen, Texas, Portland, Maine, and Poughkeepsie, N.Y.

In a reversal, more blacks moving back to South

After decades of mass exodus, blacks are returning to the South in one of the most notable migrations of the new century. It's a subtle but significant shift that experts say provides not only a snapshot of the changing economics and sociology of the nation but of an emerging new South and, in some cases, of a growing disillusionment with the Urban North.

For most of the 20th Century, blacks were buying one-way tickets out of the Jim Crow South in hopes of a better life. Nearly 6 million African–Americans followed the railroads to places like Detroit and Chicago, never dreaming that their children and grandchildren would someday lead a return migration, chasing the American dream back down the Mississippi and straight across the Mason-Dixon line.

The Great Migration slowly eased in the 1970s as the North's economic fortunes began to dim and the South's racial climate began to improve. But it wasn't until the 2000 Census, when the South posted its first black population increase in more than a century that demographers started to really take notice.

By 2010, about 57 percent of the Nation's African–Americans were living in the South—a higher percentage than at any time in 50 years.

Even at its lowest points, the South was still home to the majority of the nation's black residents, giving it a culturally and sociologically significant role in African-American history and making it, if not always comfortable, at least always familiar.

Some of the return migrants are retirees, while others are college-educated young people driven by economic realities, historical curiosity, and the old-fashioned American drive to explore new frontiers and create new worlds and the pull of a cultural homeland.

The Great Migration, the 60-year escape from segregation and racism that brought American blacks to the North, has reversed course. Better jobs and quality of life in the South are beckoning, as is the lure of something more intangible—a sense of home.

"It's no coincidence that the shift is happening as we encounter economic turmoil that is being felt disproportionately among blacks, such as mortgage foreclosures, loss of jobs and economic devastation in major Northern hubs," said Hilary Shelton, director of the NAACP's Washington bureau. "With major changes and less racial devastation in the South, people are finding their way back."

The nation's black population grew by roughly 1.7 million over the last decade. About 75 percent of that growth occurred in the South—primarily metropolitan areas such as Atlanta, Dallas, Houston,

Miami and Charlotte, N.C. That's up from 65 percent in the 1990s, according to the latest census estimates. The gains came primarily at the expense of Northern metro areas such as New York and Chicago, which posted their first declines in black population since at least 1980.

Illinois had its first decline in the black population in the state's history, with the number of African-Americans decreasing by 1.3 percent since 2000, according to official 2010 census figures released Tuesday.

In all, about 57 percent of U.S. blacks now live in the South, a jump from the 53 percent share in the 1970s, according to an analysis of census data by William H. Frey, a demographer at the Brookings Institution. It was the surest sign yet of a sustained reverses migration to the South following the exodus of millions of blacks to the Midwest, Northeast and West in the Great Migration from 1910 to 1970.

"The Great Migration of millions of disenfranchise blacks from the south to Northern cities has now completely turned around," Frey said. "Blacks now took to states like Georgia, Texas and North Carolina as the places with the most promise in the 21st century—a prospect that would have been unimaginable a generation ago."

The converts include Shelton Haynes, 33, a housing manager in Atlanta. He grew up in New York City and lived in Harlem for many years with his wife and two children before growing weary of the cost of living and hectic pace. After considering other places in the South such as Charlotte, the two settled on Atlanta, where Haynes brother, sister-in-law and parents now also live.

"We have a great support network of family and friends here, and there is good community involvement, with our kids involved in swimming, tennis and basketball," Haynes said. "In Atlanta, I also see a lot of African-Americans do very well in a variety of professions, so it was good to see things changing."

Historically, the South was home to roughly 90 percent of the nation's blacks from 1790 until 1910, when African-Americans began to migrate northward to escape racism and seek jobs in industrial centers such as Detroit, New York and Chicago during World War I. After the decades-long Great Migration, the share of blacks in the South hit a low of about 53 percent in the 1970s, before civil rights legislation and the passage of time began to improve the social climate in the region.

The current 57 percent share of blacks living in the South is the highest level since 1960.

The latest estimates show that the Atlanta metropolitan area increased by more than half a million blacks over the last decade to about 1.7 million, making it the metro area with the second-largest black population. Despite losing blacks, the New York metro area continued to be home to the largest black population, at roughly 3.2 million.

The Chicago metropolitan area, which previously was ranked No. 2 in black population, slipped to No. 3.

Broken down by state, Georgia was tops in the total number of African-Americans, edging out New York state. It was followed by Texas, Florida and California. California in recent decades has seen its black population slip or remain largely unchanged.

In December, the Census Bureau reported the nation's population was 308.7 million, up from 281.4 million a decade ago. Most of the population growth occurred in the South and West, where some states stand to gain seats in Congress to reflect their increases in population. Texas, for example, will pick up four new House seats, and Florida will gain two, while Arizona, Georgia, Nevada, South Carolina, Utah and Washington each gain one seat.

Frey noted that the continued Southern migration of blacks, who tend to vote Democratic, could have political implications as they flow into mostly Republican-leaning states. In 2008, Democrat Barack Obama was able to win in traditionally GOP-leaning states such as Virginia, North Carolina and Florida after a jump in black voter turnout.

Black power has arrived with some new challenges

Ten months after Democrats took over the Capital and the first African-American president moved into the White House, black lawmakers are in control of some of the most powerful positions in Congress...and face new challenges to using their long-sought influence.

There have been some victories...guaranteeing that stimulus money reaches some of the poorest parts of the country, expanding hate crimes legislation and moving to close health care disparities.

But "in some ways, our strategies haven't caught up with our power," said Benjamin Todd Jealous, chief executive of the NAACP.

"The civil rights community is used to passing big omnibus legislative acts," he said. "We're not so accustomed to having the power to slice and dice that into 20 pieces and attach that to various other appropriations bills."

For generations, civil rights were inseparable from black politicians. That era ended with President Barack Obama, who has declined to engage in traditional black advocacy.

So any new efforts to help blacks who remain disproportionately unemployed, incarcerated, unhealthy and undereducated will most likely come from the 42 members of the Congressional Black Caucus.

"The goal is closing all of these gaps." said Rep. Barbara Lee, chairwoman of the caucus and a member of the House Appropriations Committee, which oversees budgetary spending. "When you look at all these huge systemic gaps, there's still not equality and justice for all."

But due to recent advances among blacks. Obama's election chief among them...there is a new resistance toward efforts aimed at helping black people specifically, said University of Pennsylvania history professor Mary Frances Berry.

"We're used to being supplicants at the table," Berry said. "Now they have to be smart. If they want to do something about unemployment, they can target those who have the highest rates. If you target education, target the lowest achievement rates. Don't say, we're doing this for Black folks; you say, "we want to target where the problems are."

That strategy has been taking shape for some time, said Rep. James Clyburn, D-S-C., who as majority whip is the third-ranking member of the House. Clyburn cited an amendment in the economic recovery package that he worked on with Rep. Charles Rangel, D-N.Y., and Chairman of the Ways and Means Committee, to ensure that 10 percent of federal stimulus dollars are spent in areas where at least 20 percent of residents have lived in poverty for the last 30 years. "If I were designing a quote-unquote affirmative action program today, that's what I would be using, the 10-20-30 formula, "Clyburn said." We are finding more and more sophisticated ways of doing this on nonracial bases."

But some still say the fractious black caucus—which famously split over endorsing Obama or Hilary Rodham Clinton in the 2008 Presidential Primaries—should be doing much more to bring together leaders from the private sector, Rep. John Conyers, D-Mich., chairman of the Judiciary Committee, said recently enacted legislation expanding hate crimes protection and changes he is pushing to mandatory minimum sentencing laws are evidence of "a whole new power syndrome on the national scene."

He also said he planned to bring a bill through his committee calling for the government to study the issue of reparations to descendants of slaves. "This is not just a feel-good measure." Conyers said. "This is very serious business."

Obama opposes reparations and has said "the best reparations we can provide are good schools in the inner city and jobs for people who are unemployed."

The caucus also played a major role in pushing the House to formally rebuke Rep. Jim Wilson, the South Carolina Republican who shouted "You lie!" during Obama's health care address to Congress.

"We weren't just going to let that go and not say something about it," said Rep. Yvette Clarke, D-N.Y.

She said Clyburn's position as majority whip was crucial to this and other caucus priorities. "We're able to sort of project and amplify our voices because he's in the leadership."

Clarke said that in bills such as the stimulus package, health care reform and auto industry bailouts, caucus members affect "the chemistry of the legislation" by ensuring that provisions to help minorities are included.

For example, the House health care bill provides billions of dollars to address the substandard health care many minorities receive. It's unclear whether the provisions will remain after negotiations to reconcile the Senate health care bills.

Berry, the Penn professor, said the caucus' effectiveness should ultimately be judged by results on problems in poverty, education, unemployment and other areas.

"We're going to find out how smart they are, how committed they are and whether they have a fix on what the people need," she said.

Black voters look to leverage their loyalty

When black voters gave President Barack Obama 93 percent support on Election Day in defiance of predictions that they might sit it out this year, black leaders breathed a collective sigh of relief.

That encouraged those leaders to try to leverage more attention from both Obama and Congress. Although they waver over how much to demand from the president—particularly in light of defeated GOP challenger Mitt Romney's assertion that Obama gave "gifts" to minorities in exchange for their votes—they are delivering postelection wish lists to the president anyway.

"I think the president heard us loud and clear. The collective message was, 'Let's build on where we already are," the Rev. Al Sharpton told reporters after a White House meeting last week with a collection of advocates representing largely Democratic constituencies.

Specifically, Sharpton said, that means keeping the brunt of the looming "fiscal cliff" of tax increases and spending cuts off the backs of the middle and working class.

NAACP President Benjamin Jealous aimed that same message at Congress, especially on where tax relief is extended.

"We need Republicans to think hard and to pull back from the cliff 98 percent of our families, who make up the bulk of this nation, from seeing our taxes being raised," Jealous said.

Blacks made up 13 percent of the electorate this year, about the same as 2008, while participation among whites shrank slightly to 72 percent and Hispanics increased to 10 percent, national exit polls showed. Black leaders point to that minority participation as they sharpen their calls for initiatives to address black unemployment, which was 12.7 percent when Obama took office, peaked at 16.5 percent roughly a year later, and stood at 14.3 percent in October. The overall unemployment rate is 7.9 percent.

National Urban League President Marc Morial acknowledged in an interview that "we sweated turnout to the end," because the country's underlying economic conditions made it tougher to mobilize black voters. Within days of the election, Morial sent to Obama, House Speaker John Boehner, R-Ohio, and House Minority leader Nancy Pelosi, D-Calif., an "urgent petition" asking that Obama's second term focus on economic opportunity and income inequality.

A jobs program should emphasize infrastructure and public works, broadband technology and energy "with a special focus on those communities where unemployment is and remains stubbornly and persistently high," Moral's letter said.

"We who represent the nation's urban communities will demand a seat at the table in these discussions," he wrote.

African-American voter samples in national exit polls are not useful for providing turnout measurements. Census surveys and other analyses eventually will provide turnout numbers for specific racial groups. But exit polls can be used to examine different groups as shares of the overall vote. And there, experts say, is where the evidence can be found of how many black voters delivered for Obama.

Nationally, Obama's share of the black vote was down slightly from four years ago. But some key states, turnout was higher and had an impact, said David Bositis, an expert on black politics and voting at the Joint Center for Political and Economic Studies.

Blacks made up 15 percent of the electorate in Ohio, up from 11 percent in 2008. And 97 percent of those votes went for Obama, leading Bositis to say Obama's margin of victory in the state came from black voters.

In Michigan, the black share of the vote grew from 12 percent in 2008 to 16 percent in 2012, according to exit polls.

"Michigan was one of the states the two parties jostled around, and eventually Republicans decided they were not going to win, and one of the reasons was the big increase in the black vote," Bositis said.

In Missouri, a state Obama lost in both elections, the black vote went from 13 percent to 16 percent of all voters.

Bositis said the black share of the vote remained roughly the same at 23 percent in North Carolina, which Obama narrowly won in 2008 but lost in 2012, and 13 percent in Florida, which Obama won both times. In Virginia, which Obama won in both elections, black voters were 20 percent of all voters, he said.

Women and people from ages 18 to 29 had the strongest participation levels in the black community.

In 2008, black women had the highest turnout rate, 69 percent, of all groups. Their 2008 record created a sense of obligation among some black female leaders to take an active role against new state voting laws they said threatened to curb black voter participation. Black women made up 60 percent of the black vote this year and voted 95 percent for Obama.

The enthusiasm of black women was demonstrated in Florida when more than 250 churches marched their congregations to the polls as part of the "Souls to the Polls" early voting campaign, said Melanie Campbell, president and CEO of the National Coalition on Black Civic Participation. A large percentage of the marchers were women, Campbell said.

"Countless women stood in line for hours to vote early so they could volunteer to work at the polls to help in the fight against voter suppression," Campbell said.

Black Voters ages 18-29 made up 26 percent of the black vote nationally, a turnout close to what it was in 2008, according to the national exit poll. They voted 91 percent for Obama.

Republicans had reached out to black voters in 2004 and saw their share of the black vote increase in that election, Bositis said. But he said that in 2012, the outreach was nonexistent.

Michael Steele, former Republican National Committee chairman, said the GOP had an opportunity this election to connect with black voters on unemployment, health disparities, incarceration and other issues.

"How the heck do you win if you don't engage in the conversation?" Steele said.

12

In a first, black voter turnout rate passes whites

America's blacks voted at a higher rate than other minority groups in 2012 and by most measures surpassed the white turnout for the first time, reflecting a deeply polarized presidential election in which blacks strongly supported Barack Obama while many whites stayed home.

Had people voted last November at the same rates they did in 2004, when black turnout was below its current historic levels, Republican Mitt Romney should have won narrowly, according to an analysis conducted for "The Associated Press.

Census data and exit polling show that whites and blacks will remain the two largest racial groups of eligible voters for the next decade. Last year's heavy black turnout came despite concerns about the effect of new voter-identification laws on minority voting, outweighed by the desire to re-elect the first black president.

William H. Frey, a demographer at the Brookings Institution, analyzed the 2012 elections for the AP using census data on eligible voters and turnout, along with November's exit polling. He estimated total votes for Obama and Romney under as scenario where 2012 turnout rates for all racial groups matched those in 2004. Overall, 2012 voter turnout was roughly 58 percent, down from 62 percent in 2008 and 60 percent in 2004.

The analysis also used population projections to estimate the shares of eligible voters by race group through 2030. The numbers are supplemented with material from the Pew Research Center and George Mason University associate professor Michael McDonald, a leader in the field of voter turnout who separately reviewed aggregate turnout levels across states, as well as AP interviews with the Census Bureau and other experts. The bureau is scheduled to release data on voter turnout in May.

Overall, the findings represent a tipping point for blacks who for much of America's history were disenfranchised and then effectively barred from voting until passage of the Voting Rights Act in 1965.

But the numbers also offer a cautionary note to both Democrats and Republicans after Obama won in November with a historically low percentage of white supporters. While Latinos are now the biggest driver of U.S. population growth, they still trail whites and blacks in turnout and electoral share, because many of the Hispanics in the country are children of noncitizens.

In recent weeks, Republican leaders have urged a "year-round effort" to engage black and other minority voters, describing a grim future if their party does not expand its core support beyond white males.

The 2012 data suggest Romney was a particularly weak GOP candidate, unable to motivate white voters let alone attract significant black or Latino support. Obama's appeal and the slowly improving economy heled overcome doubts and spur record levels of minority voters in a way that may not be easily replicated for Democrats soon.

Romney would have erased Obama's nearly 5 million-vote victory margin and narrowly won the popular vote if voters had turned out as they did in 2004, according to Frey's analysis. Then, white turnout was slightly higher and black voting lower.

More significantly, the battleground states of Ohio, Pennsylvania, Virginia, Florida and Colorado would have tipped in favor of Romney, handing him the presidency if the outcome of other states remained the same.

"The 2012 turnout is a milestone for blacks and a huge potential turning point," said Andra Gillespie, a political science professor at Emory University who has written extensively on black politicians. "What it suggests is that there is an 'Obama effect' where people were motivated to support Barack Obama. But it also means that black turnout may not always be higher, if future races aren't as salient."

Whit Ayres, a GOP consultant who is advising GOP Sen. Marco Rubio of Florida, a possible 2016 presidential contender, says the last election reaffirmed that the Republican Party needs "a new message, a new messenger and a new tone." Change within the party need not be "lock, stock and barrel," Ayres said, but policy shifts such as GOP support for broad immigration legislation will be important to woo minority voters over the longer term.

"It remains to be seen how successful Democrats are if you don't have Barack Obama at the top of the ticket," he said. In Ohio, a battleground state where the share of eligible black voters is more than triple that of other minorities, 27-year-old Lauren Howie of Cleveland didn't start out thrilled with Obama in 2012. She felt he didn't deliver on promises to help students reduce college debt, promote women's rights and address climate change, she said. But she became determined to support Obama as she compared him with Romney.

"I got the feeling Mitt Romney couldn't care less about me and my fellow African-Americans," said Howie, an administrative assistant at Case Western Reserve University's medical school who is paying off college debt.

Howie said she saw some Romney comments as insensitive to the needs of the poor. "A white Mormon swimming in money with offshore accounts buying up companies and laying off their employees just doesn't quite fit my idea of a president," she said. "Bottom line, Romney was not someone I was willing to trust with my future.

The numbers show how population growth will translate into changes in who votes over the coming decade:

The gap between non-Hispanic white and non-Hispanic black turnout in 2008 was the smallest on record, with voter turnout at 66.1 percent and 65.2 percent, respectively; turnout for Latinos and non-Hispanic Asians trailed at 50 percent and 47 percent. Rough calculations suggest that in 2012, 2 million to 5 million fewer whites voted compared with 2008, even though the pool of eligible white voters had increased.

Unlike other minority groups, the rise in voting for the slow-growing black population is due to higher turnout. While blacks make up 12 percent of the share of eligible voters, they represented 13 percent of total 2012 votes cast, according to exit polling. That was a repeat of 2008, when blacks "outperformed" their eligible voter share for the first time on record.

Latinos now make up 17 percent of the population but 11 percent of eligible voters, due to a younger median age and lower rates of citizenship and voter registration. Because of lower turnout, they represented just 10 percent of total 2012 votes cast. Despite their fast growth, Latinos aren't projected to surpass the share of eligible black voters until 2024, when each group will be roughly 13 percent. By then, 1 in 3 eligible voters will be nonwhite.

In 2026, the total Latino share of voters could jump to as high as 16 percent, if nearly 11 million immigrants here illegally become eligible for U.S. citizenship. Under a proposed bill in the Senate, those immigrants would have a 13-year path to citizenship The share of eligible white voters could shrink to less than 64 percent in that scenario. An estimated 80 percent of immigrants here illegally, or 8.8 million, are Latino, although not all will meet the additional requirements to become citizens.

"The 2008 election was the first year when the minority vote was important to electing a U.S. president. By 2024, their vote will be essential to victory," Frey said. "Democrats will be looking at a landslide going into 2028 if the Hispanic voters continue to favor Democrats."

Even with demographics seeming to favor Democrats in the long term, it's unclear whether Obama's coalition will hold if blacks or younger voters become less motivated to vote or decide to switch parties.

Minority turnout tends to drop in midterm congressional elections, contributing to larger GOP victories as happened in 2010, when House control flipped to Republicans.

The economy and policy matter. Exit polling shows that even with Obama's re-election, voter support for a government that does more to solve problems declined from 51 percent in 2008 to 43 percent last year, bolstering the view among Republicans that their core principles of reducing government are sound.

The party's "Growth and Opportunity Project" report released last month by national leaders suggests that Latinos and Asians could become more receptive to GOP policies once comprehensive immigration legislation is passed.

Whether the economy continues its slow recovery also will shape voter opinion, including among blacks, who have the highest rate of unemployment.

Since the election, optimism among nonwhites about the direction of the country and the economy has waned, although support for Obama has held steady. In an October AP-GFK poll, 63 percent of nonwhites said the nation was heading in the right direction; that's dropped to 52 percent in a new AP-GFK poll. Among non-Hispanic whites, however, the numbers are about the same as in October, at 28 percent.

Democrats in Congress merit far lower approval ratings among nonwhites than does the president, with 49 percent approving of congressional Democrats and 74 percent approving of Obama.

William Galston, a former policy adviser to President Bill Clinton, says that in previous elections where an enduring majority of voters came to support one party, the president winning re-election—William McKinley in 1900, Franklin D. Roosevelt in 1936 and Ronald Reagan in 1984—attracted a larger turnout over his original election and also received a higher vote total and a higher share of the popular vote. None of those occurred for Obama in 2012.

Only once in the last 60 years has a political party been successful in holding the presidency more than eight years—Republicans from 1980-1992.

"This doesn't prove that Obama's presidency won't turn out to be the harbinger of as new political order," Galston says. "But it does warrant some analytical caution."

Early polling suggests that Democrat Hillary Rodham Clinton could come close in 2016 to generating the level of support among nonwhites as Obama did in November, when he won 80 percent of their vote. In a Fox News poll in February, 75 percent of nonwhites said they thought Clinton would make a good president, outpacing the 58 percent who said that about Vice President Joe Biden.

Benjamin Todd Jealous, president of the NAACP, predicts closely fought elections in the near term and worries that GOP-controlled state legislatures will step up efforts to pass voter ID and other restrictions to deter blacks and other minorities from voting. In 2012, courts blocked or delayed several of those voter ID laws and African-Americans were able to turn out in large numbers only after a very determined get-out-the-vote effort by the Obama campaign and black groups, he said.

Jealous says the 2014 midterm election will be the real bellwether for black turnout. "Black turnout set records this year despite record attempts to suppress the black vote," he said.

New census milestone: Hispanics hit 50 million

The Census Bureau 2010 count on race migration, detailing a decade in which rapid minority growth, aging whites and increased suburbanization were the predominant story lines. Racial and ethnic minorities are expected to make up an unprecedented 90 percent of the total U.S. growth since 2000, due to immigration and higher birth rates for Latinos. Currently the fastest growing group, Hispanics is on track to exceed 50 million, or roughly 1 in 6 Americans; among U.S. children, Hispanics are now roughly 1 in 4.

"There is excitement," said Brad Gentry, 48, of Houston, Mo., who publishes the weekly paper in Texas County, noting that the U.S. population center typically carries symbolic meaning as the nation's heartland. "It is putting a spotlight on a corner of the world that doesn't get much attention. Most residents are proud of our region and like the idea that others will learn our story through this recognition."

Based on a Pew Hispanic Center analysis, the 2010 count of Hispanics was on track to be 900,000 higher than expected as their ranks surpassed census estimates in roughly 40 states. Many of their biggest jumps were in the South, including Alabama, Louisiana, North Carolina and Louisiana, where immigrants made large inroads over the last decade.

Nationally, the number of Hispanics has soured from 9 million in 1970 to 55 million in 2014—nearly one in six Americans. In California, the number of people who identify themselves as Hispanic surpasses those who classify themselves as Hispanic surpasses those who classify themselves as white, according to a new census report. In many parts of the Midwest, Latinos are driving population growth.

Asians for the first time had a larger numeric gain than African-Americans, who remained the second largest minority group at roughly 37 million. Based on the 2010 census results released by state so far, multiracial Americans were on track to increase by more than 25 percent, to about roughly 8.7 million.

The number of non-Hispanic whites, whose median age is now 41, edged up slightly to 197 million. Declining birth rates meant their share of the total U.S. population dropped over the last decade from 69 percent to roughly 64 percent.

"This is a transformational decade for the nation," said William H. Frey, a demographer at Brookings Institution who has analyzed most of the 2010 data. "The 2010 census shows vividly how these new minorities are both leading growth in the nation's most dynamic regions and stemming decline in others."

"They will form the bulk of our labor-force growth to the next decade as they continue to disperse into larger parts of the country," he said.

The final figures come as states in the coming months engage in the contentious process of redrawing political districts based on population and racial makeup, with changes that analysts believe will result in more Hispanic-majority districts.

The population changes will result in a shift of 12 House seats and electoral votes affecting 18 states beginning in the 2012 elections. Most of the states picking up seats, which include Texas and Florida, are Republican-leaning, even as most of their growth is now being driven largely by Democrat-leaning Hispanics.

Among other findings:

In at least 10 states, the share of children who are minorities has already passed 50 percent, up from five states in 2000. They include Mississippi, Georgia, Maryland, Florida, Arizona, Nevada, Texas, California, New Mexico and Hawaii.

Over the last decade, Latino population growth was most rapid in the South, where many states have seen their Latino populations double since 2000. For the first time, Hispanic population growth outpaced that of blacks and whites in the region, changing the South's traditional "black-white" image.

More than half of the cities with the largest African-American concentrations showed black population declines in the last decade, including Chicago and Detroit. In contrast, the suburbs of growing southern metro areas like Atlanta, Dallas and Houston saw some of their highest gains.

The Census Bureau calculates the mean U.S. population center every 10 years based on its national head count. The Center represents the middle point of the nation's population distribution—the geographic point at which the country would balance if each of its 308.7 million residents weighed the same.

Plato, with a population of 109, is roughly 30 miles southwest of the present mean center in Phelps County, MO. Based on current U.S. growth, which is occurring mostly in the South and West; the center of population is expected to cross into Arkansas or Oklahoma by midcentury.

The last time the U.S. center fell outside the Midwest was 1850, in the eastern territory now known as West Virginia. Its later move to the Midwest bolstered the region as the nation's cultural heartland in the 20th century, central to U.S. farming and Rust Belt manufacturing sites.

Supreme Court Invalidates Key Part of Voting Rights Act

Washington—The Supreme Court on Tuesday June 25, 2013, <u>effectively struck down</u> the heart of the Voting Rights Act of 1965 by a 5-to-4 vote, freeing nine states, mostly in the South, to change their election laws without advance federal approval.

The court divided along ideological lines and the two sides drew sharply different lessons from the history of the civil rights movement and the nation's progress in rooting out racial discrimination in voting. At the core of the disagreement was whether racial minorities continued to face barriers to voting in states with a history of discrimination.

"Our country has changed," Chief Justice Jon G. Roberts Jr. wrote for the majority. "While any racial discrimination in voting is too much, Congress must ensure that the legislation it passes to remedy that problem speaks to current conditions."

The decision will have immediate practical consequences. Texas announced shortly after the decision that a voter identification law that had been blocked would go into effect immediately, and that redistricting maps there would no longer need federal approval. Changes in voting procedures in the places that had been covered by the law, including ones concerning restrictions on early voting, will now be subject only to after-the-fact litigation.

President Obama, whose election as the nation's black president was cited by critics of the law as evidence that it was no longer needed, said he was "deeply disappointed" by the ruling.

Justice Ruth Bader Ginsburg summarized her <u>dissent</u> from the bench, an unusual move and a sign of deep disagreement. She cited the works of the Rev. Dr. Martin Luther King Jr. and said his legacy and the nation's commitment to justice had been "disserved by today's decision."

She said the focus of the Voting Rights Act had properly changed from "first-generation barriers to ballot access" to "second-generation barriers" like racial gerrymandering and laws requiring at-large voting in places with a sizable black minority. She said the law had been effective in thwarting such efforts.

The law had applied to nine states—Alabama, Alaska, Arizona, Georgia, Louisiana, Mississippi, South Carolina, Texas and Virginian—and to scores of counties and municipalities in other states, including Brooklyn, Manhattan and the Bronx.

Chief Justice Roberts wrote that Congress remained free to try to impose federal oversight on states were voting rights were at risk, but must do so based on contemporary data. But the chances that the current Congress could reach agreement on where federal oversight is required are small, most analysts say.

Justices Antonin Scalia, Anthony M. Kennedy, Clarence Thomas and Samuel A. Alito Jr. joined the majority opinion. Justice Ginsburg was joined in dissent by Justices Stephen G. Breyer, Sonia Sotomayor and Elena Kagan.

The majority held that the coverage formula in Section 4 of the Voting Rights Act, originally passed in 1965 and most recently updated by Congress in 1975, was unconstitutional. The section determined which states must receive clearance from the Justice Department or a federal court in Washington before they made minor changes to voting procedures, like moving a polling place, or major ones, like redrawing electoral districts.

Section 5, which sets out the preclearance requirement, was originally scheduled to expire in five years. Congress repeatedly extended it: for five years in 1970, seven years in 1975, and 25 years in 1982. Congress reviewed the act in 2006 after holding extensive hearings on the persistence of racial discrimination at the polls, again extending the pre-clearance requirement for 25 years. But it relied on data from the 1975 reauthorization to decide <u>which states and localities were covered.</u>

The current coverage system, Chief Justice Roberts wrote, is "based on 40-year-old facts having no logical relationship to the present day."

"Congress—if it is to divide the states—must identify those jurisdictions to be singled out on a basis that makes sense in light of current conditions, "he wrote. "It cannot simply rely on the past."

The decision did not strike down Section 5, but without Section 4, the later section is without significance—unless Congress passes a new bill for determining which states would be covered.

It was hardly clear, at any rate, that the court's conservative majority would uphold Section 5 if the question returned to the court in the unlikely event that Congress enacted a new coverage formula. In a concurrence, Justice Thomas called for striking down Section 5 immediately, saying that the majority opinion ad provided the reasons and had merely left "the inevitable conclusion unstated."

The Supreme Court had repeatedly upheld the law in earlier decisions, saying that the preclearance requirement was an effective tool to combat the legacy of lawless conduct by Southern officials bent on denying voting rights to blacks.

Critics of Section 5 say it is a unique federal intrusion on state sovereignty and a badge of shame for the affected jurisdictions that is no longer justified.

The <u>Voting Rights Act of 1965</u> was one of the towering legislative achievements of the civil rights movement, and Chief Justice Roberts said its "strong medicine" was the right response to "entrenched racial discrimination." When it was first enacted, he said, black voter registration stood at 6.4 percent in Mississippi, and the gap between black and white registration rates was more than 60 percentage points.

In the 2004 election, the last before the law was reauthorized; the black registration rate in Mississippi was 76 percent, almost four percentage points higher than the white rate. In the 2012 election, Chief Justice Roberts wrote, "African-American voter turnout exceeded white voter turnout in five of the six states originally covered by Section 5."

The chief justice recalled the Freedom Summer of 1964, when the civil rights workers James Chaney, Andrew Goodman and Michael Schwerner were murdered near Philadelphia, Miss., while seeking to register black voters. He mentioned Bloody Sunday in 1965, when police officers beat marchers in Selma, Ala.

"Today," Chief Justice Roberts wrote, "both of those towns are governed by African-American mayors. Problems remain in these states and others, but there is no denying that, due to the Voting Rights Act, our nation has made great strides."

Justice Ginsburg, in her dissent from the bench, drew a different lesson from those events, drawing on the words of Dr. King.

"The great man who led the march from Selma to Montgomery and there called for the passage of the Voting Rights Act foresaw progress, even in Alabama," she said." "The arc of the moral universe is long, 'it bends toward justice,' if there is a steadfast commitment to see the task through to completion."

In her written dissent, Justice Ginsburg said that Congress was the right body to decide whether the law was still needed and where. Congress reauthorized the law in 2006 by large majorities; the vote was 390 to 33 in the House and unanimous in the Senate. President George W. Bush, a Republican, signed the bill into law, saying it was "an example of our continued commitment to a united America where every person is valued and treated with dignity and respect."

The Supreme Court considered the constitutionality of the 2006 extension of the law in a 2009 decision, <u>Northwest Austin Municipal Utility District Number One v. Holder</u>. But it avoided answering the central question, and it seemed to give Congress an opportunity to make adjustments. Congress, Chief Justice Roberts noted on Tuesday, did not respond.

Justice Ginsburg suggested in her dissent that an era had drawn to a close with the court's decision on the Voting Rights Act, in Shelby County v. Holder, No. 12-96.

"Beyond question, the V.R.A. is no ordinary legislation," she wrote. "It is extraordinary because Congress embarked on a mission long delayed and of extraordinary importance: to realize the purpose and promise of the Fifteenth Amendment," the Reconstruction-era amendment that barred racial discrimination in voting and authorized Congress to enforce it.

"For a half century," she wrote, "a concerted effort has been made to end racial discrimination in voting. Thanks to the Voting Rights Act, progress once the subject of a dream has been achieved and continues to be made."

"The court errs egregiously," she concluded, "by overriding Congress's decision."

Institutional Racism

The term "institutional racism" describes societal patterns that have the net effect of imposing oppressive or otherwise negative conditions against identifiable groups based on race or ethnicity.

Racism is both overt and covert, and it takes three closely related forms: Individual, Institutional, and Systemic. Individual racism consists of overt acts by individuals that cause death, injury, destruction of property, or denial of services or opportunity.

Institutional Racism involves policies, practices, and procedures of institutions that have a disproportionately negative effect on racial minorities; access to and quality of goods, services, and opportunities.

Systemic racism is the basis of individual and institutional racism; it is the value system that is embedded in a society that supports and allows discrimination.

History: The term was coined by <u>Stokely Carmichael</u> (later known as Kwame Ture) at some point during the late 1960s.

Carmichael felt that it was important to distinguish personal bias, which has specific effects and can be identified and corrected relatively easily, with institutional bias, which is generally long-term and grounded more in inertia than intent. Carmichael made this distinction because, like <u>Martin Luther King Jr.,</u> he had grown tired of white moderates and uncommitted liberals who felt that the primary or sole purpose of the civil rights movement was white personal transformation. Carmichael's primary concern, and the primary concern of most civil rights leader, were and is societal transformation—a much more ambitious goal.

Contemporary Relevance:

In the United States, institutional racism results from the social caste system that sustained, and was sustained by slavery and racial segregation. Although the laws that enforced this caste system no longer in place, its basic structure still stands to this day. This structure may gradually fall apart on its own over a period of generations, but activism is necessary to expedite the process and provide for a more equitable society in the interim.

Kings Dream, nearly fulfilled

Rev. Al Sharpton says let's pause and appreciate our progress: New York City and the U.S. are much more racially harmonious than ever before.

In April 2011, will be 43 years since the assassination of this nation's premier civil rights leader, Dr. Martin Luther King Jr. During that tumultuous and volatile time in 1968, it would have been unfathomable to even think of having an African-American president or a billionaire named Oprah Winfrey who could own an entire television network. Even as recently as the 1980s in New York, when we were forced to tackle racial outburst like those in Howard Beach and Bensonhurst, it would be difficult to imagine a day where we would be living side-by-side with one another in harmonious neighborhoods.

I still look at my scar from a stab wound at the protest in Bensonhurst, but I take comfort in the fact that I can look at my TV and see a black President salute a gay Latino congressional aide who saved the life of a Jewish member of the House of Representatives in the state of Arizona. Dr. King's vision is nearly fulfilled. As we take pride in our tremendous collective progress, we must remember to utilize all of this renewed energy and apply it toward some of the areas in which we still can equalize the playing field. We have harnessed the ability to heal and relate to one another on a very real and personal level, but now we must transfer that capability in the direction of education, employment and our criminal justice system. The vast majority of New Yorkers work alongside one another without racial or ethnic strife. We thankfully don not have open mob attacks on people nor lynching, nor segregation. But what we do have is unequal access to jobs, quality education and an imbalanced prison culture. Once we rid society of racial discrimination on an institutional level, then and only then will Dr. King's dream be fully realized.

An integral platform of my work has consistently centered on serving as a voice for the voiceless and shedding light on injustice wherever feasible. Unfortunate incidents of police brutality like those involving Abner Louima, Amadou Diallo and more recently, Sean Bell required immediate attention and action to hold the perpetrators accountable. But these horrific incidents also served as a teachable moment for everyone—despite his or her ethnic background—to acknowledge the very real existence of abusive and biased police conduct. And during these times, we were all forced to take a stern, hard look in the mirror to see how our own shortcomings and preconceived ideas may have contributed to a climate of hatred and animosity.

The violent assaults in Howard Beach and Bensonhurst during the 80s high-lighted the very real and very grave extent of racial intolerance. But these two tragic periods afforded us the opportunity to engage in honest dialogue surrounding ideas of bias, hatred and equality. We openly tackled these obstacles and thank-fully today, we do not see instances of white mobs hunting down black men—or vice-versa.

It's now 2011, and after decades of marches, non-violent protests, calls for action, education and organizing, people as a whole are finally more accepting of each other. An Indian-American female can serve as a governor, a Latino congressman can represent all of the constituents on his or her respective district and an African-American man can be elected to the highest office in the land. In our city alone, even the number of unwarranted police shootings is finally dwindling. Thanks in part to a concerted effort that forced us to confront these issues. We have been able to transcend many of the social barriers that impeded our progress just a few years ago.

So if there are no longer any polarizing conflicts like Howard Beach and Bensonhurst, why must we still continue to discuss race? If we are more socially accepting as a society, why then do we still protest and organize? If young people of color can achieve super stardom, attend Ivy League schools and serve at the highest levels of government, why is race still relevant? If we are in fact closer to sustaining racial peace now than at any other point in history, why do people like myself continue the good fight against discrimination?

The answer is really quite simple: We are still awaiting institutional justice. In the wake of the economic crises of 2008, young black men have been disproportionately hit the hardest. In cities as diverse as ours, it is an incomprehensible reality that unemployment rates within the black and Latino communities are astronomically higher than in other ethnic groups. According to several studies, nearly 50% of all young black men in New York City are unemployed. Other states put that figure even higher when taking in to account the number of under employed.

As our economy makes a slow recovery, unfortunately not everyone is feeling the effects when jobs are few and far between, oftentimes managers, executives and decision makers' will bring aboard those who most closely resemble themselves. And though we may have begun to recognize and accept one another, regrettably, certain segments of the population are still deemed as threats.

Without adequate employment and stability, a family structure diminishes, as does any notion of providing long term wealth. The racially unjust measures of the moment will have repercussions for years to come. An unfortunate reality of poverty and lack of employment is a rise in crime. Without livable wages, more and more, young people of color fall victim to a life of illegal activity. Equally disheartening, however, is the imbalanced way in which our criminal justice system operates. Receiving harsher sentences, and oftentimes unfairly profiled, these young folks are housed in overcrowded prisons that are bursting at the seams.

If we all agree that locking an individual behind bars for petty crimes only hardens him or her, we must work to seek alternatives instead of expanding our prison industrial complex.

Over the course of approximately the last two years, I spent much of my energy and time focused on another impending dilemma—our crumbling education system. Putting aside political difference and teaming up with former Republican Speaker of the House Newt Gingrich, former school Chancellor Joel Klein and Secretary of Education Arne Duncan, I focused heavily on the dire and urgent need for reform.

It should come as no surprise that much of the inequality in our education system falls along racial lines. Overwhelmingly receiving unequal access to good education from the onset, many young black and Latino students find themselves at a severe disadvantage in obtaining success. Countless studies and reports have proven that children who begin reading and writing later than average, fall years behind their counterparts. Playing a game of catch-up through high school and college, if they get there, they are consistently vying for a fighting chance when we as a society have failed them.

How can we expect greatness when we don't even provide the basic necessities for a proper education-mainly, the quality teachers every child deserves? And how can we blame these children for not attending college and bettering themselves when we deliver a message of hopelessness from the beginning? Before we criticize the youth, we must take a look at our own priorities as a nation, and as a people. Every day, I am encouraged by the changes I witness around me. And every day we inch a step closer toward racial equanimity. It took years of protest, organized marches and the sacrifices of many to achieve the success we enjoy today. As a country, we are far more accepting than ever, and racially biased incidents will hopefully be confined to the history books.

But in terms of education, employment and incarceration, much work remains. It is my hope, and the hope of many, that we can infact apply our new racial attitudes toward ensuring a new, more racially just reality in our national institution. In the spirit of our great civil rights leader Dr. King, we will continue to peacefully seek these measures so that one day we can truly say race is no longer relevant.

We as a nation have achieved ardent success; let us now continue until we see the dream all the way through. We have borne witness to the detrimental effects of Institutional Racism; let us now continue to strive for the day we experience institutional justice. Rev. Sharpton is the president of the National Action Network.

The Battle front

Institutional Racism describes any kind of system of inequality based on race. It can occur in institutions such as public government bodies, private business corporations (such as media outlets), and Universities (Public and Private). The term was introduced by Black Power activist Stokely Carmichael and Charles V. Hamilton in the late 1960s. The definition given by William Macpherson within the report looking into the death of Stephen Lawrence was "the collective failure of an organization to provide an appropriate and professional service to people because of their color, culture or ethnic origin.

The concept of institutional racism re-emerged in political discourse in the late 1990s after a long hiatus. Despite it initially seeming pivotal to New Labor's reform of policing and the antecedent of a new race equality agenda, it has remained a contested concept that has been critiqued by multiple constituencies.

Institutional racism is the differential access to the goods, services, and opportunities of society. When the differential access becomes integral to institutions, it becomes common practice, making it difficult to rectify. Eventually, this racism dominates public bodies, private corporations, and public and private universities, and is reinforced by the actions of conformists and newcomers. Another difficulty in reducing institutional racism is that there is no sole, true identifiable perpetrator. When racism is built into the institution, it appears as the collective action of the population.

Professor James M. Jones postulates three major type of racism: (1) Personally-mediated, (2) internalized, and (3) institutionalized. Personally-mediated racism includes the specific social attitudes inherent to racially-prejudiced action (bigoted differential assumptions about abilities, motives and intentions of others according to), discrimination (the differential actions and behaviors towards others according to their race), stereotyping, commission, and omission (disrespect, suspicion, devaluation, and dehumanization). Internalized racism is the acceptance, by members of the racially—stigmatized people of negative perceptions about their own abilities and intrinsic worth, characterized by low self-esteem and low esteem of others like them. This racism can be manifested through embracing "whiteness" (e.g. stratification by skin color in non-white communities), self-devaluation (e.g. racial slurs, rejection of ancestral culture, etc.) and resignation, helplessness, and hopelessness (e.g. dropping out of school, failing to vote, engaging in health-risk practices, etc.).

Persistent negative stereotype fuel institutional racism, and influence interpersonal relations. Racial stereotyping contributes to pattern of racial residential segregation, and shape views about crime, crime policy, and welfare policy, especially if the contextual information is stereotype-consistent. A great percentage of white Americans rate Black Americans and Latino Americans as less intelligent, preferring to live from welfare benefits rather than work, and "more difficult to get along with socially".

Institutional racism is distinguished from racial bigotry by the existence of institutional systemic policies, practices and economic and political structures which place non-white racial groups at a disadvantage in relation to an institution's white members. One example is public school budgets (including local levies and bonds) and the quality of teachers, which in the U.S. are often correlated with property values: rich neighborhoods are more likely to be more 'white' and to have better teachers and more money for education, even in public schools.

Restrictive housing contracts and bank lending policies have also been listed as forms of institutional racism. Other examples are racial profiling by security guards and police, use of stereotyped racial caricatures (e.g. "Indian" sport mascots), the under-and misrepresentation of certain racial groups in the mass media and race-based barriers to gainful employment and professional advancement. Additionally, differential access to goods, service, and opportunities of society can be included within the term of institutional racism, such as unpaved streets and roads, inherited socio-economic disadvantage, "standardized" tests (each ethnic group prepared for it differently, many are poorly prepared), et cetera.

Some sociological investigators distinguish between institutional racism and "structural racism" (sometimes called structural racialization). The former focuses upon the norms and practices within an institution, the latter upon the interactions among institutions. Interactions that produce racialized outcomes against non-white people. An important feature of structural racism is that it cannot be reduced to individual prejudice or to single function of an institution.

Institutional Racism in the United States

The U.S. property appraisal system, created in the 1930s originally tied property value and eligibility for government loans to race. Thus, white-majority neighborhoods received the government's highest property value ratings, and white people were eligible for government loans. Between 1934 and 1962, less than 2 percent of government-subsidized housing went to non-white people.

Government, social and educational policies also have been charged with institutional racism i.e. it affects general health care and AIDS health intervention and services in non-white minority communities. The over-representation of minorities in disease categories (including AIDS) is partly related to racism, according to J. Hutchinson. In a 1922 article, he describes how the federal government's national response to the AIDS epidemic in minority community has been slow, showing insensitivity to ethnic diversity in preventative medicine, community health maintenance, and AIDS treatment services.

Standardized testing has also been considered a form of institutionalized racism, because it is believed to be biased in favor of people from particular socio-cultural backgrounds. Some minorities (black and Hispanic) have consistently tested worse than whites on virtually all standardized tests, even after controlling for socioeconomic status. The achievement gap between white or black or Hispanic students mirrors the gap between the two groups in a variety of IQ tests, many of which are designed to be culturally neutral. In any case, the cause of the achievement gap between black, Hispanic, and white students has yet to be fully elucidated.

Although with approximately two thirds of crack cocaine users being white or Hispanic, a large percentage of people convicted of possession of crack cocaine in federal courts in 1994 were black. In 1994 84.5 percent of the defendants convicted of crack cocaine possession for powder cocaine was more racially mixed with 58% of the offenders being white, 26.7% black, and 15% Hispanic. Within the federal judicial system a person convicted of possession with intent to distribute of powder cocaine carries a five year sentence for quantities of 500 grams or more while a person convicted of possession with intent to distribute of crack cocaine faces five year sentence.

With the combination of severe and unbalanced drug possession laws along with the rates of conviction in terms of race, the judicial system has created a huge racial disparity.

Voter Suppression

The age of white dominance is coming to an end. A multiracial future beckons. Regardless of how race colors their personal views, more than a few Republican officials and operatives are seeking to stem this demographic tide, hoping to squeeze another victory, perhaps the last, out of a mono-racial coalition.

In the past, voter suppression tactics percolated in both parties. But with Republicans seeking to turn back the demographic tide rather than accommodate it, voter suppression is gaining a distinctly Republican signature. The long-term risk to the party is enormous. It's not clear how many voters in 2012 will be seriously inconvenienced or even thwarted altogether by suppression tactics. You can make a pretty good guess, however, about how long their outrage-over what happened and was responsible-will last.

There's been a concerted effort by Republicans nationwide since President Barack Obama was elected to peel back voting rights and laws improving access to the polls that had been in place since the Civil Rights era of the 1960s.

2012 election

As the incumbent president, Obama secured the Democratic nomination with no serious opposition. The Republican Party was more fractured; Mitt Romney was consistently competitive in the polls; but faced challenges from a number of more conservative contenders whose popularity each fluctuated, often besting Romney's. Romney effectively secured the nomination by early May as the economy was improving.

Obama defeated Romney, winning both the popular vote and the Electoral College, with 332 electoral votes to Romney's 206. Obama carried all states and districts (among states that allocate electoral votes by district) that he had won in the 2008 presidential election except North Carolina, Indiana, and Nebraska's 2nd congressional district. As such, his margin of victory decreased from 2008. Consequently, Obama became the first incumbent since Franklin D. Roosevelt in 1944 to win reelection with fewer electoral votes and a lower popular vote percentage.

Nonetheless, Obama also became the first two-term president since Ronald Reagan to win both his presidential bids with an absolute majority of the nationwide popular vote. Not since 1820 had three consecutive American presidents succeeded in securing two consecutive terms.

On Election Day, Latinos stood up to the Republican Party that has tormented them for years and said: "No Mas!"

They gave the GOP, in state after state, a merciless beating and helped re-elect president Obama. They also sparked a family feud within the party-about where to go from here. About 11 million Latinos voted for president. According to exit polls, Obama got 71% of the Latino vote, compared with just 27% for Romney. And they delivered three critical battle ground states Colorado, Florida and Nevada.

Black Voter Turnout:

Despite often-voiced concerns about the effect of voter turnout remained high in 2012 and, for the first time, may have topped the rate of whites, according to a new study by the Pew Research Center.

Four years ago, the rate of black voter turnout almost equaled that of whites, continuing a trend of a steady increase in black turnout rates that began in 1996. This year, with white turnout appearing to have dropped, black turnout seems very likely to have exceeded the white level, although definitive figures won't be available until the Census Bureau reports in a few months. A higher turnout rate among blacks than whites would mark an historic milestone given America's long history of disenfranchising blacks. Blacks were effectively barred from polls in many states until after passage of the federal Voting Rights Act in 1965.

In the run-up to the 2012 presidential election, a number of States with Republican-majority legislatures passed laws limiting voting hours, curtailing voter registration efforts or requiring voters to show identification. Many black leaders said those laws would disproportionately hurt elderly, poor and minority voters and accused Republicans of running a campaign of "Voter Suppression".

Republicans said the measures were needed to combat voter fraud. In a few states, Republican legislative leaders explicitly said they hoped the measure would hurt Democratic candidates or reduce the

"Urban" vote. Courts blocked some of those laws, and in the end they may have backfired as black organizations used "Voter Suppression" as a rallying cry. The perception that "people don't want you to vote "motivated many blacks, particularly young people, to turn out, said Chanelle Hardy, executive director of the National Urban League. "It was huge," she said during a recent panel discussion.

Overall, about 60% of the American eligible to register actually voted in 2012, according to data compiled by Michael McDonald of George Mason University. That would be about three points below the 2008 turnout, with much of the decline coming among white voters. The precise final number won't be known until state completes its vote count, which has been slowed by the after-effects of hurricane Sandy.

The number of voters from minority groups rose in November's election, a key factor in President Obama's reelection. But those numbers are up for disparate reasons. Among Latinos and Asians, population growth has steadily driven up the number of voters. Turnout rates also have gone up, but remain significantly lower than those of the population as a whole. The nations black population by contrast, has remained steady, but the number of black voters has continued to go up because of higher turnout rates. Blacks made up 12% of the U.S. population but were 13% of the voter turnout, according to exit polling. Whites made up about 71% of the voter-eligible population and 72% of the turnout, the exit poll indicated.

The large black turnout was critical to Obama's victory in several swing states, according to a recent analysis by Ray Texeira and John Halpin of the center for American Progress, a Democratic think tank. Their analysis pointed to Ohio, in particular, as a state in which an increase in the black share of the vote proved decisive.

U.S, stopping use of term 'Negro' for census surveys

After more than a century, the Census Bureau is drumming its use of the word 'Negro' to describe black Americans in survey.

Instead of the term that came into use during the Jim Crow era of racial segregation, census forms will use the more modern labels "black" or "African-American."

The change will take effect next year when the Census Bureau distributes its annual American Community Survey to more than 3.2 million U.S. households, Nicholas Jones, chief of the bureau's racial statistics branch, said in an interview.

He pointed to months of public feedback and Census research that concluded few black Americans still identify with being Negro and many view the term as "offensive and outdated."

This is a reflection of changing times, changing vocabularies and changing understandings of what race means in this country, "said Matthew Snipp, a sociology professor at Stanford University, who writes frequently on race and ethnicity. "For younger African-Americans, the term 'Negro' harkens back to the era when African-Americans were second class citizens in this country."

First used in the census in 1900, "Negro" became the most common way of referring to black Americans through most of the early 20th century, during a time of racial inequality and segregation. "Negro" itself had taken the place of "colored". Starting with the 1960s Civil Rights movement, black activist began to reject "Negro" label and came to identify themselves as black or African Americans.

Still, the term has lingered, having been used by Martin Luther King Jr. in his speeches. It also remains in the names of some black empowerment groups that were established before the 1960s, such as the United Negro College Fund, Now often referred to as UNCF.

For the 2010 census, the government briefly considered dropping the word "Negro" but ultimately decided against it, determining that a small segment, mostly older blacks living in the South, still identified with the term. But once census forms were mailed and some black groups protested, Robert Groves, the Census Bureau's director at the time, apologized and predicted the term would be dropped in future censuses.

When asked to mark their race, Americans are currently given a choice of five government-defined categories in census surveys, including one check box selection which is described as "black, African American, or Negro." Beginning with the surveys next year, that selection will simply say "black" or "African-American."

In the 2000 census, about 50,000 people specifically wrote in the word Negro when asked how they wished to be identified. By 2010, unpublished census data provided to the AP show that number had declined to roughly 36,000.

President Obama's Keynote address at the dedication of the Martin Luther King Jr., Statue in Washington DC.

"Our work is not done. And so on this day, in which we celebrate a man and a movement that did so much for this country, let us draw strength from those earlier struggles. First and foremost, let us remember that change has never been quick. Change depends on persistence. Change requires determination. It took a full decade before the moral guidance of Brown v. Board of Education was translated into the enforcement measures of the Civil Rights Acts and the Voting Rights Act, but those 10 long years did not lead Dr. King to give up. He kept on pushing, he kept on speaking, he kept on marching until change finally came.

And then when, even after The Civil Right Acts and The Voting Rights Act passed, African Americans still found themselves trapped in pockets of poverty across the country. Dr. King didn't say those laws were a failure, he didn't say this is too hard; He didn't say let's settle for what we got and go home. Instead he said, let's take those victories and broaden our mission to achieve not just civil and political equality but also economic justice; let's fight for a living wage and better schools and jobs for all who are willing to work. In other words, when met with hardship, when confronting disappointment, Dr. King refused to accept what I call the "isness" of today. He kept pushing toward the "oughtness" of tomorrow.

And so, as we think about all the work we must do-rebuilding an economy that can compete or a global stage, and fixing our schools so that every child-not just some, but every child—gets a world-class education and making sure our health care system is affordable and accessible to all, and that our economic system is one in which everybody gets a fair shake and everybody does their fair share, let us not be trapped by what is. We can't be discouraged by what is. We've got to keep pushing for what ought to be, the America we ought to leave to our children, mindful that the hardships we face are nothing compared to those Dr. King and his fellow marchers faced 50 years ago, and that if we maintain our faith, in ourselves and in the possibilities of this nation, there is no challenge we cannot surmount.

Martin Luther King, Jr. Memorial in Washington, DC.

The Martin Luther King, Jr. National Memorial in Washington, DC honors Dr. King's national and international contributions and vision for all to enjoy a life of freedom, opportunity, and justice. Congress passed a joint resolution in 1996 authorizing the construction of the Memorial and a foundation was created to "Build the Dream," raising the estimated $120 million required for the project. One of the most prestigious sites remaining on the National Mall was selected for the memorial for Martin Luther King, Jr., adjacent to the Franklin D Roosevelt Memorial between the Lincoln and Jefferson Memorials. It is the first major memorial along the National Mall to be dedicated to an African-American, and to a non-president. The Martin Luther King Jr. Memorial opened to the public on August 22, 2011.

The memorial's official dedication dates is August 28, 2011, the 48th anniversary of the March on Washington for Jobs and Freedom.

Dr. Martin Luther King Jr. was a Baptist minister and social activist who became a notable figure during the U.S. Civil Rights movement from the mid-1950s until he was assassinated in 1968. He played a pivotal role in ending the legal segregation of African American citizens in the U.S., influencing the creation of the Civil Rights Act of 1964 and the Voting Rights Act of 1965. He receives the Nobel Peace Prize in 1964, among other honors.

The Memorial conveys three themes that were central throughout Dr. King's life-democracy, justice, and hope. The centerpiece of the Martin Luther King Jr. National Memorial is the "Stone of Hope", a 30-foot statue of Dr. King, gazing into the horizon and concentrating on the future and hope for humanity. The sculpture was carved from 159 granite blocks that were assembled to appear as one singular piece. There is also a 450-foot inscription wall, made from granite panels, that is inscribed with 14 excerpts of King's sermons and public addresses to serve as living testaments of his vision of America.

Martin Luther King, Jr.'s message is universal: a non-violent philosophy striving for freedom, justice and equality.

Rosa Parks statue set to be unveiled at Capital

Rosa Parks is famous for her 1955 refusal to give up her seat on a city bus in Alabama to a white man, but there's plenty about the rest of her experiences that she deliberately withheld from her family.

While Parks and her husband, Raymond, were childless, her brother, the late Sylvester McCauley, had 13 children. They decided Parks' nieces and nephews didn't need to know the horrible details surrounding her civil rights activism, said Rhea McCauley, Parks' niece. "They didn't talk about the lynchings and the Jim Crow laws," said McCauley, 61, of Orlando, Fla. "They didn't talk about that stuff to us kids. Everyone wanted to forget about it and sweep it under the rug."

Parks' descendants now have a chance to be first-hand witnesses as their late matriarch makes more history, this time becoming the first black woman to be honored with a full-length statue in the Capitol's Statuary Hall. The statue of Parks joins a bust of another black woman, abolitionist Sojourner Truth, which sits in the Capitol Visitors Center.

President Barack Obama, Senate Minority Leader Mitch McConnell and House Speaker John Boehner are among the dignitaries taking part in the unveiling Wednesday. McCauley said more than 50 of Parks' relatives traveled to Washington for the ceremony.

In a pivotal moment in the civil rights movement, Rosa Parks refused to give up her seat on a city bus in segregated Montgomery, Ala. She was arrested, touching off a bus boycott that stretched over a year.

Jeanne Theoharis, author of the new biography "The Rebellious Life of Mrs. Rosa Parks," said Parks was very much a full-fledged civil rights activist, yet her contributions have not been treated like those of other movement leaders, such as the Rev. Martin Luther King Jr.

"Rosa Parks is typically honored as a woman of courage, but that honor focuses on the one act she made on the bus on Dec. 5, 1955," said Theoharis, a political science professor at Brooklyn College-City University of New York. "That courage, that night was the product of decades of political work before that and continued...decades after" in Detroit, she said.

Parks died Oct. 24, 2005, at age 92. The U.S. Postal Service issued a stamp in her honor on Feb. 4, which would have been her 100th birthday. Parks was raised by her mother and grandparents who taught her that part of being respected was to demand respect, said Theoharis, who spent six years researching and writing the Parks biography.

She was an educated woman who recalled seeing her grandfather sitting on the porch steps with a gun during the height of white violence against blacks in post-World War 1 Alabama.

After she married Raymond Parks, she joined him in is work in trying to help nine young black men, ages 12 to 19, who were accused of raping two white women in 1931. The nine were later convicted by an all-white jury in Scottsboro, Ala., part of a long legal odyssey for the so-called Scottsboro Boys. In the 1940s. Parks joined the NAACP and was elected secretary of its Montgomery, Ala., branch, working with civil rights activist Edgar Nixon to fight barriers to voting for blacks and investigate sexual violence against women, Theoharis said.

Just five months before refusing to give up her seat, Parks attended Highlander Folk School, which trained community organizers on issues of poverty but had begun turning its attention to civil rights. After the bus boycott, Parks and her husband lost their jobs and were threatened. They left for Detroit, where Parks was an activist against the war in Vietnam and worked on poverty, housing and racial justice issues, Theoharis said.

Theoharis said that while she considers the 9-foot-statue of Parks in the Capitol an "incredible honor" for Parks, "I worry about putting this history in the past when the actual Rosa Parks was working on and calling on us to continue to work on racial injustice."

Parks has been honored previously in Washington with the Presidential Medal of Freedom in 1996 and the Congressional Gold Medal in 1999, both during the Clinton Administration.

But McCauley said the Statuary Hall honor is different.

"The medal you could take it, put it on a mantel," McCauley said. "But her being in the Hall itself is permanent and children will be able to tour the (Capitol) and look up and see my aunt's face."

Legendary singer Lena Horne dies

Lena Horne the enchanting jazz singer and actress who reviled the bigotry that allowed her to entertain white audiences but not socialize with them, slowing her rise to Broadway superstardom, died Sunday May 9, 2010. She was 92.

Lena Horne was born June 30, 1917, in Brooklyn, New York. She left school at age 16 to help support her ailing mother, Horne joined the chorus line at the Cotton Club, the fabled Harlem night spot where the entertainers were black and the clientele white.

She left the club in 1935 to tour with Noble Sissie's orchestra, billed as Helena Horne, the name she continued using when she joined Charlie Barnet's white orchestra in 1940.

After having established herself as a sought after live singer, a role she would maintain throughout her life, she later signed with MGM studios and became known as one of the top African-American performers of her time, seen in such films as Cabin in the Sky and Stormy Weather.

She was also known for her work with civil rights groups and refused to play roles that stereotyped African-American women, a stance that many found controversial. She refused to play the maid and prostitute roles usually reserved for black actresses of her time, which narrowed her prospects in Hollywood.

Horne, whose striking beauty and magnetic sex appeal often overshadowed her sultry voice, was remarkably candid about the underlying reason for her success.

"I was unique in that I was a kind of black that white could accept," she once said. "I was their daydream, I had the worst kind of acceptance because it was never for how great I was or what I contributed. It was because of the way I looked."

In the 1940s, she was one of the first black performers hired to sing with a major white band, the first to play the Copacabana nightclub and among a handful with a Hollywood contract.

In 1943, MGM Studios loaned her to 20th Century-Fox to play the role of Selina Rogers in the all-black movie musical "Stormy Weather." Her rendition of the title song became a major hit and her signature piece.

On screen, on records and in nightclubs and concert halls, Horn was at home vocally with a wide musical range, from blues and jazz to the sophistication of Rodgers and Hart in songs like "The Lady is a Tramp" and "Bewitched, Bothered and Bewildered."

In her first big Broadway success, as the star of "Jamaica" in 1957, reviewer Richard Watts Jr. called her "one of the incomparable performers of our time." Songwriter Buddy De Sylva dubbed her "the best female singer of songs."

But Horne was perpetually frustrated with the public humiliation of racism. "I was always battling the system to try to get to be with my people. Finally, I wouldn't work for places that kept us out…it was a damn fight everywhere I was, every place I worked, in New York, in Hollywood, all over the world," she said in Brian Lanker's book "I Dream a world: Portraits of Black Women Who Changed America."

She won a Tony in 1981, and two years later earned an NAACP medal that had previously been awarded to Martin Luther King, Jr., Richard Wright, Langston Hughes, and Rosa Parks.

When she died in 2010 at age 92, President Barack Obama noted that she was the first black singer to tour with an all-white band and that she refused to perform for segregated audiences. "Michelle and I join all Americans in appreciating the joy she brought to our lives and the progress she forged for our country," he said.

When Halle Berry became the first black woman to win the best actress Oscar in 2002, she sobbed: "This moment is for Dorothy Dandridge, Lena Horne, Diahann Carroll... It' for every nameless, faceless woman of color who now has a chance because this door tonight has been opened." Lena Mary Calhoun Horne, the great-granddaughter of a freed slave, was born in Brooklyn June 30, 1917, to a leading family in the black bourgeoisie. Her daughter, Gail Lumet Buckley, wrote in her 1986 book "The Hornes: An American Family" that among their relatives was a college girlfriend of W.E.B. Du Bois and a black adviser to Franklin D. Roosevelt.

Horne was only 2 when her grandmother, a prominent member of the Urban League and the National Association for the Advancement of Colored People, enrolled her in the NAACP. But she avoided activism until 1945 when she was entertaining at an Army base and saw German prisoners of war sitting up front while black American soldiers were consigned to the rear. That pivotal moment channeled her anger into something useful. She got involved in various social and political organizations and—along with her friendship with Paul Robeson— got her name onto blacklists during the red-hunting McCarthy era.

By the 1960s, Horne was one of the most visible celebrities in the civil rights movement, once throwing a lamp at a customer who made a racial slur in a Beverly Hills restaurant and in 1963 joining 250,000 others in the March on Washington when

Martin Luther King Jr. gave his "I Have a Dream" speech. Horne also spoke at a rally that same year with another civil rights leader, Medgar Evers, just days before his assassination.

It was also in the mid-60s that she put out an autobiography, "Lena," with author Richard Schickel.

The next decade brought her first to a low point, then to a fresh burst of artistry.

She had married MGM music director Lennie Hayton, a white man, in Paris in 1947 after her first overseas engagements in France and England. An earlier marriage to Louis J. Jones had ended in divorce in 1944 after producing daughter Gail and a son, Teddy. In the 2009 biography "Stormy Weather," author James Gavin recounts that when Horne was asked by a lover why she'd married a white man, she replied. "To get even with him."

Her father, her son and her husband, Hayton, all died in 1970-71, and the grief-stricken singer secluded herself, refusing to perform or even see anyone but her closest friends. One of them, comedian Alan King, took months persuading her to return to the stage, with results that surprised her. "I looked out and saw a family of brothers and sisters," she said. "It was a long time, but when it came I truly began to live."

And she discovered that time had mellowed her bitterness.

"I wouldn't trade my life for anything," she said, "because being black made me understand."

14

Wealth gap widens between whites, minorities

The wealth gaps between whites and minorities have grown to their widest levels in a quarter century. The recession and uneven recovery have erased decades of minority gains, leaving whites on average with 20 times the net worth of blacks and 18 times that of Hispanics, according to an analysis of new Census data.

The analysis shows the racial and ethnic impact of the economic meltdown, which ravaged housing values and sent unemployment soaring. It offers the most direct government evidence yet of the disparity between predominantly younger minorities whose main asset is their home and older whites who are more likely to have 401 (k) retirement accounts or other stock holdings.

"What's pushing the wealth of whites is the rebound in the stock market and corporate savings, while younger Hispanics and African-Americans who bought homes in the last decade—because that was the American dream—are seeing big declines," said Timothy Smeeding, a University of Wisconsin–Madison professor who specializes in income inequality.

The median wealth of white U.S. households in 2009 was $113,149, compared with $6,325 for Hispanics and $5,677 for blacks, according to the analysis released Tuesday by the Pew Research Center. Those ratios, roughly 20 to 1 for blacks and 18 to 1 for Hispanics, far exceed the low mark of 7 to 1 for both groups reached in 1995, when the nation's economic expansion lifted many low-income groups to the middle class.

The white-black wealth gap is also the widest since the census began tracking such data in 1984, when the ration was roughly 12 to 1. "I am afraid that this pushes us back to what the Kerner Commission characterized as "two societies, separate and unequal," said Roderick Harrison, a former chief of racial statistics at the Census Bureau, referring to the 1960s presidential commission that examined U.S. race relations. "The great difference is that the second society has now become both black and Hispanic."

Stock holdings play an important role in the economic well-being of white households. Stock funds, IRA and Keogh accounts as well as 401(k) and savings accounts were responsible for 28 percent of whites' net worth, compared with 19 percent for blacks and 15 percent for Hispanics.

According to the Pew Study, the housing boom of the early to mid-2000s boosted the wealth of Hispanics in particular, who were disproportionately employed in the thriving construction industry. Hispanics also were more likely to live and buy homes in states such as California, Florida, Nevada and Arizona, which were in the forefront of the real estate bubble, enjoying early gains in home values.

But those gains quickly shriveled in the housing bust. After reaching a median wealth of $18,359 in 2005, the wealth of Hispanics—who derived nearly two-thirds of their net worth from home equity—declined by 66 percent by 2009. Among blacks, who now have the highest unemployment rate at 16.2 percent, their household wealth fell 53 percent from $12,124 to $5,677?

In contrast, the median household wealth of whites dipped a modest 16 percent from $134,992 to $113,149, cushioned in part by a stock market recovery that began in mid-2009.

The blending of socialism for the poor, corporate welfare for the rich, paper money for the government, and credit excess for the middle class that has shaped America for most of the last 40 years. What we are finding out is that a certain class of people has the power to not only protect itself from these policies but to profit as well. These people have used the last 40 years to produce massive amounts of paper wealth. And they are now desperately trying to convert those paper accounts into real wealth, which explains the exploding price of farmland and precious metals. This explosion of wealth at the top of the food chain is a kind of corruption that's hard to police because it occurs within the boundaries of the law.

The power of the system produces private profits. In this way, it provides a huge incentive to entrepreneurs and politicians to work together on behalf of the system. This is what keeps the system going. This is what keeps it from collapsing upon itself. The imbalances will grow until it implodes. The power of government to restore order will lead all of us to focus on our liberty.

"The findings are a reminder—if one was needed—of what a large share of blacks and Hispanics live on the economic margins," said Paul Taylor, director of Pew Social & Demographic Trends. "When the economy tanked, they're the groups that took the heaviest blows."

The latest data come as President Barack Obama and congressional leaders try to reach a deal to avoid a U.S. default on its financial obligations after Aug. 2. Democrats and Republicans have been wrangling over proposals that could cut trillions of dollars from programs such as Medicare and Social Security; they are divided over whether to bring in new tax revenue, such as by closing corporate tax loopholes or increasing taxes for the wealthy.

The NAACP and other black groups urged Obama to resist deep cuts to housing assistance or safety net programs, saying it would disproportionately hurt urban areas with high poverty and unemployment. The U.S. poverty rate currently stands at 14.3 percent, with the ranks of the working-age poor at the highest level since the 1960s. Some analysts believe the poverty rate will climb higher when new figures are released in September.

"Typically in recessions, minorities suffer from being last hired and first fired. They are likely to lose jobs more rapidly at the beginning of the recession, and are far slower to gain jobs as the economy recovers," said Harrison, who is now a sociologist at Howard University. "One suspects that blacks who lost jobs in the recession, or who have tried to help family members or relatives who did, have now spent whatever savings or other cashable assets they had."

Other findings:

About 35 percent of black households and 31 percent of Hispanic households had zero or negative net worth in 2009, compared with 15 percent of white households. In 2005, the comparable shares were 29 percent for blacks, 23 percent for Hispanics and 11 percent for whites.

Asians lost their top ranking to whites in median household wealth, dropping from $168,103 in 2009. Like Hispanics, many Asians were concentrated in states like California hit hard by the housing downturn. More recent arrivals of new Asian immigrants, who tend to be poor, also pushed down their median wealth.

Across all race and ethnic groups, the wealth gap between rich and poor widened. The share of wealth held by the top 10 percent of U.S. households increased from 49 percent in 2005 to 56 percent in

2009. The threshold for entry into the wealthiest top 10 percent, however, dipped lower: from $646,327 in 2005 to $598,435.

The numbers are based on the Census Bureau's Survey of Income and Program Participation, which sampled more than 36,000 households on wealth from September-December 2009. Census first began publishing wealth data from this survey, broken down by race and ethnicity, in 1984.

The continuing struggle of Racial Injustice in America

Life is better for all races since the days of Jim Crow and segregation—but the socioeconomic status of blacks in America is still substantially less than that of whites. According to a 2010 study by the U.S. Census Bureau, African-American average per Capita is $18,054 against $28,502 for whites. This disparity is a dilemma, and we cannot just sit back and allow this to occur.

A new study by Brandies University shows blacks will never gain wealth parity with whites under the current economic system. The report recognizes the "powerful role of persistent discrimination in housing, credit and labor markets"—that is, the institutionally racist crimes of financial capital. Had the survey continued past 2007, the carnage of the great recession would have revealed even more dramatically the incredibly shrining nature of Black wealth in the current era.

Enemies of all colors and sly servants of the rich will use the news of the evaporation of African–American wealth to heap blame on Black "culture." This "shaming" strategy is designed to keep Blacks looking inward for the source of their woes, and to simultaneously despair of findings salvation in our capacity for group agency. Meanwhile, the Lords of Capital devour us like piranhas-quicker than the well to do whites, who are padded with the fat of relative privilege—$95,000 worth of it, the racial wealth spread of 23 years.

Although Black parity with whites has never been on the horizon, impatient whites have insisted since 1969 or there about that "it's time" African Americans were made to "stand or fall" on their own, minus all the imagined assistance Blacks have supposedly received from phantom federal and state agencies. After all, say the anxious whites, how long is society (meaning themselves) supposed to pay for the slavery and segregation of the past? Most white folks believe, or pretend to believe, that whatever legitimate grievances Blacks might arbor against the United States stem from circumstances deep in the past. The only question is, when will blacks finally "get over it?"

"Blacks are preyed upon as a group by powerful (white) financial forces that profit from the wealth differential." The Brandies study shows that the racial wealth gap, although historically rooted in slavery and Jim Crow oppressions, has grown dramatically under post-civil rights era conditions. The gap is not simply a legacy of some ancient American apartheid, but a product of the recent past and of the present. This is a different paradigm, entirely, in which past racial wrongs are compounded by additional layers of institutionalized anti-black behavior in the 1980s, 90s, and in the 21st century-wounds so harmful they set African-Americans on a backward course in terms of wealth accumulation.

In 2004, United for a Fair Economy came out with the first of its annual "State of the Dream reports. Readers were shocked out of complacency by data that showed Blacks would not reach wealth parity with whites until the years 2099. It was surely a bummer to realize that no one then alive would see the "promised land" of evenly matched black and white median household wealth. But at least the study indicated that "we, as a people" would eventually get there, as someone famous once predicted. There are no such condolences in the Brandies data. At the rate Blacks have been falling behind in wealth since the mid-80s, the black and white median paths will diverge ever farther, never to connect under this system of economic and political rules.

Blacks cannot shop or invest or save or borrow our way to a just society. Social justice and true human equality can only be achieved through our collective political action in opposition to the current order-by any means necessary, as another famous man once urged. Racial injustice in America still occurs, and we are still quite far from Martin Luther King Jr.'s dream of racial equality. Let's be like King in the Montgomery Bus Boycotts—we must call our congressmen, senators, petition on the streets, and fight to improve the lives of every man, woman, and child in this country—no one should be left to fall by the wayside.

How Black Middle-Class Kids Become Poor Adults

Once they've grown up, African American children are more likely than their white counterparts to back slide into a lower economic group. When it comes to financial stability, black Americans are often in much more precarious financial situations than white Americans. Their unemployment rate is higher, and so is the level of poverty within the black community.

In 2013, the poverty rate among white Americans was 9.6 percent, among black Americans it was 27.2 percent. And the gap between the wealth of white families and black families has widened to its highest level since 1989, according to a 2014 study by Pew Research Center.

The facts of this rift aren't new, or all that surprising. But perhaps what's most unsettling about the current economic climate in black America is that when black families attain middle-class status, the likelihood that their children will remain there, or do better, isn't high.

"Even black Americans who make it to the middle class are likely to see their kids fall down the ladder," writes Richard Reeves, a senior fellow at the Brookings Institute. In a recent blog post Reeves says that seven out of 10 black children who are born to families with income that falls in the middle quintile of the income spectrum will find themselves with income that's' one to two quintiles below their parents' during their adulthood.

A 2014 study from the Federal Reserve Bank of Chicago, which looked at factors like parental income, education, and family structure, shows a similar pattern: Many black Americans not only fail to move up, but show an increased likelihood of backsliding. According to the study, "In recent decades, blacks have experienced substantially less upward intergenerational mobility and substantially more downward intergenerational mobility and substantially more downward intergenerational mobility than whites."

The greater probability of slipping back applies to blacks across income groups. According to the Fed study, about 60 percent black children whose parents had income that fell into the top 50 percent of the distribution saw their income fall into the bottom half during adulthood. This type of downward slide was common for only 36 percent of white children.

But the gap in mobility was significant for lower-class families as well. "For most of the bottom half of the income distribution, the racial differences in upward mobility are consistently between 20 and 30 percent," writes senior economist Bhashkar Mazumder, the study's author. "If future generations of white and black Americans experience the same rates of intergenerational mobility as these cohorts, we should expect to see that blacks on average would not make any relative progress."

The explanations for this phenomenon are varied, but largely hinge on many of the criticisms that already exist regarding socio-economies and race in the U.S. Economists cite lower educational attainment, higher rates of single-parent households, and geographic segregation as potential explanations for these trends. The latter determines not only what neighborhoods people live in, but often what types of schools children attend, which could play a role in hindering their educational and professional attainment later on. According to Reeves, "In terms of opportunity, there are still two Americas, divided by race." Still, most economists lack a clear, definitive explanation for why, after reaching the middle class, many black American families quickly loose that status as their children fall behind.

It's Still All about Race The Jena six

In the small town of Jena Louisiana, a black high school student requested the school's permission to sit beneath a broad, leafy tree in the hot schoolyard. Until then, only white students sat there. The next morning, three nooses were hanging from the tree. The black students responded en masse. Justin Purvis, the kid who first sat under the tree, told filmmaker Jacquie Soohen: "They said, 'Y'all want to go stand under? 'We said 'yeah! They said, if you go, I'll go. If you go, I'll go! One person went, the next person went, and everybody else just went."

Then the police and the district attorney showed up. Substitute teacher Michelle Rogers recounts: "District Attorney Reed Walters proceeded to tell those kids that 'I could end your lives with the stroke of a pen.' And the kids were just—it was like in awe at what the District Attorney said.

A series of incidents followed throughout the fall. In October, a black Student was beaten for entering a private all-white party. Later that month, a white student pulled a gun on a group of black student at a gas station, claiming self-defense. The black students wrestled the gun away and reported the incident to police. They were charged with assault and robbery of the gun. No charges were ever filed against the white students in either incident.

Then, in late November, someone tried to burn down the high school, creating even more tension.

Four days later, a white student was allegedly attacked in a school fight. The victim was taken to hospital and released shortly with concussion. He attended a school function that evening. Six black students were charged with attempted second-degree murder and conspiracy to commit murder, on charges that leave them facing between 20 and 100 years in jail. The defendants, ranging in age 15 to 17, had their bonds set at between $70,000 and $138,000.

The attack was written up in the local paper as fact, and DA Reed Walters published a statement in which he said, "When you are convicted, I will seek the maximum penalty allowed by law."

Elena Kagan Confirmation

Kagan, as is well known by now, clerked for Justice Thurgood Marshall, the Supreme Court's first African-American. There is no statute of limitations on the kind of attacks Marshall endured in life, and which continue seventeen years after his death. At the first day of Kagan's hearing, the Republicans seemed bent on projecting Kagan as Marshall's clone, one that would follow his "activist" judicial philosophy. Sen. John Kyl (R-AZ) laid the cards clearly on the table when he charged that "too often, it sounds to me like Ms. Kagan shares the view of President Obama and Justice [Thurgood] Marshall that the Supreme Court exists to advance the agenda of certain classes of litigants." He insisted that Kagan had the burden to demonstrate she can be "a fair and impartial justice, rather than one who would have an outcome-based approach."

Kyl and fellow Republicans Sens. Jefferson Beauregard Sessions (R-AL), Charles Grassley (R-IA), John Cornyn (R-TX), and Orrin Hatch (R-UT) invoked Marshall's name nearly forty times in two days, nearly three times more than President Obama's. They repeatedly referenced Marshall's judicial philosophy as "evidence" of Kagan's intentions. Sessions, the ranking member of the Committee, made it clear, calling Marshall "a well-Known activist." The Republicans offered no examples of how Marshall's rulings twisted the Constitution to achieve that sinister-sounding "outcome-based approach."

After the first day of hearings, a Utah newspaper asked Hatch if he would have voted for Marshall when his confirmation came up in 1967. "Well, it's hard to say," Hatch replied. Hatch projects himself as an ordinary fellow with an upright Mormon world view, and the Senate's moral voice. Some moral voice. Had Hatch opposed Marshall's confirmation in 1967, he would have had had interesting bedfellows for 10 steadfast segregationists rejected Marshall, joined by one newly-minted future of the Republican party— the never-repentant J. Strom Thurmond. There are two contexts here: the present moment of Kagan's hearing, and the historical one of Marshall's travail in is confirmation hearings.

Kagan appeared with impeccable credentials, and with smarts and savvy for running essentially a seminar with the senators. Robert Bork foolishly tried to take the lecture senators as if he were in a classroom, but only succeeded in alienation them. Kagan not only demonstrated a learned and supple mind, she showed herself to be a very human, warm individual, with a sense of humor that provided a few spontaneous moments. So, why the Republican hostility? Their not-so-subtle uses of the Marshall analogy amounted to stump speeches for the electorate back home. The senators well know their constituents' hostility toward President Obama has powerful racial overtones tat fuel the public anger so calculated for the evening television news. The Thurgood Marshall references amounted to a purposeful, well-orchestrated strategy to fire up the "base."

Deja vu all over. Nearly fifty years ago, President John F. Kennedy nominated Marshall to the Second Circuit of Appeals. Marshall came to the judiciary with an enviable record in his appearances as an advocate before the Supreme Court, winning 29 of 32 cases. He certainly did advance the "agenda of certain classes of litigants"—specifically, African–Americans determined to lift the burden of a century of formal segregation, and the national system of racial discrimination.

Marshall unique confirmation proceedings amply demonstrated the new racial component on national politics. Kennedy offered a district judgeship, but Marshall insisted on the appellate court. Robert Kennedy feared antagonizing powerful southern senators, notably Judiciary Committee Chairman, James Eastland (D-MS), but the President overruled him. Eastland indeed held the nomination until Kennedy made a recess appointment. Eastland's racism was of another era. He told President Johnson that the three missing civil rights workers in Mississippi were in Chicago; their disappearance, he insisted was a "publicity stunt." Johnson dismissed the Mississippian, saying he "could be standing right in the middle of the worst Mississippi flood ever known and he'd say the niggers caused it, helped out by the Communists."

Johnson chose Marshall Solicitor General in 1965, and his Supreme Court nomination followed in two years—not unlike the career path of Kagan. Marshall not only was the first African-American appointed to the High Court, but he also became subjected to extraordinary confirmation procedures. First, the hearings were held off for 78 days—highly unusual at the time. Most hearings began within a week of the nomination. Byron White, President Kennedy's first candidate for the Court, had been nominated and confirmed within eight days only three years earlier. Abe Fortas, President Johnson's first, had to wait only fourteen days. From the outset of the process, Marshall was different. The FBI, as well as Committee investigators, probed deep into Marshall's life—his legal career, is drinking, and marital infidelities. Former Ku Klux Klan member Sen. Robert Byrd (D-WV) asked J. Edgar Hoover about Marshall's links to Communists.

Strom Thurmond, who since 1948 never endorsed a Democratic presidential candidate, and whose party shift foreshadowed the political realignment of the South, harassed—there is no other word—Marshall with obscure historical questions. Who were the authors of the Fourteenth Amendment, he wanted to know. In a day before nominees were briefed to the point of knowing everything, Marshall honestly said he did not know. "Stupid guy," growled

Thurmond. Sen., Edward Kennedy (D-MA) then asked Thurmond to name the committee members. "I'll let you know," Thurmond grumbled.

The Republican party of 1967 was a different country. Then, 32 Republicans across their political spectrum from Jacob Javits (NY) to Roman Hruska (NB), and led by the ultimate maestro of minority maneuvering, Everett Dirksen (IL), joined 37 Democrats. Whose side would you have been on again, Senator Hatch?

Irony abounds. The noted civil libertarian Justice Hugo Black, a former Klansman, Senator from Alabama, and night court judge in Birmingham, presided at Marshall's swearing-ceremony. Four decades later, President Barack Obama delivered the eulogy for former Klansman, Robert Byrd.

Richard Nixon and his political handlers gave us his "Southern Strategy" to solidify Republican gains in the South. Strom Thurmond was his go-too man, and the President gave him two unsuccessful nominations (Clement Haynesworth and Harrold Carswell) to the Supreme Court. Just two decades earlier, President Dwight Eisenhower selected moderate Republicans for the southern federal courts in the 1950s, and they figured prominently in the civil rights revolution, aiding and abetting the Supreme Court from below. That Republican Party in the South is extinct.

For now, race remains a huge factor in Republican political strategy. Blacks may vote in southern states, but they cannot yet command consistent majorities, except in local races. Certainly the not-so-subtle racism of today's southern senators can exist only because Black political power is so fragmented and ineffective in the South. As southern Democrats wagged their party's tail for nearly a century, so now the Republican's southern base dictates their national strategy. Some believed Obama's election signaled the advent of a "post-racial "America; but not for now.

White House Blast GOP over Loretta Lynch

Loretta Lynch, born on May 21, 1959, in Greensboro, North Carolina. She went on to earn her degree from Harvard Law School. She worked as a litigator for a private law firm before becoming a prosecutor for the U.S. Attorney's office in New York's Eastern District, eventually making news as a senior prosecutor for the infamous 1997 Abner Louima police-brutality case. She served as U.S. Attorney under the administration of President Bill Clinton and Barack Obama, and in 2014 was nominated by President Obama to be U.S. attorney general, succeeding Eric Holder.

While the Senate Judiciary Committee approved Lynch's nomination by a vote of 12 to 8 in February 2015, the subsequent vote to be held by the overall Senate, with a republican majority was stalled for weeks. Republican Senator Mitch McConnell announced a delay Lynch's potential confirmation due to the parameters of an unrelated human trafficking bill waiting for approval.

With the vote taking more than five months to be held, both the presidential office and media pundits have expressed outrage.

President Obama implored the Senate to approve his nominee for Attorney General on Friday 04/17/2015, calling Loretta Lynch's confirmation process "crazy" and "embarrassing."

"What are we doing here?" Obama said in a tone at once animated and exasperated. "There is no reason for it. Nobody can describe a reason for it beyond political gamesmanship in the Senate, on an issue that's completely unrelated to her," Obama said.

"And I have to say, there are times where the dysfunction in the Senate just goes too far. This is an example of it. It's gone too far. Enough, Enough, Call Loretta Lynch for a vote. Get her confirmed. Put her in place. Let her do her job. This is embarrassing, a process like this," Obama said.

The Lynch nomination is bogged down in a debate over a human trafficking bill. Senate Republican leaders say they will vote on Lynch after Democrats lift their objections to the bill, which carries a long-standing amendment prohibiting the use of tax payer funding for abortion.

"It was Lynch or judges," said Beth Levine, a Grassley spokeswoman. "They chose judges." But Obama noted that the Lynch nomination has already been confirmed twice before by the Senate for U.S. Attorney in New York, and has now waited twice as long as the previous seven attorney general nominees combined.

Obama recited a litany of Lynch's qualifications, saying she had prosecuted terrorists and street gangs, had the support of civil rights and police groups, and was a good manager. "Nobody suggests otherwise," he said.

Senate Majority Leader Mitch McConnell (R-Ky.) is delaying the full-Senate vote until the law makers resolve the abortion issue in the trafficking bill.

Meanwhile promotions and policy decisions of the Justice Department have been put off. Announcements have slowed to a trickle. Congress is waiting for input on the agency's budget priorities.

The U.S. Senate voted on Thursday to approve Loretta Lynch as President Barack Obama's next attorney general ending a five-month deadlock that made Lynch wait longer for confirmation. The first black woman to become the top U.S. law enforcement official, Lynch, 55, was approved 56-43 vote. Ten Republicans voted for Lynch, including Senate Majority Leader Mitch McConnell. She is expected to take over as head of the U.S. Justice Department on Monday replacing Eric Holder.

The voting margin reflected many Republican's disapproval of Lynch's support for an executive order issued by Obama in November that was meant to shield millions of undocumented immigrants from the threat of deportation.

As attorney general, her earliest test will likely include handling civil rights cases stemming from deadly altercations between police and unarmed black men in several U.S. Cities. Lynch will also inherit major financial cases involving allegations that some of the world's largest banks helped clients evade U.S. taxes and manipulated the currency markets.

U.S. government considered Nelson Mandela a terrorist until 2008

Nelson Mandela is being remembered across the world for his heroic, life-long battle against apartheid and injustice in South Africa. As late as 2008, the Nobel Prize winner and former president was still on the U.S. terrorism watch list.

The apartheid regime had supported the U.S. during the Cold War and had worked closely with both the Reagan and Nixon administration to limit Soviet influence in the region.

The African National Congress, which Mandela chaired, was peppered with members of the South African Communist Party. This complicated the administration's take on South Africa. Reagan accuse the ANC of encouraging communism in a 1986 policy speech, and to rule that South Africa had no obligation to negotiate with a group bent on "creating a communist state."

After the apartheid regime in South Africa declared the ANC a terrorist group, the Reagan administration followed suit. In August of 1988, the State Department listed the ANC among "organizations that engage in terrorism." It said the group "disavows a strategy that deliberately targets civilians," but noted that civilians had "been victims of incidents claimed by or attributed to the ANC."

Five months later, in January 1989, the Defense Department included the ANC in an official publication, "Terrorist Group Profiles," with a foreword by President-elect George H.W. Bush. The ANC was listed among 52 of the "world's more notorious terrorist groups." (One of the others listed, Yasser Arafat's Fatah, is now the ruling party in the West Bank.)

The publication referred to Mandela, who had once led the ANC's military wing, as part of the "leadership," though by then he had spent more than a quarter century in prison. It also accepted the apartheid regime's claim that "ANC's operations—which heretofore had sought to avoid civilian casualties—abruptly changed. Attacks became more indiscriminate, resulting in both black and white civilian victims." Five months before the report was issued, the ANC had taken responsibility for some attacks that resulted in civilian deaths but had pledged to prevent a recurrence.

The report cited 13 attacks during the 1980s, many of which targeted government facilities, including a military command headquarters, and unfinished nuclear plant, a courthouse and SASOL, the government-owned coal-to-oil conversion facility.

Of those incidents that resulted in deaths, the biggest was a car-bombing of the South African Air Force headquarters in Pretoria that killed 19 and wounded 200.

The report also claimed significant links between the ANC and Communist countries, noting that the ANC "receives support from the Soviet Bloc, Cuba and several African nations in addition to contributions from the West." The DOD report added that the ANC received many of its weapons from the "Soviet Bloc" and listed among its "political objectives" the establishment of a "multiracial Socialist government in South Africa."

But the Defense Department stood by its language, and Mandela and other ANC officials remained on the terror list even as President Bush welcomed Mandela, newly released from prison, to the White House in 1990. Because of what was described as a "bureaucratic snafu," their names were kept on the list until 2008; 14 years after Mandela had been elected president and nine years after he had left power. He was 90 at the time.

The terrorist designation finally proved too embarrassing for the U.S. government to ignore. In April 2008, during the last year of the George W. Bush administration, Secretary of State Condoleezza Rice told a Senate committee that her department had to issue waivers for ANC members to travel to the United States.

"This is a country with which we now have excellent relations, South Africa, but it's frankly a rather embarrassing matter that I still have to waive in my counterpart, the foreign minister of South Africa, not to mention the great leader Nelson Mandela, "Rice said. Later that year, the terrorist designation was dropped after a bill, proposed by then-Senator now secretary of State John Kerry, passed both houses of Congress and was signed by President Bush.

Mandela was imprisoned in1964after being arrested and charged with sabotage, specifically a campaign against the country's power grid, and plotting to overthrow the government. No one was injured in the sabotage campaign. He was released in 1990, at age 71. He was elected president of South Africa in 1994, in the country's first full and free elections, and served until 1999.

The Tuskegee Syphilis Experiment

The U.S. government's 40-year experiment on black men with syphilis

On May 16, 1997, President Clinton formally apologized and held a ceremony at the White House for the eight remaining surviving Tuskegee study participants. He said: "what was done cannot be undone. But we can end the silence. We can look you in the eye and finally say on behalf of the American people, what the United States government did was shameful and I am sorry... To our African American citizens, I am sorry that your federal government orchestrated a study so clearly racist."

This was an infamous clinical study conducted between 1932 and 1972 by the U.S. Public Health Service. The purpose of this study was to observe the natural progression of untreated syphilis in rural African-American men in Alabama under the guise of receiving free health care from the U.S. government.

These men, for the most part illiterate share-croppers from one of the poorest counties in Alabama, were never told what disease they were suffering from or of its seriousness. Informed that they were being treated for "bad blood", a local term for various illnesses that include syphilis, anemia, and fatigue.

The data for the experiment was to be collected from autopsies of the men, and they were thus deliberately left to degenerate under the ravages of tertiary syphilis…which can include tumors, heart disease, paralysis, blindness, insanity, and death. "As I see it," one of the doctors involved explained, "we have no further interest in these patients until they die."

Using Human Beings as Laboratory Animals

The true nature of the experiment had to be kept from the subjects to ensure their cooperation. The sharecroppers' grossly disadvantaged lot in life made them easy to manipulate. Pleased at the prospect of free medical care—almost none of them had ever seen a doctor before—these unsophisticated and trusting men became the pawns in what James Jones, author of the excellent history on the subject, *Bad Blood*, identified as "the longest nontherapeutic experiment on human beings in medical history."

The study was meant to discover how syphilis affected blacks as opposed to whites—the theory being that whites experienced more neurological complications from syphilis, whereas blacks were more susceptible to cardiovascular damage. How this knowledge would have changed clinical treatment of syphilis is uncertain.

Although the PHS touted the study as one of great scientific merit, from the outset its actual benefits were hazy. It took almost forty years before someone involved in the study took a hard and honest look at the results, reporting that "nothing learned will prevent, find, or cure a single case of infectious syphilis or bring us closer to our basic mission of controlling venereal disease in the United States."

When the experiment was brought to the attention of the media in 1972, news anchor Harry Reasoner described it as an experiment that "used human beings as laboratory animals in a long and inefficient study of how long it takes syphilis to kill someone."

A Heavy Price in the Name of Bad Science

The 40-year study was controversial for reasons related to ethical standards. Researchers knowingly failed to treat patients appropriately after the 1940s validation of penicillin was found as an effective cure for the disease they were studying.

By 1947, penicillin had become the standard treatment for syphilis. Choices available to the doctors involved in the study might have included treating all syphilitic subjects and closing the study, or splitting of a control group for testing with penicillin. Instead, the Tuskegee scientists continued the study without treating any participants; they withheld penicillin and information about it from the patients. Also, scientists prevented participants from accessing syphilis treatment programs available to other residents in the area. The study continued, under numerous U.S. Public Health Service supervisors, until 1972, when a leak to the press resulted in its termination on November 16th of that year.

The victims of the study, all African American included numerous men who died of syphilis, 40 wives who contracted the disease and 19 children born with congenital syphilis. How had these men been induced to endure a fatal disease in the name of science?

To persuade the community to support the experiment, one of the original doctors admitted it "was necessary to carry on this study under the guise of a demonstration and provide treatment." At first the men were prescribed the syphilis remedies of the day—bismuth, neoarsphenamine, and mercury—but in such small amounts that only 3 percent showed any improvement.

These token doses of medicine were good public relations and did not interfere with the true aims of the study. Eventually, all syphilis treatment was replaced with "pink medicine"—aspirin.

To ensure that the men would show up for a painful and potentially dangerous spinal tap, the PHS doctors misled them with a letter full of promotional hype: "Last Chance for Special Free Treatment." The fact that autopsies would eventually be required was also concealed.

As a doctor explained, "If the colored population becomes aware that accepting free hospital care means a post-mortem, every dark will leave Macon County…" Even the Surgeon General of the United States participated in enticing the men to remain in the experiment, sending them certificates of appreciation after 25 years in the study.

Following Doctors' Orders

It takes little imagination to ascribe racist attitudes to the white government officials who ran the experiment, but what can one make of the numerous African Americans who collaborated with them? The experiment's name comes from the <u>Tuskegee Institute,</u> the black university founded by <u>Booker T. Washington.</u> Its affiliated hospital lent the PHS its medical facilities for the study, and other predominantly black institutions as well as local black doctors also participated. A black nurse, Eunice Rivers Laurie was a central figure in the experiment for most of its forty years.

Eunice Rivers Laurie was the African American nurse the USPHS hired to recruit the 399 black men in the county infected with syphilis and keep in the study while they went untreated for four decades.

Laurie was selected because she was African American and could use her standing in the community to gain the participants! Trust. She gave the men special treatment and they trusted her. The participants were told they had "bad blood" and promised free health care. The study was supposed to last three months, but the USPHS continued work and kept Laurie on to keep track of the participants and encourage them to stay in the study.

The promise of recognition by a prestigious government agency may have obscured the troubling aspects of the study for some. A Tuskegee doctor, for example, praised "the educational advantages offered our interns and nurses as well as the added standing it will give the hospital. "Nurse Rivers explained her role as one of passive obedience: "we were taught that we never diagnosed, we never prescribed; we followed the doctor's instructions!"

During World War II, 250 of the men registered for the draft and were consequently ordered to get treatment for syphilis, only to have the PHS exempt them. Pleased at their success, the PHS representative announced: "So far, we are keeping the known positive patients from getting treatment." The experiment continued despite the Henderson

Act (1943), a public health law requiring testing and treatment for venereal disease, and despite the World Health Organization's Declaration of Helsinki (1964), which specified that "inform consent" was needed for experiments involving human beings.

Blowing the Whistle

In 1966 Peter Buxtun, a PHS venereal-disease investigator in San Francisco, sent a letter to the national director of the Division of Venereal Diseases to express his concerns about the ethics and morality of the extended Tuskegee Study. The Center for Disease Control (CDC) which by then controlled the study, reaffirmed the need to continue the study until completion; i.e., until all subjects had died and been autopsied.

Buxtun finally went to the press in early 1970s. The story finally broke in the Washington Star on July 25, 1972. Senator Edward Kennedy called congressional hearings, at which Buxtun and HEW officials testified. The study was terminated.

The PHS, however, remained unrepentant, claiming the men had been "volunteers" and "were always happy to see the doctors," and an Alabama state health officer who had been involved claimed "somebody is trying to make a mountain out of a molehill."

As part of the settlement of a class action lawsuit subsequently filed by the NAACP of behalf study participants and their decendants, the U.S. government paid $10 million and agreed to provide free medical treatment to surviving participants and surviving family members infected as a consequence of the study.

The Legacy of Tuskegee

In 1990, a survey found that 10 percent of African Americans believed that the U.S. government created <u>AIDS</u> as a plot to exterminate blacks, and another 20 percent could not rule out the possibility that this might be true. As preposterous and paranoid as this may sound, at one time the Tuskegee experiment must have seemed equally farfetched.

Who could imagine the government, all the way up to the Surgeon General of the United States, deliberately allowing a group of its citizens to die from a terrible disease for the sake of an ill-conceived experiment? In light of this and many other shameful episodes in our history, African Americans' widespread mistrust of the government and white society in general should not be a surprise to anyone.

US apologizes for 1940s STD study in Guatemala

The U.S. government-funded experiment which ran from 1946 to 1948, was discovered by a Wellesley College medical historian. It was conducted to test if penicillin, then relatively new, could prevent infection with sexually transmitted diseases. The study came up with no useful information and was hidden for decades.

The government researcher who led the work in Guatemala also was involved in this country's infamous Tuskegee experiment.

"We are outraged that such reprehensible research could have occurred under the guise of public health," Secretary of State Hillary Rodham Clinton and Health and Human Services Secretary Kathleen Sebelius said of the Guatemalan project.

White House press secretary Robert Gibbs said President Barack Obama had been briefed about the situation and planned to call Guatemala's president, Alvaro Colom. "This is shocking, it's tragic, it's reprehensible," Gibbs said. "It's tragic and the U.S. by all means apologizes to all those who were impacted." Strict regulations today make clear that it is unethical to experiment on people without their consent and require special steps for any work with such vulnerable populations as prisoners. But such regulations didn't exist in the 1940s.

The U.S. government ordered two independent investigations to uncover exactly what happened in Guatemala and to make sure current bioethics rules are adequate. They will be led by the prestigious Institute of Medicine and the Presidential Commission for the Study of Bioethical Issues. And while deliberately trying to infect people with serious diseases is abhorrent today, the Guatemalan experiment isn't the only example from what National Institutes of Health Director Dr. Francis Collins on Friday called "a dark chapter in the history of medicine." Forty similar deliberate-infection studies were conducted in the United States during that period, Collins said.

In Guatemala, 696 men and women were exposed to syphilis or in some cases gonorrhea, through jail visits by prostitutes or, when that didn't infect enough people, by deliberately inoculating them, reported Wellesley College historian Susan Reverby. Those who were infected were all offered penicillin, but it wasn't clear how many were infected and how many were successfully treated. She reported that the U.S. had gained permission from Guatemalan officials to conduct the study, but did not inform the experimental subjects.

Reverby's work was first reported by NBC News. She uncovered the records of Dr. John Cutler, a prominent government scientist of the 1940s, while researching the Tuskegee experiment for a recent book. She posted on her website a copy of an article about the findings that is to be published in January in an academic journal. A speech she gave on her findings last spring alerted government health officials to her findings, resulting in Friday's apology.

Ala. Leaders apologize for handling of 1944 rape

Nearly 70 years after she was raped by a gang of white men, Recy Taylor got an apology Monday from leaders of a rural southeast Alabama community who acknowledged that her attackers escaped prosecution because of racism and an investigation bungled by police. "It is apparent that the system failed you in 1944, "Henry County probate judge and commission chairwoman Joann Smith told several of Taylor's relatives at a news conference at the county courthouse.

Taylor's case has been a symbol of the sexual violence black women suffered for decades. The Alabama Senate joined the state House in passing a resolution for an official State apology to Recy Taylor, 91, who was raped by seven white men in Abbeville, Ala., in 1944.

Taylor's case has for decades lingered as an icon of the sexual violence black women suffered from white men in the South. At the time, her case became a rallying point for a movement to end impunity for that violence.

Today, Federal law enforcement officials have reopened dozens of civil rights era murders, but have not revisited the rapes and sexual assaults that went un-prosecuted. Taylor who is now in her 90's said through her brother "that she wants apologies from the state and from the County and City where the rape occurred and was covered up.

In 1944, in the face of a state investigation, the Henry County sheriff and an Abbeville policeman took part in covering up the rape.

"What happened to my sister way back then… couldn't happen today," Robert Corbitt said. "Boy, what a mess they made out of it. They tried to make her look like a whore and she was a Christian lady." Taylor was 24, married and living in her native Henry County when she was gang-raped in Abbeville. She was walking home from church when she was abducted, assaulted and left on the side of the road in an isolated area.

Taylor's story, along with those of other black women attacked by white men during the civil rights era, is told in "At the Dark End of the Street," a book by Danielle McGuire released last year. McGuire said Monday she would eventually like to see more formal apologies from the state, city and county, but views the statements from officials, prompted by publicity about her book, as a good first step." The fact that they are acknowledging that this happened is important," said McGuire, a history professor at Wayne State University in Detroit.

The case got the attention of NAACP activist Rosa Parks in the 1940s, a decade before she became an icon by refusing to give up her seat on a Montgomery city bus. Parks interviewed Taylor in 1944 and later recruited other activists to create the "Alabama Committee for Equal Justice for Mrs. Recy Taylor." Those efforts were later overshadowed by other civil rights battles. Corbitt said he felt like his sister's case was forgotten until he started doing some research several years ago and found out about the work that McGuire was doing. Mayor Ryan Blalock, who was among those apologizing Monday, said he had not heard about the case until recently.

"It felt good that the mayor said he is sorry about it," Corbitt said. Blalock got emotional when he told Taylor's family that Abbeville is now a good place to live and that white people and black people respect each other and work and play together. "My 8-year-old son has as many black friends as he does white friends," said Blalock, who is white. "They are welcome at our place and he is welcome in their homes."

15

Political Corruption of America

The link between welfare, education, crime and politics

On January 8, 1964, during his State of the Union address President Johnson introduces legislation to fight poverty. Congress passes the Economic Opportunity Act, which established the Office of Economic Opportunity (OEO) to administer the local application of Federal funds targeted against poverty.

Johnson believed in expanding the federal government's roles in education and health care as poverty reduction strategies.

Johnson claimed that his programs would bring to an end the "conditions that breed despair and violence," those being "ignorance, discriminations, slums, poverty, disease, not enough jobs."

He was concern with the high rate of black poverty. He felt the problems plaguing black Americans could not be solved by self-help.

From 1965 to 2008, nearly $16 trillion of taxpayer money was spent on means—tested welfare programs for the poor.

Many whites viewed Great Society programs as supporting the economic and social needs of low-income urban minorities. It effectively subsidized the dissolution of the black family by rendering the black man's role as a husband and a father irrelevant, invisible and disposable. Several generations of blacks born into broken homes and broken communities experiencing social, moral and economic chaos. Some of the major disasters that plaguing minority communities including drugs, higher incarceration rates and a rise in unwed mothers.

But besides the soaring rhetoric, besides the promise of a "chicken in every pot," what have these programs achieved? The wholesale destruction of urban communities across America, communities that are overwhelmingly African American. If these programs had intended to destroy black communities, you could have hardly done more damage than the last 50 plus years of Democratic policy.

According to the NAACP, Texas taxpayers spent $175 million in 2009 to imprison residents from a small part of Houston-only 10 zip codes out of 75. Thus, people from neighborhoods that are home to only about 10% of the city's population account for more than 33% of the state's entire $500 million annual prison spending. These neighborhoods are overwhelmingly poor African Americans.

In Pennsylvania, taxpayers will spend $290 million in 2009 to imprison residents from just 11 of Philadelphia's neighborhoods, representing about 25% of the city population. On this relatively small urban area, the state will spend roughly half its $500 million prison budget. These neighborhoods are overwhelmingly poor and African American.

In New York, taxpayers will spend $539 million to imprison residents from only 24 of New York City's 200 different neighborhoods. Only 16% of the City's population lives in these areas, but they will account for nearly half of the state's $1.1 billion prison budget. These neighborhoods are overwhelming poor and African American.

America has many problems…but these neighborhoods represent more than a society in decline. **Life in these places reflects a complete collapse of Western Civilization.** What's happening in these communities? A breakdown of the family and the resulting collapse of the school system.

What you have left is crime—violent and political.

In Detroit, only 27% of the black male students in the school system graduate from these same schools. What's causing this problem? A complete breakdown of society. When communities can no longer teach their children the most basic academic skills, such as reading, math, history literature, and economics…what future can we expect? And what kind of society do you expect after several generations of total ignorance?

These problems are still found primarily in urban areas, but they are spreading across the country. In Pinellas County, Florida, only 21% of black male students graduate from high school. In Palm Beach County, Florida, you can find a similar number. Likewise Duval County, Florida…and Jefferson Parish, Louisiana…and Charleston County, South Carolina. In Nebraska, only 40% of black male students graduate from high school. In Nevada, only 45%. In New York State, only 25%.

What opportunities are available in America to people without even a basic education? The New York Times reports almost 70% of black males without a high school diploma are unemployed in the United States. In many predominantly black, urban communities, the actual unemployment rate is close to 100% for young dropouts. Given these figures, it isn't surprising that many of these people end up in jail. These are the two primary reasons nearly one in 11 adult black men are either in jail or on parole. How did this all happen? How did we end up with expensive schools that can't teach? How did we end up with young mothers who aren't married? How did we end up with entire generations of people who won't—and probably can't—work in the labor force? How did we end up with a skyrocketing prison population? The prison population in America has soared from less than half a million people in 1980 to more than 2.5 million people today. More than 7 million adults are in prison or on parole in the United States. We have an incarceration rate that's seven times higher than any other industrialized nation.

The land of the free?

Let's ask the most basic question: what has the gigantic increase in welfare spending and education spending done for the underclass of America? It seems apparent that growth in federal spending has caused far more harm than good. When you study these neighborhoods, what you find is a horrifying story that's been repeated, generation after generation since the early 1960s. It's a story of families who have been destroyed by their dependency on the state.

As provisions in welfare laws offered ever—increasing economic incentives for shunning marriage and avoiding the formation of two-parent families, illegitimacy rates rose dramatically. A mother generally received far more money from welfare if she was single rather than married. Once she took a husband, her benefits were instantly reduced by roughly 10 to 20 percent.

The truly extraordinary part is that all these things happened after these neighborhoods began voting and electing their own (typically black and Democratic) leadership. The socialism they voted for themselves led most directly to the destruction of their communities. It was their mayors, ward leaders, and congressmen who chose this path for these communities.

Welfare policies pushed by liberal do-gooders have created a perpetual dependent class—good for winning elections but bad for the overall health of black families.

Welfare has led to the disintegration of the black family similar to how slavery affected the black family structure. Welfare family disintegration is worse than slavery because politicians and so-called black leaders believe that welfare is a right that is due blacks because of slavery. The welfare has done more to harm poor people than slavery ever did.

None of this is to indict all blacks. There is a developing black middle and upper class in the United States. Their rise came about despite economic hardships, prejudice, bigotry, and outright racism. They didn't use these as excuses to explain failure in the black community. They fought against it.

How socialism came to America... and destroyed Detroit.

Louis C. Miriani was an American politician who served as Mayor of Detroit, Michigan (1957-62) He was the last republican mayor of Detroit. He was best known for completing many of the large-scale urban renewal projects financed by federal money. He was convicted of federal tax evasion.

Jerome Cavanagh became mayor in 1961 largely by African-American support. Cavanagh criticized Miriani's handling of Detroit's financial affairs and race relations with the city's African-American Community. Many in the black community believed Miriani condoned police brutality. On election-day, black voters turned out in force to defeat Miriani. Seeing the political advantage to serving this community's interests, he did all he could to bring government benefits and government spending to Detroit's black community.

He installed aggressive affirmative action policies at City Hall. And most critically, he greatly expanded the role of the government in Detroit, taking advantage of President Lyndon Johnson's "Model Cities Program"—the first great experiment in centralized urban planning.

Mayor Cavanagh was the only elected official to serve on Johnson's task force, and Detroit received wide spread acclaim for its leadership in the program, which attempted to turn nine-square-mile section of the city (with 134,000 inhabitants) into a model city.

More than $400 million was spent trying to turn inner cities into shining new monuments to government planning. In short, the feds and democratic city mayors were soon telling people where to live, what to build, and what businesses to open or close. In return, the people received cash, training, education and health care.

Unfortunately, as with all socialist programs, lots of folks simply don't like being told what to do.

Lots of folks don't like being plundered by the government. They don't like losing their jobs because of their race.

In Detroit, they didn't like paying new, large taxes to fund a largely black and democratic political hegemony. And so, in 1966, more than 22,000 middle- and upper-class residents moved out of the city.

In July 1967, police attempted to break up a late-night party in the middle of the new "Model City." The scene turned into the worst race riot of the 1960s. The violence killed more than 40 people and left more than 5,000 people homeless. One of the first stores to be looted was the black-owned pharmacy. The largest black-owned clothing store in the city was also burned to the ground.

On this particular night, at this particular club, the community was celebrating the return of two Vietnam War veterans. More than 80 people had packed into the club. The police decided to arrest everyone present, including the two war vets. This outraged the entire neighborhood, which began to riot.

Mayor Cavanagh didn't do anything to stop the riots, fearing a large police presence would make matters worse. Five days later, President Johnson sent in two divisions of paratroopers to put down the insurrection.

The situation destabilized the entire city. Most of the people who could afford to leave did. Over the next 18 months, 140,000 upper- and middle-class residents—almost all of them white—left the city.

And so, you might ask…after five years of centralized planning, higher taxes, and a fleeing population, what did the government decide to do with its grand experiment? You'll never guess.

Seeing it had accomplished nothing but failure. The government expanded the Model City program with 1974's Community Development Block Grant Program. Here again, politicians would decide which groups (and even individuals) would receive state funds for various "renewal" schemes. Later, big business was brought into the fold. In exchange for various concessions, the Big Three automakers "gave" $488 million to the city for use in still more redevelopment schemes in the mid-1990s.

What happened? Even with all of their power and all of the money, centralized planners couldn't succeed with any of their plans. Nearly all of the upper- and middle-class citizens left Detroit. The poor fled, too. The Model City area lost 63% of its population and 45% of its housing units from the inception of the program through 1990.

Even today, the crisis continues. At a recent auction of nearly 9,000 seized homes and lots, less than one-fifth of the available properties sold, even with bidding starting at $500. You literally can't give away most of the property in Model City areas today. The properties put up for sale represented an area the size of New York's Central Park. Total vacant land in Detroit now occupies an area the size of Boston. Detroit properties in foreclosure have more than tripled since 2007.

None of this is surprising. It's exactly what you'd expect to see given the implementation of a socialist scheme like a Model Cities' program. Quite simply, coercion doesn't work for economic development. You cannot tax yourself into prosperity. It might buy votes…but sooner or later the voters will realize all that's been promised was a lie. Won't they? Maybe not.

You see, the failure of the Model Cities program and of the War on Poverty wasn't surprising. What is surprising is that every single mayor of Detroit since 1961 has been a Democrat. And extremely liberal, black politicians have filled almost every major political office in the city since the mid-1960s. For example, John Conyers, Jr. has represented most of Detroit's worst neighborhoods since 1965. Today, Conyers is the second-longest serving congressman in the House. Conyers doesn't merely win all of his election campaigns. He wins by margins that aren't explainable in a normal, two-party system.

He defeated Republican Robert Blackwell in 1964, getting 84% of the vote. He was re-elected 13 times in a row from that district, all with a greater margin of victory than 85%. Ironically, the district was so ill-served by his socialistic policies that about half of the people moved away. The population losses led to redistricting. From then on, his margin of victory has fallen…to "only" around 80%. These election results don't seem reasonable, do they? They aren't. By controlling the state legislature in Michigan, the Democrats can draw the congressional districts in a way that guaranteed them almost permanent control. It's no different than what despots do all over the world. They hold an "election." But it's only for show.

And what do the Democrats do with this power? They push a form of American socialism. This political system features transfer payments, government jobs, and lucrative government contracts to voters in exchange for political support—and in many cases, outright bribes. They do all of these things under the cover of "progressive" politics and "social justice."

These kinds of people and their political philosophy have destroyed what was once America's fourth-largest city. There is almost nothing left of what was the capital of America's industrial heartland. It's not hard to understand what has happened. When you start taxing people at extremely progressive rates to pay for socialist "benefits".when you start telling them which schools their children must attend…when you start giving jobs away to people based on political patronage, race, or anything other than ability, you quash human freedom, you create dependency. And you deter capital and investment…which bogs down productivity and economic growth. If continued for long enough, it leads to social collapse.

Prison System

The United States is seen by social critics, including international and domestic human rights group and Civil Rights organizations, as a state that violates fundamental human rights, because of disproportionately heavy, in comparison with other countries, reliance on crime control, individual behavior control (civil liberties), and societal control of disadvantaged groups through a harsh police and criminal justice system. The U.S. penal system is implemented on the Federal, and in particular on the state and local levels. This social policy has resulted in a high rate of incarceration, which affects Americans from the lowest socioeconomic backgrounds and racial minorities the hardest.

Some have criticized the United States for having an extremely large prison population, where there have been reported abuses. As of 2004 the United States had the highest percentage of people in prison of any nation. There were more than 2.2 million in prisons or jails, or 737 per 100,000 population, or roughly, out of every 136 Americans. According to the National Council on Crime and Delinquency, since 1990 the incarceration of youth in adult jails has increased 208%. In some states youth-juveniles is defined as young as 13 years old. The researchers for this found that juveniles often were incarcerated to await trial for up to 2 years and subjected to the same treatment is often subjected to a highly traumatic environment during this development stage.

The long-term effects are often irreversible and detrimental.

"Human Rights Watch believes the extraordinary rate of incarceration in the United States wreaks havoc on individuals, families and communities, and saps the strength of the nation as a whole.

Police Brutality

Police brutality is one of several forms of police misconduct, which includes: false arrest, intimidation, racial profiling, political repression, surveillance abuse, sexual abuse, and police corruption. Although illegal, it can be performed under the color of law.

In March of 1991, members of the Los Angeles Police Department harshly beat an African American suspect, Rodney King. This led to extensive media coverage and criminal charges against several of the officers involved.

According to data released by the Bureau of Justice Statistics (2011), between 2003 and 2009 at least 4,813 people died in the process of being arrested by local police. Of the deaths classified as law enforcement homicides, 2,876 deaths occurred of which 1,643 or 57% of the people who died were "people of color."

Since 1999, at least 148 people have died in the United States and Canada after being shocked with tasers by police officers, according to a 2005 ACLU report.

In one case, a handcuffed suspect was tasered nine times by a police officer before dying, and six of those taserings occurred within less than three minutes. The officer was fired and faced the possibility of criminal charges.

Race in the United States Criminal Justice System

There have been different outcomes for different racial groups in convicting and sentencing in the United States criminal justice system. Experts and analysts have debated the relative importance of different factors that have led to these disparities. Minority defendants are charged with crimes requiring a mandatory minimum prison sentence more often, in both relative and absolute terms (depending on the classification of race, mainly in regards to Hispanics), leading to large racial disparities in incarceration.

Some argue that the decision to criminalize the use of drugs was driven by racial considerations. Cocaine was associated with African Americans, Opium was associated with Chinese Americans, and Marijuana was associated with Chicanos. The argument is based largely on the fact that these minority-linked drugs have the same potential for harm as other drugs that are not treated the same way by the criminal justice system or viewed the same way by the general public.

African American communities have a higher percentage of adult males behind bars. That means fewer fathers, grandfathers and mentors for young men to look up to. Without a stable father figure, young men are more likely to follow the paths of their father.

The "war on drugs" has traditionally targeted low-income, minority communities where many street dealers live instead of the often white and well to-do suppliers. A criminal record reduces one's opportunities for employment; thus, they are more likely to turn to crime again.

At the end of 2002 the Bureau of Justice released data stating there were 3,042 black male prisoners per 100,000 black males, 1,261 Hispanic male prisoners per 100,000 Hispanic males and 487 white male prisoners per 100,000 white males within the United States.

Likelihood of incarceration

The likelihood of black males going to prison in their lifetime is 28% compared to 4% for white males and 16% for Hispanic males. Some factors used to attempt to explain the racial disparities in the criminal justice system besides race itself include socioeconomic status, the environment in which a person was raised, and the highest educational level a person achieves.

For the Baby Boomers, some 1.2% of white men 9% of black men had been imprisoned by 2004, according to Bruce Western, a Harvard sociology professor. Out of those born in the 1970s, 3.3% of white men and 20.7% of black men had been in prison.

Most of the growth in incarceration rates is concentrated at the very bottom, among young men with very low levels of education. In 1980, around 10 percent of young African American men who dropped out of high school were in prison or jail. The significant growth of incarceration rates among the least educated reflects increasing class inequality in incarceration through the period of the prison boom.

In many urban neighborhoods where millions of dollars are spent to lock up residents, the education infrastructure is crippled. As the prison population skyrocketed in the past three decades, researchers began to notice that high concentrations of inmates were coming from a few selected neighborhoods. Primarily poor communities of color…in major cities.

Effect of race on likelihood of conviction

Various studies have shown that, in recent decades, there has been no noticeable disparity in black vs white conviction likelihood for those accused in black-run vs. white-controlled cities, say Atlanta vs San Diego. In the largest counties, the rates of prosecution for accused blacks was slightly less than the prosecution rates for whites, for example. "The only hint of racial disparity was to the advantage, not disadvantage, of blacks accused of crimes."

The Sixth Amendment to the U.S. Constitution establishes the right of a defendant charged with a crime to a trial by an impartial jury. The history of U.S. criminal justice is replete with cases where the abstract promise of jury impartiality has been called into question. Of special concern are settings where a minority member of a population is tried in a location in which few, if any, members of the same minority are likely to serve on the duty. This concern has arisen repeatedly in the context of race, as blacks generally constitute a small fraction of the population.

The proportion of blacks in the prison population is almost four times that in the general population. Evidence shows that: juries formed from all-white jury pools convict black defendants significantly more often than white defendants and this gap in conviction rates is eliminated when the jury pool includes at least black member.

The findings imply that the application of justice is highly uneven and raise obvious concerns about the fairness of trials in jurisdictions with a small proportion of blacks in the jury pool.

False imprisonment

False imprisonment is a growing problem throughout the U.S. When someone has been a victim of a false arrest chances are they have lost their job, their social status and reputation within the community. You must also consider the effects it has on a child or significant other. This can mean financial ruin for some families not to mention the mental effect it can have on their love ones.

False imprisonment is a violation of a person's most fundamental civil rights. Not only can false imprisonment result in physical injury, it can result in extreme trauma, humiliation, degradation and anxiety. It can lead to physical, emotional and psychological problems. When you are a victim of a false imprisonment you are entitled to seek money damages for your injuries and the violation of your legal rights.

In 1974 at the young age of 18, James Bain was arrested and later convicted of breaking, kidnapping and raping a nine-year old boy. He was sentenced to life in prison. After spending 35 years in prison, the court agreed to DNA testing, which proved that Bain couldn't have committed the rape. The state vacated his sentenced and at 54 years old, he found himself a free man.

The state of Florida awarded Bain a paltry $50,000 for each year he was incarcerated, which totaled $1.75 million. There are numerous cases where black men are being freed after decades of false imprisonment and have to be compensated by the states.

Race and the death penalty

Various scholars have addressed what they perceived as the systemic racial bias present in the administration of capital punishment in the United States. There is also a large disparity between races when it comes to sentencing convicts to Death Row. The federal death penalty data released by the United States Department of Justice between 1995-2000 shows that 682 defendants were sentenced to death. Out of those 682 defendants, the defendant was black in 48% of the cases, Hispanic in 29% of the cases, and white in 20% of the cases.

Racial bias has always been a significant issue in death penalty debates. There have been many careful statistical studies indicating that race plays a significant role in determining who lives and who dies. For example, a study released in 2003 by the University of Maryland concluded that race, along with geography, is an important factor in death penalty decisions in that state.

Prosecutors are more likely to seek the death penalty when the race of the victim is white and less likely when the race of the victim is African-American

Anthony Ray Hinton

Anthony Ray Hinton, a man condemned to death in 1985 for killing two people in Alabama, was freed after spending 30 years in jail for a crime that a new trial found he did not commit.

Hinton's case goes back to 1985, when there was a wave of violent robberies in fast-food restaurants of the area and the managers of two of them were murdered. A worker who was wounded in a third robbery identified Hinton as the shooter and with that testimony and a gun found in the home of the suspect's mother, prosecutors made a case against him that led to the death penalty.

According to the prosecution, that gun was used to kill the two managers and to wound the victim at the third establishment who testified against him. Hinton was sentenced despite having no criminal record, successfully passing a polygraph test and having an alibi for the night of the third assault—his boss and fellow workers said he couldn't possibly have done it because he was at work.

Hinton spent 30 years on death row in a 5X8 cell. He communicated with other inmates by banging on the bars with their cups and plates. You could tell when someone got executed by the scent of burning flesh that get into your nostril and stay for days.

While in prison, Anthony Ray Hinton said "his mother reminded him that he should trust in God to set him free. He reference: Mark 11:24, Therefore I tell you, whatever you ask for in prayer, believe that you have received it, and it will be yours.

In 2002 his attorneys of the Equal Justice Initiative proved the gun found at the home of Hinton's mother was not used in the murders. The

U.S. Supreme Court ordered a new trial. The defense also introduced evidence that the prosecutors in the case had a history of racial discrimination and that the attorney assigned to defend Hinton at the time did not adequately represent him.

The court stated his court appointed lawyer should have known state money was available to hire a better firearms expert than the one eyed, unqualified expert who testified on Hinton's behalf.

Hinton is the 152nd prisoner to be freed after spending time on death row, according to the Death Penalty Information Center, or DPIC.

Equal Justice Initiative director Bryan Stevenson, who waged a 16-year fight for Hinton's release, said while the day was joyous, the case was tragic.

An Alabama legislative committee is reviewing a request to give $1.5 million to compensate Hinton. Despite being freed after new testing on the alleged murder weapon, a few state officials still question Hinton's claims of innocence and whether he is eligible for that money.

As he left the jail, Hinton said he would pray for the victim's families as he has done for the past 30 years. They have suffered a "miscarriage of justice" as well, he said. He had less kind words for those involved in his conviction.

"When you think you are high and mighty and you are above the law, you don't have to answer to nobody. But I got news for them, everybody who played a part in sending me to death row, you will answer to God," Hinton said.

Justice Department flawed evidence prior to 2000

The steps outlined in a joint statement with the Innocence Project and the National Association of Criminal Defense lawyers, follow revelations of flawed testimony by specialized FBI examiners in cases.

Of the 268 trials that have already been reviewed in which hair evidence was used against a defendant, more than 95 percent contained flawed testimony by specialized examiners. Besides, 26 of 28 FBI specialist provided flawed statements at trial or produced lab reports with errors.

"The department (of Justice) and the FBI also are committed to ensuring the accuracy of future hair analysis testimony, as well as the application of all disciplines of forensic science."

When corruption, carelessness, or racial prejudice interferes, the consequences can be devastating to the defendants and their families. This phenomenon is more apparent in NYC. In 2014, numerous lawsuits have been filed against the city by wrongfully convicted criminal defendants—a disproportionate number of whom are black.

The increasing prevalence of DNA testing over the years has played a crucial role in clearing charges for previously convicted "criminals."

National Registry currently cites a total of 1,417 exonerations—the majority of which are attributed to black defendants.

Defendants and prosecutors in 46 states, along with the District of Columbia, are being advised of the findings, which could result in appealing of convictions, the newspaper said. The cases with overstated evidence included 32 that resulted in death sentences, and 14 of those defendants have been executed or died in prison.

The Post first raised the question of flawed testimony in 1980s and 1990s trials in a story in July. Peter Newfeld, co-founder of the Innocence Project, said the FBI's hair analysis in that period was "a complete disaster" but praised the bureau and the Justice Department for collaborating in the review.

The FBI and Justice Department issued a statement vowing to continue addressing cases, notify affected defendants and ensure accuracy in future cases.

Advancement in Forensic and Technology

Advances in Forensic provide tools for solving crimes. Forensic—the application of science to matters of law—has made great strides in recent years, as advances in technology have given forensic scientist a variety of new tools. DNA analysis is unlocking the mysteries of human identity. Image enhancement technologies are enabling investigators to read clues such as finger prints, foot prints and bite marks.

Computer science is enabling police to collect evidence from e-mail and other digital files. Police mine narcotics dealers' hard drives for records of their transactions, and they examine the e-mail correspondence of murder victims to uncover motives and identify suspects. Police have software and hardware technology that enables them to look at the hard drive forensically. They can recreate deleted files and recover instant messaging chats.

DNA science has solved crimes considered otherwise unsolvable. DNA has ended the careers of serial rapists and serial killers, identified the remains of soldiers missing in action, established paternity in many instances, helped medical detectives to track diseases, and illuminated countless other controversies involving biological issues.

Police today commonly use DNA analysis and other technologies. They are less dependent on traditional crime-solving methods that have fallen into disfavor, such as interrogating suspects, talking with informers or relying on witness identification.

Until recently, DNA analysis had been used mostly in serious criminal cases such as murder, rape, terrorism or genocide. Since advances have streamlined DNA procedures and cut their cost, however, they are being used increasingly to investigate other offenses such as hit-and-run, burglary, robbery and white collar crime.

"Whether it's DNA, finger prints, e-mail or other evidence, technology is giving us new tools that are helping not only to solve crimes, but also to prove the innocence of those wrongly accused.

Contributing factors to the rise in the penal population

In 2013, the United States had the highest rate of incarceration in the world. In the 1980s U.S. legislation issued some new drug laws with stiffer penalties that ranged from drug possession to drug trafficking. Many of those charged with drug crimes saw longer prison sentences and less judicial leniency when facing trial. The war on drugs has furthered the boom in prison population even though violent crime has continued to steadily decrease. A lot of urban areas in the U.S. have a majority black population. With crime tendencies high in these areas, drugs are also prevalent. This means that a greater percentage of those in prison are going to be black because law enforcement is already concentrated in the areas with high violent crime and drug crime. With this new drug legislation, the U.S. government has increased the use of incarceration for social control which has resulted in "sharper disproportionate effects on African Americans.

Factors affecting incarceration rates

Blacks had a higher chance of going to prison especially if they drop out high school. If a Black male dropped out of high school, he had an over 50% chance of being incarcerated in his life time, as compared to an 11% chance for white male high school drop outs. Socio-economic, geographic, and educational disparities, as well as alleged unequal treatment in the criminal justice system, contributed to this gap in incarceration rates by race. Failure to achieve literacy (reading at "grade level") by the third or fourth grade makes the likelihood of future incarceration twenty times more likely than other students. Some states use this measurement to predict how much prison space they will require in the future. It appears to be a poverty issue rather than a race issue.

Effects on families and neighborhoods

With violent crime on the rise in the late 20th century coupled with the war on drugs violations, penal population growth sent shockwaves through the most fragile families and neighborhoods that were least equipped to deal with the problem. Since the majority of people in the prison population are minorities and lower class individuals, the people they leave behind have to deal with extraordinary circumstances. This burden has left families broken and children are the victims of single-parent homes which increases the percentage of these children going to jail earlier than most. With the majority of the prison population being men, "women are left in free society to raise families and contend with ex-prisoners returning home after release. Children raised in single-parent homes are less supervised which leads to less emphasis on education and self-determination.

The result of this situation is that society is damaged and has to take on the financial burden of children growing up in crime ridden neighborhoods and going to prison. When a family member is arrested, the family loses not only that person's income, but also acquire additional expenses involved in keeping contact with the incarcerated family member. The current prison complex serves as a punitive system in which mass incarceration has become the response to problems in society. Field studies regarding prison conditions describe behavioral changes produced by prolonged incarceration, and conclude that imprisonment undermines the social life of inmates by exacerbating criminality or impairing their capacity for normal social interaction. Moreover, this racial disparity in imprisonment, particularly with African American, subjects them to political subordination by destroying their positive connecting with society. Institutional factors—such as the prison Industrial Complex itself—become enmeshed in everyday lives, so much so that prisons no longer function as "law enforcement" systems.

Crime in poorer urban neighborhoods is linked to increased rates of mass incarceration, as job opportunities decline and people turn to crime for survival. Crime among low-education men is often linked to the economic decline among unskilled workers. These economic problems are also tied to reentry into society after incarceration. Data from Washington State Department of Corrections and employment insurance records show how "the wages of black ex-inmates earn 10 percent less than white ex-inmates post incarceration.

Black Women

Since 1980 the number of women in prison has increased at nearly double the rate for men. The number of people in women's prison rose almost twice as fast (4.8%) as the growth of the number of men imprisoned (2.7%). Prisons have increased eight-fold from 12,300 in 1980 to 107,500 in 2005. African American women make up 30% of the women prisoners and 16% are Latinas. Black women are incarcerated at 4 times the rate of white women.

Women of color, who are disproportionately poor and often bear the primary responsibility for raising their children, are disproportionately dependent on the government to satisfy their basic human needs through programs like Public Housing, Temporary Assistance for needy families and Medicaid, and therefore are particularly impacted by governmental bans on receiving such assistance base on prior drug conviction.

In 1997, 65% of women in state prisons were parents of minor children, compared to 55% of men. Two-thirds of mothers incarcerated in state prison lived with their children before their arrest. Approximately 37% of women and 28% of men in prison had monthly incomes of less than $600 before their arrest.

Nearly a quarter of women in state prisons have a history of mental illness. Nationally 3.6% of women in state prisons were HIV positive in 2000, compared to 2% of men. More than half of the women in state prisons have been abused, 47% physically abused and 39% sexually abused.

Women also are affected by policies targeting members of their families who are involved in the criminal justice system. For example, women who live in public housing may be evicted if a member of their household engages in criminal activity, and people with criminal histories are frequently denied admission to public housing in the first place.

Furthermore, this system can disintegrate familial life and structure. Black and Latino youth are more likely to be incarcerated after coming in contact with the American juvenile justice system. In a study Victor Rios, 75% of prison inmates in the United States are Black and Latinos between the ages of 20 and 39. Furthermore, societal institutions—such as schools, families, and community centers can impact youth by initiating them into this system of criminalization from an early age. These institution, traditionally set up to protect the youth, contribute to mass incarceration by mimicking the criminal justice system.

Having parents in prison can have adverse psychological effects as children are deprived of parental guidance, emotional support, and financial help. Because many prisons are located in remote areas, incarcerated parents face physical barriers in seeing their children and vice versa. Societal influences, such as low education among African American men, can also lead to higher rates of incarceration. Imprisonment has become "disproportionately widespread among low-education black men "in which the penal system has evolved to be a "new feature of American race and class inequality." Scholar Pettit and Western's research has shown how incarceration rates for African Americans are "about eight times higher than those for whites, "and prison inmates have less than "12 years of completed schooling" on average.

The 40-year-old "war on crime and drugs" has been a war of little success but huge casualties. The collateral damage of this war far exceeds any benefits. It's time for our government to work to improve the lives of our community rather than continuing to fight this war against poor women of color and their children.

Post Release

These factors all impact released prisoners who try to reintegrate into society. According to a national study, within three years of release, almost 7 in 10 will have been rearrested. Many released prisoners have difficulty transitioning back into societies and communities from state and federal prisons because the social environment of peers, family, community, and state level policies all impact prison reentry; the process of leaving prison or jail and returning to society. Men eventually released from prison will most likely return to their same communities, putting additional strain on already scarce resources as they attempt to garner the assistance they need to successfully reenter society. Due to the lack of resources, these same men will continue along this perpetuating cycle.

A major challenge for prisoners re-entering society is obtaining employment, especially for individuals with a felony on their record. A study utilizing U.S. Census occupational data in New Jersey and Minnesota in 2000 found that "individuals with felon status would have been disqualified from approximately one out of every 6.5 occupations in New Jersey and one out of every 8.5 positions in Minnesota. "As African Americans and Hispanics are disproportionately affected by felon status, these additional limitations on employment opportunity were shown to exacerbate racial disparities in the labor market.

Without change, the continual racist image of blacks and colored minorities in ideologies, the culture, and the media upholds the racial stereotype of African Americans and other minorities. For those who were arrested to successfully reenter, abolitionist alternatives propose that the community unlearn that all individuals arrested should be punished rather than rehabilitated. Consequential damages are those that are not a direct result of an act, but a consequence of the initial act. Through the abolition of collateral consequential laws, improvements can be made for ex-inmates to turn their lives around after their release from prison. This action will, in turn, improve the lives of families and black communities that are currently devastated by the harsh repercussions of collateral consequential laws.

New Justice Department Policy will cut Federal drug sentences

Attorney General Eric Holder will announce a new policy on Thursday that may shorten sentences for federal drug offenders as part of his "Smart on Crime" initiative. Holder is set to testify in front of the U.S. Sentencing Commission on Thursday and endorse changes to the Commission's Drug Quantity Table. The changes would mean a two-level reduction in ranges of sentences for people convicted of federal drug crimes. For example, someone convicted of trafficking more than one Kilogram of heroin, five Kilograms of cocaine or 280 grams of crack would now trigger a Level 32 sentence—121 months to 151 months. If the Sentencing Commission passes the changes, it would reduce that punishment to a sentence of 97 months to 121 months.

In the meantime, Holder is instructing federal prosecutors not to object to any request for sentence reductions based on the guideline being considered by the Commission. That means people serving time for federal drug crimes who ask for a reduction based on the proposed guidelines should receive one. The government said the proposed change will affect 69.9 percent of drug trafficking offenders and will reduce the average sentence of a drug offender by about 11 months, or 17.7 percent of the average sentence.

May 12, 2017

Democratic and Republican officials alike took up the banner of criminal justice reform over the past five years, hoping to reduce the nation's unprecedented prison population and scale back the harshest punishments of the tough—on crime era. Now Attorney General Jeff Sessions has taken a major step toward rolling back their efforts. In a memo released Friday, Sessions instructed federal prosecutors nationwide to seek the strongest possible charges and sentences against defendants they target.

"It is a core principle that prosecutors should charge and pursue the most serious, readily provable offense, "he wrote. "This policy fully utilizes the tools congress has given us.

By definition, the most serious offenses are those that carry the most substantial guidelines sentence, including mandatory-minimum sentences."

Friday's policy change effectively rescinds Obama-era guidelines for federal prosecutors that were designed to curtail the harshest sentences for defendants charged with low-level drug offenses. The previous memo, first promulgated by then—Attorney General Eric Holder in 2013, reserved the

most severe options in the federal sentencing guidelines for "serious, high-level, or violent drug traffick-
ers" instead of defendants charged with lower-level
offenses.

Holder's changes addressed longstanding criticisms of the federal posture toward drug crimes. "In
some cases, mandatory-minimum and recidivist-en-
hancement statutes have resulted in unduly harsh
sentences and perceived of actual disparities that do
not reflect or principles of Federal Prosecution," he
wrote at that time.

"Long sentences for low-level, non-violent
drug offenses do not promote public safety, deter-
rence, and rehabilitation." To that end, he instructed
prosecutors not to list the quantity of drugs seized
when charging a defendant unless he or she was "an
organizer, leader, manager, or supervisor of others
within a criminal organization, "had used violence,
or had a lengthy criminal history. Prosecutors should
also consider, he said, if their charges "would create
a gross sentencing disparity" compared with other
defendants.

Session's new memo effectively rejects that
stance, insisting on seeking the maximum punishments lawfully possible. Prosecutors must disclose to
the sentencing Court all facts that impact the sentencing guidelines or mandatory-minimum sentences,
and should in all cases seek a reasonable sentence
under the factors "prescribed by federal drug laws, he
wrote. Any deviations from the policy require "super-
visory approval" from the justice department.

In a statement shortly after Session's memo was issued, Holder castigated his successor's move. "The policy announced today is not tough on crime," he said. "It is dumb on crime. It is an ideologically motivated, cookie-cutter approach that has only been proven to generate unfairly long sentences that are often applied indiscriminately and do little to achieve long-term public safety."

Monday's "absurd reversal," Holder added, "is driven by voices that have not only been discredited but until now have been relegated to the fringes of this debate."

The memo is expected to be the first of many breaks the attorney general makes with Obama-era policies on high-profile criminal justice matters. Sessions previously ordered a comprehensive review of the Justice Department's consent decrees with local police departments. Those agreements were among the Obama Justice Department's most valued tools in reforming troubled law-enforcement agencies. Sessions, however, has been a frequent critic of the decrees in general, describing them as unnecessary federal intrusion into local policing practices.

Following Donald Trump's victory in the 2016 elections, stock prices for CCA and GEO Group surged.

On February 23, 2017 the DOJ under Attorney General Jeff Sessions overturned the ban on using private prisons. According to Sessions, "the (Obama administration) memorandum changed long-standing policy and practice, and impaired the bureau's ability to meet the future needs of the federal correctional system. Therefore, I direct the bureau to return to its previous approach."

Issuing of Clemency

The Federal prison population has increased 800 percent over the past 30 years and currently totals nearly 216,000 inmates, more than half of whom are drug offenders. The federal prison system currently operates at 33 percent over capacity system-wide. The Department of Justice spent about 6.5 billion on prisons, law enforcement agents in their fight against violent crime, drug cartels, public corruption, financial fraud, human trafficking, child exploitation, to name a few.

Public safety is going to suffer if the federal prison population is not addressed. In addition to getting low-level drug offenders out of prison, the Justice Department also is focused on "reentry" programs that prepare inmates for life on the outside. Inmates with limited skills and inadequate education will have to be trained to become supportive and productive members of their community with good paying livable wage, obtain housing and able to put their lives together.

The goal is to give these prisoners a fresh start. Inmates qualified for clemency will be nonviolent low-level drug offenders who were not involved in gangs or cartel activity; first time offenders, and those without an extensive criminal history. Qualified candidates should have a "clean record in prison," not pose a threat to public safety and face life or "nearlife" sentences that are "excessive under current law".

A growing number of states are pushing inmates out of prison in early release programs designed to reduce over-crowding and save money. But faced with a tight job and few employers willing to hire someone with a criminal record, many former inmates are likely to end up right back behind bars.

California began releasing prisoners deemed at low risk for re-offending. Colorado, Oregon, Kentucky and Connecticut, all wracked with budgetary issues, have instituted similar moves as a way to cut costs, while others, including Michigan and Mississippi, are considering similar initiatives.

The cost of housing, feeding and providing medical care for America's prison population has surged over the past two decades, from $11 billion a year to more than $50 billion, as states passed tough laws that put more offenders behind bars.

Holder to Issue Revised Racial Profiling Rules with New Limits

Attorney General Eric Holder, who has long spoken out against racial profiling, has been under pressure from civil-rights and civil-liberties groups to broaden rules put in place in 2003 that banned profiling based on race and ethnicity. The new guidelines will also prohibit profiling based on national origin, sexual orientation, and gender identity.

"Profiling by law enforcement is not only wrong, it is profoundly misguided and ineffective because it wastes precious resources and undermines the public trust," Holder said in a statement that previewed the policy changes, which the Justice Department was set to make public today.

The new rules come amid mass demonstrations over the use of deadly force by police against two unarmed black men, in Ferguson, Missouri, and New York City. Local grand juries declined to indict the two officers involved in those incidents, sparking more protests in recent weeks.

The Justice Department is conducting civil rights investigations of the incidents, and Holder and President Barack Obama have called for better relations between police and the communities they serve.

Divisive Issue

Racial profiling has been a divisive issue for decades, and authorities have long tried to find ways to curb police and federal agents from using race, ethnicity, gender or sexual orientation in deciding whether to target people for traffic stops, searches or other actions.

Despite pressure for groups like the American Civil Liberties Union, it has taken the Justice Department five years to update the rules. Holder said that the policy's release is coming at the right time.

"In light of certain recent incidents we've seen at the local level—and the widespread concerns about trust in the criminal justice process, which so many have raised throughout the nation—it's imperative that we take every possible action to institute strong and sound policing strategies," Holder said.

The new policy will require new training and data collection to monitor whether officers or agents engage in profiling. Holder will encourage state and local police departments to adopt the federal rules, according to a Justice Department statement.

"With this new guidance, we take a major and important step forward to ensure effective policing," Holder said in the statement.

Emmett Till 07/25/1941-08/29/1955

Emmett Till was an African-American teenager whose brutal murder in Mississippi is often cited as the catalyst for the start of the Civil Rights movement in the United States. Emmett Till was born and raised in Chicago. He went down to Mississippi to visit his relatives. On August 24, 1955, Emmett went to a grocery store in town to buy bubble gum and allegedly whistled at the white woman working there, Carolyn Bryant.

Roy Bryant the husband of Carolyn and J.W. Milam his half-brother were accused of murdering Emmett because he allegedly whistles at Carolyn. They went on trial in a segregated court house in Sumner Mississippi. On September 23, the all-white jury deliberated for less than an hour issuing a verdict of "NOT GUILTY," explaining that they believed the state had failed to prove the identity of Emmitt's body.

Emmett was abducted at gun point from his uncle's home on August 28, 1955 by Roy Bryant and J.W. Milam because they wanted to teach him a lesson. They tortured, beat and shot him in the head.

After their acquittal, both Bryant and Milam boasted about what they had done to Till, saying they had no choice but to kill him for behaving in such an obscene way towards Bryant's wife.

Carolyn Bryant Donham, the woman who accused Emmett Till of lewd and lascivious acts has reportedly confessed for the first time that she fabricated part of her testimony in a 2007 interview with Vanity Fair.

In Washington, a tree planting ceremony was held in honor of Emmett Till at the U.S. Capitol. Senator Susan Collins sponsored the U.S. Capitol Grounds Memorial Tree in honor of 14-year-old Emmett Till, whose brutal murder in 1955 in Money, Mississippi for whistling at a white woman helped spark the civil rights movement. Till was buried at Burr Oak Cemetery in Alsip, Illinois.

Senator Collins, U.S.Attorney General Eric Holder, Architect of the U.S. Capital Stephen T. Ayers, Janet Lunghart Cohen, author of the play "Anne and Emmett," and others were at the tree planting ceremony.

James Byrd 05/02/1949-06/07/1998

On June 7, 1998, Byrd, age 49, accepted a ride from Shawn Berry, Lawrence Russel Brewer and ex-convict John William King. Berry who was driving knew Byrd from around town. Instead of taking him home, the three men took Byrd to a remote country road out of town, beat him severely, urinated on him and chained him by his ankles to their pickup truck before dragging him for approximately 1.5 miles.

Byrd died after his right arm and head were severed when his body hit a culvert. Berry, Brewer and King dumped the mutilated remains of the body in front of an African-American church on Huff Creek Road, then drove off to a Barbecue.

Since Brewer and King were well-known white supremacist, law enforcement officials along with Jasper's District Attorney determined the murder was a hate crime.

Berry, Brewer and King were tried and convicted for Byrd's murder. Brewer and King received the death penalty, while Berry was sentenced to life in prison. Brewer was executed on September 21, 2011 while King remains on Texas death row.

The 77th Texas legislature passed the James Byrd Jr. Hate Crime Act. The Act became state law in 2001. In 2009, the Matthew Sheppard and James Byrd Jr. Hate Crimes Prevention Act expanded the 1969 limited States federal hate-crime law to include crimes motivated by a victim's actual or perceived gender, sexual orientation, gender identity, or disability.

Ramarley Graham

On February 2, 2012, officers from a special narcotics unit chased Ramarley Graham, 18, from White Plains Road and East 228th Street to his home at 719 E. 229th Street in Wakefield because cops investigating a drug deal believed Graham had a gun in his waistband. The officers alleged that they witnessed Graham adjusting and tugging at his waistband, which they said led them to believe he was carrying a gun. The officers then began to follow Graham as he left the bodega and went into an apartment building, reporting over their radio that they saw the "butt of a gun" on the teen.

There was no evidence that this statement was true. The officers claimed that they approached Graham when he left the building, identifying themselves as police officers and telling him not to move.

Then, the officers stated in their official report, Graham started to run from them toward his home, a claim that was later retracted by police after surveillance footage showed Graham walking not running. It is unclear whether Graham was aware that the officers were pursuing him when he reached his home.

After officers tried unsuccessfully to kick down the front door of the apartment building, two officers went to the back of the building, where they were let in by a first floor tenant. They went to the door of Graham's apartment and proceeded to kick it in. According to the NYPD, Graham and the officers spotted each other and Graham ran into a bathroom, where he allegedly tried to flush a small bag of marijuana down the toilet. Officer Haste shot Graham in the chest because he thought he was reaching for a gun in his waistband. No weapon was found.

Haste's attorneys have said that multiple communications from fellow officers that Graham had a gun determined Haste's actions that day. Supreme Court Justice Steven L. Barrett dismissed the manslaughter indictment against Haste on a legal technicality. A second grand jury declined to indict Haste.

City Law Department spokesman Nick Paolucci said. "This was a tragic case. After evaluating all the facts and consulting with key stakeholders such as the NYPD, it was determined that settling the matter was in the best interest of the City."

The family of Ramarley Graham has agreed to a $3.9 million settlement with New York City. In a lawsuit filed a year ago, Graham's family sought damages for emotional distress and their treatment by the police.

Besides emotional damages, the family also sought compensation for their alleged mistreatment by police who detained them after the shooting. After Graham was gunned down in the bathroom, cops allegedly threatened to shoot his grieving grandmother, according to the suit filed in Bronx Supreme Court.

The suit also accused the NYPD of trying to cover up the killing, failing to properly train officers and engaging in racial discrimination through the stop-and-frisk policy. Graham's death sparked numerous protests in the Bronx and other parts of the city by demonstrators calling for justice.

Trayvon Martin

Trayvon Benjamin Martin was a 17 year-old African American from Miami Gardens, Florida who was fatally shot by George Zimmerman, a neighborhood watch volunteer, in Sanford, Florida. Martin had gone with his father on a visit to his father's fiancee at her townhouse at The Retreat at Twin Lakes in Sanford. On the evening of February 26, Martin went to a convenience store and purchased candy and juice. As Martin returned from the store, Zimmerman spotted him and called the Sanford Police to report him, saying he looked suspicious. Moments later, there was an altercation between the two individuals in which Martin, who was unarmed, was shot in the chest. Zimmerman was not charged at the time of the shooting by the Sanford Police, who said that there was no evidence to refute his claim of self-defense and that Florida's stand your ground law prohibited law-enforcement officials from arresting or charging him. Zimmerman was eventually charged and tried in Martin's death and a jury acquitted Zimmerman of second-degree murder and manslaughter in July 2013.

His killing ignited a wave of intense protests that denounced police brutality and ultimately birthed the **Black Lives Matter movement.**

Travon's parents Sybrina Fulton and Tracy Martin mourn the loss of their son every day, and some days are more difficult to endure than others which is why they admit it took them five years to put their feelings into words in the form of their book. While several books focus on Trayvon and his death, his parents say they don't adequately capture the details of Trayvon's life because, simply, no one ever knew him like they did.

The two plans to continue to fight for equality, uplift communities of color, identify ways to police the police and help others heal through times of devastation. "They want to make change."

Months later, George was quoted saying that president Obama amped up racial tensions by allowing the Justice Department to investigate him. He criticize Obama for his comment that, "If I had a son, he would look like Trayvon." "For him to make incendiary comments as he did, and direct the Department of Justice to pursue a baseless prosecution, he by far over-reached. The President was criticized for playing the race card and dividing the country.

Death of Eric Garner

On July 17, 2014, In Staten Island, New York, United States, Eric Garner died of a heart attack while police officers were arresting him for the suspected sale of untaxed cigarettes. Garner previously had been arrested for selling untaxed cigarettes. When a police officer attempted to arrest Garner, he had broken up a fight which brought additional police units to the scene. He was approached by police officer Justin Damico. A New York Police Department officer, Daniel Pantaleo, put Garner on the ground by the use of force, which included the use of a chokehold, backed by video evidence of the event.

Garner died some minutes later. NYPD union leader Patrick Lynch challenged that chokehold claim. On August 1, 2014, medical examiners concluded chokehold and chest compression as the primary cause of Garner's heart problems, obesity and asthma as additional factors. As a result of Garner's death, four EMTs and paramedics who responded to Garner's death were suspended without pay on July 21, 2014, and officers Justin Damico and Daniel Pantaleo were placed on desk duty, the latter stripped of his service gun and badge.

The medical examiner concluded that Garner was killed by "compression of neck (choke hold), compression of chest and prone positioning during physical restraint by police." No damage to Garner's windpipe or neck bones was found. The medical examiner ruled Garner's death a homicide. According to the medical examiner's definition, a homicide is a death caused by the intentional actions of another person or persons, which is not necessarily an intentional death or a criminal death.

The event stirred public protests and rallies with charges of police brutality and was broadcast nationally over various media networks. Mayor Bill de Blasio held a roundtable meeting with police officers and political officers and in a statement on August 1, called for dialogue to heal old wounds and create trust and respect between the police and the community.

On December 3, 2014, the Richmond County grand jury decided not to indict Pantaleo.

The City of New York made an out-of-Court settlement to pay the Garner family $5.9 million.

New York City mayor says he would veto police chokehold ban

New York City Mayor Bill De Blasio said on Wednesday January 14, 2015, he would veto a bill by city lawmakers that would make it illegal for a police officer to put a person in a chokehold during an arrest. The maneuver, which has come under intense scrutiny since an unarmed New Yorker died last July after a policeman gripped him around the neck, already is banned under the police department's internal rules.

De Blasio said ensuring officers follow those rules was sufficient, while still allowing for "exceptional" instances where the hold could be justified. "One officer and one perpetrator in a death struggle—in that instance the officer has the right to use all tools he can to save his life," De Blasio said when asked about the bill during an unrelated news conference. "I'm not going to agree to a situation where an officer is in that life-and-death struggle, thank God survives, and then faces criminal charges. That's unacceptable."

The proposed law would make a chokehold during an arrest punishable by up to a year in prison or a fine of $2,500.

Stephen Davis, the police department's chief spokesman, has said that other wrestling-style holds the city teaches police can sometimes inadvertently slip into a chokehold during an unpredictable street struggle.

The Council's bill was prompted by the death of unarmed Eric Garner, 43, who was killed by Officer Daniel Pantaleo compressing his neck while arresting him for selling loose cigarettes on a sidewalk. A grand jury voted against indicting Pantaleo.

The mayor's support for protesters angered by Garner's death has led to an acrimonious rift with police that he has struggled to heal.

Louis Turco, president of the city's Lieutenants Benevolent Association, said in an interview he welcomed the mayor's veto promise as an encouraging step.

Rory Lancman, a Democratic co-author of the bill, said Garner's death and other instances of chokeholds showed the department had failed to eradicate the practice. "In many circumstances it's not a maneuver of last resort," Lancman said in an interview. "It's the first technique that they applied."

Asked about the mayor's "death struggle" objection, Lancman said an officer in that scenario probably would not even be indicted because state law allowed a self-defense justification. No date for a vote on the bill has been set. The Council can override a mayor's veto if two-thirds of its members vote to do so.

De Blasio said that retraining cops on the protocol is "the best way to handle that." "What's going to happen is the retraining of the entire police department on a variety of approaches, including the fact that the choke hold is not an appropriate tool to use," de Blasio said.

The mayor previously expressed his opposition to any effort to make a choke hold an illegal police action, saying that "there has to be some flexibility" for police. He explained the argument further saying that cops must be able to take such an action in a life-or-death situation.

"There are some exceptional situations," He said. "I want to respect our men and women in uniform who may be put into a life-and-death situation; one-on-one, them and a perpetrator who could… Mean to kill them; and they have to defend themselves—and that might involve a choke hold."

Mayor Bill De Blasio approval ratings

De Blasio publicly supported protest over white police violence against black men created a backlash in his approval ratings. Blacks and Hispanics overwhelmingly approved of the job he's doing whereas whites disapprove almost two-to-one. Everyone agrees that a race relation in New York since the Mayor took office is slightly better than worse. Overall, 48 percent of voters approved of the way de Blasio is handling relations between blacks and whites compared to 42 percent who disapproved. Overall, 49 percent of New York City voters supported the mayor. His predecessor Michael Bloomberg had a higher rating for the same period.

Mayor de Blasio's education initiatives will go a long way towards improving his approval ratings. Unemployment rate in New York has dropped to 5.4% with 177,000 new jobs in 2016.

He has created universal Pre K for all by taxing those making more than $500,000.

Mr. de Blasio calls for luring 700 literacy specialists and distributing them in elementary schools throughout the system. The mayor's goal of having, within six years, at least two-thirds of students reading fluently by the end of second grade is a laudable one, given that currently only 30 percent of third graders are proficient in reading.

Another proposal calls for adding Advanced Placement Courses, through which students can get college credit, in over 100 high schools that do not have them. Still another proposal calls for providing computer science education throughout the school system, paid for by a public-private partnership.

Mayor de Blasio also promised to raise the City's graduation rate from the current 68 percent to 80 percent within 10 years.

Manufacturing Jobs

Today, manufacturing contributes $2.18 trillion to the U.S. economy. Manufacturing is a thriving, productive, dynamic industry. Robots and the Internet of Things improve our productivity, the power of data cuts waste, the advancement of 3-D printing makes us more responsive to customers and digital modeling solves problems before they arise. But these advancements don't happen on their own. They require engineers, technicians, programmers and scientists. They require modern manufacturing workers. Without them, our progress could be in jeopardy.

Today, as many as 350,000 manufacturing jobs are unfilled. By 2025, manufacturers expect 3.5 million job openings but 2 million of them could sit unfilled-promising good wages and rewarding work but lacking candidates. This is more than a manufacturing challenge. It is an American challenge. The strength of our economy hangs in the balance.

Leading the way

Manufacturing employers are working hard to close the skills gap, forging partnerships with community colleges as well as local and regional organizations. Many offer on-the-job training and apprenticeships so that workers can earn and learn at the same time. Apprentices take home a pay check and, over time, a credential or a degree. They gain valuable knowledge while the company gains a talented worker. Manufacturing companies see a person's potential whatever his or her age, experience or situation—regardless of whether a person is a recent graduate or looking for a midlife career change.

Manufactures are working hard to bring people of all backgrounds onto shop floors and teams, including underrepresented groups such as women, young people, veterans, minorities and those who can benefit from new opportunities, such as people recently released from prison who have served their time and want to be productive member of society.

Taking Action

Manufacturers alone can only do so much. Everyone, including parents, teachers and elected officials, has a role to play. Our public officials must reject old models of education. The modern economy is changing too fast to stick to rigid, outdated systems. We need flexibility and a focus on the STEM fields (science, technology, engineering and math).

Teachers and parents, who wield outsized influence with students regarding their career paths, need to recognize that modern manufacturing doesn't look like the manufacturing industry of the past.

Manufacturers are, however, making it easier for them to see the difference. The first Friday of October is manufacturing Day, and manufacturers across the country will open their shop floors to welcome students, teachers, parents and the public to see what modern manufacturing looks like. Every year, participants report gaining a better perspective of the industry and having a more positive view of the opportunities available. Students say they are more likely to see a future in manufacturing.

NYPD'S difficulties recruiting African-Americans.

African-Americans comprise 16% of NYPD officers. The percentage has not risen in decades while the percentage of other minorities in particular Hispanics and Asians has increased.

Other law enforcement agencies—such as Correction or Housing and Transit Police before their merger with the NYPD—were able to attract African-Americans officers.

Although 19% of blacks pass the entrance exam, only 10% are selected. The reason: Many don't follow through the cumbersome process that can take three to four years and require applicants to go to three different locations.

"It's us," said a high-ranking NYPD official. "We give them no support," the official said. "We haven't looked at our systems. We've blamed external forces. Now we have to look inside ourselves."

The new class of NYPD recruits being sworn in October is expected to be comprised of more than 30% Hispanic officers, the highest such proportion in city history. Black candidates are expected to be close to 17% of the new hires, Asians about 10% and women more than 18%, said an NYPD official familiar with the hiring.

The department is pushing to increase minority hiring by shortening the application and screening process, which can take up to four years.

Higher percentages of Hispanics, blacks, Asians and females will be the new norm, said the official about future police academy classes.

The City's top cop, speaking one day after his controversial comments about the difficulties of hiring black officers were published, said he expects to see an increase over the next year.

Mayor de Blasio offered the police Commissioner a vote of support for both his job performance and his comments about the difficulties of recruiting black candidates. Some black leaders criticized Bratton for saying that hiring African American officers was an issue because a large number were disqualified by criminal records.

De Blasio added that he wanted to join Bratton in setting the record straight. "You can be a New York police officer even if you were once stopped," said de Blasio, "you can be a New York police even if you once had a misdemeanor… We want to encourage all people in this City to be a part of this police force.

Bratton added that dropping the minimum age for would-be cops to 21 was under consideration, but he had no plans to scratch the required two years of college.

Shooting of Michael Brown

The shooting of Michael Brown occurred on August 9, 2014, in Ferguson, a suburb of St. Louis County, Missouri, United States. Brown, an 18-year-old black man, was fatally shot by Darren Wilson, 28, a white police officer of the Ferguson Police Department. The disputed circumstances of the shooting and the resultant protests and civil unrest received considerable attention in the United States and abroad, and have sparked debate about law enforcement's relationship with African Americans and police use of force doctrine.

The shooting sparked unrest in Ferguson. The "hands up" account was widely circulated within the black community immediately after the shooting and it contributed to the strong protests and outrage about the killing of the unarmed man. The U.S. Department of Justice did not conclude that the "hands up" account was inaccurate until months later. Believing accounts that Brown had his hands up in surrender when he was shot, protesters chanted, "hands up, don't shoot." Protests, both peaceful and violent, along with vandalism and looting, continued for more than a week in Ferguson.

DOJ investigation into the Ferguson Police Department

On September 5, 2014 the U.S. Department of Justice began an investigation of the Ferguson, Missouri police force to examine whether officers routinely engaged in racial profiling or showed a pattern of excessive force. The investigation was separate from the Department's other investigation of the shooting of Brown. The results of the investigation were released in a March 4, 2015, report, which concluded that police officers in Ferguson routinely violated the constitutional rights of the City's residents, by discriminating against Africans Americans and applying racial stereotypes, in a pattern or practice of unlawful conduct within the Ferguson Police Department that violates the First, Fourth, and Fourteenth Amendments to the United States Constitution, and Federal Statutory Law.

Brown family Lawsuit

On April 23, 2015, the Brown family filed a wrongful death lawsuit in state court against Wilson, Jackson, and the City of Ferguson, asking for damages over $75,000 as well as attorney's fees. On May 27, 2015, the lawsuit was moved from state court to federal court. The trial is scheduled for May of 2017.

On June 20, 2017 the parents of black teenager Michael Brown have settled a lawsuit with Ferguson,

Missouri, over his fatal shooting by a white city police officer in 2014, according to a federal court document filed on Monday. Terms of the wrongful death settlement between Ferguson and Brown's parents, Michael Brown Sr. and Lesley Mc Spadden, were not disclosed. The judgement was approved by U.S. District Judge E. Richard Webber.

Moss appointed Police Chief

On May 9, 2016 Delrish Moss, a Miami law enforcement veteran and expert in community relations, was sworn in as the first permanent African American chief in Ferguson. He acknowledged that his challenges will include diversifying the police force and dramatically improving community relations.

At the culmination of a tumultuous day, President Obama spoke from the White House on the decision made in Ferguson not to prosecute the police officer who shot and killed an 18-year-old African American man this past August.

"We need to accept that this decision was the grand jury's to make," Obama said Monday night. "There are Americans who agree with it, and there are Americans who are deeply upset, even angry. It's an understandable reaction. But I join Michael's parents in asking anyone who protests this decision to do so peacefully."

A St. Louis County grand jury decided not to indict Ferguson police Darren Wilson in the shooting of Michael Brown, the unarmed 18-year-old who was killed by Wilson's gunfire in August. County Prosecutor Bob McCulloch announced the news Monday evening in a press conference. The decision has been months in the making, and threatens to reignite tensions in Ferguson between heavily-armed police and protesters in the area.

"The fact is, in too many parts of this country, a deep distrust exists between law enforcement and communities of color. Some of this is the result of the legacy of racial discrimination in this country. And this is tragic because nobody needs good policing more than poor communities with higher crime rates," Obama said, highlighting-the need for criminal justice reform. "We need to recognize that this is not just an issue for Ferguson, this is an issue for America."

Already, there are reports of possible gunshots in Ferguson among large crowds. Obama asked police in the area "to show care and restraint in managing peaceful protests that may occur," While saying that police have a "tough job" to do, he asked that "as they do their jobs in the coming days, they need to work with the community, not against the community, to distinguish the handful of people who may use the grand jury's decision as an excuse for violence."

The grand jury's decision has implications far beyond Ferguson. Gallup Polling has found that African-Americans have less confidence in the criminal justice system than white Americans, while a W.W. Kellogg Foundation report found that 68% of

Latinos report being worried about police brutality. Wilson walking free will likely reinforces the views among communities of color that our justice system is unfair. And when significant segments of our population lose faith in our justice system, our democracy is weakened. The Ferguson decision reflects poorly on prosecutor McCulloch. His flawed grand jury proceedings ensured that justice was not served for Michael Brown.

It took a full-bore investigation after the death of Michael Brown for the Justice Department to document that the Ferguson courts, prosecutors, and police department were awash in institutional racism.

Justice Dept. finds racial bias in Ferguson police practices

The violent protest in Ferguson was driven by the image of an unarmed black teenager, Michael Brown, lying in the street after a white police officer, Darren Wilson, shot him dead. Allegations that Ferguson's largely white police force were deeply, systematically and violently prejudiced against black residents.

A Justice Department investigation opened after Brown's shooting has found routine patterns and practices of racism in Ferguson, including the excessive use of force and unjustified arrests. In 88 percent of the cases in which the department used force, it was against African Americans. In all of the 14 canine-bite incidents for which racial information was available, the person bitten was African American.

In Ferguson court cases, African Americans are 68 percent less likely than others to have their cases dismissed by a municipal judge, according to the Justice review. In 2013, African Americans accounted for 92 percent of cases in which an arrest warrant was issued.

The Justice Department has little enforcement power to fix the problems it finds. As a rule, it enters into contracts with the offending force, which agrees to increase transparency and data collection and to provide better training and supervision.

In Pittsburg, New Jersey and Los Angeles, Justice Department investigations led to successful reforms. They've established a national standard for what good policing looks like.

Eric Holder has identified the problem in Ferguson. The town that came to symbolize 21st century police racism in America needs to buy-in to the reforms.

Nationwide protests of police actions that resulted in deaths of African Americans in Ferguson, New York and Cleveland laid bare racial tensions and what President Barack Obama called "simmering distrust" between police and communities.

The report's findings vindicate critics who have cited a pattern of abuse in Ferguson. But they are unlikely to restore full trust in the Ferguson police by citizens who were angered when a grand jury decided not to indict Brown's killer, officer Darren Wilson. Wilson, who said he acted in self-defense, is also unlikely to face criminal charges in a separate Justice Department investigation.

Mayor James Knowles said Ferguson was committed to making improvements. Knowles spoke to Reuters after a cursory read through a roughly 100-page report the Justice Department presented to Ferguson officials on Tuesday.

"The city has always been committed to making sure we have the very best police department and any training and improvements or reforms we make to help improve service to the community, we are interested in," Knowles said.

Civil rights attorney Jerryl Christmas, who has represented people who have clashed with Ferguson police and city officials, said he was not surprised by the findings, and he hopes to see Ferguson Police Chief Tom Jackson fired.

"We already knew all this was going on. The problem is nobody is being prosecuted, nobody has been terminated," Christmas said.

Jackson did not respond to a request for comment.

The Ferguson Municipal Court, which Attorney General Eric Holder has previously criticized for unfairly penalizing the city's poor, issued the majority of its warrants for minor violations such as parking, traffic and housing code violations.

Ferguson Committeewoman Patricia Bynes said she was outraged at a section of the DOJ report that outlined racially biased emails that federal officials said were written "by certain Ferguson police and municipal court officials in multiple emails on official Ferguson email accounts."

"The fact that police officers and municipal court officials are using their public emails to tell racial jokes that just reeks of arrogance and ignorance" said Bynes. "It's astounding. They think they are untouchable. The taxpayers have been paying for that racial bias."

Holder Slams Ferguson Cops for Racists, Money-Grubbing Practices

Ferguson, Missouri, police fostered a "highly toxic environment" of racism and misconduct that turned the city into a "powder Keg" that was ready to explode after the fatal shooting of unarmed teenager Michael Brown last year, Attorney General Eric Holder said Wednesday—even though the officer who shot Brown was determined to have committed no crime.

In a lengthy explanation of the Justice Department's two investigations in Ferguson—of police in general and of former Officer Darren Wilson's shooting of Brown in August specifically—Holder agreed with a local grand jury that declined to indict Wilson, stressing that "the facts do not support the filing of criminal charges."

"Michael Brown's death, though a tragedy, did not involve prosecutable conduct on the part of Officer Wilson," Holder said.

A visibly disturbed Holder said "it is not difficult to imagine how a single tragic incident set off the city of Ferguson," which he described as "defined by mistrust and resentment, stoked by years of bad feelings and spurred by illegal and misguided practices."

Those illegal practices included constitutional violations and excessive and dangerous use of force disproportionately targeted against African Americans St. Louis County Prosecutor Robert McCulloch, who was widely criticized by activists and critics of local law enforcement, told reporters later, "I don't feel any need to be vindicated," saying it was Wilson who was vindicated by the physical evidence and the consistency of witnesses' statements.

"Those who say that, well, charges should be filed just so we can have a trial—we don't operate that way in this country," McCulloch said.

McCulloch said he had not had a chance to read the second report, documenting misconduct by Ferguson police. But "we've all got a long way to go to restore and build that trust in the community."

In his remarks, Holder said the systemic problems in Ferguson went far beyond just the police department. A trove of work emails from not only police but also other city officials revealed "racist comments or gender discrimination, demonstrating grotesque views and images of African Americans in which they were seen as the 'other,' called 'transient' by public officials and characterized as lacking personal responsibility," he said.

The Justice Department report further denounced the emails as unequivocally derogatory, dehumanizing and demonstrative of impermissible bias. It found that none of the officers or court clerk employees who wrote them was ever disciplined. Senior Justice Department officials said some of them were still employed by Ferguson.

Holder said the flagrant bias was coupled with determination to squeeze every possible penny out of overzealous enforcement of minor violations—"to use law enforcement not as a public service, but as a tool for raising revenue."

Holder said the Justice Department found that the unconstitutional practices extended to nearly every level of Ferguson's law enforcement system. Ferguson Police issued nearly 50 percent more citations in the last year than they did in 2010, even though there was no rise in crime, he said.

Ferguson officers routinely charge multiple violations for the same conduct, competing to see who can issue the most citations during a single stop.

In one particular egregious example, he cited the case of a woman for example, who received two parking tickets in 2007-8 that totaled $152. But so far, she has paid $550 in fines and fees, has been arrested twice for having unpaid tickets and has spent six days in jail—and "yet she still inexplicably owes Ferguson $541," he said.

From October 2012 to July 2014, African–Americans accounted for 85 percent of all charges brought by Ferguson Police, and they made up more than 90 percent of those-charged with highly discretionary offenses like "manner of walking along roadway," Holder said. In every case in which records recorded the race of a person bitten by a police dog, the subject was African-American.

The fallout is an "unsustainable situation that has not only severely damaged relationships between law enforcement and members of the community but [has] made professional policing vastly more difficult—and unnecessarily placed officers at increased risk," he said.

The Justice Department called on the Ferguson police and courts to immediately start tracking, and analyzing police stops, searches and arrests practices; involve civilians in police decision-making; and develop effective procedures to respond to allegations of officer misconduct. And it said the use of arrest warrants to collect fines and fees should cease.

Holder said that the Justice Department "reserves all of its rights" to force change in Ferguson, suggesting a federal lawsuit could be in the future.

"It is time for Ferguson's leaders to take immediate wholesale and structural corrective action," he said.

In a statement, Brown's parents, Lesley McSpadden and Michael Brown Sr., said they were disappointed that Wilson would not be "held accountable for his actions." But they said they were "encouraged that the DOJ will hold Ferguson Police Department accountable for the pattern of racial bias and profiling they found in their handling of interactions with people of color." "If that change happens, our son's death will not have been in vain," they said.

Civil Rights

Relatives of a Hispanic teen shot dead by a white City of New York police officer are headed back to court in January after filling a lawsuit in a case that could set the stage for the family of slain teenager Michael Brown. A day after Missouri grand jury declined to indict the white police officer in Brown's death, a jury hearing civil cases in Bronx Supreme Court unanimously decided on Tuesday that the City of York and NYPD sergeant Robert Barnett were liable in the 2005, death of 19-year-old Leonel Disla.

The Bronx Court will reconvene with a new jury in January to decide how much it will award in damages to the family of Disla, who was born in the Dominican Republic, the family's attorney, LLaan Maazel, said on Thursday. Maazel drew a parallel with the Brown case, which has sparked national turmoil over police relations with minority communities.

Ferguson police said Brown was unarmed but tried to get hold of the officer's weapon, while New York police said Disla waved a 7-inch knife blade at officers trying to break up a fight-a version of events Maazel challenged at the Civil trial.

Barnett fired twice at Disla, inflicting a fatal wound to the abdomen. The young man died a few hours later at a local hospital Like in Brown case; no criminal charges were filed against Barnett, a veteran officer who said he acted out of fear for his safety. "In both cases no special prosecutor was investigating the police, and I think that's a problem," Maazel said, "police have a hard job but it's so important that when a police officer violates the law that he's held accountable."

While no criminal charges were filed, the teen's mother, Candida Disla, pressed a civil suit. "The family has waited a very long time to get some justice in this case," Maazal said. Tuesday's verdict finding the City and Barnett liable was the result of a successful appeal reversing a verdict two years ago that cleared them of liability.

A lawyer for the city, Patrick Mantione, said he opposed the second jury's decision. "We respectfully disagree with the second jury's verdict and will evaluate our options, "he said.

12-year-old shot and killed by police in Cleveland

A 9-1-1 Caller, who was sitting in a nearby gazebo, reported that someone, possibly a juvenile, was pointing "a pistol" at random in the Cudell Recreation Center. The caller twice said the gun was "probably fake." According to police spokesman, it was unclear whether or not that information had been relayed to the dispatched officers. When the officers showed up at the park. They ordered Tamir Rice to put his hands up. They thought he was reaching for his gun and they shot him. The officers later found the gun to be an Airsoft gun which are replicas of a real gun and are designed to shoot non-lethal plastic pellets. Rice was 12 years old.

The dispatcher who took the 911 call before the Tamir Rice shooting received an eight day suspension for failing to relay that a caller said the slain boy's gun was "probably fake," and was "probably a juvenile," contributed to the death. That omission of the information has been cited as a reason why Officer Timothy Loemann shot and killed the 12-year-old.

The boy's death sparked protest in Cleveland and around in Cleveland and around the country as part of the Black Lives Matter movement.

On December 5, 2014, Rice's family filed a wrongful-death suit against officers Loehmann, Garmback and the City of Cleveland in the United States District Court for the Northern District of Ohio. The lawsuit was settled on April 25, 2016 for $6 million.

A Cop's plea: Stop calling in "suspicious activity" every time you see a black person. These types of calls are a genuine problem, especially when the full details aren't relayed to dispatch officers.So not only can these phone calls be a waste of time for Cops, but they can lead to dangerous confrontations.

"Police departments around the country have begun adopting small body-worn cameras for police officers on patrol. These cameras provide a visual and audio record of interactions with the public, so that in the event of a confrontation or police-involved shooting, such as the one that occurred in Ferguson, there is an inalterable record of the events. There are also indications that the presence of body cameras has a civilizing effect on both police officers and the public, resulting in lower incidents of excessive force complaints and deescalating tense situations before they become violent. Perhaps most importantly, cameras can instill greater trust in police departments on the part of the public they are sworn to protect. In communities with frayed police-community relations, cameras demonstrate a commitment on the part of the local police department to transparency and accountability, while protecting officers from false or frivolous complaints. For all these reasons, the adoption of body cameras has been well received in the jurisdictions that have begun to use them, both by the public and the officers wearing the cameras."

Police officers in these cases appeared to overestimate the threat posed by their victims which may be a result of subconscious racial biases. Studies show officers are quicker to shoot black suspects in video game simulations. Josh Correll, a University of Colorado at Boulder psychology professor who conducted the research, said it's possible the bias could lead to more skewed outcomes in the field. "In the very situation in which [officers] most need their training," he said, "we have some reason to believe that their training will most likely fail them."

Walter Lamar Scott

A white police officer in North Charleston, S.C., was charged with murder after a video surfaced showing him shooting in the back and killing an unarmed black man while the man ran away.

The officer, Michael T. Slager said he had feared for his life because the man had taken his stun gun in a scuffle after a traffic stop. A video, however, shows the officer firing eight times as the man, Walter Lamar Scott fled.

The shooting came on the heels of high-profile instances of police officers' using lethal force in New York, Cleveland, Ferguson, Mo., and elsewhere. The deaths have set off a national debate over whether the police are too quick to use force, particularly in cases involving black men.

North Charleston was named one of America's most dangerous Cities in 2006. The North Charleston Police Department responded by swarming high-crime areas, stopping more drivers and questioning more people on the street. The murder rate went down but complaints shot up.

Of the complaints from 2008 to mid-2012 in which the race of the parties is identified, 62% were filed by African-Americans against white officers. A 2007 survey shows that the police department was 80% white that year—in a city that is currently made up of 47% black residents.

At a press conference on Wednesday 04/08/15, North Charleston Mayor Keith Summey said all of the City's police officers would soon wear body cameras. But many residents weren't sure those cameras would go a long way toward ending what they feel is systemic mistreatment of black people.

Residents of North Charleston said that the video of Walter Scott's death is not surprising. When it comes to daily life, some black residents said they're victims of racial profiling and sometimes, as in Scott's case much worse.

Dylann Roof

On June 18, 2015, Dylann Roof went into the historic African-American church in Charleston and killed nine people, three males and six females at a Bible-study meeting.

Roof crime cannot be divorced from the ideology of white supremacy which long animated his state nor from its potent symbol—the Confederate flag.

That the Confederate flag is the Symbol of White supremacists is evidenced by the very words of those who birthed it:

> Our new government is founded
> upon exactly the opposite idea;
> its foundations are laid, its cor-
> ner-stone rests, upon the great
> truth that the Negro is not equal
> to the white man, that slavery

subordination to the superior race is his natural and normal condition. This, our new government, is the first, in the history of the world, based upon this great philosophical and moral truth…

This moral truth—"that the Negro is not equal to the white man"—is exactly what animated Dylann Roof. More than any individual actor, in recent history, Roof honored his flag in exactly the manner it always demanded—with human sacrifice.

Dylann Roof, the alleged killer, the president said, thought he would "incite fear and recrimination." He "could have never anticipated the way the families of the fallen would respond when they saw him in court, during unspeakable grief, with words of forgiveness."

Obama spoke of grace, and didn't gloss over the political truth. "For too long, we were blind to the pain that the confederate flag stirred in many of our citizens," he said. "But that flag was a reminder of systemic oppression and racial subjugation." But that flag was a reminder of systemic oppression and racial subjugation."

The symbol's removal from the South Carolina Capitol "would be an acknowledgement that the cause for which they fought, the cause of slavery was wrong."

"Perhaps this tragedy causes us to ask some tough questions about how we can permit so many of our children to languish in poverty or attend dilap-idated schools or grow up without prospects for a job or a career," he said. "Perhaps it causes us to examine what we are doing to cause some of our children to hate."

The blood bath in Charleston gave him no choice. Even before investigators found white supremacist pornography on Roof's laptop, we knew that his words as he opened fire spoke to the hateful propaganda he inhaled. "You rape our women, "he shouted, "and you're taking over our country."

George Wallace couldn't have said it more clearly. The former governor of Alabama, upset by desegregation and Civil Rights legislation, put up the Confederate flag to thumb his nose at a federal government trying to give former slaves rights that would recognize their humanity and restore their full and equal status as citizens.

It took excerpts from Roof's manifesto to con-vince many that he wasn't just a mentally unsta-ble loaner-or even, some suggested, a hater of Christians—but was intent on starting "a race war."

South Carolina Gov. Nikki Haley called Monday for the removal of the confederate flag from the Statehouse grounds. "It's time to move the flag from the Capitol grounds," Haley said to applause at a news conference, while flanked by the state's con-gressional delegation and other leaders.

Haley's impassioned speech follows Wednesday's killing of nine black church members by a white gun-man who allegedly expressed racist sentiments. The massacre prompted many in the state to question whether the flag's presence on public property delivered a not-so-subtle message of bigotry.

President Obama, who will travel to Charleston on Friday to deliver the eulogy for one of the victims, the Rev. Clementa Pinckney, has said the flag should be removed and placed in a museum.

President Obama delivers Eulogy for Rev. Clementa Pinckney

Obama: By taking down Confederate flag, 'we express God's grace'. Pinckney was one of nine people slain at Emanuel African Methodist Episcopal Church.

With a rousing eulogy and chorus of "Amazing Grace," President Barack Obama called on the country Friday to honor the nine victims of the South Carolina Church massacre by working toward racial healing. He said that includes removing the Confederate flag from the State House grounds, which he said would be not an act of political correctness but a "meaningful balm" for the unhealed wounds of slavery and the Jim Crow era.

"It's true, the flag did not cause these murders," Obama said, but "we all have to acknowledge the flag has always represented more than just ancestral pride. For many, black and white, that flag was a reminder of systematic oppression and racial subjugation. We see that now".

"By taking down that flag," he said, "we express God's grace."

"Out of this tragedy, God visited grace upon us for he has allowed us to see where we've been blind," he said. "If we can find that grace anything is possible. If we can tap that grace anything can change."

The president has every reason to keep reminding us how far we've come, but Friday's eulogy, he showed us how far we still need to go.

Columbia, SC: The South Carolina Senate has given final approval to a bill to remove to remove the Confederate flag from the grounds of the Capitol. The 36-3 vote Tuesday now sends the bill to the house, where it faces a less certain future. Republicans met behind closed doors Monday and struggled to reach a consensus on what to do next.

The Senate bill would remove the Confederate flag flying in front of the State house and the flagpole as soon as the governor signs it. Republican Gov. Nikki Haley urged lawmakers to remove the flag after the killing of nine black people in a historic African-American church in Charleston last month by a gunman police say was motivated by racial hatred. The suspect was photographed several times with the Confederate flag.

On July 8, 2015 the South Carolina House approved a bill removing the Confederate flag from the Capitol grounds, a stunning reversal in a state that was the first to leave the Union in 1860 and raised the flag again at its Statehouse more than 50 years ago to protest the Civil rights movement. The House approved the Senate bill by a two-thirds margin, and the bill now goes to Republican Gov. Nikki

Haley's desk. She supports the measure, which calls for the banner to come down within 24 hours of her signature. Now the United Nations Ambassador—recognized the cruel symbolism of the Confederate flag flying at the state house and agreed to pull it down.

The national board of directors of prominent U.S. civil rights group the NAACP voted on Saturday to end its 15-year boycott of South Carolina prompted by the display of the Confederate battle flag on State Capitol grounds. The resolution was approved during the NAACP's annual convention in Philadelphia.

The Confederate flag was raised atop the South Carolina State House dome in 1961 as part of Centennial Commemorations of the American Civil War. Critics said its placement was a sign of opposition by politicians to the black civil rights movement at the time.

In 2000, the NAACP announced an economic boycott of South Carolina and protesters marched on the State capitol. The group maintained its boycott even after lawmakers agreed to move the flag to a monument to confederate war dead on the capitol grounds. The NAACP said any move to prematurely end the boycott would have emboldened elements of society seeking to "perpetuate the hatred and history of oppression associated with the Confederate flag."

List of Confederate monuments and memorials

The monuments and memorials honor Confederate leaders, soldiers, or the Confederate States of America in general during the American Civil War. At least 1,503 symbols of the Confederacy can be found in public spaces across the country. The monuments and memorials have become increasingly controversial due to differing interpretations of their meaning and importance. Many confederate monuments were erected in the former confederate States and border States in the decades following the Civil War, in many instances by the United Daughters of the Confederacy, Ladies Memorial Associations, and other memorial organizations. Other Confederate monuments are located on Civil War battlefields.

Historians have found that Confederate monuments were not built primarily as historical markers, but were instead intended to glorify and commemorate the Confederacy. Most Confederate monuments were built in periods of racial conflict, such as when Jim Crow Laws were introduced at the start of the 20th century or during the Civil Rights Movement of the 1950s and 1960s. New Confederate monuments continued to be proposed in recent years and some have been built.

Robert E Lee was against erecting Confederate memorials

Based on his writings, Lee was not a fan of statues honoring Civil War generals, fearing they might "keep open the sores of war." And the ill will war engendered, which he thought should be consigned to "oblivion."

He expressed his views in two famous letters that are now recirculating widely in the wake of Charlottesville.

The First was to Thomas Rosser, a former Confederate general who in 1866 queried Lee about a proposed commemorative monument.

"My convictions is, "Lee wrote, "that however grateful it would be to the feelings of the South, the attempt in the present condition of the Country, would have the effect of retarding, instead of accelerating its accomplishments; and of continuing, if not adding to, the difficulties under which the Southern People labour."

The Second came in 1869, when Lee declined an invitation from the Gettysburg Battlefield Memorial Association to help mark the positions of the troops in that 1863 battle with granite memorials.

He responded that his "engagements will not permit me to be present."

Lee, "believed countries that erased visible signs of Civil War recovered from conflicts quicker. He was worried that by keeping these symbols alive, it would keep the divisions alive.

Mitch Landrieu, the New Orleans mayor gave a remarkable speech after the city dismantled the last of its Confederate monuments in May 2017. "The Confederacy was on the wrong side of history and humanity," he said. "It sought to tear apart our nation and subjugate our fellow Americans to slavery. This is the history we should never forget and one that we should never again put on a pedestal to be revered."

J. Marion Simms

A statue of Doctor J. Marion Sims, credited by many as the father of modern gynecology, is being considered for removal, under the City's push to oust symbols of hate on city property. East Harlem residents and City officials have long advocated for the statue's removal, asserting that it honors Sim's medical achievements while overlooking that between the years 1845 and 1849, he performed gynecological exams on 12 enslaved women without anesthesia. He repeatedly performed surgery on black women without anesthesia because, according to him, black women don't feel pain.

The renewed call for the statue's removal comes after the marches, protests, and attacks at a "Unite the Right" rally led by white nationalist groups in Charlottesville, Virginia.

In New York, a plaque commemorating Confederate general Robert E. Lee was removed from a tree in Brooklyn, busts of Lee and Confederate general Thomas "Stonewall" Jackson were removed from Bronx Community College's Hall of Fame For Great Americans, and the MTA has vowed to remove tile resembling the Confederate flag in a subway station near Times Square.

The museum of the City of New York praises Mayor de Blasio for initiating a 90-day review of 'symbols of hate on New York City property and we join the East Harlem Community in asking that the statue of Dr. J. Marion Sims be included in this review.

Freddie Gray

Freddie Carlos Gray, Jr. a 25-year-old African–American man was arrested by the Baltimore Police Department for possessing what the police alleged was an illegal switchblade under Baltimore law. While being transported in a police van, Gray fell into a coma and was taken to a trauma center. He died of a spinal injury on April 19, 2015. The incident has led to protest in Baltimore. Six Baltimore police officers have been suspended with pay.

Baltimore officials approved a $6.4 million deal to settle all civil claims tied to his death.

Justice Department report

Baltimore police officers routinely discriminate against blacks repeatedly use excessive force and are not adequately held accountable for misconduct. The report, the culmination of a year-long investigation into one of the country's largest police forces, also found that officers make large numbers of stops mostly in poor black neighborhoods—with dubious justification and unlawfully arrest citizens for speech deemed disrespectful.

Physical force is used unnecessarily, including against the mentally disabled, and black pedestrians and drivers are disproportionately searched during stops—Among the findings—The report represents a damning indictment of how the City's police officers carry out the most fundamental of policing practices, including stops and searches and responding to First Amendment expressions. The Justice Department is seeking a court-enforceable Consent decree to force the police agency to commit to improving its procedures to avoid a lawsuit.

Among the findings: Black residents account for roughly 84 percent of stops though they represent just 63 percent of the city's population

The statement of charges filed by Officer Garrett Miller against Gray accused him of possessing a switchblade. Miller wrwote, "The defendant was arrested without force or incident." Officers also reported "that he suffered a medical emergency during transport."

In the following week, according to the Gray family attorney, Gray died, was resuscitated, remained in a coma, and underwent extensive surgery to save his life. He lapsed into a coma after his spine was "80% severed" at his neck and his voice box was injured. He died the following Sunday, April 19, 2015.

Protesters have been holding near-daily demonstration over the death of Freddie Gray. Protesters vowed to "shut down" the city by marching through the streets and snarling traffic.

Malik Shabazz of Black Lawyers for Justice said, "It cannot be business as usual with that man's spine broken, with his back broken, with no justice on the scene." He also demanded the arrest of six officers involved in the arrest of Gray.

Gray asked for medical help several times, beginning before he was placed in the van. After a 30-minute ride that included three stops, paramedics were called. Authorities have not explained how or when Gray was injured.

Commissioner Anthony Batts said Gray might have been hurt before the van ride or during a "rough ride"—where officers hit the brakes and take sharp turns to injure suspects in the back of the vans.

"We know he was not buckled in the transportation wagon as he should have been. There's no excuse for that, period," Batts said. "We know our police employees failed to give him medical attention promptly multiple times.

Mayor Stephanie Rawlings-Blake said she has many questions. "I still want to know why the policies and procedures for transport were not followed," she said. "I still want to know why none of the officers called for immediate medical assistance despite Mr. Gray's apparent pleas.

Police killings in 2015

Police shot and killed 986 people in 2015.

The Washington Post's year-long project tracking on-duty police killings, by firearm, an issue that has taken on new urgency after many high-profile killings of unarmed African American men.

The Post found that the vast majority of those shot and killed by police were armed and half of them were white.

Still, police killed blacks at three times the rate of whites when adjusted for the populations where these shootings occurred. And although black men represent 6 percent of the U.S. population, they made up nearly 40 percent of those who were killed while unarmed. Regardless of race, about a quarter of those killed displayed signs of mental illness.

The Data from Killed by police...net show that white people are the largest group of killed by police. But when taken together, the number of people of color killed by police...Latino, Black, Asian and indigenous people—surpasses the number of whites.

Young black men are 21 times more likely to be killed by cops than young white men.

The data also show that California, Texas and Florida lead the U.S. in terms of deadly police encounters.

New Research shows one big change when cops wear cameras.

Cameras worn on police uniforms have been lauded as a possible solution to many of the problems facing officers on the line of duty, from violence against law enforcement to the unnecessary use of force. The US Department of Justice recently announced a plan to spend $20 million on Body Cameras for cops in 32 states. The cameras are controversial, as all surveillance technology tends to be. And until recently, there's been little hard evidence about how effective body cameras are.

Study shows less violence, fewer complaints when cops wear body cameras. Use of force and civilian complaints fell dramatically when officers and civilians knew they were being recorded.

Equipping police with body cameras may be an effective way to improve the behavior of officers and the public with which they interact a new study finds.

The University of South Florida release their report after a year-long body—worn camera pilot program at the Orlando Police Department, in which they randomly selected 46 officers to wear the devices and compared them against 43 officers who did not.

The study also showed significant reductions in the number of civilian injuries by officers wearing body cameras, and of injuries to the officers themselves. Officers who didn't wear body cameras in the study also used force fewer times over the year, though the drop-off was less substantial.

The study comes amid a nationwide effort to outfit more police forces with body cameras following high-profile police killings and instances of misconduct, which have spurred calls for improved transparency and accountability. President Barack Obama announced a $75 million initiative to help departments cover the cost of expanding their programs.

Many officers reported that the equipment changed citizen behavior and helped to de-escalate confrontations between civilians and police. They also said body cameras improved evidence collection, and helped them more accurately recollect events and fill out reports. Most officers felt that the camera made them better officers.

Racial Disparities exist in All Parts of the U.S.

Racial disparities in social and economic outcomes exist in all parts of the United States. Black Americans make about 62 cents for every dollar earned by white Americans. Black Americans are also twice as likely to be unemployed and considerably more to live in poverty and five times more likely to go to prison. These disparities are entirely attributable to residential segregation, which in turn is attributable to deliberate, racially conscious, government policies implemented over the 20th century. During this time, the Federal Housing Administration financed thousands of suburban development projects with the explicit requirement that no homes be sold to African Americans.

In some places, these disparities are even more pronounced. In many of the worst states for black Americans, there are opportunities to get a good job, earn good pay, and buy a home in a good community. However, these opportunities are not uniformly accessible across racial lines. Based on an examination of several socio-economic measures, 24/7 Wall Street identified the worst states for black Americans.

According to Dr. Valerie Wilson, Program Director on Race and Ethnicity in the Economy at the Economic Policy Institute, "You're never going to find a state or city where the outcomes for blacks are better than for whites." For centuries, there have been stark differences in the conditions and opportunities black Americans have faced.

The Civil Rights Movement led to hopes that racial inequality would soon end. The movement led to a series of reforms, including the Civil Rights Act of 1964, the Voting Rights Act of 1965, and other legislation, known as the "Great Society." Over the following 50 years, however, further advances have been modest at best.

According to Dedrick Asante-Muhammad, Senior Director of the Economic Department at the NAACP Financial Freedom Center "its one thing to end segregation, but it's another thing to talk about billions of dollars of investment." When the United States invested in a middle class in the 1940s and 1950s, it was in a white middle class, explained Asante-Muhammad. However, the country was "never willing to do that same type of investment to create a middle class that would be inclusive of African Americans."

The effects of this unwillingness to invest in the black community are clear in the racial economic outcome gaps. According to the Bureau of Labor Statistics, for example, the national jobless rate for November was 5.8% nationwide. Among white Americans, the figure was 4.9%. Among black Americans it was 11.1%.

Segregation also creates different communities with different social services. The quality of schools, property values, the quality of services available, and the quality of food are all "legacies of racially segregated neighborhoods in this country," said Wilson. Six of the worst states were home to nearly half of the 30 most segregated U.S. cities, according to a University of Michigan Institute for Social Research study on racial segregation in large metropolitan areas.

Few factors do more to improve people's livelihoods than access to good jobs. High employment rates contribute to higher incomes, better health insurance coverage, as well as lower poverty rates. In eight of the worst states for black Americans, the difference between black unemployment rates and that of the whole workforce was higher than the national difference. Black Americans in these states also tended to have higher poverty rates, lower incomes, and lower educational attainment rates than both their white peers and black residents in other states.

The Worst States for Black Americans

To determine the 10 worst states for black Americans, 24/7 Wall St. created an index of 12 measures from a variety of data sources. The index was designed to assess race-based gaps in access to resources and opportunities in each state, rather than measure the availability of resources and opportunities in those states. Creating the index in this way ensured that states were ranked based on differences between black and white Americans and not levels of socioeconomic development. We ranked the size of the race gap for each measure, with the largest gap receiving the worst score. We excluded states where black residents comprised less than 5% of the population.

To construct the index, we considered data from the U.S. Census Bureau on median household income, poverty rates, educational attainment rates, homeownership rates, and the percentage of people without health insurance. Unemployment figure came from the Bureau of Labor Statistics. Data on incarceration rates and disenfranchisement came from The Sentencing Project and are for the most recent available year. We also considered age-adjusted death rates and infant mortality rates per 100,000 people from the Centers for Disease Control and Prevention.

Additionally, we considered an analysis of racially-segregated metropolitan areas authored by William Frey of the Brookings Institution in partnership with the University of Michigan's Institute for Social Research. Educational outcomes for African-American children came from the Annie E. Casey Foundation's 2014 report, Race for Results: building a path to opportunity for all children.

Arkansas

Pct. Residents black: 15.7%
Black homeownership rate:
42.8% (15th highest)
Black incarceration rate: 2,432 per 100,000 people (24th highest)
Black unemployment rate: 16.5% (tied 4th highest)
Unemployment rate, all people: 7.8% (14th highest)

Arkansas is among the worst states for black Americans. Nearly 16% of Arkansas' population identifies as black. Yet, the state does not have a single black representative in Congress. In addition to limited representation, black Arkansas residents are disproportionately likely to be unemployed. Last year, the state's unemployment rate for black workers was 16.5%, versus a 7.8% unemployment rate of the state's labor force. In general, upward income mobility is more limited for Americans living in the South, according to research from the Equality of Opportunity Project. In Arkansas' largest urban area, Little Rock, the odds of reaching the top income quintile for a person born in the bottom quintile was just 5.4%, well-below the U.S. rate overall. Economic mobility may be even more difficult for black Americans, who, on average, earn less than 60% the median household income of white Americans.

Kansas

> **Pct. Residents black: 5.8%**
> **Black homeownership rate: 36.1%**
> **(22nd lowest)**
> **Black incarceration rate: 3,306 per 100,000 people (9th highest)**
> **Black unemployment rate: 11.8% (14th lowest)**
> **Unemployment rate, all people: 5.6% (12th lowest)**

A typical black household in Kansas made 60.2% of the median white household income in 2013, slightly wider than the national income gap. Lower incomes among the state's black population are due in part to the relatively large gaps in educational attainment and incarceration rates compared to white residents, among other measures. Nearly 32% of white state residents had attained at least a bachelor's degree in 2013, while black Americans were 5.12 times more likely to go to prison than their white peers across the U.S., in Kansas, black residents were nearly eight times more likely to go to prison, one of the higher disparities nationwide. As in several other states on this list, Kansas residents are also not represented at all by black congressmen in the U.S. Congress.

New Jersey

> **Pct. Residents black: 13.7%**
> **Black homeownership rate: 39.1% (23rd highest)**
> **Black incarceration rate: 1,992 per 100,000 people (13th lowest)**
> **Black unemployment rate: 13.0% (21st lowest)**
> **Unemployment rate, all people: 8.2% (7th highest)**

Nearly 16% of New Jersey's black population lived in poverty in 2013. This figure is lower than the national poverty rate of 17.1% and partially reflects the fact that the state is among the wealthiest in the country. Yet, the typical black household made only 58% of the typical white household, a wider income gap than across the county. Only one in five black residents had at least a bachelor's degree in 2013, much lower than the nearly 40% of white adults who had held at least such a degree. As Wilson explained, without economic opportunity people often turn to alternatives that may be illegal. Blacks were more than nine times as likely to be imprisoned in 2013, nearly twice the national ratio. Homeownership is another issue that many black Americans face. While more than 75% of white households owned their own home in 2013, fewer than 40% of black house-hold did, a much larger disparity than across the U.S.

Connecticut

> **Pct. Residents black: 10.3%**
> **Black homeownership rate: 35.0%**
> **(21st lowest)**
> **Black incarceration rate: 13.3% (20th Highest)**
> **Black Unemployment rate: 13.3% (20th highest)**
> **Unemployment rate, all people: 7.7% (15th highest)**

Connecticut is home to a relatively high number of highly segregated metro areas, according to an analysis of 2010 Decennial Census data by Brookings Institution's demographer William Frey. All three of Connecticut's metro areas—Bridgeport, Hartford, and New Haven—are also among the 30 most racially segregated in the country. In addition to living in different neighborhoods, black state residents are far less likely to own their home. The nearly 41 percentage point gap between black and white homeownership rates—35% and 75.8% respectively—was among the worst in the nation. Similarly, the state had among the worst gaps other key measures of social outcomes. Just 19.2% of black residents had at least a bachelor's degree, versus 39.7% of the state's white 25 and older population. Further, Connecticut had one of the largest disparities in incarceration rates in the nation, with black residents 9.38 times more likely than white residents to be incarcerated.

Michigan

Pct. Residents black: 13.9%

Black homeownership rate: 42.6% (16th highest)

Black incarceration rate: 2,169 per 100,000 people (18th lowest)

Black unemployment rate: 16.5% (tied-4th highest)

Unemployment rate, all people: 8.6% (6th highest)

For every 100,000 black Michigan residents, more than 965 died last year, a higher rate than in all but a handful of states. The same rate for white state residents was lower by 214, nearly the widest gap by this measure in the country. Poor health and the generally higher death risk among black Michigan residents can be partly explained by economic and social factors. For example, 16.5% of black workers in the state were unemployed last year. A relatively high level of unemployment tends to lower health insurance coverage and exacerbate health risks. The jobless rate for black residents was also nearly 8 percentage points higher than the rate for white Michigan residents, which was one of the wider gaps reviewed. African-American children in Michigan also had among the worst educational outcomes compared to most of the nation. Additionally, Michigan reported 31 racially-motivated hate crimes per 100,000 people—many of which likely targeted black residents—

the second-highest rate in the nation last year. While Detroit represents a small percent of Michigan's total population, it was identified as nearly the most racially-segregated city in the United States.

Pennsylvania

> **Pct. Residents black: 11.0%**
> **Black homeownership rate: 43.1% (14th highest)**
> **Black incarceration rate: 3,269 per 100,000 people (10th highest)**
> **Black unemployment rate: 14.4% (15th highest)**
> **Unemployment rate, all people: 7.5% (20th highest)**

While some 28% of Pennsylvania's black population did not have health insurance last year, only 8.5% of the white population did not, a difference of 20 percentage points. Also, as in the majority of the states on this list, African-American children faced larger obstacles to opportunities than their white classmates—much more than black children faced nationwide. Geographical segregation may partly explain the discrepancy in educational outcomes. Some Pennsylvania cities, including Philadelphia, Pittsburgh, and Harrisburg, were identified in a recent analysis by the University of Michigan's Institute for Social Research as among the nation's 20 most racially-segregated cities. Also, black state residents were nearly nine times more likely than their white peers to go to prison, a larger incarceration rate gap than the vast majority of states.

Illinois

> **Pct. Residents black: 14.2%**
> **Black homeownership rate: 38.5%**
> **(25 highest)**
> **Black incarceration rate: 2,128 per 100,000 people (17th lowest)**
> **Black unemployment rate: 17.0% (3rd highest)**
> **Unemployment rate, all people: 9.1% (3rd highest)**

Social and health outcomes for Illinois' black residents are far worse than for white residents. As of 2013, 17% of black workers were unemployed, versus 9.1% of the state's workforce. Also, the incarceration rate for black Americans in the state, at 2,128 per 100,000 people, was more than eight times that for white residents. Tragically, Illinois had one of the largest gaps in death rates between white and black Americans. As of 2012, the death rate for white residents was 711.8 per 100,000 people, far better than the 925.6 deaths per 100,000 black residents. According to data from the University of Michigan's Institute for Social Research, as of 2010, Chicago was among the most segregated metro areas in the nation, despite considerable improvements in the past 20 years.

Rhode Island

> **Pct. Residents black: 6.4%**
> **Black homeownership rate: 29.4% (10th lowest)**
> **Black incarceration rate: 1,884 per 100,000 people (11th lowest)**
> **Black unemployment rate: 16.0% (6th highest)**
> **Unemployment rate, all people: 9.2% (2nd highest)**

While typical black households earned 62.3% of the white median household income across the nation, black Rhode Island households made just 52.5% of white households in the state. Such disadvantage can lead to a variety of negative outcomes, including higher poverty and death rates. Last year, there were 234 more deaths per 100,000 people among the black population in Rhode Island than among the white population, nearly the largest gap nationwide. More than 23% of black Rhode Islanders lived in poverty last year, while less than 11% of white residents lived in poverty, a difference of more than 12 percentage points, among the larger gaps nationwide. Another particularly detrimental area of inequality is the housing market. While 67.2% of white households in the state were homeowners, only 29.4% of black households were. The 38 percentage point was wider than the gap nationwide of nearly 30 percentage points.

Minnesota

> **Pct. Residents black: 5.4%**
> **Black homeownership rate: 25.7% (5th lowest)**
> **Black incarceration rate: 2,321 per 100,000 people (22nd lowest)**
> **Black unemployment rate: 15.0% (tied-11th lowest)**
> **Unemployment rate, all people: 4.9% (9th lowest)**

A typical black household in Minnesota earned less than half the median income of white households in 2013, well below the 62.3% nationwide. Low incomes among the black population are likely due in part to a high unemployment rate. While 15% of black workers in the state were unemployed in 2013, fewer than 5% of the total workforce did not have a job, a gap nearly twice as large as the national gap. High unemployment rates tend to lead to higher rates of people without health insurance, as a majority of Americans receive health insurance through their employers. While only 6.9% of white residents did not have health insurance in 2013, nearly 33% of blacks were uninsured. Additionally, black Minnesotan households were three times less likely than white households to own their homes, a rate nearly twice as high as the rest of the nation. Across the country, black Americans were also more likely to be disenfranchised as a result of the criminal justice system. In 2013, more than 7% of Minnesota's black population was barred from voting as a result of felony convictions or imprisonment.

Wisconsin

> **Pct. residents black: 6.2%**
> **Black homeownership rate: 28.1% (7th lowest)**
> **Black incarceration rate: 4,042 per 100,000 people (3rd highest)**
> **Black unemployment rate: 15.0% (tied-11th highest)**
> **Unemployment rate, all people: 6.7% (21st lowest)**

Based on our index, Wisconsin is the worst state for black Americans. Typical black Wisconsin household made roughly half the white median household income, a wider income gap than in the majority of states. Wisconsin's black residents were also far less likely than white residents to have health insurance, with a gap of more than 30 percentage points. Black

Americans in Wisconsin are at a much greater risk of death than their white peers as well, which could be due in part to poor health coverage. There were 980 deaths per 100,000 people among Wisconsin's black population—one of the highest rates nationwide. This figure represents 288 more deaths than the comparable rate for white residents, nearly the largest gap reviewed. Black Wisconsin residents were also nearly 10 times more likely than white residents to go to prison, nearly the largest gap. Black children in Wisconsin had worse educational outcomes than both their white classmates and their black peers in other states. Milwaukee led the nation of most racially-segregated U.S. cities, which may make the problem in Wisconsin more a problem for Milwaukee, where the vast majority of the state's black population lives. Half of all black men in Milwaukee County have a suspended driver's license today. Why? Because in Wisconsin, any unpaid driving fine or fee can result in a two-year license suspension—more than twice as long as the suspension for a drunk-driving conviction. Being short of $50 may be the defining factor of whether you can drive to work tomorrow and in the suburbs public transportation is lacking. And of course you can know that black men are stopped more than any other racial/ethnic group, such is the case in Milwaukee, where black drivers are stopped seven times more often than white drivers.

Is it any wonder, then, that in Wisconsin unemployment for black men is 20%? That is four times the national average. No community that has unemployment that high isn't angry. Can't work, can't drive, can't own a home, no freedom of movement, no ability to provide for a family, high exposure to violence—this anger builds and builds. Very few people can thrive under these conditions. When the society you live in constantly reminds you that your wants and needs don't matter, that your well-being doesn't matter, you read that as being told that your life does not matter.

Wisconsin has the highest percentage of incarcerated black men in the nation, with more than half of African American men in Milwaukee County in their thirties having served time in prison. Inner city schools are under-funded and black students are suspended at rates double the national average.

The anger was already there, from the experiences of people being born into a system that actively works against them. Those are just a few of the statistics to illustrate that a lot of blacks in Milwaukee are hurting and angry, and their anger is justified.

Cities where African-Americans are doing the best economically

At the top of the list is Atlanta, long hailed as the unofficial capital of Black America. The city, which in the 1960s advertised itself as "the city too busy to hate," has long lured ambitious African-Americans. With its well established religions and educational institutions, notably Spelman and Morehouse, which are ranked first and third, respectively, by US News among the nation's historically black colleges, the area has arguably the strongest infrastructure for African–American advancement in the country.

Some 46.9% of the black population owned their own homes. African-Americans have a median household income of $41,800, also considerably above the major metro average, while their rate of self-employment, 17.1% is second only to New Orleans.

No 2 Raleigh, NC: median household income $42,285, Home ownership rate: 46.7%.

No 3 Washington, DC. As in Atlanta, black community has strong institutions of culture and higher education. The District is home to Howard University, the nation's second-ranked historically black university. The median black household income in the metro area is $64,896 more than $20,000 above that of Atlanta and other top-ranked Southern cities. Home ownership rates at 49.2%, are also the highest in the nation.

No 4 Baltimore, MD: median household income $47,898, Home ownership rate 46.2% which is due to federal jobs.

No 5 Charlotte NC: median household income $36,522, Home ownership rate: 43.9%

No 6 Virginia Beach-Norfolk, VA: median household income $40,677, Home ownership rate: 43.8%.

No 7 Orlando, FL: median household income $33,982, Home ownership rate: 43.8%

No 8 Miami, FL: median household income $36,749, Home ownership rate: 44.9%

No 9 Richmond, VA: median household income $38,899, Home ownership rate: 47.8%

No 10 San Antonio, TX: median household income $41,681, Home ownership rate: 40.8%

African American Women-Owned Businesses Numbers and Characteristics

There are 911,728 African Americans women-owned businesses in the United States. This reflects a tremendous 66.7% increase in number since 2002 and a 191.4% increase since 1997. In comparison, African American men owned businesses grew 93.1% from 1997 to 2007.

African American women-owned firms across the country have total receipts of $36.8 billion.

The total receipts of African American women-owned firms grew 78.1% since 2002.

Women owned firms make up 47.4% of all African American nonfarm businesses across the country.

A full 96.5% of these firms are non-employers firms, with average receipts of $15,618. The remaining 3.5% of the firms have paid employees, employing a total of 245,474 people across the country with a payroll of 5.6 billion. These employer firms have average receipts of $718,374.

Geography

Slightly more than one in 10 (11.7%) of all women-owned firms across the country are owned by African American women.

The South has the highest representation (17.2%) followed by the Midwest and Northeast (both 11.1%) and the West (4.4%).

The States with the largest number of African American women-owned business are New York (98,877), Georgia (88,920), and Florida (86,001).

18

Black Lives MatterMovement—A Racial Justice Project for Black People

Addressing systemic racism and redefining the political process: Tracing its roots to the fatal 2012 shooting of 17-year-old Trayvon Martin in Florida, the Black Lives Matter Movement gained national ground after 18-year-old Michael Brown was shot and killed by a white police officer in Ferguson, Missouri. Since then, deaths of other unarmed black males at the hands of law enforcement officers have inspired protests under the "Black Lives Matter" moniker. Co-founders Alicia Garza, Patrisse Cullors and Opal Tometi

Since 2013, Black Lives Matter has moved from social media platforms to the streets, morphing into an organization and a movement that gained national recognition during demonstrations after the 2014 police-involved killings of Michael Brown and Eric Garner.

How does Black Lives Matter work?

What set Black Lives Matter apart from other social justice groups, however, is its decentralized approach and reliance almost solely on local, rather than national leadership. Cullors said organizing is often spontaneous and not directed by one person or group of people. "We don't get (people) onto the streets, they get themselves onto the street," she said.

Black Lives Matter is made up of a network of local chapters who operate mostly independently. Chelsea Fuller of the Advancement Project, a non-profit that works with grassroots justice and race movements, said that local organizing is a powerful way to address poverty, access to housing and jobs, community policing and other issues that intersect with systemic racism.

"We can't affect national narrative, we can't affect national legislation that comes down and affects local people if local people don't push back and take a stand about what's happening in local communities," Fuller said.

What does Black Lives Matter stand for?

The most important directive of Black Lives Matter, Cullors said, is to deal with anti-black racism, to "push for black people's right to live with dignity and respect" and be included in the American democracy that they helped create.

"This is about the quality of life for black people, for poor people in this country," said Umi Selah, co-director of Dream Defenders in Miami. Though not officially affiliated, Dream Defenders and similar social justice groups often align themselves with Black Lives Matter.

"The conception that all we're mad about is police and policing is a strong misconception," Selah said. Black Lives Matter released a statement last week condemning the shooting in Dallas as counter to what the movement is trying to accomplish.

Cullors also hears claims that Black Lives Matter lacks direction of strategy. But Cullors said the strategy is clear-working to ensure that black people live with full dignity of their human rights.

"We are not leaderless, we're leaderful," she said. "We're trying to change the world…developing a new vision for what this generation of black leaders can look like."

<u>Why so many critics of President Obama insists that he hates police officers.</u>

His critics accuse him of secretly hates Christianity, secretly hates the Constitution, he secretly hates America itself.

He's also accused of Anti-Cop rhetoric:

In the first year of Obama's term, Historian Henry Louis Gates, who is black, was arrested while trying to force his way into his own home in Cambridge, Mass. The incident gained national attention, Obama weighed in, saying that the arresting officer had "acted stupidly" for handcuffing and booking Gates.

The politics of defending police officers created a stir in congress, where congress man Thaddeus Mc Cotter introduce a resolution in the House demanding that Obama apologize for his comments.

The National Republican Senate Committee used Obama's remarks to mobilize its base, asking Americans to sign a petition if they thought it was inappropriate for "our nation's Commander in chief to stand before a national audience and criticize the men and women in law enforcement who put their lives on the line every day" Obama defused the controversy in part by inviting Gates and the arresting officer to a "beer summit" at the White House.

In 2011, critics of the President decried his inviting the rapper Common to the White House as part of an event celebration poets. Critics of Obama seized upon Common's track "A song for Assata," dedicated to Assata Shakur, who was convicted of killing a police officer and who then fled to Cuba. It was a New Jersey police officer whom Shakur was convicted of killing and a New Jersey State Police spokesman criticized Obama for extending an invitation to someone who defended "a fugitive who killed one of our own."

In November 2013, Obama nominated Debo Adegbile to a position in the Department of Justice. Opponents quickly seized upon Adegbile are having signed a friend-of-the-Court petition on behalf of Mumia Abu-Jamal, who was convicted of the murder of a Phi8ladelphia Police officer in 1982. The nomination was blocked by the Senate focusing on the Abu-Jamal filing.

In 2014, the Death of Michael Brown and Eric Garner kicked the Obama-hates-cops sentiment into overdrive. Brown's death prompted Obama to release a statement offering his condolences to the family and calling for calm. The failure of grand juries to indict the officers in either man's death gave rise to the Politically contentious Black Lives Matter movement which itself was blamed for the murders of two police officers in a patrol car in New York that December.

Former New York City mayor Rudy Giuliano traced those officers' deaths back to the president. "We've had four months of propaganda, starting with the president," he said on "fox News Sunday" that month, "that everybody should hate the police.

There was no evidence Obama said anything of the sort. (Joe Walsh also argued that Obama was to blame.)

In October 2015, for example, Obama was criticized for supporting changes to police practices and for meeting with members of the Black Lives Matter movement who "appear to hate all cops."

It's impossible not to note that each of these incidents centers in some way on race: Gates, rap music, Black Lives Matter, that Obama has been receptive to the concerns of protesters is amplified by how Obama is himself black and that he has framed some of what police departments need to improve upon in explicitly racial terms.

Some small part of the interest in siding with the police in opposition to Obama—if one chooses to look at the two in opposition—is probably motivated by race-based assumptions. More broadly, though, it's Obama's focus on problems in police work that happen to deal with race, which are blended into a sense that he opposes law enforcement broadly.

The Dallas police killings that occurred July 7th 2016 was horrific. Walsh was by no means alone in suggesting that the fault lay with Obama—unsurprising given how long Obama has been surrounded by criticisms of his views of law enforcement.

With obvious exception of calling the actions of the police in Cambridge "stupid," though, Obama's comments about police have been positive even as he has called for improvements. That call for improvement is, to many, enough to suggest that the president broadly dislikes all American police officers. Which seems to say far more about our politics than it does about Obama?

Police are safer under Obama than they have been in decades

Data from the <u>Officers down Memorial Page,</u> which tracks law enforcement officer fatalities in real time, illustrates the point. During the Reagan years, for instance, an average of 101 police officers were intentionally killed each year. Under George H. W. Bush that number fell to 90. It fell further, to 81 deaths per year, under Bill Clinton, and to 72 deaths per year under George W. Bush.

Under Obama, the average number of police intentionally killed each year has fallen to its lowest level-yet-an average of 62 deaths annually through 2015. If you include the 2016 police officer shootings year-to-date and project it out to a full year, that average of 62 deaths doesn't change.

Reforming the Criminal Justice System

President Obama gave a speech at the NAACP's 2015 national convention about reforming the criminal justice system.

America is home to 5% of the world's population, but 25% of the world's prisoners. America keeps more people behind bars than the top 35 European countries combined.

In 1980, there were 500,000 people in American jails. Today, there are 2.2 million. Many belong, but too many are non-violent offenders.

The $80 billion we spend each year to keep people incarcerated could pay for universal pre-k for every 3-year-old and 4-year-old in America. The $80 billion we spend each year on incarcerations could double the salary of every high school teacher in America. We could eliminate tuition at every public college and university in America with the $80 billion we spend each year on incarcerations. Mass incarceration doesn't work. Let's build communities that give kids a shot at success and prisons that prepare people for a 2nd chance.

Directly comparing incarceration with other expenditures, Obama is making a point many criminal justice experts now agree with: Mass incarceration reached the point of diminishing returns by the 1990s—there are only so many serious criminals out there, and by then the people getting put in prison weren't people who'd be committing crime after crime on the street.

So it would be better for the US to spend money on other measures, some of which could even do a better job at fighting crime.

America is now the World's leader in incarceration

Starting in the 1970s, America's incarcerated population began to rise rapidly. In response to a tide of higher crime and drug use over the preceding decade, state and federal lawmakers passed measures that increased the length of prison sentences for all sort of crimes, from drugs to murder. This tough-on-crime mentality continued to the 1990s, when President Bill Clinton approved a crime law that imposed tougher prison sentences, increasing funding for prisons, and put more cops on the streets.

No single state escaped the rise of incarceration, but Southern States have stood out. States like Louisiana and Mississippi have been slower in reducing their prison populations.

In 1971 President Nixon officially declared the war on drugs. The high drug use is one of the reasons law makers passed tougher prison sentences for drug possession and trafficking, which helped fill America's prisons with drug offenders.

In 1986 President Ronald Reagan pass the AntiDrug Abuse Act, which greatly elevated prison sentences for drugs, especially crack.

In response to higher drug use, federal lawmakers passed very strict mandatory minimum sentences for drugs. Many states followed with their elevated drug sentences. This meant that not only did the crack down on drugs put more people in prison, but they would be doomed to stay in prison for longer, as well.

It wasn't just drug offenses that saw higher sentences—practically all crimes resulted in higher prison time after the 1980s. This was also a result of mandatory minimum sentences that states and the federal government enacted on crimes in the 1980s and 1990s. One particularly harsh form of sentencing was the "three-strikes" laws, which force people to serve 25 years to life after they're convicted of any third felony. Lawmakers also passed "truth-in-sentencing" laws that require inmates to serve most of their prison sentences—typically 85 percent—before qualifying for parole.

It's not just that prison sentences got longer; more crimes also began to be punished by life sentences, including life without parole, as prosecutors and judges embraced tougher sentences on some of the worst convicts. So not only are there more people in prison, but a record number are expected to spend the rest of their lives there.

Prosecutors are driving mass incarceration

Prosecutors were more likely to go after people with longer criminal records, who now existed in greater numbers because of the war on drugs and other tough-on-crime polices enacted in the 1980s and 90s that pushed more people into the corrections systems.

The number of plea bargains, when a defendant pleads guilty to avoid trial, has steadily increased over the past few decades—helping fill America's prisons with people who never went through a full trial. There have been many cases in which someone who's not guilty of a crime pleads guilty-out of fear, for example, that the jury of judge might make the wrong call and sentence him to prison for much longer than a plea bargain does.

In a 2012 survey among 40 States, the average inmate cost about $31,000 each year. With studies showing that incarceration doesn't significantly reduce crime, many lawmakers feel they're not getting much bang for their buck when they spend more on prisons.

Minority Americans are much more likely to be incarcerated

Black people are nearly six times as likely to be incarcerated as white people, and more than twice as likely to be incarcerated as their Latino counterparts. This leads to enormous inequities over lifetimes: The Sentencing Project estimated that one in three black men born in 2001 will be imprisoned at some point in their lives, compared with one in 17 white men and one in six Latino men.

Part of this disparity is explained by socioeconomic factors, including poverty and unemployment that make black Americans more likely to commit crime than their white counterparts. But a review of the research by the Sentencing Project concluded that the higher crime rates in black communities only explained about 61 to 80 percent of black over-representation in prisons. This means that other factors, such as racial bias, were behind as much as 39 percent of the disparate rates of imprisonment for black people.

The numbers show that mass incarceration didn't just put more Americans in prison—but, in effect, more black Americans. Mass incarceration has drained 1.5 million black men from their communities.

Poorer, Black neighborhoods are much more policed

These neighborhoods indeed tend to have more crime. But there's a long history behind that: The shackles of slavery deprived black Americans of any freedom, and then segregation ensured wealthier neighborhoods and better job prospects remained out of reach once they were free. When Jim Crow policies finally began collapsing under civil rights movement, black communities were left mired in socioeconomic stagnation after decades of oppression—which led many to turn to crime as their only outlet for making ends meet.

So as the war on drugs and tough-on-crime policies kicked in, black neighborhoods were more likely to be consumed by crime—and residents have faced the brunt of police enforcement and mass incarceration as a result.

American Civil Liberties Union study shows that only two States—Maine and Vermont—allow everyone to vote regardless of criminal record.

As a result, more than 5.8 million Americans weren't legally allowed to vote due to their criminal records in 2012, according to data analyzed by the Sentencing Project. The black disenfranchisement rate topped 20 percent in Florida, Kentucky and Virginia.

Other examples of collateral effects of prison include restriction on unemployment, bans on receiving welfare benefits, accessing Public housing, or qualifying for student loans for higher education

Bill Clinton Concedes His Crime law jailed too many for too long.

Its true Bill Clinton did not start Mass Incarceration. But don't be fooled Clinton has never been a friend, fan or hero of the Black Community.

Mass Incarceration is as American as apple pie, from Slavery to Jim Crow, Black Codes and the War on Drugs.

The War on Drugs: Nixon declared the War on Drugs in the 1970s. It was expanded by Reagan and Bush senior. But Bill Clintons 1994 Crime Bill took things to another level.

Five provisions in the 1994 Crime Bill that crippled the black community and exploded the Prison Industrial Complex.

#1 10.8 billion in federal matching funds to local government to hire 100,000 new police officers over 5 years. Who were focused primarily on the Black community? This continues to this day.

#2 $10 billion for the construction of new federal prisons. All this money spent on shiny new facilities, they had to be filled. As we know they are now filled with black people.

#3 An expansion from two to eight in the number of federal crimes to which the death penalty applied.

#4 A three strike proposal that mandate life sentences for anyone convicted of three "violent" felonies, 25 to life!! In practice this just didn't apply to violent crimes, many drug trafficking and possession charges were attached.

#5 A section that allowed children as young as thirteen to be tried as adults. Black youth seems to be the target, now many are in the system with no way out.

Today there are more African American men incarcerated in the U.S. than the total prison population of India, Argentina, Canada, Lebanon, Japan, Germany, Finland, Israel and England combined.

These nine country in total represent 1.5 billion people. In contrast, there are only 18.5 million black males in the United Stated, including children

Addressing a convention of the NAACP a day after President Obama called for a wholesale overhaul of the criminal justice system, Mr. Clinton embraced the idea. He agreed that the law he enacted in 1994 played a significant part in warping sentencing standards and leading to an era of mass incarceration. "I signed a bill that made the problem worse," Mr. Clinton said' "And I want to admit it."

The law Mr. Clinton signed in 1994 committed to putting 100,000 more police officers on the street, banned certain assault rifles, enacted background checks for many gun purchases and increased resources to fight violence against women.

"But in that bill, there were longer sentences," Mr. Clinton told the NAACP gathering in Philadelphia. "And most of these people are in prison under state law, but the federal law set a trend. And that was overdone. We were wrong about that." But the damage has been done and the evidence irrefutable.

Republicans wants Criminal Justice Reform

President Obama called for an overhaul of how we treat low-level offenders. It was a move that brought a chorus of applause from across the political spectrum. The President's commitment to change was both highly personal and clear: "Mass incarceration makes our country worse off, and we need to do something about it."

Hope has been building among those behind bars, their families, Communities and Justice Reform advocates nationwide.

House Speaker John Boehner announced his commitment to getting people out of prison "who don't need to be there" and signaled his commitment to bringing justice reform legislation before the full House Chamber for a vote.

In the U.S. Senate, leaders are working together across the aisle on a deal. President Obama and speaker John Boehner are in rare agreement.

According to a recent poll of likely voters released by the ACLU, the next majority of Republicans, Democrats and Independents believe we need to rethink our approach to punishment. Rep. Elijah Cummings, D-Maryland, said at the Bipartisan Summit on Criminal Justice Reform in March of 2015, "the stars have aligned." Our major leaders acknowledge that our justice system is broken. The only question is how to fix it.

America is ready for strong, smart reforms that reduce the overly harsh punishment for nonviolent drug offenders. As outlined in the Coalition for Public Safety's "Fair sentencing and Fair Chances" effort and as discussed at the Bipartisan Summit on

Criminal Justice Reform earlier in the year, there are many more areas with strong bipartisan consensus:

- Ensuring fair and appropriate treatment of juveniles and young adults.
- Reform federal and state sentencing laws and reducing mandatory minimum sentences.
- Expanding alternatives to incarceration, reducing recidivism and safety reducing prison and jail populations.
- Enabling prisons to offer programs that allow people to make a positive transition back into their communities.

Decades of failed policies and wrongheaded politics brought us here. It will undoubtedly take years to transform the Justice System. While solutions will not come overnight, we have—at long last—reached a tipping point in the quest for justice.

Justice Department to release 6,000 inmates from federal prisons

The Justice Department will release 6,000 inmates from federal prisons beginning at the end of October 2015 as part of new sentencing guidelines for drug crimes established last year.

Poll Shows Most Americans Think Race Relations Are Bad

Seven years ago, in the gauzy afterglow of a stirring election night in Chicago, commentators dared ask whether the United States had finally begin to heal its divisions over race and atone for the original sin of slavery by electing its first black president. It has not, not even close.

A new NY Times/CBS News Poll reveals that nearly six in 10 Americans, including heavy majority of both whites and blacks, think race relations are generally bad and that nearly four in 10 think the situation is getting worse. By comparison, two-thirds of Americans surveyed shortly after president Obama took office said they believed that race relations were generally good.

The swings in attitude have been particularly striking among African-Americans. During Mr. Obama's 2008 campaign, nearly 60 percent of blacks said race relations were generally bad, but that number was cut in half shortly after he won. It has now soared to 68 percent, the highest level of discontent among blacks during the Obama years and close to the numbers recorded in the aftermath of the riots that followed the 1992 acquittal of Los Angeles police officers charged in the beating of Rodney King. Only a fifth of those surveyed said they thought race relations were improving, while about 40 percent of both blacks and whites said they were staying essentially the same.

Respondents tended to have much sunnier views of race relations in their communities. For instance, while only 37 percent said they thought race relations were generally good in the United States, more than twice that share—77 percent—thought they were good in their communities, a number that has changed little over the past 20 years. Similarly, only a third thought that most people were comfortable discussing race with someone of another race, but nearly three-quarters said they were comfortable doing so themselves.

The nationwide telephone poll of 1,205 people, which focused on racial concerns, was conducted from July 14 to July 19, at the midpoint of a year that has seen as much race-related strife and violence as perhaps any since the desegregation battles of the 1960s. It came one month after the massacre in Charleston, S.C., of nine black worshippers at Emanuel A.M.E. Church apparently by a white supremacist, and after a yearlong series of shootings and harassments of blacks by white police officers that were captured by smartphone cameras.

The Charleston shootings, which took place during Bible study on June 17, generated a national outpouring of outrage and grief. The suspect's embrace of the Confederate battle flag in internet photographs prompted South Carolina's Republican governor, Nikki R. Haley, and its Republican-controlled legislature to order the flags removal from the grounds of the State House in Columbia.

But despite the perception that the shootings inspired a moment of empathy and reconciliation, the poll suggests that attitudes toward the flag remain deeply divided between whites and blacks, and not just in the south.

When asked how they regarded the battle flag, 57 percent of whites said they considered it mostly an emblem of Southern pride, while 68 percent of blacks said they saw it more as a symbol of racism. The view that the flag represents heritage more than bigotry was shared by 65 percent of white Southerners, including three-fourths of white Southern men. About four in 10 whites—and one in 10 blacks—said they disapproved of the decision to lower the flag in Columbia, while 52 percent of whites and 81 percent of blacks favored it.

Nearly half of white Southerners disagreed with the decision. Four in 10 blacks said they would be less likely to shop with a retailer who sold Confederate flags and merchandise, but only 17 percent of whites said so.

In the aftermath of the Charleston shootings, many Americans were deeply moved when relatives of five of the victims told the suspect in the killings, Dylann Roof, at a court hearing that their faith directed them to forgive him. The poll found that about half of those surveyed, including 49 percent of whites and 41 percent of blacks, could not have brought themselves to do the same.

Mr. Obama delivered perhaps his most pointed reflection on race in late June when he eulogized the

Rev. Clementa C. Pinckney, the pastor of Emanuel A.M.E. "For too long," he said, "we've been blind to the way past injustices continue to shape the present." But Mr. Obama has largely succeeded in persuading the country that, as he asserted in 2012, he is "not the president of black America" but rather "the president of the United States of America." Two-thirds of those surveyed said his administration's policies treated whites and blacks the same.

Yet in 2010, 83 percent of Americans said the administration did not favor one race over the other. Still, almost half of those questioned said Obama presidency had not affect bringing the races together, while about a third said it had driven them further apart. Only 15 percent said race relations had improved. Seventy-two percent of blacks said they approved of the way Mr. Obama is handling race relations, compared with 40 percent of whites.

The President won 95 percent of the black vote and 43 percent of the white vote in 2008, according to exit polling, and 93 percent of the black vote and 39 percent of the white vote in his re-election. His job approval ratings also demonstrated a deep racial divide.

The divide, seen in the answers to virtually every question in the poll, was stark when respondents were asked whether they thought most Americans had judged Mr. Obama more harshly because of his race. Eighty percent of blacks said yes, while only 37 percent of whites agreed.

Deep racial schisms also were evident in responses about law enforcement and the criminal justice system. About three-fourths of blacks said they thought the system is biased against African–Americans, and that the police are more likely to use deadly force against a black person than a white person. Only 44 percent of whites felt that the system is biased against blacks.

Views of the police are informed by personal experience. Four in 10 blacks—and nearly two-thirds of black men—said they felt they had been stopped by the police just because of their race or ethnicity, compared with only one in 20 whites. Fully 72 percent of blacks said they had suffered what they perceived as racial discrimination, compared with 31 percent of whites.

At a time when the unemployment rate for blacks is double that for whites and black households earn 40 percent less, blacks continue to assert they do not enjoy an equal shot at attaining financial success. The share of blacks who said whites have a better chance to get ahead rose by 14 percentage points in about a year to 60 percent.

More than half of whites said blacks have equal opportunities, compared with a third of blacks who said so.

But in a finding that may highlight class divisions more than racial ones, identical majorities of blacks and whites, 59 percent, said the economy enabled only a few people at the top to get ahead.

More than 80 percent of blacks favored affirmative action programs for minorities, a figure that has largely stayed static for nearly two decades. Only half of whites supported special efforts for minorities. This fall, the Supreme Court is scheduled to hear a new challenge to affirmative action policies in college admissions.

In large measure, the poll found that blacks and whites live in separate societies. Most whites say they do not live (79 percent), work (81 percent), or come in regular contact (68 percent) with more than a few blacks. While the numbers have not changed among whites in the past 15 years, the poll suggested some erosion in residential segregation among blacks. Only a third of blacks surveyed said that almost all of the people who lived near their homes were of the same race, compared with half who said so in a 2000 Times Poll.

The long history of black officers reforming policing from within

The war has been ongoing at the local level for over a half-century, with African American officers working to mitigate racial bias and abuse of power from within the profession after decades of being ineligible for top positions, some black law enforcement leaders today try to shape how officers think about racism and inequality.

Historian W. Marvin Dulaney details this progression in cities across the country in his book Black Police in America. During slavery and Reconstruction, a few cities and states in the South hired black officers to fill undesirable positions or increase departments' size, but their brief tenures often ended in backlash from white citizens. (During slavery, the officers were freedmen.) In the North and Midwest, newly elected mayors appointed some of the first African American police as a reward for black votes in the late 1800s and early 1900s. States in the Deep South that had previously outlawed black police officers during Reconstruction didn't hire them again until the 1930s or 1940s, after protests from African American communities.

Across the country, more black officers joined during the Jim Crow era, and they were commonly assigned to patrol only black neighborhoods. "They were often denied promotions and transfers to other division. In some cases they were not allowed to wear their uniform to or from work for fear of some altercations that could occur with a white citizen," said Alan Thompson, a University of Southern Mississippi criminal-justice professor. Their treatment of minorities was shaped by social norms and growing up in segregated communities; through the early 1900s, black officers were often aggressive toward minorities. But by the 1930s and 1940s, there were new cohorts of black police who actively adopted a more respectful posture toward people of color and began building ties to black community organizations like the NAACP.

In the social upheaval of the 1960s—as departments had to "back away from explicit practices" segregating police—some started relying on black officers to deescalate tensions between police and black communities, and to improve their reputations. As the first black mayors of major cities were elected in the late 1960s and early 1970s, some of them appointed their cities, first black police chief.

"I think we can't make changes if we're not part of the system," said Jefferson County Sheriff Zena Stephens, the first African American female sheriff elected in Texas. "If I have a skillset that can prevent this misunderstanding or this train wreck that seems to be happening in society, then I think I have a responsibility to do so."

During the Obama administration, the Fraternal Order of Police, the largest police union in the United States, promotes a defend-at-all-costs culture, some suggested. When something controversial goes on with the police in Chicago, the media interviews the union President—who's not even part of the administration of the police department. In recent years, the F O P has offended some of its black members by investing in the defense fund for Darren Wilson, the Ferguson, Missouri, officer who shot Michael Brown. In 2014; hiring Jason Van Dyke, the Chicago Officer who was fired for shooting Laquan Mc Donald 16 times in 2014; and endorsing Trump's candidacy.

During the Obama administration, the FOP butted heads with members of the Presidential Task Force on 21st Century Policing and publicly opposed measures like Barack Obama's executive order curtailing police access to military weapons. In August, the FOP cheered as Attorney General Sessions announced Trump could nullify the directive.

"Day to day, [Black law enforcement leaders] are putting out fires. But those with a long-term vision are trying to do what others did for them, which is bring along the next generation. They are slowly chipping away at the stone."

Maya Angelou
Poet, Author, Civil Rights Activist (1928-2014)

Maya Angelou was an American author, poet, dancer, actress and singer. She published seven autobiographies, three books of essays, and several books of poetry, and was credited with a list of plays, movies, and television shows spanning over 50 years. She received dozens of awards and more than 50 honorary degrees. Angelou is best known for her series of seven autobiographies, which focus on her childhood and early adult experiences. The first, I Know Why the Caged Bird Sings, tells of her life up to the age of 17 and brought her international recognition and acclaim.

NY Public Library getting Maya Angelou's papers

More than 300 boxes of Maya Angelou's papers, including letters from Malcolm X and James Baldwin and several scribbled revisions of the poem she wrote to celebrate President Bill Clinton's inauguration, will be made public at a New York library, the author said.

The Schomburg Center for Research in Black Culture plans to announce the papers' acquisition this week.

Angelou, 82, said she sought out the Harlem institution—a research unit of the New York Public Library—as a home for works that include notes for her acclaimed autobiography "I know Why the Caged Bird Sings" and the 1993 inaugural poem "On the Pulse of Morning."

Angelou said Tuesday that she revised the poem about 10 times before getting it right. "I had to continue to go back for the melody of the language," she told The Associated Press in a telephone interview.

"People all over the world use words; (then) the writer comes along and has to use these most-in-use objects, put together a few nouns, pronouns, verbs, adjectives…and put them together and make them bounce, throw them against the wall and make people say, 'I never thought of it that way."

The Schomburg Center said the poem's draft is in one of nearly 350 boxes containing personal and professional correspondence, drafts, manuscripts and fan mail. It said that it has barely skimmed the surface of the material and that processing it will take up to two years.

"This is the essence that covers her literary career," Schomburg director Howard Dodson said.

The deal was sealed after a two-year negotiation, said Dodson, who has known Angelou for 20 years. He declined to reveal the terms. Deciding to put her collection at the Schomburg was a "no-brainer," Angelou said. "It is the principal repository in the world of literature and affairs for, by and about African-Americans, in particular, and Africans anywhere in the diaspora."

Angelou, who has homes in Harlem and Winston-Salem, N.C., said her many scribbled drafts are proof of how she can agonize over her writing. "I want to write so well that the reader is 20 pages in a book of mine before she knows she's reading," she said.

For example, a typewritten draft of "On the Pulse of Morning" shows that she changed "Welsh" to "Irish" in the line: "The Irish, the Rabbi, the Priest, the Sheikh." Angelou is the author of 31 books of fiction, poetry, nonfiction and children's books, as well as a cookbook scheduled for release in December. She has won three Grammys for her spoken-word albums and was nominated for a Pulitzer Prize for her screenplay and score for the 1972 movie "Georgia, Georgia."

The collection contains manuscripts, typescript, proofs of galleys for a number of her published works, including "A Song Flung Up to Heaven" and "All God's Children"; correspondence with writers Marshall Davis, Mari Evans and Chester Himes; photographer Gordon Parks; and jazz singer Abbey Lincoln.

In a six-page letter written Nov. 20, 1970, Baldwin—the author of "Go Tell it on the Mountain" and "Native Son" who died in 1987—begins with the salutation "Dear, dear Sister," and continues: "I didn't know how much I needed to hear from a solid, loving funky.friend."

"This is a truly remarkable human being," Dodson said. "The life record that she's created, especially as a writer, is of great significance…not only of the times, but as an understanding of ourselves as human beings."

In a July 11, 1964, letter, typed on letterhead from the University of Ghana, where she was teaching, Angelou told Malcolm X: "Malcolm, I'm sure that we have not had a leader like you since the dead days of Frederick Douglas."

Five years before the publication of "I Know Why the Caged Bird Sings," Malcolm X foretold her literary success.

"Your analysis of our peoples (sic) tendency to talk over the head of the masses in a language that is too far above and beyond them is certainly true. You can communicate because you have plenty of (soul) and you always keep your feet firmly rooted on the ground," he told her in a Jan. 15, 1965, letter.

In terms of scholarly relevance, Angelou said she hoped some of her papers would show that Martin Luther King Jr. and Malcolm X were "were not demigods."

"Both those men were good men, strong and courageous, but they were men," she said. "I hope that in my papers people will find evidence that some of the people they would like to sit on pedestals were just like them, and so each of us has the possibility of being effective in changing our world, even if it's just the world around us."

The Schomburg archive also contains the papers of Malcolm X; Nobel Peace Prize winner Ralph Bunche; singer Nat King Cole; "A Raison in the Sun" playwright Lorraine Hansberry; and tennis great Arthur Ashe.

National Black History Museum

President Barack Obama heralded a new national black history museum as "not just a record of tragedy, but a celebration of life "as he marked Wednesday's ground breaking of the long-sought-after museum on the National Mall.

During his brief remarks, Obama said the museum—the 19th in the Smithsonian Institution—would help future generations remember the sometimes difficult, often inspirational role, that African Americans have played in the nation's history. And he said it was fitting that a museum telling the history of black life, art and culture would be located on the National Mall in the capitol city.

"It was on this ground long ago that lives were once traded, where hundreds of thousands once marched for jobs and freedom," Obama said. "It was here that the pillars of democracy were built often by black hands."

The President was joined by wife Michelle Obama and former first lady Laura Bush to celebrate the start of construction on the National Museum of African American history and culture. It will be built between the Washington Monument and the National Museum of American History as a seven-level structure with much of its exhibit space below ground. A bronze-coated "corona, "a crown that rises as an inverse pyramid, will be its most distinctive feature. Organizers said the design is inspired by African-American metal work from New Orleans and Charleston, S.C., and also evokes African roots.

Some exhibits will eventually include a Jim Crow-era segregated railroad car, galleries devoted to military and sports history and Louis Armstrong's trumpet, among thousands of items. There will also be a court for quiet reflection, Museum Director Lonnie Bunch said.

"We will have stories that will make you smile and stories that will make you cry, "Bunch told the Associated Press. "In a positive sense, this will be an emotional roller coaster, so you want to give people chances to reflect and to think about what this means to them."

In many ways, the museum already exists. It has staff collecting artifacts and working to raise $250 million to fund the construction. Congress pledged to provide half of the $500 million construction cost. The museum is scheduled to open in 2015. It already has a gallery at the Smithsonian's American history museum with rotating exhibits to showcase its new collection and test different themes and approaches with visitors.

The newest exhibit explores Thomas Jefferson's lifelong ownership of slaves and his conflict and advocacy against slavery, while also looking at the lives of six slave families who lived on his Monticello plantation in Virginia, to humanize the issue of slavery.

Telling such stories has been taboo at many museums in the past and missing from the National Mall. Bunch said that by presenting a fuller view of history and dealing directly with difficult issues like race, the Smithsonian can present a fuller view of history and what it means to be an American.

"What this museum can do is if we tell the unvarnished truth in a way that's engaging and not preachy, what I think will happen is that by illuminating all the dark corners of the American experiences we will help find reconciliation and healing," he said.

Curators estimate that 15,000 to 20,000 artifacts already are in hand. Bunch estimates they will need about 35,000 artifacts to choose from to create the museum's permanent galleries. The staff is working to collect more materials on popular culture and music, earlier materials from military history from World War I and earlier and artifacts to tell stories from the 19th century, including slavery and reconstruction.

In Washington, the black history museum will follow major museums devoted to the Holocaust and Native American history. Legislation has also been introduced in Congress to create a Smithsonian American Latino Museum. Actress Phylicia Rashad, famous from TV's "The Cosby Show," hosted the groundbreaking ceremony Wednesday. In an interview, she said African-American history is interconnected with many other groups "this is what makes America great and unique is that different peoples are living here who come together as one people, she said, adding that she hopes to be surprised by what the new museum can offer. "I would like to see some stories I've never imagined. I'd like to see some stories that aren't so well talked about but that have documentation to back them.

The ground breaking also marks the start of a public fund raising campaign to build the museum. "Officials revealed about $100 million has been raised to date in private funds. This includes $5 million gifts from Wal-Mart, American Express, Boeing, Target and United-Health Group. The Bill and Melinda Gates foundation and the Lilly Endowment each gave $10 million in recent years. Some celebrities also re supporting the project, including Quincy Jones and Oprah Winfrey, whose foundation gave $1 million.

Delphia Dickens, the museum's associate director for fund raising, said the museum will begin a regional campaign targeting key markets of New York, Los Angeles, Houston, Dallas, Chicago, Atlanta and Washington. They are modeling the strategy to seek individual donors on the recent effort to build a Martin Luther King Jr. Memorial and on Obama's 2008 presidential campaign, she said.

"This is a museum for everybody," she said. "We want to model it such that everybody can say they had a part in making this a reality."

Civil rights veteran Rep. John Lewis of Georgia introduced legislation for many years to create a black history museum. "We must tell the story, the whole story," Lewis said, "a 400-year story of African Americans' contributions to this nation's history from slavery to the present—without anger or apology."

Smithsonian curators scout for Obama artifacts

As crowds descended and the inauguration unfolded, a few museum curators in Washington kept watch for symbols and messages that would make history.

The Smithsonian's National Museum of African American History and Culture will open during President Barack Obama's second term, and one section will feature a large display about the first black president. Curators have been working since 2008 to gather objects, documents and images that capture his place in history.

Curator William Pretzer ventured into the crowd Monday, mostly looking for memorabilia that had a personal touch—beyond the T-shirts and buttons hawked by vendors. Pretzer was most interested in handmade items, but he didn't find much. "There's so much commercially produced stuff that people don't go to the trouble anymore," he said. "It's the personal expression, as opposed to the commercial" that the museum most wants to display.

Among the masses of people, Ollie Parham, 55, and her fellow travelers stood out in their bright yellow Alabama NAACP sweatshirts. She rode all night in a tour bus, nearly 19 hours from Huntsville, Ala., to witness Obama's oath-taking. Pretzer told her about the museum's collection effort and asked whether Parham might donate any memorabilia later. She said she would think about it; she had another all-night drive home to get through first.

Shortly afterward, the curator stopped Larry Holmes, 56, of Washington, who was waving an American flag with an inauguration seal imprinted on the stripes. Holmes bought a similar souvenir flag at Obama's 2009 inauguration. Pretzer took Holmes' picture and handed him a donation card, in case he might donate the flags later.

When Peggy Shamley Christian, a retired teacher from Chesapeake, Va., heard about the collection effort, she dug through her purse to find an Obama magnet, Pretzer gladly accepted the tiny gift. Christian said she worked to mobilize voters for Obama's re-election and was thrilled to celebrate the inaugural. "It just makes me feel like I'm a part of something wonderful," she said.

"Instead of being considered a second-class citizen, we all have it going on now," added Christian, who is black. "We all can stand up and be proud." Keeping an eye out for the unusual, Pretzer spotted a man pulling two life-sized cutouts of the president and first lady on a cart through the crowd. He flagged down Ian Davis, 43, of Baltimore and asked whether he might donate the cutouts later.

Davis had been allowing visitors to take pictures with the "Obama" for a donation. "You gotta make a dollar," he said, adding that he hauled the cutouts onto the National Mall "so I can see it, be it and participate." Police eventually kicked him off the mall for asking for money. Now, Davis' cardboard images might be fit for a museum. He said he would donate them if his wife approves.

The museum has amassed more than 300 Obama-related items, including furniture from a 2008 campaign office in northern Virginia and a cloth banner from Tanzania with an Obama portrait and message reading "Congratulations Barack Obama." Curators might also try to acquire items from the inauguration platform, including, perhaps, the invocation written by Myrlie Evers-Williams, the widow of slain civil rights activist Medgar Evers. Evers was gunned down 50 years ago in the driveway of his Mississippi home. That history became a link between Obama and the civil rights era. When the museum opens in 2015 near the Washington Monument, one floor will be devoted to a chronology of African-American history, from 16th century slavery through the Civil War, Reconstruction, the Civil Rights era and beyond. The timeline will end with Obama and the 2008 election as a symbolic moment.

"Portraying a living individual is always more challenging," Pretzer said. "You don't have the perspective, and you don't have all the evidence."

The exhibits can evolve later to show Obama's impact and what comes next. In planning for the future display, Pretzer and other curators listened closely to Obama's inauguration speech. "Part of the dynamic is no longer, if it ever were, white and black. The dynamic is now generational. It is gender; he mentioned gay rights, so sexuality; as well as race," Pretzer said. "It was an 'E Pluribus Unum' speech. It was 'out of many, one.'"

Museum Director Lonnie Bunch said Obama's speech was more progressive and aggressive than his first inaugural. It framed the ongoing issues of women's rights, gay rights and immigration in the context of the historic struggle for equality. "It reminded people that the story of America is not just about today and tomorrow, but it's also about yesterday." Bunch said. "The question becomes, how effective is his administration as a model for what the presidency can accomplish?

New Smithsonian Museum Chronicling African American history opens

America's first national museum dedicated to African-American history and culture opened Saturday September 24, 2016. President Obama said he hoped the stories contained inside will help everyone "walk away that much more in love" with their country.

In an impassioned speech, President Barack Obama pointed out the highs and lows of being black in America, from slavery and Jim Crow segregation to voting rights and economic leaders. That duality lingers still, Obama said, through successes such as his presidency, and trials such as the Police killings of black men. "We are not a burden on America. Or a stain on America… We are America. And that's what this museum explains," Obama said.

He and first lady Michelle Obama joined Ruth Bonner, a 99-year-old direct descendent of a slave, and her family as they rang a bell from the historic First Baptist Church of Williamsburg, Virginia, to signal that the museum was officially open.

Millions of donors contributed to the $315 million in private funding raised before the museum's opening. Some of the biggest donors' names adorn the walls inside, including the Oprah Winfrey Theater; the Michael Jordan Hall: Game Changers; and the Robert F. Smith Explore Your Family History Center, named for the CEO of investment firm Vista Equity Partners after a $20 million gift.

As part of the opening ceremony, Winfrey and actor Will Smith read lines of famous black writers, from Maya Angelou to Langston Hughes, Toni Morrison and Martin Luther King Jr.

A Canadian's View on our Disrespect of President Obama's Presidency

America—he's your President for goodness sake by William Thomas

There was a time not so long ago when Americans, regardless of their political stripes, rallied around their president. Once elected, the man who won the White House was no longer viewed as a republican or a democrat, but the President of the United States. The oath of office was taken, the wagons were circled the country's borders and it was America versus all the people at the helm.

Suddenly President Barack Obama, with the potential to become an exceptional president has become the glaring exception to that unwritten, patriotic rule. Four days before President Obama's inauguration, before he officially took charge of the American Government, Rush Limbaugh boasted publicly that he hoped the president would fail the country. Of course, when the president fails the country flounders. Wishing harm upon your country to further your narrow political views is selfish, sinister and a tad treasonous as well.

Subsequently, during his state of the union address, which is pretty much a pep rally for America, an unknown congressional representative from South Carolina, later identified as Joe Wilson, stopped the show when he called the President of the United States a liar. The President showed great restraint in ignoring this unprecedented insult and carried on with his speech. Speaker Nancy Pelosi was so stunned by the slur, she forgot to jump to her feet while clapping wildly, 30 or 40 times after that.

Last spring, President Obama took his wife Michelle to see a play in New York City and republicans attacked him over the cost of security for the excursion. The President can't take is wife out to dinner and a show without being scrutinized by the political opposition? As history has proven, a President in a theatre without adequate security is a tragically bad idea.

Remember, "apart from that, Mrs. Lincoln, how did you enjoy the play?" At some point, the treatment of President Obama went from offensive to ugly and then to downright dangerous. The HealthCare debate, which looked more like extreme fighting in a mud pit than a national dialogue, revealed a very vulgar side of America. President Obama's face appeared on protest signs white-faced and blood-mouthed in a satanic clown image. In other tasteless portrayals, people who disagreed with his position distorted his face to look like Hitler complete with mustache and swastika. Odd, that burning the flag makes Americans crazy, but depicting the president as a clown and maniacal fascists is accepted as part of the new rude America.

Maligning the image of the leader of the free world is one thing, putting the president's life in peril is quite another. More than once, men with guns were videotaped at the health-Care rallies where the president spoke. Again, history shows that letting men with guns get within range of a president has not served America well in the past.

And still the "birthers" are out there claiming Barack Obama was not born in the United States, although public documentation proves otherwise. Hawaii is part of the United States, but the Panama Canal Zone where his electoral opponent Senator John McCain was born? Nobody's sure.

Last month, a 44-year-old woman in Buffalo was quite taken by President Obama when she met him in a chicken wing restaurant called Duff's. Did she say something about a pleasure and an honor to meet the man or utter encouraging words for the difficult job he is doing? No. Quote: "You're a hottie with smoking 'little body." Lady that was the President of the United States you were addressing, not one of the Jonas Brother's. He's your president for goodness sakes, not the guy driving the Zamboni at "Monster Trucks on Ice. "Maybe next it'll be, "Take your President to a Topless Bar Day."

In President Barack Obama, Americans have a charismatic leader with a good and honest heart. Unlike his predecessor, he's a very intelligent leader.

And unlike that president's predecessor, he's a highly moral man.

In President Obama, Americans have the real deal, the whole package and a leader that citizens of almost every country around the world look to with great envy. Given the opportunity, Canadians would trade our leader, hell, most of our leaders for Obama in a heartbeat.

What America has in Obama is a head of State with vitality and insight and youth. Think about it, Barack Obama is a young Nelson Mandela. Mandela was the face of change and charity for all of Africa but he was too old to make it happen. The great things Obama might do for America and the world could go on for decades after he's out of office.

America, you know not what you have.

The man is being challenged unfairly, characterized with vulgarity and treated with the kind of deep disrespect to which no previous president was subjected. It's like the day after electing the first black man to be president, thereby electrifying the world with hope and joy, Americans sobered up and decided the bad old days were better. President Obama may fail but it will not be a Richard Nixon default with larceny and lies. President Obama, given a fair chance, will surely succeed but his triumph will never come with a Bill Clinton caveat—"if only he'd got control of that zipper."

Please. Give the man a fair, fighting chance. This incivility toward the leader who won over Americans and gave hope to billions of people around the world that their lives could be enhanced by his example, just naturally has to stop. Believe me, when Americans drive by the White House and see a sign on the lawn that reads: "No shirt. No shoes. No service," they'll realize this new national rudeness has gone way, way too far.

Obamas welcomed at Buckingham Palace

President Barack Obama and wife Michelle Obama were welcomed to Buckingham Palace in grand royal style Tuesday by Queen Elizabeth II as they began their official state visit to Britain, a rare honor for a U.S. president.

The queen and her husband Prince Philip greeted the Obamas on a sunny, windy afternoon in London. Following a private tour of the palace, the two couples emerged on the ceremonial steps of the West Terrace for a 41-gun salute. The queen, dressed in a powder blue suit and matching hat, stood with the president, as ranks of Scots Guards in red jackets and tall hats played the Star-Spangled Banner in honor of the American president and his wife. A longer 62-gun salute at the Tower of London could be heard throughout the city heralding the Obamas' arrival.

The Obamas will spend two nights at the palace as guests of the queen, staying in a six-room suite last used by Prince William and Kate Middleton on their wedding night. The newlyweds, now known as the Duke and Duchess of Cambridge, had a brief, private meeting with the Obamas Tuesday before the palace arrival ceremony, but will not attend a lavish banquet being held in the Obamas' honor Tuesday night.

The Obamas were to lunch privately with the queen, then head to London's famous Westminster Abbey for a wreath laying. The president and first lady began the day greeted by Prince Charles and his wife Camilla at Winfield House, the stately mansion in Regent's Park that is the residence of the U.S. ambassador. The Obamas stayed there Monday night after leaving Ireland early instead of spending the night in Dublin because of safety concerns over a volcanic ash cloud being blown toward Britain from Iceland.

There was no avoiding domestic issue, either. From Europe Obama was monitoring fallout from the massive tornado that struck Missouri, and before meeting the queen Tuesday he announced plans to tour the damage on Sunday after he return to the states.

While Obama will tackle prickly foreign policy matters in the coming days, the opening rounds of his four-country European tour are all about the personal politics that made him so beloved on this continent as a presidential candidate and in the early days of his term in office. While in Ireland, Obama embraced the touch of Irish in his family history, drinking a pint of Guinness with a distant cousin in the hamlet of Moneygall and delivering a rousing speech on the ties between the U.S. and Ireland before tens of thousands crammed into the center of Dublin.

In London, the Obamas will fully embrace the tradition and history of the royal family, which is experiencing resurgence in popularity following Prince William's wedding. Royal watchers say the queen has taken a liking to the Obamas ever since meeting the couple during their 2009 visit to London, Mrs. Obama created a stir in Britain when she wrapped her arm around the queen—a faux pas, according to royal etiquette experts—only to have the queen respond with her show of affection and a reciprocal embrace.

Obama will meet briefly with British Prime Minister David Cameron on Tuesday, though their most substantial talks will come the following day, when Afghanistan, Libya and the global economy are all on the agenda. Obama's mission, in part, is to reassure Britain and the rest of Europe that the traditional U.S. allies still have a central role in a U.S. foreign policy that has become increasingly focused on Asia and other emerging markets. "I think this is, in part, way to bring back the special bonds of this relationship," said Heater Conley, director of the Europe program at the Washington-based Center for Strategic and International Studies.

In a joint editorial for Tuesday's edition of the British newspaper The Times of London, Obama and Cameron cast the relationship between the U.S. and Britain as one that makes the world more secure and more prosperous. "That is the key to our relationship. Yes, it is founded on a deep emotional connection, by sentiment and ties of people and culture. But the reason it thrives, the reason why this is such a natural partnership, is because it advances our common interests and shared values." The leaders wrote.

Still, the two allies don't always agree on every issue, a reality sure to expose itself in talks on national security and foreign policy. When it comes to the NATO-led bombing campaign in Libya, for example, some British lawmakers have expressed concern that European countries, including Britain, have carried an unfair share of the burden in an effort the U.S. has made clear it does not want to run.

After his two-day stop in Britain, Obama will head to France for a meeting of the Group of Eight Industrialized nations and then to Poland, a schedule the White House says the president intends to keep despite the approaching ash cloud.

Obama tried to get to Poland last year for the funeral of its president. But that trip was cancelled because of an ash cloud.

Amelia Platts Boynton Robinson, August 18, 1911-August 26, 2015

Amelia Boynton Robinson was an American activist who was a leader of the American Civil Rights Movement in Selma, Alabama and a key figure in the 1965 Selma to Montgomery marches. She was a voting rights activist in the 1930s and was a friend of Martin Luther King Jr., Rosa Parks and other civil rights leaders in the 1950s and 1960s. She lived long enough to attend President Obama's State of the Union address in January and to accompany the president across the Edmund Pettus Bridge in March, commemorating the 50th anniversary of the Selma march that almost claimed her life.

When President Lyndon B. Johnson signed the Voting Rights of 1965, she was one of his guests.

Racist History of Police Unions

Outraged by New York City Mayor Bill de Blasio's statement concerning the killing of Eric Garner, Patrick Lynch, the longtime leader of the New York City Patrolmen's Benevolent Association (PBA), the NYPD's officers union, recently made the outrageous assertion that the Mayor had "blood on his hands" for the murder of the two NYPD officers.

In Milwaukee this past fall, the Police Association called for, and obtained, a vote of no confidence in MPD Chief Ed Flynn after he fired the officer who shot and killed Dontre Hamilton, an unarmed African American; subsequently, the Union's leader, Mike Crivello, praised the District Attorney when he announced that he would not bring charges against the officer.

In Chicago, the Fraternal Order of Police (FOP), a longtime supporter of racist police torturer Jon Burge, is now seeking to circumvent court orders that preserve and make public the police misconduct files of repeater cops such as Burge, by seeking to enforce a public contract provision that calls for the distruction of the files after seven years. And in a show of solidarity with the killer of Michael Brown, Chicago FOP is soliciting contributions to the Darren Wilson defense fund on its website.

Such reactionary actions by police unions are not new, but are a fundamental component of their history, particularly since they came to prominence in the wake of the civil rights movement. These organizations have played a powerful role in defending the police, no matter how outrageous and racist their actions, and in resisting all manner of police reforms.

Police Union's leader hopes to Direct Slew of Police Reforms

The leader of the nation's largest law enforcement union has a plan for how to repair the sinking reputation of police officers and departments across the country.

The deaths of black men in New York, South Carolina, and Baltimore has led the Fraternal Order of Police executive director, Jim Pasco, to develop a strategy to renew the image of the in the face of controversy.

While there is a call for reform from law makers, Pasco first wants Congress to form a commission to investigate the alleged problem and propose recommendations.

On the agenda for Pasco is stopping a bill that is aimed at restricting the amount of militarytype weapons and supplies available to police departments and stopping investigations by the Justice Department.

Anthony Batts

Baltimore's Police Commissioner Anthony Batts told CNN he was "probably surprised" about the charges in the case of Gray, who died of injuries he sustained in police custody. Batts says he knows the community doesn't trust law enforcement-and police have to accept "we are part of the problem."

"The community needs to hear that, he tells CNN." They need to hear from us that we haven't been part of the solution, and now we have to solve. Now we have to change." He says he wants to start a program modeled after one in Los Angeles to have police working inside housing complexes.

"It's going to be a long journey," he said. "This isn't going to be a short journey. You can see the distrust that's out there, and we have to find inroads to sit down with people—to show care, to show empathy."

Baltimore Mayor Stephanie Rawlings-Blake replaced Anthony Batts as the City's top cop amid anger over his handling of protests and a startling rise in crime.

Batts drew widespread criticism for his response to the riots that erupted after the April death of

Freddie Gray. The move came as the City's police union said in a report that the riots were preventable and fueled by the "passive stance" adopted by Batts and top commanders.

Racial Bias in Policing

Rev. Al Sharpton announced his plans to March on Washington from Baltimore as riots erupted over the death of Freddie Gray by the hand of Police.

"The march will bring the case of Freddie Gray, Eric Garner, Walter Scott, Eric Harris to the new Attorney General, Loretta Lynch.

The march is to ramp up pressure on federal officials to take action on racial bias in policing.

Sharpton has used his platforms as a radio and T.V. host to raise issues of police brutality and racial discrimination against back men in police forces around the country as high-profile deaths in Cleveland, New York and Ferguson, Missouri shook the nation.

Before the tragic killing of Michael Brown by a police officer in August 2014, Ferguson already had evidence of racially biased policing. The Missouri attorney general had published data showing that although Ferguson police were twice more likely to search blacks than whites after initiating a stop, whites were far more likely to be found with contraband. That meant police were targeting blacks for stops and searches, but getting it wrong more often than they were for whites. But the police did not reform.

ACLU Racial Justice Program

The Boston ACLU recommends opportunity for police reform by Accountability, Constitutionality and Transparency.

Accountability: All officers who engage in any police-civilian encounters to wear and use body-worn cameras during every interaction with the public. It should also provide documentation—i.e., a receipt—to any civilian involved in a stop, frisk, and search, even if purportedly consensual.

Constitutionality: Police department should adopt department-level training on implicit bias and supervision to identify and correct racial bias. This will help ensure respect for the right to equal protection under the law.

Transparency: Police Department should publish quarterly electronic data on all police-civilian encounters, including demographic information and the officer's basis for the encounter and action. Openness will rebuild badly damaged public trust, permit researchers to continually test data for evidence of racial bias, and help identify solutions

Racial Bias in Policing

The law enforcement system has enormous discretionary power discretionary power in determining who is stopped, searched, arrested, prosecuted, and how punishment is dispensed.

The image of racial discrimination in the exercise of police authority was most vividly etched in the public's mind by three widely publicized cases: Rodney King, a 26-year-old African-American who was severely beaten by four Los Angeles Police Department officers, Abner Louima, the 30-year-old Haitian immigrant who was brutally assaulted by a group of New York Police Department officers, and Amadou Diallo, a 22-year-old unarmed West African immigrant who was shot forty-one times by four New York City policemen in front of his home.

These dramatic instances of excess in the exercise of police authority touch a raw nerve in American Civic life-the possibility that racial bias causes unequal treatment in the criminal justice system. Is it racial bias that explains the police's disparate use of force in dealing with minorities, especially young black men? Under what circumstances might race influence police officers' decision making? And how do we present racial discrimination in the exercise police authority?

A New Alliance between Social Scientists and the Police.

Over the last few years, however, a new generation of law enforcement officials has emerged, with a leadership willing to entertain closer scrutiny of police department efforts to improve relationships with the minority communities that they serve and to prevent racial profiling. The working group was created to take advantage of the tools that social science has developed in the content of experimental and survey research (especially in the field of social psychology), together with the data that some police departments are now willing to share, to shed light on how law enforcement might change its officer recruitment, hiring, and training decisions to reduce racial bias.

Economic backlash from race riots and urban unrest

The 1992 Los Angeles riots, over the police beating of Rodney King, left 52 dead and 1,000 building in ruins. One study put the business cost at 8.3 billion in lost sales over the next 10 years. There were 2500 injuries, $446 million in property damage.

Watts riot of the 1960's, thousands of National Guard troop were brought into the city. The guardsmen restored order after six days of rioting during which 34 people died, 1,032 were injured and 3,192 were arrested. Property damage was estimated at $183 million (1992 dollars). Of the 600 buildings damaged, 200 were destroyed. Ferguson riots cost over 20 million.

Rioting is related to Community level grievances with racially prejudiced police officers.

President Obama criticizes black deaths by police and also rioters.

Urging Americans to "do some soul-searching," President Barack Obama expressed deep frustration Tuesday over recurring black deaths at the hands of police, rioters responding with senseless violence and a society that will only "feign concern" without addressing the root causes. "This is not new. It's been going on for decades," Obama Said from the White House a day after rioting erupted 40 miles north in Baltimore following the funeral for Freddie Gray who died of spinal cord injury after being arrested.

Gray is the latest black man to die at the hands of police, prompting protests and calls for criminal justice reform. Some have criticized America's first black president for not speaking out forcefully enough as he tries to avoid criticism of law enforcement, and he responded by calling the deaths "a slow-rolling crisis."

"We have seen too many instances of what appears to be police officers interacting with individuals, primarily African-American, often poor, in ways that raise troubling questions. It comes up, it seems like, once a week now," Obama said.

He said although such cases aren't unprecedented, there's new awareness as a result of cameras and social media. "We shouldn't pretend that it's new."

Still, Obama showed no sympathy for rioters, saying those who stole from businesses and burned buildings and cars should be treated as criminals. Obama said they distracted from days of peaceful protest focused on legitimate concerns from days of peaceful protest focused on legitimate concerns "over the possibility that our laws were not applied evenly in the case of Mr. Gray and that accountability needs to exist."

"There's no excuse for the kind of violence that we saw yesterday," Obama said. "It is counterproductive, when individuals get crowbars and start prying doors to loot, they're stealing." But he also criticized a society that doesn't do enough to uplift poor minority communities. He said the solution to deep-seeded problems that spur violence include early education, criminal justice reform and job training, while suggesting that kind of a response is out of reach with a Republican Congress. "I'm under no illusion that out of this Congress we're going to get massive investments in urban communities," Obama said.

"It's too easy to ignore those problems or to treat them just as a law-and-order issue as opposed to a broader social issue," Obama said.

The president spoke during a state visit with Japanese Prime Minister Shinzo Abe, at one point apologizing to his guest for taking nearly 15 minutes of their news conference to discuss it. "I felt pretty strongly about it," he said.

The White House sought to show that it is keeping abreast of the fluid situation, announcing that Attorney General Loretta Lynch and Obama senior adviser Valerie Jarrett had held a conference call Tuesday with more than 50 local leaders, including urban Mayors Michael Nutter of Philadelphia, Tom Barrett of Milwaukee and Karen Freeman-Wilson of Gary Indiana.

Obama also taped an interview Tuesday with "The Steve Harvey Morning Show," which targets primarily African-American radio audiences. The White House said the interview would air Wednesday Morning.

At the news conference, Obama said America should not just pay attention to these communities "when a CVS burns" or when "a young man gets shot or has his spine snapped." He said he can't force police departments to retrain their officers, but he can work with them and help pay for body cameras to improve accountability.

"In those environments, if we think that we're just going to send the police to do the dirty work of containing the problems that arise there, without a nation and as a society saying what can we do to change those communities, to help lift those communities and give those kids opportunity, then we're not going to solve this problem," he said. "And we'll go through the same cycles of periodic conflicts between the police and communities and the occasional riots in the streets. And everybody will feign concern until it goes away and then we go about our business as usual.

The Real Reason behind Baltimore Uprising

The death of Freddie Gray at the hands of Baltimore Police sparked outrage and protest by thousands of Baltimore residents and people of color around the world. It seems that almost daily, the headline "Unarmed Black man killed by Police" has pulled back the veil on what many white Americans, liberal and conservative alike, have been blinded to by privilege; racism is real in American society.

With the 2008 election of Barack Obama, the success of entrepreneurs like Oprah and Tyler Perry, and the increase in African Americans attendance in College, about half of white American's have wrongly concluded that the U.S. has entered a "post-racial" phase, where race is no longer the determining factor in inequality. This couldn't be further from the truth.

What can we do to change those communities, to help lift up those communities and give those kids opportunity, then we're not going to solve this problem, "he said. "And we'll go through the same cycles of periodic conflicts between the police and communities and the occasional riots in the streets. And everybody will feign concern until it goes away and then we go about our business as usual.

The crux of much debate surrounding the death of Freddie Gray and the subsequent civil unrest by both moderate and conservative media and pundits lay the blame squarely on the backs of the protestors and victims of such assaults. They contend that these deaths and protest are a result of those unwilling to take responsibility for their actions. That criminal activity and arrests are a result of poor choices and poor moral character. That, in this post racial society; everyone has equal ability to change their circumstances if only they try hard enough.

What happens when we try to qualify those beliefs? Well, we find that blacks and whites use marijuana at similar rates, but blacks are four times more likely to get arrested for it, and six times more likely to go to prison. This certainly proves that arrest has a whole lot more to do with what you look like than the actual crime.

Or what about when we compare resumes, and find that identical resumes sent to the same employer have a 50 percent less chance of being called if they have a "black sounding" name. This certainly demonstrates unequal ability to change your circumstances. Want to complain about all of this to your local Congressperson? Good luck. People with black sounding names consistently see less response from their representatives—in both parties. So much for taking responsibility!

The truth is, Jim Crow grew up, cleaned up, and started writing laws. Laws that create institutionalized racism without having to have a sign that reads "whites only." Our current policies and criminal justice system do that implicitly. To get a real handle on what is going on in Baltimore, Ferguson and around the nation; to understand why people feel stuck, angry frustrated, we have to be willing to face the fact that racism has not disappeared. It has instead morphed into less conspicuous white privilege and social and economic inequality. One that many American whites are unwilling to face out of guilt and the belief that they have somehow "earned" a position in life that they have inherited under simply being white.

If America wants to hold onto the belief that what we inherit is unabashedly what we deserve, then we must be willing to acknowledge that we force minorities to inherit inequality at no fault of their own.

Kathy Miller a Donald Trump campaign chair in Ohio. In an interview said there was "no racism" during the 1960s and claimed black people who have not succeeded over the past half century only have themselves to blame. If you're black and you haven't been successful in the last 50 years, it's your fault. "You've had every opportunity, it was given to you," she said.

"You've had the same schools everybody else went to. You had benefits to go to college that white kids didn't have. You had all the advantages and didn't take advantage of it. It's not our fault, certainly." Miller added: "I don't think there was any racism until Obama got elected. We never had problems like this… Now, with the people with the guns, and shooting up neighborhoods, and not being responsible citizens, that's a big change, and I think that's the philosophy that Obama has perpetuated on America."

She was dismissed over her "insane comments."

President Obama: Let's 'Work Harder' to 'Heal' Police Community Rifts.

President Barack Obama honored police officers killed in the line of duty, and consoled their grieving families, saying they must be remembered as "heroes, because that's what they are."

The comments come in the wake of an alarming rise in police fatalities.

In 2013, 27 law enforcement officers were feloniously slain on the job. In 2014, there were 51, according to preliminary statistic released by the FBI.

President Obama addressed the tensions between police and communities, and vowed to try to "work harder" to heal the rift.

"We can do everything we have to do to combat the poverty that plagues too many communities in which you have served," he said. "We can work harder as a nation to heal rifts that exist in some places between law enforcement and the people you risk your lives to protect."

FBI Director James Comey also noted that more work needed to be done. "I think it's very, very important for all of us that we do our absolute best to try to see those people we serve and to look for opportunities to have them see us—see the nature and character of the people who are in law enforcement and why we do the work that we do," Comey said.

President Obama will announce $163 million in new Department of Justice grants to promote "community policing" practice at local departments, such stronger policies against racial profiling and increased transparency about officer-related incidents. The Justice Department will also offer a "tool Kit" to encourage more police departments to use body cameras in the field. One of the most popular reforms to emerge after Ferguson was the widespread use of body cameras by police.

The White House has launched a limited program that would equip 50,000 police officers with the cameras, but has stopped short of calling for their mandatory use.

The announcements come on the same day Obama is visiting Camden N.J., which the White House has touted as an antidote to Ferguson.

Camden's troubled police department was eliminated in 2012, and a new county-run force has been credited with improving community relations while driving down crime.

The city is one of 20 jurisdictions participating in a police data-sharing program that makes public information about use of force, traffic stops and officer-involved shootings. In April 2015, the Obama administration selected Camden as one of eight new "Promise Zones," a federal program that gives preferential treatment to struggling municipalities applying for anti-poverty, health and crime-prevention grants.

It also participates in the White House's My Brother's Keeper Community Challenge, which sets educational standards for young minority males.

During the visit, the president will meet with the Camden County Police Chief Scott Thompson and tour the department's tactical operations center. He will also visit a group of police officers and young people and speak at a Salvation Army community center.

"Camden is an example of a lot of good things happening, a lot of things moving in the right direction," White House Domestic Policy Council Director Cecilia Munoz said Sunday on a conference call with reporters.

Chicago OK's $5.5M in reparations for Police torture victims

Chicago's leaders took a step Wednesday May 6, 2015, typically reserved for nations trying to make amends for slavery or genocide agreeing to pay $5.5 million in reparations to the mostly African–American victims of the city's notorious police torture scandal and to teach school children about one of the most shameful chapters of Chicago's history.

Chicago has already spent more than $100 million settling and lowing lawsuits related to the torture of suspects by detectives under the command of disgraced former police Commander Jon Burge from the 1970s through the early 1990s. The City Council's backing of the new ordinance marks the first time a U.S. city has awarded survivors of racially motivated police torture the reparations they are due under international law, according to Amnesty International.

"It is a powerful word and it was meant to be a powerful word. That was intentional, "Alderman Joe Moore said of the decision to describe it as reparations.

Before the council unanimously backed the deal, the names of more than a dozen victims were called out, and those men and their families were given a standing ovation.

"This stain cannot be removed from our city's history, but it can be used as a lesson in what not to do" said Mayor Rahm Emanuel, who stressed that Chicago had to do more than just pay the victims if it is to get beyond this stain in our history.

"While the payment is important…it cannot stand alone, it has to stand associated with and part of a city that will say it's sorry, it's wrong when it's wrong, and we need to right a wrong when we find it," he said.

Each of the approximately 80 victims will be eligible to receive up to $100,000 of the money Also, the ordinance calls for the council to issue a formal apology for the construction of a memorial to the victims and for the police torture scandal to be added to the city's school history curriculum. Victims will receive psychological counseling and free tuition at some community colleges and, in recognition of the lasting damage the torture did to the victims and their families, some of the benefits will be available to victim's children and grandchildren.

Will Porch, who spent nearly 15 years in prison for a robbery after he says he was tortured into giving a false confession, said that although he's pleased he might receive money under the new ordinance, the apology and other actions the city is taking are just as important, particularly out-side of Chicago.

"Going forward for other cities and other states, now they have a template of what to do," Porch said.

New York City settled with the family of Eric Garner, agreeing to pay $5.9 million to resolve the claim over his killing by the police last July on Staten Island. Mr. Garner died on July 17 after a police officer, placed him in a choke hold. The medical examiner ruled the death a homicide, citing the chokehold and the compression of Mr. Garner's chest by the police.

A $6.4 million deal with David Ranta, who was imprisoned for 23 years after a wrongful murder conviction. A deal was also reached for $2.25 million with the family of Jerome Murdough, who died in an overheated jail cell at Rikers Island.

In 2001, a suit brought by Abner Louima, a Haitian man tortured with a broomstick while in police custody at a Brooklyn precinct station house in August 1997, was settled for $8.75 million, with the city paying $7.125 million and the police officers' union, the Patrolmen's Benevolent Association, which was accused of conspiring to cover up the assault, paying Mr. Louima another $1.625 million.

Nearly five years after the killing of Amadou Diallo in 1999, the City settled with his relatives for $3 million. The City settled a suit over the 2006 fatal shooting of Sean Bell for $3.25 million.

In January 2015, Scott M. Stringer, the New York City comptroller agreed to pay $17 million to settle wrongful conviction claims brought by three defendants whose cases involved Louis Scarcella, a retired homicide detective whose investigative tactics have come under scrutiny and are under review.

"This is not about people getting money," Rev. Al Sharpton said on Monday. "This is about justice. We've got to restructure our police departments and how we deal with policing nationwide."

21

President Obama and first lady Michelle Obama will honor Dr. King's birthday Monday Jan. 19th.

In his proclamation of the holiday, Obama said King's life, work, and courage continue to inspire the nation to "continue climbing toward the Promised Land" of justice and equality.

> "Our Nation has made undeniable progress since his time, but securing these gains requires constant vigilance, not complacency," Obama Said. "We have more to do to bring Dr. King's dream within reach of all our daughters and sons. We must stand together for good jobs, fair wages, safe neighborhoods, and quality education."

The Proclamation added:

"With one voice, we must ensure the scales of justice work equally for all-considering not only how justice is applied, but also how it is perceived and experienced.

Obama's emotional speech in Selma

It is a rare honor in this life to follow one of your heroes. And John Lewis is one of my heroes.

Now, I have to imagine that when a younger John Lewis woke up that morning fifty years ago and made his way to Brown Chapel, heroics were not on his mind. A day like this was not on his mind. Young folks with bedrolls and backpacks were milling about. Veterans of the movement trained newcomers in the tactics of non-violence; the right way to protect yourself when attacked. A doctor described what tear gas does to the body, while marchers scribbled down instructions for contacting their loved ones. The air was thick with doubt, anticipation, and fear. They comforted themselves with the final verse of the final hymn they sung:

> No matter what may be the test,
> God will take care of you;
> Lean, weary one, upon His
> breast, God will take care of you.

Then, his knapsack stocked with an apple, a toothbrush, a book on government—all you need for a night behind bars—John Lewis led them out of the church on a mission to change America.

President Bush and Mrs. Bush, Governor Bentley, Members of Congress, Mayor Evans, Reverend Strong, friends and fellow Americans:

> There are places, and moments in America where this nation's destiny has been decided. Many are sites of war—Concord and Lexington, Appomattox and Gettysburg. Others are sites that symbolize the daring of America's character—Independence Hall and Seneca Falls, Kitty Hawk and Cape Canaveral.

Selma is such a place.

In one afternoon fifty years ago, so much of our turbulent history—the stain of slavery and anguish of civil war; the yoke of segregation and tyranny of Jim Crow; the death of four little girls in Birmingham, and the dream of a Baptist preacher—met on this bridge.

It was not a clash of armies, but a clash of wills; a contest to determine the meaning of America.

And because of men and women like John Lewis, Joseph Lowery, Hosea Williams, Amelia Boynton, Diane Nash, Ralph Abernathy, C.T. Vivian, Andrew

Young, Fred Shuttles worth, Dr. King, and so many more, the idea of a just America, a fair America, an inclusive America, a generous America—that idea ultimately triumphed.

As is true across the landscape of American history, we cannot examine this moment in isolation. The march on Selma was part of a broader campaign that spanned generations; the leaders that day part of a long line of heroes.

We gather here to celebrate them. We gather here to honor the courage of ordinary Americans willing to endure billy clubs and the chastening rod; tear gas and the trampling hoof; men and women who despite the gush of blood and splintered bone would stay true to their North Star and keep marching toward justice.

They did as Scripture instructed: "Rejoice in hope, be patient in tribulation, be constant in prayer." And in the days to come, they went back again and again. When the trumpet call sounded for more to join, the people came—black and white, young and old, Christian and Jew, waving the American flag and singing the same anthems full of faith and hope. A white newsman, Bill Plante, who covered the marches then and who is with us here today, quipped that the growing number of white people lowered the quality of the singing. To those who marched, though, those old gospel songs must have never sounded so sweet.

In time, their chorus would reach President Johnson. And he would send them protection, echoing their call for the nation and the world to hear:

"We shall overcome."

What enormous faith these men and women had. Faith in God—but also faith in America.

The Americans who crossed this bridge were not physically imposing. But they gave courage to millions. They held no elected office. But they led a nation. They marched as Americans who had endured hundreds of years of brutal violence, and countless daily indignities—but they didn't seek special treatment, just the equal treatment promised to them almost a century before.

What they did here will reverberate through the ages. Not because the change they won was preordained; not because their victory was complete; but because they proved that nonviolent change is possible; that love and hope can conquer hate.

As we commemorate their achievement, we are well-served to remember that at the time of the marches, many in power condemned rather than praised them. Back then, they were called Communists, half-breeds, outside agitators, sexual and moral degenerates, and worse—everything but the name their parents gave them. Their faith was questioned. Their lives were threatened. Their patriotism was challenged.

And yet, what could be more American than what happened in this place?

What could more profoundly vindicate the idea of America than plain and humble people—the unsung, the downtrodden, the dreamers not of high station, not born to wealth or privilege, not of one religious tradition but many—coming together to shape their country's course?

What greater expression of faith in the American experiment than this; what greater form of patriotism is there; than the belief that America is not yet finished, that we are strong enough to be self-critical, that each successive generation can look upon our imperfections and decide that it is in our power to remake this nation to more closely align with our highest ideals?

That's why Selma is not some outlier in the American experience. That's why it's not a museum or static monument to behold from a distance. It is instead the manifestation of a creed written into our founding documents: "We the People…to form a more perfect union."

"We hold these truths to be self-evident, that all men are created equal."

These are not just words. They are a living thing, a call to action, a roadmap for citizenship and an insistence in the capacity of free men and women to shape our destiny. For founders like Franklin and Jefferson, for leaders like Lincoln and FDR, the success of our experiment in self-government rested on engaging all our citizens in this work. That's what we celebrate here in Selma. That's what this movement was all about, one leg in our long journey toward freedom.

The American instinct that led these young men and women to pick up the torch and cross this bridge is the same instinct that moved patriots to choose revolution over tyranny. It's the same instinct that drew immigrants from across oceans and the Rio Grande; the same instinct that led women to reach for the ballot and workers to organize against an unjust status quo; the same instinct that led us to plant a flag at Iwo Jima and on the surface of the Moon.

It's the idea held by generations of citizens who believed that America is a constant work in progress; who believed that loving this country requires more than singing its praises or avoiding uncomfortable truths. It requires the occasional disruption, the willingness to speak out for what's right and shake up the status quo.

That's what makes us unique, and cements our reputation as a beacon of opportunity. Young people behind the Iron Curtain would see Selma and eventually tear down a wall. Young people in Soweto would hear Bobby Kennedy talk about ripples of hope and eventually banish the scourge of apartheid. Young people in Burma went to prison rather than submit to military rule. From the streets of Tunis to the Maidan in Ukraine, this generation of young people can draw strength from this place, where the powerless could change the world's greatest superpower, and push their leaders to expand the boundaries of freedom.

They saw that idea made real in Selma, Alabama. They saw it made real in America.

Because of campaigns like this, a Voting Rights Act was passed. Political, economic, and social barriers came down, and the change these men and women wrought is visible here today in the presence of African-Americans who run boardrooms, who sit on the bench, who serve in elected office from small towns to big cities; from the Congressional Black Caucus to the Oval Office.

Because of what they did, the doors of opportunity swung open not just for African-Americans, but for every American. Women marched through those doors. Latinos marched through those doors. Asian–Americans, gay Americans, and Americans with disabilities came through those doors. Their endeavors gave the entire South the chance to rise again, not by reasserting the past, but by transcending the past.

What a glorious thing, Dr. King might say.

What a solemn debt we owe.

Which leads us to ask, just how might we repay that debt?

First and foremost, we have to recognize that one day's commemoration, no matter how special, is not enough. If Selma taught us anything, it's that our work is never done—the American experiment in self-government gives work and purpose to each generation.

Selma teaches us, too, that action requires that we shed our cynicism. For when it comes to the pursuit of justice, we can afford neither complacency nor despair.

Just this week, I was asked whether I thought the Department of Justice's Ferguson report shows that, concerning race, little has changed in this country. I understand the question, for the report's narrative was woefully familiar. It evoked the kind of abuse and disregard for citizens that spawned the Civil Rights Movement. But I rejected the notion that nothing's changed. What happened in Ferguson may not be unique, but it's no longer endemic, or sanctioned by law and custom; and before the Civil Rights Movement, it most surely was.

We do a disservice to the cause of justice by intimating that bias and discrimination are immutable, or that racial division is inherent to America. If you think nothing's changed in the past fifty years, ask somebody who lived through the Selma or Chicago or L.A. of the Fifties. Ask the female CEO who once might have been assigned to the secretarial pool if nothing's changed. Ask your gay friend if it's easier to be out and proud in America now that it was thirty years ago. To deny this progress—our progress—would be to rob us of our agency; our responsibility to do what we can to make America better.

Of course, a more common mistake is to suggest that racism is banished, that the work that drew men and women to Selma is complete, and that whatever racial tensions remain are consequences of those seeking to play the "race card" for their purposes. We don't need the Ferguson report to know that's not true. We just need to open our eyes, and ears, and hearts, to know that this nation's racial history still casts its long shadow upon us. We know the march is not yet over, the race is not yet won, and that reaching that blessed destination where we are judged by the content of our character—requires admitting as much.

"We are capable of bearing a great burden," James Baldwin wrote, "once we discover that the burden is reality and arrive where reality is."

This is work for all Americans, and not just some. Not just whites. Not just blacks. If we want to honor the courage of those who marched that day, then all of us are called to possess their moral imagination. All of us will need to feel, as they did, the fierce urgency of now. All of us need to recognize, as they did, that change depends on our actions, our attitudes, the things we reach our children. And if we make such effort, no matter how hard it may seem, laws can be passed, and consciences can be stirred, and consensus can be built.

With such effort, we can make sure our criminal justice system serves all and not just some. Together, we can raise the level of mutual trust that policing is built on—the idea that police officers are members of the communities they risk their lives to protect, and citizens in Ferguson and New York and Cleveland just want the same thing young people here marched for—the protection of the law. Together, we can address unfair sentencing, and overcrowded prisons, and the stunted circumstances that rob too many boys of the chance to become men, and rob the nation of too many men who could be good dads, and workers, and neighbors.

With effort we can roll back poverty and the roadblocks to opportunity. Americans don't accept a free ride for anyone, nor do we believe in equality of outcomes. But we do expect equal opportunity, and if we mean it, if we're willing to sacrifice for it, then we can make sure every child gets an education suitable to this new century, one that expands imaginations and lifts their sights and gives them skills. We can make sure every person willing to work has the dignity of a job, and a fair wage, and a real voice, and sturdier rungs on that ladder into the middle class.

And with effort, we can protect the foundation stone of our democracy for which so many marched across this bridge—and that is the right to vote. Right now, in 2015, fifty years after Selma, there are laws across this country designed to make it harder for people to vote. As we speak, more of such laws are being proposed. Meanwhile, the Voting Rights Act, the culmination of so much blood and sweat and tears, the product of so much sacrifice in the face of wanton violence, stands weakened, its future subject to partisan rancor.

How can that be? The Voting Rights Act was one of the crowning achievements of our democracy, the result of Republican and Democratic effort. President Reagan signed its renewal when he was in office. President Bush signed its renewal when he was in office. One hundred Members of Congress have come here today to honor people who were willing to die for the right it protects. If we want to honor this day, let these hundred go back to Washington, and gather four hundred more, and together, pledge to make it their mission to restore the law this year.

Of course, our democracy is not the task of Congress alone, or the courts alone, or the President alone. If every new voter suppression law was struck down today, we'd still have one of the lowest voting rates among free peoples. Fifty years ago, registering to vote here in Selma and much of the South meant guessing the number of jellybeans in a jar or bubbles on a bar of soap. It meant risking your dignity, and sometimes, your life. What is our excuse today for not voting? How do we so casually discard the right for which so many fought? How do we so fully give away our power, our voice, in shaping America's future?

Fellow marchers, so much has changed in fifty years. We've endured war, and fashioned peace. We've seen technological wonders that touch every aspect of our lives, and take for granted convenience our parents might scarcely imagine. But what has not changed is the imperative of citizenship, that willingness of a 26 year-old deacon, or a Unitarian minister, or a young mother of five, to decide they loved this country so much that they'd risk everything to realize its promise.

That's what it means to love America. That's what it means to believe in America. That's what it means when we say America is exceptional.

For we were born of change. We broke the old aristocracies, declaring ourselves entitled not by bloodline, but endowed by our Creator with certain unalienable rights. We secure our rights and responsibilities through a system of self-government, of and by and for the people. That's why we argue and fight with so much passion and conviction, because we know our efforts matter. We know America is what we make of it.

We are Lewis and Clark and Sacajawea—pioneers who braved the unfamiliar, followed by a stampede of farmers and miners, entrepreneurs and hucksters. That's our spirit.

We are Sojourner Truth and Fannie Lou Hamer, women who could do as much as any man and then some; and we're Susan B. Anthony, who shook the system until the law reflected that truth. That's our character.

We're the immigrants who stowed away on ships to reach these shores, the huddled masses yearning to breathe free—Holocaust survivors, Soviet defectors, the Lost Boys of Sudan. We are the hopeful strivers who cross the Rio Grande because they want their kids to know a better life. That's how we came to be.

We're the slaves who built the White House and the economy of the South. We're the ranch hands and cowboys who opened the West, and countless laborers who laid rail, and raised skyscrapers, and organized for workers' rights.

We're the fresh-faced GIs who fought to liberate a continent, and we're the Tuskegee Airmen, Navajo code-talkers, and Japanese-Americans who fought for this country even as their liberty had been denied. We're the firefighters who rushed into those buildings on 9/11, and the volunteers who signed up to fight in Afghanistan and Iraq.

We are the gay Americans whose blood ran on the streets of San Francisco and New York, just as blood ran down this bridge.

We are storytellers, writers, poets, and artists who abhor unfairness, and despise hypocrisy, and give voice to the voiceless, and tell truths that need to be told.

We are the inventors of gospel and jazz and the blues, bluegrass and country, hip-hop and rock and roll, our very own sounds with all the sweet sorrow and reckless joy of freedom.

We are Jackie Robinson, enduring scorn and spiked cleats and pitches coming straight to his head and stealing home in the World Series anyway.

We are the people Langston Hughes wrote of, who "build our temples for tomorrow, strong as we know how."

We are the people Emerson wrote of, "who for truth and honor's sake stand fast and suffer long;" who are "never tired, so long as we can see far enough."

That's what America is. Not stock photos or airbrushed history or feeble attempts to define some of us as more American as others. We respect the past, but we don't pine for it. We don't fear the future; we grab for it. America is not some fragile thing; we are large, in the words of Whitman, containing multitudes. We are boisterous and diverse and full of energy, perpetually young in spirit. That's why someone like John Lewis at the ripe age of 25 could lead a mighty march.

And that's what the young people here today and listening all across the country must take away from this day. You are America. Unconstrained by habits and convention. Unencumbered by what is, and ready to seize what ought to be. For everywhere in this country, there are first steps to be taken, and new ground to cover, and bridges to be crossed. And it is you, the young and fearless at heart, the most diverse and educated generation in our history, who the nation is waiting to follow.

Because Selma shows us that America is not the project of any one person.

Because the single most powerful word in our democracy is the word "We." We the People. We Shall Overcome. Yes We Can. It is owned by no one. It belongs to everyone. Oh, what a glorious task we are given, to continually try to improve this great nation of ours.

Fifty years from Bloody Sunday, our march is not yet finished. But we are getting closer. Two hundred and thirty-nine years after this nation's founding, our union is not yet perfect. But we are getting closer. Our job's easier because somebody already got us through that first mile. Somebody already got us over that bridge. When it feels the road's too hard, when the torch we've been passed feels too heavy, we will remember these early travelers, and draw strength from their example, and hold firmly the words of the prophet Isaiah:

> "Those who hope in the Lord will renew their strength. They will soar on wings like eagles. They will run and not grow weary. They will walk and not be faint."

We honor those who walked so we could run. We must run so our children soar. And we will not grow weary. For we believe in the power of an awesome God, and we believe in this country's sacred promise.

May He bless those warriors of justice no longer with us, and bless the United States of America.

On Race, Obama seeks steady gains within the system

During racially tense moments that have beset the nation recently many Americans have longed for President Obama to display some of the passion and rhetoric that made the Rev. Martin Luther King Jr. a civil rights legend.

Kings speeches in the 1960s were clarion calls for justice, action and civil disobedience. Obama has sounded calls for restraint, lawful demonstrations, commissions of inquiry and slow steady progress toward reform. On race as on the economy, a "resurgent America" has made great progress but still requires greater inclusiveness.

Rather than making pressing demands for economic justice like those of that defined King's crusade, Obama will make a pitch for a tax package that will aid lower-and middle-class households and serve as modest tools for economic advancement for both whites and blacks. Obama has inherited King's legacy of economic inequality, and with only two years left in office, he will likely bequeath it to the next president.

In 1967, 1 in 7 Americans lived below the poverty line. Today that's still the case. And among African Americans, more than 1 in 4 do.

In 2013, 27 percent of African Americans lived in poverty, well over twice the 10 percent rate for white Americans, according to census data collected by the Kaiser Family Foundation.

Nearly a third of African American high school students do not graduate on time, double the rate of whites and Asian Americans. Black households on average bring in less than 60 cents for every dollar earned by whites—a difference only slightly smaller than it was in the mid-1960s.

The crippling recession has helped widen the wealth gap, leaving African Americans with a dollar for every $18 held by whites.

Once-soaring black incarceration rates are indeed declining and black high school graduation rates are inching up. A small but growing number of African Americans sit atop corporations, such as

Kaiser Permanente and the board of software titan Microsoft.

But despite that headway, the federal government estimates that 1 in 3 black men can expect to go to prison in their lifetime.

"The disparities in wealth, incarceration rates and residential segregation levels were the same on the day before and the day after the election of our nation's first African American President."

A decade ago, in "The Audacity of Hope, "Obama wrote that health-care reform" would do more to eliminate health disparities between whites and minorities than any race-specific programs we might design." He wrote that the idea "of rising tide lifting minority boats" was true, and that "growing incomes and a sense of security among whites made them less resistant to minority claims to equality."

Finally, after a deep recession and slow recovery, the economic tide is rising. But so far, a large number of "minority boats" are still stuck on the rocks.

John Conyers

Four days after the assassination of Martin Luther King Jr., a junior member of Congress introduced a bill to establish a federal holiday to honor the slain Civil Rights leader. Five decades later, the holiday is on the calendar and that lawmaker Rep. John Conyers (D-Mich.), is now the longest-serving member of Congress. Monday presents a unique bit of historical symmetry for Conyers, who marked 50 years in Congress in January 2015. Both his longevity and the holiday are testaments and by products of the civil rights struggles led by King. For the first time, the 85-year-old will observe the Martin Luther King Jr. Day holiday as Dean of the house, the ceremonial title for the longest-serving member of the House of Representatives.

Middle Class Economics

The Oxfam international, the British antipoverty organization has released a report outlining how within the next 12 months the richest one percent will take ownership of over 50 percent of the planets wealth.

Obama, In State of the Union, highlights tax reform, Community College plans

President Obama focused on helping the middle class in his state of the Union address Tuesday night 01/20/15, highlighting his tax proposals targeting the wealthy and big banks even as Republicans voiced opposition.

"Will we accept an economy where only a few of us do spectacularly well?" the president said in his speech, which was released before he addressed a joint session of Congress.

"Or will we commit ourselves to an economy that generates rising incomes and chances for everyone who makes the effort?"

"That's what middle-class economics is—the idea that this Country does best when everyone gets their fair shot, everyone does their fair share, and everyone plays by the same set of rules." Obama said in a reprise of one of the key themes that animated his reelection campaign in 2012.

Dalton Conley wrote:

On the one hand, the Civil Rights era officially ended inequality of opportunity. At the same time, civil rights legislations did nothing to address the underlying economic and social inequalities that had built up through hundreds of years of discrimination.

The one statistic that best captures the state of racial inequality in America today is wealth, or net worth. Today, the average white family has eight times the net worth of the average Black family. That difference has grown since the 1960s, and is not explained by other factors like education, earnings rates, and savings rates. It's the legacy of racial inequality from generations past. No other measure captures the cumulative disadvantage of race, or cumulative advantage of race for Whites, than net worth or wealth.

Economist has shown that 50 to 80 percent of our lifetime wealth accumulation is attributable, in one way or another, to past generations.

The house, the Cadillac, the big bank account—these aren't just the pot of gold at the end of the game, they're also the starting point for the next generation. Until we address the underlying inequalities and structures that advantage whites at the expense of other groups, we're stuck with this paradoxical idea of a color blind society that is unequal by color.

"Promised Land" of justice and equality.

We know that it's just a matter of time before black people and other minorities will achieve justice and equality, good jobs, fair wages, safe neighborhoods and quality education.

In 2015, undergraduate enrollment is projected to expand by 2.6 million, 80% of these being minority students. White undergraduate enrollment is projected to decrease from 70.6% in 1995 to 62.8% in 2015 with a corresponding increase in the percentage of minority students from 29.4% in 1995 to 37.2% in 2015. As the white, non-Hispanic proportion of the total population decreases from 73.6% in to a projected 52.8% in 2050. The traditional male white work force will shrink by an estimated 11% while the minority workforce will expand rapidly. By 2028, it is expected that there be a shortage of 19 million skilled workers to fill jobs in the U.S. (U.S. Census Bureau)

Now is the time to do something about it. We can encourage our youth to pursue STEM careers. We can develop our children's interest in these fields at an early age by taking them to museums, doing fun at-home experiments with them, taking them to the library and watching movies and documentaries that expose them to the possibilities of these careers.

US News concluded that careers in science and technology are the "best jobs," with the top 15 being in one of those fields. The chance to advance and be professionally fulfilled, and the ability to meet financial obligations are all possible.

President Obama continues to tout a new "green" economy built on renewable energy, climate change solutions, and sustainability. This economy will require a new generation of professionals that understand changing weather patterns, climate science, Wind and Solar, Engineering, Environmental Sustainability, and mitigation-adaptation strategies.

Connect Students with funding Sources

Money is a major concern for Black students trying to make it to college, let alone for a STEM degree. But there are many federally-funded programs like the NSF-funded Louis Stokes Alliances for Minority Participation or the Diversity Climate Network which offer funding to attract minority students to STEM fields. Find those resources and take advantage of them.

Obama brings a moral clarity to his leadership reserved for those who have had to work for everything they've gotten and has to do twice as well as the person standing next to them because of the color of their skin, his experience of succeeding despite his color, social background and prejudice could have been embittering or one that fostered a spiritual rebirth of forgiveness and enlightenment. Obama radiates the calm inner peace of the spirit of forgiveness. Doubters from the left and right just look cranky by comparison.

A hundred years from now Obama's portrait will be placed next to that of George Washington, Abraham Lincoln and Franklin Roosevelt. Long before that we'll be telling our children and grandchildren that we stepped out in faith and voted for a young black man who stood up and led our country back from the brink of an abyss. We'll tell them about the power of love, faith and hope. We'll tell them about the power of creativity combined with humility and intellectual brilliance.

We'll tell them that President Obama gave us the gift of regaining our faith in our country. We'll tell them that we all stood up and pitched in and won the day. We'll tell that President Obama restored our standing in the world. We'll tell them that by the time he left office Health Care was reformed! We'll tell them that our schools were on the mend, our economy booming, that we'd become a nation filled with green energy alternatives and we're leading the world away dependence on carbon-based destruction.

Here comes Donald Trump

Trump wants to erase Obama not only from the political landscape but also from the history books. In 2011, Donald J. Trump mischievously began to question president Obama's birthplace aloud in television interviews. "I'm starting to think that he was not born here," he said at the time. In 2012, he took to twitter to declare that "an 'extremely credible source'" had called his office to inform him that Mr. Obama's birth certificate was "a fraud."

Mr. Obama released his short form birth certificate from the Hawaii Department of Health in 2008. Surrounded by and in many ways shielded by decorated veterans in his new Washington hotel, Mr. Trump could not resist indulging in another falsehood—that is opponent, Hillary Clinton, had started the so-called birther movement. She did not.

Running for President with campaign promise

- Build a wall and make Mexico pay for it

- Temporarily ban Muslims from entering the U.S.
- Bring manufacturing jobs back
- Impose tariffs on goods made in China and Mexico
- Renegotiate or withdraw from the North American free trade agreement and Trans Pacific Partnership
- Full repeal of Obamacare and replace it with a market-based alternative
- Renegotiate the Iran deal
- Leave Social Security as is
- Cut Taxes
- 'Bomb' and/or 'take the oil' from ISIS

Paris Climate Agreement

Nearly 200 nations, including the United States under President Barack Obama's administration, agreed in 2015 to voluntarily reduce their greenhouse gas emissions to combat climate change. The countries each set their own emissions targets, though these goals are not legally binding. A priority "is to strengthen the global response to the threat of climate change keeping a global temperature rise this century well below 2 degrees Celsius above pre-industrial levels and to pursue efforts to limit the temperature increase even further to 1.5 degrees Celsius," according to the United Nations Framework Convention on Climate Change (UNFCCC).

Developed nations are also supposed to offer financial aid to developing ones so they can move toward cleaner energy sources. The U.S. pledged to lower its annual greenhouse gas emissions in 2025 by 26 to 28 percent below 2005 levels, which would be a reduction of about 1.6 billion tons of annual emissions.

The U.S. is the world's second-largest emitter of carbon, while China takes the top spot. Beijing, however, has reaffirmed its commitment to meeting its targets under the Paris accord, recently canceling construction of about 100 coals-fired plants and investing billions in massive wind and solar projects.

The Obama administration pledged as much as $3 billion to less wealthy nations by 2020, with the U.S. giving $1 billion. A total of 195 parties sign the agreement.

Syria and Nicaragua are the only nations that didn't sign Paris Agreement. Nicaragua said it wasn't tough enough.

Four claims Trump used to justify pulling the U.S. out of the Paris agreement

- The Paris Agreement was costly and ineffective.
- The agreement wasted taxpayer money
- Withdrawal is a demonstration of leadership
- Withdrawal is good for American energy competitiveness

<u>Trump override of Climate Plan</u>

President Trump has moved to kill an Obama-era effort to limit carbon emissions from coal-fired Power Plants. Environmental Protection Agency Administrator Scott Pruitt said he would be issuing a new set of rules overriding the Clean Power Plan, the centerpiece of President Barack Obama's ddrive to curb global climate change.

"The war on coal is over," Pruitt declared, adding that no federal agency should ever use its authority to "declare war on any sector of our economy". Republicans had criticized the Obama administration for issuing the ruling.

Attorney General Eric Schneiderman said "the Trump Administration's persistent and indefensible denial of climate change—and their continued assault on actions essential to stemming its increasing devastation—is reprehensible, and I will use every available legal tool to fight their dangerous agenda." Pruitt was among about two dozen attorney generals who sued to stop Obama's 2014 push to limit carbon emissions, stymieing the limits from ever taking effect. Closely aligned with the oil and gas industry in his home state, Pruitt rejects the consensus of scientists that manmade emissions from burning fossil fuels are the primary driver of global climate change.

President Donald Trump, who appointed Pruitt and share his skepticism of established climate science, promised to kill the clean Power Plan during the 2016 campaign as part of his broader pledge to revive the nation's struggling coal mines.

Obama's plan was designed to cut U.S. carbon dioxide emissions to 32 percent below 2005 levels by 2030. The rule dictated specific emission targets for states based on power-plant emissions and gave officials broad latitude to decide how to achieve reductions. The Supreme Court put the plan on hold in 2016 following legal challenges by industry and coal-friendly states. Even so, the plan helped drive a recent wave of retirements of coal-fired plants, which are also being squeezed by low cost natural gas and renewable power.

In the absence of stricter federal regulations curbing greenhouse gas emissions, many states have issued their mandates promoting energy conservation.

The withdrawal of the Clean Power Plan is the latest in a series of moves by Trump and Pruitt to dismantle Obama's legacy on fighting climate changes including the delay or roll back of rules limiting levels of toxic pollution in smokestack emissions and wastewater discharges from coal-burning power plants.

Despite the rhetoric about saving coal, government statistics show that coal mines currently employ only about 52,000 workers nationally—a modest 4 percent uptick singe Trump became president. Those numbers are dwarfed by the jobs created by building such clean power infrastructure as wind turbines and solar arrays.

"Trump is not just ignoring the deadly cost of pollution, he's ignoring the clean energy deployment that is rapidly creating jobs across the Country," said Michael Brune, executive director of the Sierra Club.

Deferred Action for Childhood Arrivals (DACA)

The Trump administration said it ended DACA because Obama overstepped his constitutional authority by creating the policy without Congressional approval. Mr. Obama created the Deferred Action for Childhood Arrivals program in June 2012 aiming to protect from deportation undocumented immigrants who were brought to the United States as children. The so-called Dreamers who have benefited from the program now number approximately 800,000.

What Mr. Trump has done: Mr. Trump repeatedly railed against the program on the campaign trail. After taking office, he ordered an end to the program in September, calling it an "amnesty-first approach." Mr. Trump called on Congress to pass a replacement plan within six months, before the program is to be fully phased out. Since then, he has said he is willing to "revisit" his decision if Congress does not come up with a fix.

In early October, Mr. Trump delivered to Congress a list of hard-line demands on immigration policy that may make building Democratic support for a deal more difficult.

Before agreeing to provide legal status for 800,000 young immigrants brought here illegally as children, Mr. Trump will insist on the construction of a wall across the southern border, the hiring of 10,000 immigration agents, tougher laws for those seeking asylum and denial of federal grants to "sanctuary cities," the use of the E-Verify program by companies to keep illegal immigrants from getting jobs, an end to people bringing their extended family into the United States, and a hardening of the border against thousands of children fleeing violence in Central America.

Such a move would shut down loopholes that encourage parents from Guatemala, El Salvador and Honduras to send their children illegally in the United States, where many of them melt into American communities and become undocumented immigrants.

In a letter to lawmakers, Mr. Trump said his demands would address "dangerous loopholes, outdated laws and easily exploited vulnerabilities" in the immigration system, asserting that they were "reforms that must be included" in any deal to address the Dreamers.

Mr. Trump is also calling for a surge in resources to pay for 370 additional immigration judges, 1,000 government lawyers and more detention space so that children arriving at the border can be held, processed and quickly returned if they do not qualify to stay longer.

Advocates acknowledge that more resources are necessary to speed up those hearings. But they argue that White House efforts to demand quick decisions are likely to merely result in many children being sent back to places where they are raped, beaten or killed.

If the children are not deported quickly, officials say, many will never leave, eventually becoming a new population of sympathetic young immigrants who seek amnesty. That could create lasting cycles in which illegal immigrants demand to be given a legal status, the official say.

Confronting the NFL players

Several athletes, including a handful of NFL of players have refused to stand during "The Star-Spangled Banner" to protest of the treatment of blacks by police. Quarterback Colin Kaepernick, who started the trend last year when he played for the San Francisco 49ers, hasn't been signed by an NFL team for the 2017 season. Trump took credit for the fact that Kaepernick hadn't been signed.

Trump, during an extended riff at a rally speech in Huntsville, Alabama, said those players are disrespecting the flag and deserve to lose their jobs. "That's a total disrespect of our heritage. That's a total disrespect of our heritage. That's a total disrespect of everything that we stand for," he said, encouraging owners to act. "Wouldn't you love to see one of these NFL owners, when somebody disrespects our flag, you'd say, "getthat son of a bitch off the field right now. Out! He's fired, "Trump said to loud applause.

He recently suggested police officers should be tougher with criminals and shouldn't protect their heads when pushing them into squad cars.

Athletes—mostly black—from every team in the country knelt, stood arm in arm, sat or refused to take the field for the national anthem. They even took it abroad with the first protest taking place in England, in a game that represents the NFL's effort to broaden the league's appeal. And it's all because of president Trump.

Former San Francisco 49ers quarterback Colin Kaepernick was the first to make the controversial statement last year, before Trump's election, over police violence in black communities. When Trump weighed in, it gave the movement new life. It became about freedom of speech—and a anti-Trump protest. This is about where this moment in history, with a president like President Trump at the helm of the country, fits in.

It's another chapter in a divisive history of sports, politics and race. "Trump told reporters that this had nothing to do with race or anything else. This has to do with respect for our country and respect for our flag." Almost two-thirds of whites disapproved of not standing for the anthem, while three-quarters of African-Americans approved of the tactic.

The same poll found 70 percent of whites approve of the job the police are doing, while two-thirds of blacks do not.

Athletes in the NFL are overwhelmingly black—70 percent of the league. Black athletes have used the megaphone sports provide to protest for a long time.

Jesse Owens and 17 other black American Olympians went into the 1936 Olympics in Germany and won medal after medal in front of Adolf Hitler. Those 18 black athletes accounted for a quarter of the entire U.S. team's medals in Berlin. But nearly all faced racism, backlash and a lack of fully integrated rights as citizens back home in a segregated America.

Thirty-two years later, Tommie Smith and John Carlos, American gold and bronze medal winners at the 1968 Olympic Games, donned black gloves and raised their arms in a black power salute from the medal podium in Mexico City. 1968 was another inflection point year in American political and social history. Violence was spilling out in the Civil rights and integration movement. Cities had been burned from rioting the year before. Martin Luther King Jr. and Robert F. Kennedy had been assassinated. Like today, the country was divided politically and along racial lines.

After their wins, Smith and Carlos were stripped of their medals by the head of the International Olympic Committee. There was Mohammad Ali, born Cassius Clay, the champion boxer converted to Islam in 1964, and when drafted into the Vietnam War in 1967, he refused to go, listing religious convictions. Ali was convicted of draft evasion, sentenced to five years in prison and banned from boxing for three years. The U.S. Supreme Court overturned his conviction in 1971.

Around the same time, Curt Flood of the St Louis Cardinals made history in 1969 by challenging a clause in professional baseball that essentially said players were teams' property. Flood called himself a "well-paid slave." That triggered mass backlash among whites, but it also helped bring the issue of free agency to the forefront. The NFL adopted similar free agency in 1992 and the NBA in 1996.

In 1992 Flood received the Jackie Robinson Award for contributions by black athletes.

By calling players "sons of bitches," questioning their patriotism and right to free speech and calling for their firings, struck a nerve and had an ironic unifying effect across the league. Owners stood with players arm in arm.

The remarks landed him right back into the race and culture wars, just a month after his widely criticized response to white Supremacists, Nazis and the KKK marching in Charlottesville, Va. And his handling of race relations, Charlottesville and Twitter, are three of the least popular things Trump has done.

Kaepernick "I am not going to stand up to show pride in a flag for a country that oppresses black people and people of color," Kaepernick told NFL Media at the outset of the controversy. "To me, this is bigger than football and it would be selfish on my part to look the other way. There are bodies in the street and people getting paid leave and getting away with murder."

The 49ers stated Kaepernick's decision: "The national anthem is and always will be a special part of the pre-game ceremony. It is an opportunity to honor our country and reflect on the great liberties we are afforded as its citizens. In respecting such American principles as freedom of religion and freedom of expression, we recognize the right of an individual to choose and participate, or not, in our celebration of the national anthem.

Colin Kaepernick receives Muhammad Ali Legacy Award from Sports Illustrated

In an essay, Sports Illustrated's Michael Rosenberg wrote, "In the last 16 months, Kaepernick's truth has been twisted, distorted and used for political gain. It has cost him at least a year of his NFL career and the income that should have come with it. But still, it is his truth. He has not wavered from it. He does not regret speaking it. He has caused millions of people to examine it. And, quietly, he has donated a million dollars to support it."

California NAACP President

National Anthem has racist third stanza

California's NAACP is pushing for state lawmakers to support a campaign to remove "The Star Spangled Banner" as the country's national anthem.

The group says the song, which has been a point of controversy in the NFL, is "one of the most racist, pro-slavery, anti-black songs in the American lexicon." "This song is wrong," state President, Alice Huffman told a CBS affiliate in Sacramento. "It shouldn't have been there, we didn't have it 'til 1931, so it won't kill us if it goes away."

"The Star-Spangled Banner" became the nation's anthem when President Herbert Hoover signed a congressional act making it the song of the United States. Huffman told the CBS affiliate the NFL protests led her to look at the lyrics of the anthem—finding a little—noticed third stanza includes the phrase: "no refuge could save the hireling and slave from the terror of flight or the gloom of the grave."

Huffman said some interpretations conclude it celebrates the deaths of black American slaves fighting for freedom. "It's racist; it doesn't represent our community; it's anti-black," she said.

By taking a stand for civil rights, Kaepernick, 28, joins other athletes, like the NBA's Dwayne Wade, Chris Paul, LeBron James and Carmelo Anthony and several WNBA players in using their platform and status to raise awareness to issues affecting minorities in the U.S.

"By definition, an anthem is a song or hymn of praise or loyalty for or to something else. The anthem comes to mean something more than its words and music, but acts as a musical or lyrical tribute to, or affirmation of, something else—the United States, the flag, and their underlying ideals. "By participating, individuals adhere to and adopt the ideas symbolized in the song itself; by not participating, they send a different, contrary message.

University of New Hampshire law professor Michael Mc Cann, who is a recognized expert in sports law, wrote that an NFL team that fired a player for protesting would not only need to deal with the players' union and the arbitration process, but the terminated player could file a discrimination complaint with the Equal Employment Opportunity Commission or possibly file a defamation lawsuit.

Gun Control advocates slammed President Donald Trump on Monday November 6, 2017 as a hypocrite for having signed a bill earlier in February 2017 that rolled back a regulation making it harder for people with mental illnesses to buy firearms even as he blamed the shooting in Texas over the weekend on "a mental health problem."

"One of his first actions as president trashed a new regulation that would have prevented potentially irresponsible and mentally incompetent people from being able to buy guns."

The rule, which had been finalized in December 2016, added people receiving Social Security checks for mental illnesses and people deemed unfit to handle their financial affairs to the national background gun check database. Had the rule fully taken effect, the Obama administration predicted it would have added about 75,000 names to the database.

The National Rifle Association applauded Trump for signing the bill. Chris Cox, the group's chief lobbyist, said at the time that it marked "a new era for law-abiding gun owners, as we now have a president who respects and support our arms."

Obama proposed the now-nullified regulation in a 2013 memo following the mass shooting at Sandy Hook Elementary School. At the time the measure was hotly contested by gun rights advocates who said it infringed on Second Amendment rights.

It isn't clear whether the now-eliminated rule would have applied to the gunman in the Texas church shooting, identified as Devin Patrick Kelley. Kelley had a turbulent past, including a court-martial from the Air Force for assaulting his first wife and child, an animal cruelty arrest and a habit of harassing ex-girlfriends. Earlier, Monday, Trump said that Sunday's mass shooting at a Texas church—the largest in the state's history—"isn't a guns situation" "but instead" a mental health problem at the highest level."

The massacre left 26 people dead, including up to 14 children, and 20 more injured. "Mental health is your problem here." Said Trump. In the end the

Air Force failed to report on Kelley domestic violence charges. The Air Force's failure to alert federal authorities Delvin Kelley was convicted of a crime, which might have kept him from buying the military style rifle he used in the massacre of 26 churchgoers Sunday.

The debate on gun control cannot wait, according to a piece by the New York Times editorial board. The board cited the Texas church shooting in Sutherland Springs, calling it an "unthinkable tragedy at the hands of a mass murderer and his guns."

"Still, Republican leaders in Congress do nothing. Ok, so far they've done the same thing they have always done: offered thoughts and prayers, the board wrote. Soon, they will offer warnings not to 'politicize' a tragedy by debating gun controls that might prevent such mass killings from happening again."

Trump ramps up Obama care sabotage

President Trump's administration has taken steps to undermine the Obamacare market place. It's responsible for managing. The Federal Centers for Medicare and Medicaid Services announced that it's making drastic cuts in spending on advertising for the 2018 open enrollment period on the Affordable Care Acts health insurance exchanges, as well as significant cutbacks in funding for local organizations that help consumers navigate the buying process.

Trump himself repeatedly has said he wants to let or make the health insurance exchanges collapse, and his administration has taken several actions to destabilize them.

That's above and beyond his advocacy for the Affordable Care Act's repeal.

Chief among the destabilizing steps has been Trump threatening to withhold billions owed to health insurance companies serving poor enrollees, which has contributed to large rate hikes for the next year.

The department of Health and Human Services also has used its Websites and social media channels to criticize the Affordable Care Act at tax payer expense. And the administration previously cancelled other outreach and education programs President Barack Obama's administration created to help get out the word about coverage options and provide in-person assistance to people seeking help signing up. The Trump administration also cut the open enrollment period for next year to half its length from last year, giving customers less time to weigh their options,

Trump told HHS to deny request to fix Iowa Obama care market

President Trump told the head of the centers for Medicare and Medicaid Seema Varma to deny a request from the Republican-Controlled state of Iowa to fix their health-care market place, according to the Washington Post. Iowa officials sought for months to get federal permission to fix health insurance markets in their State, but they were shut down by Trump administration officials. Democrats have called on the White House to stop undermining the Health Care Law.

Senate Republicans and the administration failed twice this year to fulfill a seven-year campaign promise to repeal and replace Obamacare.

The Mandate requiring most Americans to have health insurance or pay a tax penalty is easily the most unpopular piece of the 2010 health law. Only Congress can strike the mandate, but many viewed the executive order Trump issued on his first day in office instructing agencies to weaken Obamacare as a sign to stop enforcing the penalties.

The mandate hasn't convinced enough young and healthy people to buy insurance, but health plans see it as a crucial tool to keep markets stable. Without it, premiums could unexpectedly spike or carriers could exit markets altogether, accelerating a trend that began this year.

Senate Minority Leader Chuck Schumer "the Trump administration is deliberately attempting to sabotage our health care system," Schumer said in a statement. "When the number of people with health insurance declines and cost skyrocket the American people know who's to blame."

<u>White house to end health care subsidies</u>

After three high profile failed GOP repealand-replace efforts in Congress, President Trump decided to end health care subsidies. Trump argues the subsidies are illegal because they are not appropriated by Congress. House Republicans sued the Obama administration hoping to stop the payments. A Court sided with the House GOP, but agreed to leave the subsidies in place until a government appeal could be heard. The Trump administration, however, decided to drop the appeal, thereby ending the payments. Trump's move came a day after he took yet another step to undermine Obamacare by signing an executive order allowing groups of small businesses and associations to band together to buy health insurance.

According to Bloomberg politics Trump's new Obamacare killer to cost Uncle Sam $194 billion. President Trump thinks by halting some Obamacare subsidies would be a big money saver for taxpayers. The move could force the government to dole out almost $200 billion more on health insurance over the next decade.

The insurer payouts Trump cut off aren't the only government funds financing the program. Consumer also can get help with their insurance premiums when the insurer subsidies are discontinued, those premiums are pushed higher—and because the consumer subsidies are far bigger than those given to insurers, that's a costly trade.

More than eight in ten individuals who buy Obamacare Plans get help paying their premiums directly from the federal government. Those subsidies effectively cap how much people have to pay for insurance as a percentage of their income.

Even if premiums climb, people who receive those benefits won't pay more out of their own pockets. The subsidies are available to people making as much as four times the federal poverty level, or just over $97,000 for a family of four.

That means that those most likely to be hurt by the president's action aren't low-income people who will still get help with their costs. Instead, consumers who make much money to qualify for subsidies will now have to pay a much higher price for their health plans. It all adds up to a hefty bill for taxpayers for as long as the Affordable Care Act is the law of the land.

The Congressional Budget Office estimated that ending the cost-sharing payments would increase the U.S. fiscal shortfall by $194 billion over the next decade as subsidy outlays jump.

Trump said "I've been saying for the last year and a half that the best thing we can do politically speaking is let Obamacare explode," It is exploding right now." Experts said that the ACA wasn't "exploding" but that it needed fixes to help incentivize insurers to stay in market places. The moves he has taken risk blowing up the individual markets by making insurance too expensive for lower and middle-class families. Trump's actions, however could backfire politically, threatening to shift blame for the health care act's shortcomings from former President Barack Obama and Democrats to Trump and Republicans.

Trump Border Wall

Trump administration is finding ways to reduce the number of foreigners living in the United States. Those who are undocumented and those here legally and overhaul the U.S. immigration system for generations to come.

Across agencies and programs, federal officials are wielding executive authority to assemble a bureaucratic wall that could be more effective than any concrete and metal one. While some actions have drawn widespread attention, others have been put in place more quietly. The administration has moved to slash the number of refugees, accelerate deportations and terminate the provisional residency of more than a million people, among other measures.

On Monday 11/20/17, the Department of Homeland Security said nearly 60,000 Haitians allowed to stay in the United States after a devastating 2010 earthquake have until July 2019 to leave or obtain another form of legal status. "He's building a virtual wall by his actions and rhetoric," said Kevin Appleby, migration policy for the Center for Migration Studies, a nonprofit think tank. Trump administration officials say they are simply upholding laws their predecessors did not and preserving American jobs. Previous Republican and Democratic administrations were too soft on enforcement, they sat and too rosy in their view of immigration as an unambiguously positive force.

"For decades, the American people have been begging and pleading with our elected officials for an immigration system that's lawful and serves the national interest," Attorney General Jeff Sessions said in Austin last month, "Now we have a president who supports that."

Bob Dane, executive director of the Federation for American Immigration Reform, which has pushed for many of the Trump administration's main goals on immigration, said the president has "really scaled back this expansive view of immigration that occurred under the Obama administration."

The new restrictions could significantly reduce the number of foreign-born workers in the U.S. labor force, but demographic experts say there is little chance they will alter the country's broader racial and ethnic transformation, which Trump's critics say is his goal. Census projections show the United States will no longer have a single racial or ethnic majority by mid-century, according to the Pew Research Center.

Still, by erecting tougher, taller administrative hurdles for foreigners seeking to move to the United States or remain in the country after arriving illegally, the White House is attempting to shift the country back toward the tighter controls on immigration in place before the 1960s. "Within the administration there are several key players who are just looking for every opportunity, every program…every administrative or regulatory leeway they have to restrict entry into the United States," said Linda Hartke, president and chief executive of the Lutheran Immigration and Refugee Service, which resettles refugees.

Even as they fight court orders seeking to halt parts of Trump's immigration agenda, Sessions, White House senior adviser Stephen Miller and other key players are finding ways to shrink the immigration system. Miller was an aide to Sessions before both men joined the administration; in less than a year their immigration policy prescriptions have move from the realm of think-tank wish lists to White House executive orders. In October, the White House—in a plan led by Miller—said it had conducted a "bottom-up review of all immigration policies" and found "dangerous loopholes, outdated laws, and easily exploited vulnerabilities in our immigration system—current policies that are harming our country and our communities."

Trump has endorsed GOP legislation to cut annual, legal immigration by half, reducing the number of green cards issued annually from about 1 million to 500,000. More weight would be given to immigrants with job skills, as opposed to those with extended family in the United Stated.

The president cut the number of refugees the United States is willing to accept annually from 110,000 to 45,000, the lowest level since 1980, and ordered the implementation of a time-consuming "extreme vetting" system that could mean the number of refugees cleared each year is much lower. In October, 1,242 refugees arrived in the United States, down from 9,945 in October 2016.

Trump also eliminated a smaller program specifically for refugees fleeing violence in Central America. The Pentagon, citing concerns about vetting, suspended a recruitment program offering skilled foreigners a fast track to citizenship if they serve in uniform. Muzaffar Chishti, the director of the Migration Policy Institute at the New York University School of Law, said nearly 350,000 of the newcomers who arrive legally to the United States each year are the spouses and minor children of U.S. Citizens and permanent residents. Since barring those arrivals is not under consideration, Chishti said, the government would have to eliminate or sharply restrict almost all other avenues to reduce the annual number of immigrants to 500,000.

In addition to this week's decision on Haitians, the government earlier this month declined to renew Temporary Protected Status, a form of provisional residency, for about 2,500 Nicaraguans. The State Department says condition in Central America and Haiti that had been used to justify the protection for as long as two decades no longer necessitate a reprieve. Decisions on more than 250,000 Hondurans and Salvadorans with the provisional residency permits are pending.

Trump is also ending Deferred Action for Childhood Arrivals, or DACA, the Obama administration program that granted work permits to

690,000 young immigrants brought here as children. Trump's administration is expanding immigration courts and detention Centers and has ratcheted up deportations from the interior of the United States, where millions of undocumented immigrants with U.S. born children and no serious criminal records held little fear of expulsion under President Barack Obama.

Arrest by Immigration and Customs Enforcement are up more than 40 percent this year, and the agency wants to more than double its staff by 2023, according to a federal contracting notice published this month. ICE is calling for a major increase in agreements with state and local governments that want to help arrest and detain undocumented residents. If you're in this country illegally and you committed a crime by entering this country, you should be uncomfortable," Thomas Homan, the top official at ICE, told Lawmakers this year. "You should look over your shoulder. And you need to be worried.

The president and his aides have pressed forward despite an outcry form advocates and Democratic lawmakers, who in states such as California and Illinois have instructed Police and public officials to shun cooperation with ICE. The Trump administration has threatened to strip such "Sanctuary" jurisdictions of federal in an escalating legal standoff. Trump's tough talk alone appears to be one of the administration's best bulwarks: Illegal crossings along the border with Mexico have plunged to their lowest in 45 years, and U.S. Agents are catching a far greater share of those attempting to sneak in.

Applications for H-1B skilled visas and new foreign student enrollment have also declined. William Frey, a demographer at the Brookings Institution, said that until now U.S. immigration rates have largely spared the country from the challenges facing advanced industrial nations such as Japan and Germany that can't replace aging workers fast enough. By slashing immigration, Frey said, the country could end up with labor shortages and other workforce issues.

But although some of Trump's most fervent supporters see curbing immigration as a way to turn back the United States' rapid racial and ethnic transformation, Frey said it is an unrealistic goal.

By 2020, census projections show minorities will account for more than half of the under-18 U.S. population, because of higher birthrates in nonwhite populations. And by 2026, the number of whites is projected to begin declining in absolute numbers, he said, as deaths exceed births. "You can slow the rate of Latino and Asian immigration, but it won't make the population whiter," Frey said. "It will just become less white at a slower pace."

Trump continues to insist his administration will build a border wall, despite exorbitant cost projections and senior DHS officials saying a 2,000mile structure is impractical. His supporters say they admire the president plowing ahead in his overhaul efforts and see a historic, generational shift underway.

"There is more than one way to get to the goal," Dane said. "Legislative solutions are all great, but the administration has done things behind the scenes… The results have been dramatic."

Generation Z

The oldest members of a new generation after the Millennials are becoming adults. This generation makes up 25.9% of the United States population. By 2020, they will account for one-third of the U.S. population.

Parkland, Florida School shooting is heralding the arrival of the younger generation. Racial diversity, attitudes toward religion and culture, their digital fluency and their political priorities might shake American life even more profoundly than the millennials. On February 14, 2018, a mass shooting was committed at Marjory Stoneman Douglas High School in Parkland, Florida by Nikolas Cruz. Seventeen people were killed and seventeen more were wounded, making it one of the world's deadliest school massacres.

Since the February 14th shooting at Parkland, 8 states have changed their laws, while 5 cities and counties have tried to push for changes. Meanwhile, 7 companies tweaked their policies related to guns and 18 businesses have cut ties with gun lobbying groups.

On March 24, 800,000 protesters attended the gun-control demonstration in Washington, D.C. on Saturday. The event was the largest single-day protest in the history of the nation's Capital. This was the March for Our Lives by students in an attempt to sway law makers to act to stop future gun violence, as well as an effort to inspire additional marches in other parts of the country.

The rallies are aiming to persuade Congress to tighten the US's notoriously lax firearm laws, which have made gun massacres a regular part of American life.

"David Hogg, a student, was urging protesters to register to vote. When Politicians send thoughts and prayers we say no more!" he said. "I say to politicians: get your resumes ready! "Chants of "vote them out" punctuated the event. Martin Luther King Jr's granddaughter, Yolanda Renee King, said: "I have a dream that enough and that this should be a gun free world, Period." Organizers want the U.S. Congress to ban the sale of assault weapons like the one used in the Florida rampage and to tighten background checks for gun buyers.

The Revolution has started: Barack Obama tweeted: "Michelle and I are so inspired by all the young people who made today's marches happen. Keep at it. You're leading us forward." Oprah Winfrey, Steven Spielberg. Kate Capshaw, George

Clooney and Amal Clooney made sizeable donations to March for Our Lives.

Here are the laws that student gun-control activists from Parkland want to pass.

Ban "assault weapons", prohibit high-capacity magazines, close background-check loopholes.

- Slap a 10% tax on all fire arms sales
- Raise the minimum federal age of gun ownership and possession to 21
- Increase spending for mental healthcare programs.

The death of Stephon Clark, an unarmed black man who was shot and killed by two Sacramento police officers on March 18th, in his grandparents' backyard. With the city on edge after a series of volatile protest last week over the Clark shooting Attorney General Becerra announced the State Department of Justice will also review use-of-force policies, training and other practices of the Sacrament Police Department. "There have been federal investigations before of police killings," said Tanya Faison of Sacramento's Black Lives Matter Chapter. NAACP leaders, at a press conference that included members of Clark's family, demanded that charges be filed against the two officers who shot Clark, and called for the U.S. Justice Department to intervene. Black leaders urged the community to stay calm, saying Sacrament could distinguish itself from other cities, where major violence has erupted after police shooting of a black man. "Sacramento will be a role model, "said Dr. Ollie Mack, a Sacramento physician speaking on behalf of the fraternities and sororities.

"A greater goal has to be preventing incidents like this in the future," Becerra said. "We have to dig deep to see what that takes."

The Sacramento Kings owner and chairman said "we recognize that it's not just business as usual, and we are going to work hard to bring everybody together to make the world a better place, starting with our community, and we're going to work hard to prevent this kind of a tragedy from happening again." It's time to love thy neighbor.

The strategy on how to combat police brutality, racial violence and systematic injustice in America requires sustained protests for awareness. To make it a priority for change.

We must boycott cities, states, businesses and Institutions which are either willfully indifferent to police brutality and racial injustice or are deliberately destructive partners with it. Passively complying with slavery, genocide or widespread injustice is a form of support. We have crossed a line in this country right now where this must no longer be tolerated on our watch.

In a nation that became possible through slavery among other things, the gun was central to a particular notion of racial power. If gun enthusiasts were seriously concerned about state they would have been marching alongside Black Lives Matter demonstrators protesting police shootings and calling for the mass armament of poor black neighborhoods. That's not the kind of tyranny they object to.

Gun control advocates, for the most part, want to change laws. Gun-rights advocates, by and large, believe they are preserving "essential truths" that make the country what it is. They have proved themselves more motivated because long after those distressing scenes from Vegas are a distant memory. These myths will remain vivid.

Americans need new gun laws. But to get them they will have to start telling themselves a new story about the country it is, has been and want to be. Their lives depend on it. Garry Young-Guardian.

Notes

Holder to Issue Revised Racial Profiling Rules With New Limits. Copy right 2014 Bloomberg News.

Loving v. Virginia—Wikipedia, the free encyclopedia Black people and The Church of Jesus Christ of Latter-day Saints-Wikipedia, the free encyclopedia

List of African-American firsts—Wikipedia, the free encyclopedia

Slavery in the United States—Wikipedia, the free encyclopedia

African-American Civil Rights Movement (1955–1968)—Wikipedia, the free encyclopedia

The Corruption of America—Investment Advisory

The Upset-Harlem Globetrotters vs. Minneapolis Lakers, 1948. Written by Ben Green.

Hispanics to hit 50 million—AP News

Blacks seek new clout in once—white suburbs—AP News

Ala. Leaders apologize for handling of 1944 rape— AP News

US apologizes for 1940s STD study in Guatemala— AP News

The Tuskegee Syphilis Experiment—Infoplease.com

NY Public Library getting Maya Angelou's papers—AP News

Legendary singer Lena Horne dies—AP News

Wealth gap widens between whites, minorities—AP News

William R. Hudgins, 100, Who Led Black-Owned Bank, Dies—New York Times

The History of Black History Month—CNN—Infoplease.com

Race in the United States Criminal Justice System-Wikipedia, the free encyclopedia

Rosa Parks statue set to be unveiled—AP News

Why Hollywood Tells Troubled Stories about Blacks—Newsweek

Smithsonian curators scout for Obama artifacts—AP News

Obamas welcomed at Buckingham Palace—AP News Ignoring Black American Veterans—Black Press USA Benjamin F Chavis Jr.

US government considered Nelson Mandela a terrorist until 2008—Robert Windrem NBC News IT'S STILL ALL ABOUT RACE—Stanley Kutler Report says too many whites, men leading military—AP News

Black party identification—Wikipedia, the free encyclopedia

The 1964 Civil Rights Act to the Present—Infoplease.com

Malcolm X—Infoplease.com—Brainy Quote

Marshall, Thurgood—Infoplease.com

Integrating the Armed Forces-www. Digital History

The UFT and the civil rights movement—Susan Amlung

Black power has as arrived—with some new challenges—AP News

What does it mean to be politically independent?—www.articlesalley.com

Obama signs law for Indian tribes black farmers—AP News

Bachman criticizes black farmer settlement—AP News

Voting rights acts of 1965—www.core-online.org

March on Washington—www.core-online.org

Eric Holder—www.infoplease.com

Supreme Court invalidates Key Part of Voting Rights Act—NYTimes.com

Promises kept—www.Barackobama.com

Top 50 colleges for Black Students—www.infoplease.com

In a first, black voter turnout rate passes whites—AP News

In a reversal, more Blacks moving back to south—AP News

The Journal of Blacks in Higher Education—www.jbhe.com/news.

Census estimates show more blacks moving to South—AP News

The Historical Black Colleges and University—Hannah Purnell

African Americans by the Numbers—Infoplease.com New York City had most Black-owned businesses—Johnson Publishing Co.

Black segregation in US drops to lowest in century—AP News

Black voters look to leverage their loyalty—AP News Famous Firsts by African Americans—www.infoplease.com

African Americans in government—www.answers.com 8 political takeaways from the census—www.cnn.com Barack Obama—Infoplease.com

Affirmative Action: Factious Past, Uncertain Future—NPR News

Race in the United States Criminal Justice System—Wikipedia, the free encyclopedia

The Ten Worst States for Black Americans—Thomas C. Frohlich, Alexander Kent, Alexander E.M. Hess, Douglas A. McIntyre and Ashley C. Allen Jay Timmons president and CEO, national associations of manufacturers.

Maria Sacchetti is the Post immigration reporter Washington Post.

About the Author

Derrick St Thomas is a retired veteran and a father of six. Two girls and four boys and a grandfather of ten. He served in the U.S. Air Force during the Vietnam era. He graduated from the University of Connecticut with a BS degree in Management and Labor Relations. After college he started his career in Insurance and Investment and a business owner. Throughout his career he took part in ventures that were successful and rewarding. This is the first book that he has written to show the struggles of Black people when it comes to equal rights and what Black people must do to achieve that goal.

Mistreatment of Black people in the judicial and police system has been a reminder that the dreams of the civil rights movement have not been realized. Many Americans still have racist tendencies or feelings of superiority to people of color.

We must strive for a society where racial differences don't matter when it comes to issues of the law or basic fairness. We must approach each other with respect and even interest in our diverse backgrounds, rather than try to ignore them. It would mean opening our eyes instead of actively wishing to be blind.

My first taste of the good life was back in 1983. I was on top of my game and people respected me because I was a success and I was shown some respect. I was striving to be somebody. I had a lot of white friends that treated me with respect because I was successful. I was making money like them and they respected that. When I lost everything I was depressed and couldn't get back in the game and I became ordinary. When I got back on my feet I was willing to start over because I believed I had something to offer. It's like falling from the top and when you hit bottom it's a whole different world. This book is my inspiration to get us to the Promise Land and participating in the game of life. Be a beacon of light to inspire people to do the right thing and follow their dreams. We only go around once.

I attributed my never give up attitude to my parents. My mother was a nurse and my father was an educator in the New York City school system. He always stressed the benefits of a good education. He had a Master Degree from NYU. They were an inspiration to me because they were always positive. They didn't believe in mental slavery. They loved America and believed in working hard. My father owned a house in Amityville long Island. He bought it for 14,000 dollars in 1956. When he sold it in 1982 to retire in South Carolina his net worth sky rocketed. My mother had her house in Staten Island New York and my sister owns it.

My upbringing did not allow me to fail. I could improve my surroundings or I could stay the same but not go downward. Let's face it. "It's about the money." Not having it can cause a lot of the problems we see today. Plus the system is out to get you. You have to be responsible. For example, your inspection sticker for your car expired. I guarantee that the cops will come around your house to give you a ticket if the car is parked on the street. As the saying goes "Only in America".

I love America, it's the best country to live in. I love my black brothers and sisters. I also love my white brothers and sisters. We are all God's children and we have to talk and listen to each other. We as parents should raise our children to be law abiding citizens, have respect for each other and provide for them. Instill values in them to help them to help them become successful and take their rightful place in society and be productive. Education and wealth creation is essential. Wealth and financial freedom for the next generation must be part of the plan. It's the meal ticket to economic freedom and the good life in contrast to poverty and incarceration. Everybody loves a winner. It's about respect and love.